The Testing Ground

Volume 1

The Cave

Louis Evan Grivetti
Sargent Thurber Reynolds

Published by EditPros LLC
423 F Street, Suite 206
Davis, CA 956167
www.editpros.com

Cover design by Erin Michele Childs

ISBN-10: 1937317218
ISBN-13: 978-1-937317-21-8
Library of Congress Control Number: 2015944429
Printed in the United States of America

CATALOGING INFORMATION:

Grivetti, Louis Evan, and Reynolds, Sargent Thurber

The Testing Ground: Volume 1 – The Cave
Filing categories:
    Fiction: Science Fiction - General
    Fiction: Science Fiction - Adventure
    Fiction: Action & Adventure
    Survivalist Thriller

TABLE OF CONTENTS

PRE-WORD: INITIAL DISCOVERY AND EXPLORATION

Expedition Date: 3012 (New Calendrical Calculation)
Log Scribe: Senior Lieutenant Jackson James, Navigation Specialist
Entry: Third work shift, 673rd Relative Day, PDC (post-departure calculation)

Oh, the tedium of stellar exploration!

For days on end we have continued our search for an inhabitable orbital within our assigned sector A-38-M-19. We have discovered nothing – nothing except boredom, lethargy, and tedium.

Our journey has been without variation. Our tasks remain routine. We experience the endless cycles of repeated activities.

The relative days, post-departure, merge into one monotonous mass of time interrupted only by flashing integers and changing light sequences that appear on our craft's sensors and computer screens. Our edibles and beverages are terrible, without flavor and texture. The initial packaged meals seem as unidentifiable dehydrated and reconstituted piles of glop (as we call the tasteless, formless, masses that pass for food).

Conversations with crew members have passed through stages, from interesting exchanges to oft-repeated stories. The words we speak have become strained as each relative day passes aboard our craft, the *KosMa ExPlorer*, with nothing new to report. Over and over – time and time again – the same tales are repeated of past activities, exploits, and events. The Vistal Horizon films supplied by our sponsors projected in the crew lounge each evening for group entertainment have grown stale as well. The computerized Eze-mags with their three-dimensional feelies no longer attract our interest. Still, we continue our assignments as we venture through the vastness of sector A-38-M-19.

(CLOSE LOG: Jackson James, senior lieutenant, navigation specialist.)

Expedition Date: 3012
Log Scribe: Senior Lieutenant Jackson James, Navigation Specialist
Entry: Second work shift, 717th Relative Day, PDC

And on and on we travel through the great void of sameness ... until ... Unbelievable!

We will always celebrate the moment when the unnamed orb's image appeared on our external rotational sensors, projected on our central command deck screen.

Upon receipt of the first image, Ad-Miral Franklin Egenda initiated sector coordination calculations. We neared the orb, slowed, and slipped into the standard circumgyration arc.

Below us loomed a sphere enveloped by a kaleidoscope of colors – blues, browns, greens, and whites – patterns of light and dark almost forgotten during our long outward journey.

After completion of two orbital circuits, the Ad-Miral issued the descent command. We slowed and dropped through a gap in the swirling cloud cover. Exposed before us was an extraordinary landscape, similar in appearance to our far distant home but different in ways difficult to describe. We hovered briefly over a broad river valley bounded by frozen moisture-capped mountain peaks.

Our external life sensors revealed a reasonable mix of botanicals and zoologicals. The ratio of botanicals was similar: 392 plants tagged as potentially toxic, compared to 428 identified as safe edibles. Of the 46 surface zoologicals, only seven were classified at levels 3a or above (potentially dangerous/lethal), with the balance of 39 registered as potential food resources.

Our sensors revealed numerous freshwater resources: lakes, rivers, and streams abounding with swimming and crawling creatures. Overhead circled flocks of winged animals, some exhibiting feathers of extraordinary colors that shimmered in the reflected light. The grassy meadowlands below were filled with herds of beasts that grazed and ambled about – types not before seen during previous exploration cycles.

We offered thanks to our guardian spirit, Pas JmoDk (may Its name forever be honored) for guiding us to this orb and granting the opportunity to re-amplify and replenish our tasteless company-supplied ersatz beverages and rations.

What joy! Throughout the later stages of our journey, we had longed for real water and suitable food. Now, at last, we will be satisfied.

Our Ad-Miral gave orders to set down, and the *KosMa ExPlorer* landed just inside the rim of the sheltered valley, bisected by a wide, strong-flowing river. Tall forests, glades, and meadows graced the nearby horizon. Our vista scanners surveyed the immediate area: no biped units were identified within the valley or beyond for a distance up to 150 kilo-miles.

(CLOSE LOG: Jackson James, senior lieutenant, navigation specialist.)

Expedition Date: 3012
Log Scribe: Senior Lieutenant Jackson James, Navigation Specialist
Entry: Third work shift, minimal comments, 718th–723rd Relative Days, PDC

Within this valley haven we took our relaxation. For five relative days we completed minor repairs and tended to our usual tasks. On the sixth relative day we rested, as was traditional in our culture.

(CLOSE LOG: Jackson James, senior lieutenant, navigation specialist.)

Expedition Date: 3012
Log Scribe: Senior Lieutenant, Jackson James, Navigation Specialist
Entry: Second work shift, 724th Relative Day, PDC

My gender opposite, Junior Science Officer Janice Upton, and I received our Ad-Miral's permission to explore the mountainside rising in the near distance along vector N-68. We hiked upslope at a reasonable pace and at mid-elevation encountered an unusual rock formation. The site was characterized by angular boulders and detritus of mixed vegetal and mineral composition, possibly loosened from the primary rock face by a strong tectonic jolt. The smaller rock pieces and scree had been subjected to extensive erosional drainage and sediment redistribution.

As Upton circumvented these loose materials, she noticed a small opening in the cliff face partially hidden by overgrown vegetation. Our sensors identified no creatures therein, so we cleared away the loose rocks and entered. We crawled inside, and with voice commands switched on our phospho-light beam canisters. Deep within the cavern was an unexpected surprise. Hundreds of items were strewn over the cave floor. There were metal cases of different sizes stacked three to four high, other objects were in neat piles, while hundreds of others of variable shapes and colors were strewn here and there.

Upton and I initially were attracted to the well-designed compact cases. Each was sealed and labeled with short clusters of unrecognizable symbols, probably identifying the contents. I selected one that appeared different from the rest, took my laser-tech tool, and opened the lid.

Found therein was another unexpected surprise.

Inside were hundreds of small pages covered with unintelligible symbols. My cordon-sensor identified their composition as a mix of vegetable and textile constituents. Remembering my cadet training, I recalled several orb exploration reports that similar materials in the distant past sometimes were known as pay-per (or something akin).

My eyes were drawn to a thick multi-sheaf cluster of this pay-per substance, a collection of sheets bound and protected on the outside by a composite material that resembled stiff animal hide. Upon first glance, the package contained at least 400 sheets – each covered with unintelligible symbols. Inserted among the pay-per pages were 15 additional thin metal sheets, also covered with symbols. My cordon-sensor could not identify the composition of these metal items.

Upton and I continued to inspect the cave, and we completed a quick scan-map of its interior. We debated whether or not to remove any of the items to take them back to the craft. Ultimately, we decided to take the bound multi-sheaf cluster with us, and retraced our steps downslope to camp. We presented the bundle to Ad-Miral Egenda, who received it with interest and thanked us

We were de-briefed regarding the cave location, and projected the scan-map images of the interior that showed the several stacks of metal cases and what appeared to be numerous relics prepared of variable substances – primarily metal, stone, and wood. Some items were wrapped in protective cloth and had been stored inside smaller metal containers (apparently for safekeeping). Other objects merely had been piled on the ground at scattered sites – perhaps done so in haste. Several objects of intricate design, carved images of bipeds presented in unfamiliar modes of dress, had been set inside alcoves carved into the cavern walls. Still other items appeared to be weapons, and some reminded Upton and me of objects of veneration. Numerous small machines of different complex designs and unusual configurations also were scattered across the cave floor.

As we projected the scan-map many thoughts came to my mind.

Some of the items inside the cave had a special aesthetic appeal to me, not dissimilar to elements common to our own culture. Others appeared to be more utilitarian, perhaps items used regularly by these early bipeds and preserved for unknown reasons. Still others appeared unknown. Throughout the scan-map presentation we speculated about their uses.

The Ad-Miral thanked us, then handed the bundle of pay-per and metal, and my scan-map sensor to Senior Security Officer Adele Franklin.

(CLOSE LOG: Jackson James, senior lieutenant, navigation specialist.)

Expedition Date: 3012
Log Scribe: Senior Lieutenant Jackson James, Navigation Specialist
Notation: Second work shift, 725th Relative Day, PDC

The morning after discovery of the cave site, the Ad-Miral assigned Upton and me to lead Security Officer Franklin and a select group of crew members to the cave site. Our orders were to retrieve a representative selection of the pay-per documents, and prepare a master list of the cave contents. We were to determine the elemental composition of the various items, and complete detailed image-scans of the relics and machines stashed therein, for later visual and origin analysis.

As we sorted through the metal cases, we located collections of images of what appeared to be family-related activities taking place at various homes and work locations. These were printed old-style on flat surfaces that resembled glass. In one of the metal cases, we discovered more than 2,000 small rectangular units that puzzled us initially, until Technical Ensign Orson Lebow related that such objects once had been called Fl-Ash Dri-Ves and were used by some bipeds to store encrypted data. We hoped that this finding would provide us with additional essential documentation regarding the purpose of the cave storage and the objects herein, and provide information about the daily activities and lives of these early residents as practiced on this orb.

Some of the contents of other cases jolted my memory, as they appeared to resemble objects that I had seen as a child when my parents had taken me to a history museum at our settlement where objects from past battles on our home orb had been placed on display. A number of these items I recalled as military hardware – belt buckles, buttons, insignia patches, and rings – each distinctive with unrecognizable symbols, and many inset with what appeared to be gemstones. Several of these items I sketched in my log:

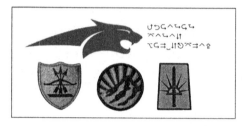

We returned to our craft and presented our materials to the Ad-Miral. Senior Security Officer Adele Franklin summarized our activities, and the details were entered into the master log. Upton and I, along with the other crew members who had assisted, were told that all the materials would be placed in security storage, and the pay-per documents and materials with other symbolic images would be scanned by our craft's acoastal-5-scanner/ translator. The Ad-Miral assured us that the translations would be made available to all in due order.

Upton and I were joined by several others. We gathered in the mess quarters, where we discussed our morning activities and speculated as to the origin and purpose of the cave and its contents:

What was this place?

Why were these documents and relics secreted inside the mountain?

Certainly we had stumbled upon a treasure, a collection of unusual importance, but most questions remained unanswered.

After we had snacked and consumed several intox-waters, Upton and I retired to our cubicle. In the quiet of the ultra-darkness, we pondered the circumstances that led to the cave discovery. Was it luck and happenstance, or had our path to the cave site been guided by an unseen force?

Given the geographical setting, it was obvious that the site had remained sealed and protected against entry. If the presumed tectonic jolt had not revealed the cave opening, the pay-pers and relics would not have been recovered by our exploration team.

Even more interesting, had Janice and I climbed a different route or had chosen to explore the mountainous terrain along vectors 82 or 147, or had ventured along the mountains on the opposite side of the valley, then the depository site would not have been located by our exploration crew.

(CLOSE LOG: Jackson James, senior lieutenant, navigation specialist.)

Expedition Date: 3012
Log Scribe: Senior Lieutenant Jackson James, Navigation Specialist
Notation: Second work shift, 726ᵗʰ – 727ᵗʰ Relative Days, PDC

General craft-board tasks: no news from the Ad-Miral or Chief Security Officer Franklin regarding translations from the cave objects.

(CLOSE LOG: Jackson James, senior lieutenant, navigation specialist.)

Expedition Date: 3012
Log Scribe: Senior Lieutenant Jackson James, Navigation Specialist
Notation: Second work shift, 728ᵗʰ Relative Day, PDC

Same. Upton and I, along with several of the crew who had explored the cave with us, were curious why news about the find had not been forthcoming.

(CLOSE LOG: Jackson James, senior lieutenant, navigation specialist.)

Expedition Date: 3012
Log Scribe: Senior Lieutenant Jackson James, Navigation Specialist
Notation: Second work shift, 729ᵗʰ Relative Day, and for 730–745 RDs, PDC following

Morning and afternoon tasks the same. During evening mealtime, we heard the crackle and initial static of the intercom. The Ad-Miral spoke and asked us to assemble in the central great room (although his request was a level 8B polite command, all were required to attend).

We could scarcely have envisioned that what we were to learn this evening would change our lives forever.

The room was abuzz as the Ad-Miral entered and greeted us. As we grew attentive, he projected the first image onto the central screen of the great room. Along the right side of the image were multiple lines of unknown symbols; opposite along the left side were the translations that all could read and understand.

We in the audience were captivated and sometimes startled by the content of this document. The translation was read aloud by the Ad-Miral – document by precious document – each different, enlightening, and astonishing.

During this first evening and for the following 15, we eagerly assembled, viewed the documents, and listened to the Ad-Miral's readings. Through these sessions, we learned about and began to understand the life forms that once inhabited this orb, especially the advanced biped units that had produced these cryptic symbols – a record of their behaviors and actions.

At the conclusion of each evening's presentation, the Ad-Miral invited all those interested to come forward and examine the original documents. While most attending did not, my gender opposite, Janice Upton, and I regularly accepted our Ad-Miral's invitation.

By touching these pay-per and thin metal sheets, both Janice and I somehow felt connected across time and space with the orb inhabitants who had created these documents and the associated relics. What she and I learned during these reporting sessions challenged us to consider our own place and purpose in the vast Kos-Mos that we had been assigned to explore.

NOTE: I remember thinking at the time as the readings continued – may the events described, the questions raised, the difficult decisions made by former inhabitants of this orb, allow us to lead better lives so that our culture will continue to flourish now and eons into the future, and not end as it once did here.

(CLOSE LOG: Jackson James, senior lieutenant, navigation specialist.)

CHAPTER 1: FIRST EVENING READING

Cave Location: Case 43-B

In the Beginning

And thus began the Ad-Miral reading on the first evening.

In the Beginning

Before all else there was chaos
Dust and matter swirled therein
Etowah flowed within the Great Void
Etowah without form and shape
All alone the Great Void filled

Yanna wanna yanna a wey hey yanna
A wey hey yanna hey
Hey yo wey!

Great Spirit Etowah cried aloud
I am who I am I am
I alone will fill the Great Void
I alone will take shape and form
I am who I am I am

Louis Evan Grivetti & Sargent Thurber Reynolds

Yanna wanna yanna a wey hey yanna
A wey hey yanna hey
Hey yo wey!

Etowah grew in strength and substance
Great Spirit Etowah took shape and form
Inside Etowah grew three seeds
Seeds of conflict, pain, and war
Ever growing through the eons

Yanna wanna yanna a wey hey yanna
A wey hey yanna hey
Hey yo wey!

Great Spirit Etowah expelled the seeds
Gas and matter churned ever outward
Filled the darkness of the void
Clusters formed from gas and matter
Became orbs and arcs of light

Yanna wanna yanna a wey hey yanna
A wey hey yanna hey
Hey yo wey!

Etowah breathed upon the orbs
Etowah's breath turned orbs to stone
Arcs of light around them circled
Faster spinning life emerging
Etowah observed and found it good

Yanna wanna yanna a wey hey yanna
A wey hey yanna hey
Hey yo wey!

On orbs of stone the seeds found roots
Conflict mixed with soil and water
Seeds of pain took faster root
War seeds flourished upon the ground
Growing through the eons passing

Yanna wanna yanna a wey hey yanna
A wey hey yanna hey
Hey yo wey!

Great Spirit Etowah expelled more seeds
Seeds of goodness, trust, and care
Over orbs of stone were scattered
Mixed with conflict seeds that grew
Which would dominate the other?

Yanna wanna yanna a wey hey yanna
A wey hey yanna hey
Hey yo wey!

Great Spirit Etowah formed the O-Os
Observers 6 – Overseers 12
O-Os watched life evolve and change
Watered seeds of conflict – seeds of care
Which seeds would survive the competition?

Yanna wanna yanna a wey hey yanna
A wey hey yanna hey
Hey yo wey!

(Source: *Creation Chant: Our Beginnings,* William Black Eagle. Summer Solstice Ceremony, Bison Camp, Solar Cycle 4.)

And it was that Great Spirit Etowah created all there is and ever will be throughout time and space. And it was that Great Spirit Etowah created six Observers and twelve Overseers

And it was that Great Spirit Etowah selected Observer A'-Tena Se-Qua and Overseer K'Aser L'Don, then assigned them to the Testing Ground to examine, record, and evaluate the sequences of life and extermination cycles (LECs).

And it was that Overseer K'Aser L'Don assessed, catalogued, and reported to Observer A'-Tena Se-Qua, who relayed information from the Testing Ground to Great Spirit Etowah for final decisions (may their names and their work forever be honored):

Cycle 1: The Overseer swam the vast seas and filled them with brachiopods, crinoids, and trilobites. But it came to pass that these creatures gave the Overseer and the Observer no great pleasure, so they were exterminated and the Testing Ground was cleansed.

Cycle 2: The Overseer then swam the vast seas and filled them with bryozoans, eurypterids, and placoderms. But it came to pass that these creatures gave the Overseer and the Observer no great pleasure so they too were exterminated and the Testing Ground was cleansed once more.

Cycle 3: The Overseer then swam the vast seas and walked the great land masses arising from the Testing Place and filled them with ammonites, dinosaurs, and plesiosaurs. But it came to pass that these creatures gave the Overseer and the Observer no great pleasure, so they too were exterminated and the Testing Ground was cleansed once more.

Cycle 4: The Overseer then walked the great land masses arising from the Testing Place and filled them with warm-blooded creatures. And it came to pass that these beasts pleased the Overseer and the Observer. They watched together as the warm-blooded animals evolved, changed, and transformed. One group emerged as dominant, and all was well ... for a time.

But it came to pass that the Observer and the Overseer found the masters of the Testing Ground had become corrupt with evil and violence within their hearts. So Great Spirit Etowah sent a flood, and the Testing Ground was again cleansed.

Cycle 5: Etowah, through the Observer and the Overseer, caused the swirling waters to recede. As family members of survivors assembled, Etowah through the wind spoke these words:

Listen and remember forever
I am who I am, I am and always will be;
Follow the Noble Seven and you will flourish;
Disregard and ignore at your peril.

Listen and remember forever
I am who I am, I am and always will be;
This I say to you; practice the Noble Seven;
Disregard and ignore at your peril.

1. Aid the weak and helpless;
2. Treat women and men equally;
3. Appreciate differences;
4. Reject behaviors that degrade or harm others;

5. *Welcome each newborn to the family hearth;*

6. *Respect and honor your mating partner;*

7. *Celebrate those who help you through life's passages.*

I am who I am, I am and always will be;
Know and understand me well.
Follow the Noble Seven and you shall thrive;
Disregard or ignore them and you shall perish.

Thus spoke Etowah through
A'-Tena Se-Qua and K'Aser L'Don.
(may their names be blessed through eternity.)

Ijano Esantu Eleman

NOTES: Written by Jackson James, senior lieutenant, navigation specialist, during the evening of the first reading, relative day 729, PDC (post-departure calculation).

We in the audience listened intently to our Ad-Miral's reading and translation of this initial document. What were we to make of the content? Was their Great Spirit ⊥↑∧ᗐ̣ᗑᴴᕮ (Etowah) akin to our worshiped one, Pas JmoDk (may Its name forever be written)?

The text certainly was a creation document, one that considered the formation of what we call the Kos-Mos, and is it not curious their word – ⊥⊥ᗐ᙮Uᗐ᙮ (Cosmos) is so similar to our own?

Coincidence or not?

The text recalled the traditional battles between good and evil, similar to the epics we recited regularly to our children describing how the dual components of life struggled for domination with uncertain outcomes – sometimes good winning, sometimes not. But there were significant differences between our lives and those who created this text.

Who were the entities ᗐ╤᙮⊥↑ᗐ̣⊥↑ᗐ᙮ (Observers) and ᗐ̣⊥↑ᗐ᙮⊥↑⊥↑ᗐ᙮ (Overseers) identified in the document? The text suggested that each was created by Great Spirit, ⊥↑∧ᗐ̣ᗑᴴᕮ (Etowah), but no further information was provided regarding their tasks – except that they watched events unfold on the orb during the endless battles between good and evil.

Were these entities gods or demi-gods? Did they reside on this orb or elsewhere in the Kos-Mos? Were they invisible, essentially spirits, or did they have bodies and specific shapes? Did they dictate and direct the behavior of the orb's life forms, or do they allow free choice? Were they merely watchers of events, or did they intervene and direct specific life outcomes?

Answers to these questions were not considered in this document.

Near the beginning there appears a suite of repeated terms that make no sense in our language as translated by our acoastal-5-scanner. These appear to be rhythmic sounds that accentuate the previous text lines, but for what purpose? Do they sanctify the words as a form of blessing, or are there other purposes? Perhaps we will learn more as additional translations are presented and revealed.

Other terms translated as ⊏⁻☖⊏⁻∩↓↑⋏(cycles) characterize the middle portion of the document. I deduced that the word was used to describe a sequential series of exterminations of different life types on the orb. The context seems to be: organisms were created, allowed to develop and evolve, then were destroyed in different ways, according to the whim of their Great Spirit, ↓↑⋏⌐⌐‿⊦⊨(Etowah). If correct, this analysis suggests that the orb has been a location for testing qualities and behaviors of numerous life types; in essence, the orb has served as a testing ground. But for what purpose?

Why would life be created, allowed to evolve, and then eliminated? Why would other life types be permitted to remain and flourish? Could it be that the best of these tested life forms – after proving themselves and surviving on the orb – were transported elsewhere within the Kos-Mos by forces unknown to us to re-seed and re-populate other orbs where life had become extinct?

The document identifies seven commandments issued to the later inhabitants of the orb. I find that this commandment cluster, called the ᏳᏅ╤∩↓↑ ⋏↓↑‿↓↑Ᏽ (Noble Seven), is reasonable and in accord with my own social practices and traditions (and would be so with most of the inhabitants of my home orb). However, at the conclusion of the seventh commandment, a warning is issued: if individuals disregard the Noble Seven, then the penalty is harsh. The phrasing of this line allows further interpretation that individuals who diverge will perish, and that potential mass extinctions may follow.

How could this be so?

Laws of reason and logic suggest that unanimity in thought and action among bipeds never has existed. It would be reasonable that some bipeds would disregard the Noble Seven, even when the vast majority – perhaps even when the 99.99 percenters – kept the commandments. Why then would their Great Spirit Etowah implement mass extinction, based upon the actions and behaviors of a minority, since the process also would eliminate those who honored the Noble Seven?

After the initial reading by Ad-Miral Egenda, a number of us officers and crew members retired to the mess hall, where we speculated long into the night. Who were these orb inhabitants? How and when did they originate? Were their social practices similar or different from our own? Who were the scribes who left this astonishing collection of pay-per and metallic documents, and relics? What principles and values can be learned from these previous inhabitants that may help us as we progress through our own lives? And the most intriguing question of all: while our vista-scanners have shown no evidence that biped units have survived, at least within their 12 kilo-mile range, did any survive elsewhere on this orb?

Upton recalled that at the end of the Ad-Miral's presentation, he pointed to a line in the document where a cryptic phrase appeared, one not translated into our language. The text was written as:

Ꝫ⼊⼝ᏳᏳ ⼃⼂ᕁᏳᏳ⼂⽹⼛ ⼃⼂᎓⼃⼃ᕻᏳᏳᏳᏳ (*Ijano Esantu Eleman*).

Both she and I remembered that when the Ad-Miral spoke this phrase aloud as he finished his reading, we immediately sensed an undefined feeling of calm and wonder that somehow we were akin to these biped units. What the phrase meant and why it evoked such strong feelings within us and other crew members we could not answer at the time.

As Upton and I retired to our rest cubicle, we looked forward with great anticipation to next evening's presentation by the Ad-Miral. Each of us was filled with further questions.

CHAPTER 2: EVENING READING 2

Document 2
Cave Location: Case 43-B
The Mole

How could it be that a sequence of numbers, letters, and symbols caused global destruction?

Question asked by Alecia Jenkins, fourth-year student, Bison Camp Communal School, New NorthWest Configuration

Pre-Note

I, Jensen Gravens, attest that I am the chief psychologist, Stockton Federal Prison. Warden Thomas Cranston appointed me to interview Farid al-Saif abd al-Karim four days before his scheduled execution date of Day 3, Week 2, Month 4, Solar Cycle 2. Assisting me in this duty was Nancy Fowler, chief legal stenographer, Stockton Federal Prison, who prepared the verbatim transcript of the interview sessions. I attest that the following presentation is accurate and based upon the verbatim notes taken made at the time.

Jensen Gravens   Certified: 6-1-4-2

Jensen Gravens
Date: Day 6, Week 1, Month 4, Solar Cycle 2

Preliminary Statement: Jensen Gravens

When Farid al-Saif abd al-Karim entered the interview room, he was not what I expected. This man, who had designed and injected what became known as the attack virus (AV), had contaminated and destroyed the global banking system. What he set into motion subsequently precipitated the atomic destruction of the religious centers of Mecca and Medina, Jerusalem, and Vatican City. It was he who forced the re-shaping of all behavior – how could the person before me be him? The prisoner was slight of build, not more than 170 centi-inches, perhaps 142 kilo-pounds, dark hair, and striking blue eyes. He appeared as an average man, but he was not. He had created and unleashed the AV and nothing ever again was the same. He sat in a wooden chair across the table opposite me. He seemed uncomfortable at first, and several times adjusted his arm and leg chains.

Why had I been chosen to conduct this interview, to confront face-to-face and question the most hated and despised being on earth? He who had initiated the Ripple Event that expanded nationally across the former United States of America, then globally, and the horrible sequence of events that resulted in the Dark Times and the ultimate deaths of an estimated 95 percent of the world's population?

He lifted his head and smiled. What I saw reflected in his eyes has continued to haunt me.

Interview Part I: Day 6, Week 1, Month 4, Solar Cycle 2

Gravens: *You know who I am?*

Farid: *Yes.*

Gravens: *Is there anything you want to ask me before we start?*

Farid: *No.*

Gravens: *Tell me about your family.*

As he spoke I recorded his statement and took extensive notes. These are summarized and presented here.

Farid al-Saif abd al-Karim was raised in a poor but loving family. His father Twarik traced his family line back several generations to a well-known progenitor, Mohammed abd al-Karim, who was active in the *Ikwan* resistance movement that intended to expel the British and end colonial rule in Egypt. Mohammed had joined the famed Brotherhood in 1928 (old solar cycle) shortly after the group was founded by Hassan al-Banna. Mohammed had attended a rally held at a secluded site on the outskirts of Giza, west of central Cairo. It was there that he first heard al-Banna's philosophy of resistance. Mohammed joined the Brotherhood the following week, and soon after became a mid-level member of the el-Arish Confederation and spoke at numerous events to spread news of Banna's revolt.

By the time World War II had started in Europe, Mohammed already was being watched by the Egyptian secret police and was followed at times by a British A-4 officer attached to the Embassy in Garden City, just south of Tahrir Square.

One night a squad of Egyptian soldiers led by British A-4 Officer, Captain Eric McDonald, arrested Mohammed abd al-Karim as he emerged from the Excelsior Restaurant just off Soliman Pasha Street in central Cairo. There was no confrontation. He offered no resistance but asked Captain McDonald about the charges:

Fomenting revolution and encouraging anti-government activities.

Mohammed was taken by military van to the notorious Ansar Prison just south of Cairo on Sharia Salah Salem west of the Citadel. There, he was incarcerated and languished in a damp filthy cell for 14 days with only limited access to food and water. On the 15th day, he was rousted from sleep, beaten, and led to his first interrogation. During the subsequent five days, he was tortured repeatedly to reveal what he knew about the Brotherhood activities and membership lists. On the 20th day of his incarceration, he was clubbed to death. Throughout his time in the Ansar Prison, Mohammed was allowed no visitors; no family communication – to them he had died at the moment of his arrest.

Gravens: *How do you know this?*

Farid: *Because Mohsen el-Ghani informed me. Mohsen was a prisoner in an adjacent cell. He counted the 20 days before the British interrogators killed Mohammed.*

Gravens: *Let us continue.*

Mohammed's family? He had six sons and three daughters. The second of Mohammed's sons, Said, was Farid's father. Said al-Karim was literate, a kind man who cared for his family. Their village, Kalama, was blessed with fertile fields. The families' holdings were limited; they cultivated just eight feddans.

(NOTE INSERTED IN MARGIN: 1 feddan = 0.42 hectares or 1.038 acres.)

Year after year, Said's family worked the family fields where they grew cotton, rotated with fava beans, onions, and leafy vegetables. Three seasons formed their annual activities: planting, harvest, and flood. When the River Nile flooded, no agriculture could be pursued. At these times, Said provided for his family and took day-work at Shubra, one of the northern suburbs of Cairo.

Farid revealed a memory from his childhood:

Farid: *During flood season my friends and I played in the flood zone west of Kalama where we splashed in the waters left behind by the Nile. As the floodwaters gradually receded day by day we gathered fish by hand, capturing the slippery forms left behind by the retreating waters of Nahr al-Nile. We called these activities the annual "fish harvest." We would roast the fish we collected on spits made from trimmed cotton stalk stems.*

As he spoke, Farid smiled as he remembered the pleasure of eating these seasonal foods.

Farid: *Other foods were scarce during the flood season. I grew up in poverty; my riches came from the love of my family.*

He continued …

Farid: *When time came for me to enter Primary School, there was no school in our village. The nearest was at Sindion, a wealthier village some five kilo-miles to the north. The Sindion Primary School was at that time only for boys.*

Farid related that his father approached Sheik Ibrahim the *Omdah* (i.e., mayor) of Sindion, and asked for an audience. He related how Farid's grandfather had fought for Egyptian independence and had died at the hands of British interrogators. He appealed to the *Omdah* using the following words:

Said: *In the name of God, the Compassionate, and the Merciful – might an exception be made for my son to enter into your blessed Primary School at Sindion?*

Sheikh Ibrahim thought for a moment and then replied:

Ibrahim: *If I grant entrance for your son, what will you do for me?*

Said: *Whatever you desire, Effendi. I will work for you and hold you in highest esteem.*

And so it came to be ...

Farid was accepted into Sindion School along with two other boys from Kalama. Their names Aarif al-Salam and Salem ibn Tarik. Throughout the first through sixth grades, the three Kalama boys were harassed as the students from Sindion made fun of them as outsiders. Through it all the three withstood the taunts and slurs of their classmates. Together, they resisted fighting back and held their anger inside. They remembered and would not forget. They recalled the weekly, sometimes daily incidents and catalogued them for future dealings. The Kalama-*Talata*, or Kalama-three as they became known, finished the sixth grade and returned to their village to resume agricultural activities with their respective families.

The time came when the Egyptian Revolution land reforms were implemented. Lands formerly held by those in power during the era of British occupation had their fields confiscated and their lands re-distributed. None of these "take-and-give" scenarios, however, filtered down into poor delta villages like Kalama, since none of the families here had "pull" or "influence" with the new cadres of social reformers: one group of oppressors merely had been replaced by another.

Farid finished the sixth grade as the best student at Sindion Primary School, and was nominated by the headmaster for admission to the Secondary School at Qaliub, a delta city about 20 kilometers to the south. This nomination was a special honor, but posed a potential serious financial hardship. Farid recalled that at this time a bus system for transporting children to school did not exist. He continued:

Farid: *If I were to accept this special educational opportunity, I*
           would either have to ride on the commercial delta bus line,
           which I could not afford, or find a family at Qaliub that
           would house me, where perhaps in exchange for rent I could
           clean, cook, or help the family in some other way.

And it came to be that a member of the Brotherhood who knew Farid's grandfather was a respected resident of Qaliub. He volunteered to take the young pupil under his supervision, doing so out of respect for what Mohammed had accomplished during the British Occupation. This man, unnamed by Farid, is known in subsequent documents only as the Qaliub Tutor (QT). Farid never identified the name of this individual: he has remained unknown.

This chance to live at Qaliub – an opportunity facilitated by family friendship between an elder former statesman and a young energetic student – allowed Farid to flourish and later expand his education beyond Qaliub Secondary School. The opportunity ultimately would lead to college and graduate school opportunities – advanced education at both Cairo University and the American University in Cairo, and later in the United States of America at the University of California, Davis.

Farid stood out from his other classmates at the Qaliub school. He was studious, well-behaved, well-mannered, and best in his classes. Mathematics and language courses were his favorite subjects. After daily class assignments had been completed, he continued his education at home during the evenings working with QT, who tutored him in a broad range of "real world" knowledge.

Together, they explored the modern history of Egypt, starting with the period of Arabi Pasha, the initial revolt against the British; the battle at Tel-el-Kebir; the rule of King Fouad; the debauchery and inconsequential reign of King Farouk; the Revolution of 1952 led by Gamal abdel Nasser and the Free Officer Movement (FOM); the assassination of Anwar al-Sadat; the Arab Spring, the administration of Abdel Fattah el-Sisi, and subsequent leaders.

Through the days and nights after school, QT tutored Farid in economic and political subjects: the colonial aspirations of European nations; the obtuse political wiles of the United States; the inconsistencies and terror of Soviet Communism; economic differences between north and south/east and west; the endless political issue of Palestine and Israel; and especially the role of petroleum and other natural resources in global economics and politics – who had it, who wanted it, who took it.

The discussions he liked best, however, focused on the importance of computers and the reliance of the global banking system on machines. Farid pondered how easily financial transfers were conducted instantly using the correct code numbers followed by the touch of an electronic button on a keyboard.

QT: *Yes my son, have more tea and we will talk further about this subject long into the night.*

And with more tea and under the tutelage of his grandfather's friend, Farid also learned of his family line and heritage. The history of the al-Karim clan in Egypt could be traced to the time of Amr ibn al-As, who invaded the eastern delta region in CE 641 (old solar cycle). It was unclear whether or not the family progenitor had entered Egypt with the invading Arab army, or arrived during subsequent decades. The family originally had been granted lands in Sharkaia Province, east of the Nile Delta, long before construction of the Suez Canal. Farid learned that members of his family once were wealthy, but lost their lands and economic holdings because they challenged the trustworthiness of the Ottoman Bey who administered Sharkia Province. The Bey retaliated against the family and stripped the clan of their lands, forcing them to evacuate and leave Sharkia. They migrated westward into the southern delta region, where they found anonymity and safety at Kalama – at that time an even smaller and even more insignificant farming village. And it was at Kalama in subsequent generations that Mohammed, the grandfather of Farid, had been born.

In the month before graduation from Secondary School, Farid received the Egyptian State Award as the top student at Qaliub Secondary School. When he sat for the National Placement Examination, he scored in the 97th percentile, making him eligible for state-sponsored scholarships to attend Cairo University and to major in any subject of his choosing. He was but 17 years old.

Thus it was that Farid left the Qaliub Secondary School and the home of his respected tutor and entered Cairo University, where he declared his major in political economics with a minor in computer language and creative web design.

Interview Part II (continued): Day 6, Week 1, Month 4, Solar Cycle 2

The first days on the Cairo University campus were hectic: understanding class schedules, room locations, rushing here and there among the more than 30,000 students attending. In class and outside the classroom, Farid met students with diverse social and political agendas for the first time. Some espoused beliefs, experiences, and values similar to those he had gained from QT. Others were more anti-European, anti-American, and anti-government in general (anarchists). He exchanged views with his classmates but usually avoided controversial political subjects.

His economic and computer science courses captivated him; he once said to a classmate:

Learning is my destiny; so much to learn in so little time.

With the first year of classes successfully passed, he returned to Kalama in the summer to help his family oversee the seasonal harvest. He reconnected with his friends who had attended Sindion School together. They remembered their treatment at the hands of some Sindion students, and discussed the taunts and assaults they had suffered. They drank tea at the village refreshment hut, and sat outside on the worn, rickety chairs remembering the shame. The subject of revenge was brokered: how easy it would be to waylay one or more of the most hated students. How easy it would be to cut the throats of these sanctimonious idiots and watch them squirm on the ground as their life essence flowed onto the earth.

Aarif:	*Let it pass Farid. Let it pass.*
Farid:	*But they were dishonorable, were they not?*
Salem:	*But of course – but they knew no better.*
Farid:	*But the headmaster allowed them to treat us badly.*
Aarif:	*But of course Farid – but let it pass; God will judge them at the appropriate time.*

Years two and three on campus passed quickly. Farid had less and less time for home visits, and returned to Kalama only during the feasts of Mulid en-Nebi and the Eid al-Adha. Love from his mother and father continued to envelop and sustain him through the loneliness of distance being away from Kalama and his family.

Bayida:	*How you have grown and matured into a fine young man.*
Farid:	*Yes, Mother. How I love you, Father, and our family.*
Bayida:	*Bring us joy and honor, son; I remember well the day of your naming.*
Farid:	*Yes, Mother.*
Bayida:	*You are my golden son, the golden one who will continue to bring honor to our clan.*
Farid:	*Yes, Mother.*

During his fourth year, Farid had an uneasy sense that he was being watched – but from afar. During the second week of class, he was approached by an older student. Farid would not provide the name of the contact. This individual, a middle-age male, appears in some documents we have on file only as the initial campus contact (ICC), but otherwise has remained unidentified.

This first contact had the appearance of an accidental meeting, but planning the event took more than a year. After a brief introduction and handshake, Farid and the older student agreed to have lunch in downtown Cairo at Groppi Café. They met at a table on the upstairs veranda. They initially spoke about general subjects, nothing political at first, nothing anti-American. Farid recalled that the conversation was about world events, but nothing in-depth. They selected nicely cut sandwiches and cakes from the luncheon cart and continued to sip their tea. After the plates had been cleared from the table, and more tea ordered, the conversation changed. Using carefully selected vocabulary – lest others on the veranda overhear and mark them for further scrutiny – Farid learned of a special organization for people like himself, those who were intelligent and with bright futures. The ICC invited him to join and attend the next meeting.

Several months passed. Additional meetings were held with his contact and others (also not named) to gain a sense of Farid's personality and ambition. In late spring, Farid and his contact met openly on the middle span of Victory Bridge leading to Dokki, just across the Nile from Cairo. With no possibility to be overheard, the first stages of the plan were voiced:

Contact:	*You have expressed interest in helping our group. May we suggest the following possibilities?*
Farid:	*Go on.*

And so it came to pass that events were set into motion to bring about destruction of the Western banking system. Select professors at Cairo University – advisors to the group – urged Farid to continue his education at the American University in Cairo (AUC) to gain a better understanding of the American education system. There, he also could "mingle" with American exchange students and wealthy Egyptians – get to know them, and develop a first-hand sense of how individuals from rich families thought about the poor and destitute.

Admission application forms were completed and letters of recommendations supplied. A letter was sent, and Farid was accepted into graduate school at AUC in the department of economics. His thesis advisor and computer instructor at AUC, Dr. Fahmi el-Badawi, was a respected Egyptian economist from the older generation. El-Badawi was known for his monographs on wealth redistribution and monetary reforms after the 1952 Revolution. His fame extended internationally for his seminal papers on economic disparity between Northern Tier and Southern Tier nations.

Farid met regularly with Professor el-Badawi in his campus office, where they reviewed his academic and thesis research progress. Several months passed and there came a time when Dr. el-Badawi invited Farid to his home for evening coffee.

Farid thought initially that the invitation had been directed only to him. Upon his arrival at el-Badawi's residence, three additional students from AUC also were present, students whom he recognized: Ali Maksur, Ghazi Ibn Maksoud, and Rayhan Musa. Professor el-Badawi prepared coffee, allowing the four students to introduce themselves and engage in small talk. He returned to the sitting room and, when all were seated, he carefully poured the coffee so that no bubble "eye" formed on the surface of the tiny cups.

El-Badawi: *I have asked each of you to join me this evening; I have some thoughts to share with you.*

Dr. El-Badawi informed the four students that each had been vetted, their family backgrounds checked, and their student activities at Cairo University and AUC monitored.

El-Badawi: *We know of your extracurricular activities and of your political-religious beliefs; you have been watched from afar for more than three years. Our proposal for you to consider is this:*

For the next three hours Professor el-Badawi and the four students exchanged views that subsequently changed their lives forever.

As the students left the apartment, el-Badawi spoke to them again:

El-Badawi: *Now that you accepted my conditions and support our cause, there is a colleague I want you to meet soon; you will know him only by his code name – Fyodor.*

And it came to pass that the four met with Dr. el-Badawi and Fyodor several times the following month. The AUC graduate students received their code designation: Delta Cadre (DC). Their initial tasks outside the classroom were to develop and refine their computer scripting skills. They already were well beyond HTML, JavaScript, and sever-side scripting abilities. They explored and practiced simple languages, like PHP, Python, and Perl-Ruby before moving on to BetaTheorems, SigmaTesting, RDBMS, and Auto-Presaging. The simplicity of Auto-Value Substitution and the MySQL tutorials allowed extensive self-modification and integer substitution. Under the tutelage of Dr. el-Badawi and Fyodor, members of Delta Cadre were exposed to the highest levels of code extensions.

Farid related how easy it was to develop scripts whereby software could integrate and talk to programs far beyond the geo-political boundaries of Egypt. They honed and practiced their skills well: they entered and placed backdoor signatures in computers located in dozens of countries, among them Austria, Australia, and Afghanistan; Belgium, Bahrain, and Benin. Each of the institutions or businesses attacked thought they were protected with unhackable firewalls, but accessing and downloading their content for data segmenting and fragmenting became simple tasks for the Delta Cadre members.

By mid-semester they had developed their stealth skills to such an extent that they brought down Bentoit's Pharmaceuticals, a corporation located in Brussels, and easily uploaded the names and ID data of more than 800,000 Bentoit's credit card customers. This initial attack was followed by multiple simple text bombs that caused targeted computers in five major cities of the world to crash and hard drives to lose configuration and data storage.

These were simple projects: more challenging ones followed.

The DC members were introduced to Shell scripting and, coupled with training from Fyodor, they practiced developing applications with complex user interactions. Firefox Extensions linked to Lifehacker were their preferred platforms. These were modified and frameworks developed, whereby Delta Cadre members could park and hang their probing activities. They practiced debugging texts to correct mistakes in the computer programs they wrote. Their hexadecimal conversions flowed with ease and became second languages, something that they practiced in daily lives, in which simple phrases like "coffee with sugar" written on a restaurant napkin during morning class breaks became:

A 63 6f 66 66 65 65 20 77 69 74 68 20 73 75 **67** 61 72

Farid laughed when Ali Maksur made a simple coffee/sugar text mistake, and transcribed the triennial digit as 68 instead of 67.

A 63 6f 66 66 65 65 20 77 69 74 68 20 73 75 **68** 61 72

Because of this simple error, Ali's program froze and would not activate.

Farid smiled then showed his friend that by simply placing four two-digit couplets at the end of the numerical stream along with a lower-case Greek letter T (tau), followed by a semicolon, the program would reactivate:

A 63 6f 66 66 65 65 20 77 69 74 68 20 73 75 **68** 61 72 38 14t;

Simple? Perhaps.

Night after night they practiced their skills, designing executable programs. They developed communication algorithms and tested self-created worms that briefly infected the computer platforms on the Cairo University campus for short periods of time – then laughing, they would inject a cleansing variable byte text that scrubbed the offending worm and returned function to the campus computers.

They developed a range of additional standalone malware – an advanced set of techniques to infect other computers, evade firewalls, and cause security failures. They learned how to target specific files within a host system and mastered variable backdoor entry techniques that they practiced daily.

Fyodor taught the Delta Cadre members how to avoid detection by reducing network scans, creating false signatures, and re-routing the launches from different geographical points of origin.

As their skills grew they expanded their activities.

Fyodor departed for Belarus, then after two weeks returned to Egypt, bringing with him three black boxes especially constructed for the highest level of training for launching viral and worm constructs. These black boxes were exceptional: composed of carefully crafted high-density plastic, and manufactured to evade airport security. Fyodor easily passed them through the lax Egyptian police officer security and luggage X-ray stations.

Each member of Delta Cadre was presented with one of Fyodor's gifts.

First use of these new pieces of equipment brought down the firewall of the Egyptian Western Desert Agricultural Union (EWDAU), where the Delta Cadre retrieved more than 45,000 user codes that members carelessly had left unprotected.

This attack on the EWDAU achieved notice in the Cairo press when the newspaper *al-Ahram* ran a story of the "hack" on the sixth page. The tone of the article, however, was more humorous than serious. The location of the report buried inside revealed to Delta Cadre that the authorities had not taken the event seriously.

Fyodor praised the Delta Cadre members for this initial success.

> Fyodor: *You will have an exciting and profitable life, but be cautious.*
> *Leave no entry signatures that can be traced to your*
> *platforms. He laughed and then quoted the well-known*
> *Belarus idiom known to all hackers in his nation:*
>
> *"A different computer each day keeps the trackers away."*

At these words, Farid and the other members of Delta Cadre laughed and, in return, Professor el-Badawi quoted the seventh-century Arabic idiom quoted in the medieval saga of Antar ibn al-Shadad:

> *"A hero will rise to confront evil and bring justice to the poor."*
> (translation)

Farid graduated and received his master's degree in economics and computer science from AUC. His family in Kalama was ecstatic. Now their son would have a fine position working in Egypt for the betterment of the nation and for their village. He would bring honor to the al-Karim clan. He would be a true *Ragel ad-Dahab* – a man of gold.

But their wish would not be satisfied.

Based upon the high quality of Farid's master's degree research, several AUC professors urged him to consider continuing his education and going abroad for his Ph.D. His major professor, Dr. el-Badawi, was most proud of his fine student.

> El-Badawi: *I suggest that you attend the University of California, Davis. There, you will excel and achieve greatness!*

The depth of darkness in Professor el-Badawi's eyes revealed that his words were not a suggestion, but a requirement. In order to provide cover for the preferred designation, Farid applied to 10 graduate schools in the United States with the University of California, Davis (UC Davis), among them. In this way, his desired path would not be revealed, just in case others were tracking his intent.

Farid was accepted at nine of the American universities, and offered international scholarships, teaching assistantships, or grant funding from six. The University of California, Davis, through its Department of Economics, was one of two campuses that offered him full financial aid. Funding sources for air transportation and initial settling-in were covered in the usual way.

(NOTE INSERTED AFTER INTERVIEW: Despite continued probing, Farid's transportation funding source was not described during the interview; logically it would have been supplied by Farid's handlers.)

On the day of departure, Farid's parents were very proud. But at the same time they were saddened by his decision to go abroad for further training. They would miss him dearly. Both parents realized the honor and prestige that completing his doctorate would bring to the family, so tears of sadness gradually were replaced by tears of joy. The villagers at Kalama also were proud and wished him the best. All saw Farid as a golden boy (now a man) – one who would work for justice, equality and, with God's help, improve the economic and living conditions in Kalama.

His going-away party was hosted by Professor el-Badawi at the Estoril Restaurant in downtown Cairo. After all the well-wishers had departed, Dr. el-Badawi approached Farid and whispered:

> El-Badawi: *Once you settle in Davis, you will be contacted. You are the leader that we envisioned; we place our hopes with you. May God's blessing be upon you.*

Then it was goodbye to parents and villagers. Tears of excitement, mixed with tears of sadness, all flowed as his new venture was about to begin – one characterized by external appearances of education and knowledge, but with the primary objective of bringing justice to the poverty-stricken, downtrodden peoples of the Third World.

Farid departed Cairo and flew to Frankfurt. He transferred to United Airlines flight 8829 on to San Francisco, then the short hop to Sacramento. Upon arrival, he was met by the UC Davis international student representative and welcomed to the United States of America.

Interview Part III (continued): Day 7, Week 1, Month 4, Solar Cycle 2

Farid arrived in California during late August, a month before the start of instruction. He was met at the Sacramento International Airport by a staff assistant from the international student office at UC Davis. On the drive into Davis, Farid was informed he would have temporary housing at the Orchard Park facility, located on the west side of campus.

He settled in the small, one-bedroom apartment, which was sparsely furnished but adequate. Neighbors kept to themselves, which pleased him, as he wished to focus on his studies.

In the days and weeks that followed, Farid familiarized himself with the campus and nearby town facilities, especially the Farmers Market that was held in Central Park, and the nearby restaurants and shops. During registration week, he was invited to a campus welcome event at International House, where he met other foreign students, along with American student and faculty member hosts.

Farid held initial meetings with Dr. Ariel Blackman, professor of economics, who had agreed to serve as his major professor and guide Farid's research. Professor Blackman's research group consisted of three other graduate students, each working on topics related to the theme of economic disparity in Third World regions. He was introduced to the team and made to feel welcome.

Orientation week followed, and the campus quickly filled with an overflow load of 35,000 students. Farid met with his academic advisor, Professor Sheila Graham, who reviewed the standard suite of courses in the Department of Economics that he would be expected to take. With the advice of Professors Graham and Blackman, Farid was encouraged to continue and expand upon his previous coursework in computer program design and digital languages – tools that would be added to his skillset as he began research on his dissertation topic.

The first academic quarter went very well: Farid's GPA was 3.92 – his one A- grade had been in Advanced Vector Analysis. All courses he readily mastered, to the delight of Professor Blackman. Farid spoke up at group team meetings, and it was clear to all attending that he was exceptionally bright and able.

(NOTE INSERTED AFTER INTERVIEW: In subsequent depositions from Blackman's graduate students, they would relate that it had been a pleasure to interact with Farid in the classroom, during study breaks, and over meals taken at the Memorial Union on campus. When asked, none of the students interviewed believed that it could have been Farid who launched the attack virus. Blackman's students related:

> *He was our friend – a really nice guy – quiet and reserved but pleasant to be around. No, it could not have been him.*

Farid was drawn slowly into the social life of American graduate students. He made friends with selected students living at Orchard Park, and they would invite him to dinner, invitations that he sometimes accepted, sometimes not. Graduate students in the Department of Economics regularly held weekend socials to which he was invited and enjoyed the relaxed atmosphere. He did not drink alcohol, but had no problem associating and mingling with the students who did. When alcoholic beverages were pushed onto him by well-meaning students (ignorant of the Islamic prohibition toward alcohol), he would gently reply:

Farid: *Thank you; I will have a soda or juice if you don't mind.*

Most often, however, he dined alone and spent the majority of his time either on campus or at his small apartment at Orchard Park. When he had free time, Farid read extensively and mastered several additional computer languages and acquired technical skills well beyond those he had learned in Egypt.

Many evenings were spent at the campus computer laboratory in the basement of Haring Hall, where he became widely known and recognized as a "regular." He enjoyed discussing technical skills with the talented computer programmers, who openly shared their knowledge with him – little knowing how the information provided ultimately would be put to use.

At one of the departmental social events, he met Frank (last name uncertain), a pre-veterinary major minoring in economics. Frank had brought his girlfriend Sapha Stone to the event and introduced her to Farid. Sapha was a graduate student majoring in ethnobotany and plant science. As the three exchanged pleasantries, she asked Farid questions about his views on Middle East issues. He deflected her inquiries with a smile saying:

Farid: *As you know, the Middle East is complicated.*

Frank and Sapha sensed that Farid did not want to speak with them further, so they thanked him then walked off and joined another group in which they felt more comfortable discussing UC Davis football and local events.

(NOTE INSERTED AFTER INTERVIEW: When Sapha and Frank subsequently were interviewed at Bison Camp by Data Collector Theodore Johnson, she could not recall that specific social meeting with Farid, although her boyfriend at the time (Frank – who ultimately became her formal mate – recalled the incident and the exchange.)

Farid prepared for and passed successfully his Ph.D. oral examination. It appeared to others in the research group that he was spending most of his time focused on his dissertation topic. He apparently was making good progress, and his major professor, Dr. Blackman, was very pleased.

Days passed into weeks until the evening of the contact telephone call. The voice began with standard pleasantries, then used the code term DC (Delta Cadre) twice in the same sentence and requested a meeting off campus at Mishka's Coffee House in downtown Davis.

Contact had been made!

Three days after the meeting at Mishka's coffee shop, Farid met his contact at Slide Hill Park in East Davis and received his instructions.

The contact (not identified by Farid) informed him that other members of Delta Cadre had been positioned at key locations at other universities in the United States, saying only that one member was in the northeast, one in the southeast, and one was in the Great Lakes region. Each member already had recruited a triad of assistants with their identities not to be shared in order to compartmentalize and reduce exposure if one were arrested by the authorities.

The contact informed Farid that the time had come for him to recruit three members in order to complete the UC Davis triad. The contact asked Farid when the attack virus would be completed.

Farid: *I told the contact that I already had identified three students sympathetic to our goals, and they could be recruited this week. They will be told that their focal efforts are to organize data comparing standards of living and health-related statistics; this they will do quickly. I then will take these data and design the injection point – the specific vent for introducing the attack virus. These students will know nothing of our goals and intent. Praise be to God! I will expect a messenger to meet me within 10 days to collect the code package. He will deliver copies of the attack virus for distribution to the other Delta Cadre members. The injection was planned to coincide with the fourth Thursday of November – a day when Americans are lax and thinking inward about their lives, filling themselves with food, and not respecting the poor and starving unfortunates elsewhere.*

Contact: *You have done well, Farid. You have exceeded our expectations. Your name will be known forever for your works.*

And so it happened that within the time frame mentioned, Farid recruited three students to assist with gathering the necessary global economic data. Two hours later, the attack virus was completed.

(NOTE INSERTED AFTER INTERVIEW: Although I pressed Farid

numerous times for the names of these three students, he would not reveal them.)

The messenger, who would coordinate the event in the four geographical regions, arrived in Davis on Monday, November 24. Farid met the messenger at a coffee shop in South Davis, where he delivered the package containing the code. Both men then went outside and walked to a secluded spot behind Nugget Market, where they could not be seen. They embraced, then raised their arms in reverent supplication and spoke the following words:

> *Do not consume one another's wealth unjustly.*
>
> *(Koran. Surat al-Baqarah. 2:188).*

Without further conversation, the messenger departed. Farid returned to his room at Orchard Park, and spent the remainder of the afternoon in prayer. The code he had written was designed to interrupt the banking system of the West, an action that would force the West into a re-examination of global business practices and produce economic justice forthe less fortunate. In two days, he would inject the virus.

And the waiting began.

After-Word

In the late evening of November 26 – the eve of Thanksgiving Day in the United States, the day of celebration with family and friends – Farid al-Saif abd al-Karim entered the basement of Hutchison Hall on the University of California, Davis, campus where the master computer and servers were housed.

There, he encountered three graduate students studying and working on their research: Frank Costello, Adam Jones, and Sarah Jenkins. Farid spoke briefly with each and exchanged pleasantries. He left the table where they had been sitting and walked through the southwest corridor of the computer center where no one was present.

Looking about to make certain that no one was nearby who could observe, he removed the flash drive containing the attack virus and inserted it into the operational slot of the Unisys XPCL Mainframe.

Ten milliseconds later, the electron flow encountered the first firewall that easily was circumvented, then the next, the next, the next, and . . .Virus implementation was initiated at 12:00:01 on the early morning of November 27. . . And the world changed forever!

NOTE: Comment on the metal document that follows ...

Presented here is the translation of the first metal sheet that formed part of the overall collection of documents initially removed from the cave by expedition crew members Jackson James (senior lieutenant, navigation specialist) and Janice Upton (science officer). Symbols on the metal sheets initially defied translation by our craft's acoastal-5-scanner/translator. It has been reported that Ad-Miral Franklin Egenda held this initial sheet of metal and noticed a large eye-like symbol at the bottom. As he ran his fingers over the symbol the metal glowed, shimmered, and the symbols shifted into our language allowing them to be read.

The document is a report that begins with a short statement regarding solar exploration and the responsibility of gathering information for assessment and evaluation. The text continues by identifying two individuals, or forces, and names them by category ⊃ᗡ⋏⇂↟♥_↟↟♥ (Observer), and ⊃_↟↟♥⋏↟↟↟↟♥ (Overseer), who have been assigned to work together on the orb where our craft landed.

The most important information from the document reveals that the orb where we landed has served (and continues to serve) as a testing ground for different life forms, from simple to most complex – identified in the initially scanned document already presented on the first evening.

The present document is a short discussion between Observer 6, known as ↳⊀∧⇌↔⇨ ⋏⇨⊀∪▶⇨ (A'-Tena Se-Qua), and Overseer 3, titled ⇂⇂↳⋏↟♥ ∩⇋⊃⊂ (K'Aser L'Don), regarding the emergence of innocent life and what are called the parallel tracks that the biped units select, where one path diverges from righteousness into the darkness of evil-doing – or the reverse – born evil but adopting a life of kindness and helping others.

The text ends with the assumption that further reports on the biped units will be forthcoming, and with the cryptic phrase ∃⇂⇂↳⊂⊃ ⇂⋏↳⊂∧⊻ ⇂↟∩⇂↟∪↳⊂ (Ijano Esantu Eleman), whose meaning is unclear. When our Ad-Miral touched the eye-like symbol, the following translation was obtained:

Metal Sheet #1

Inscription and Translation

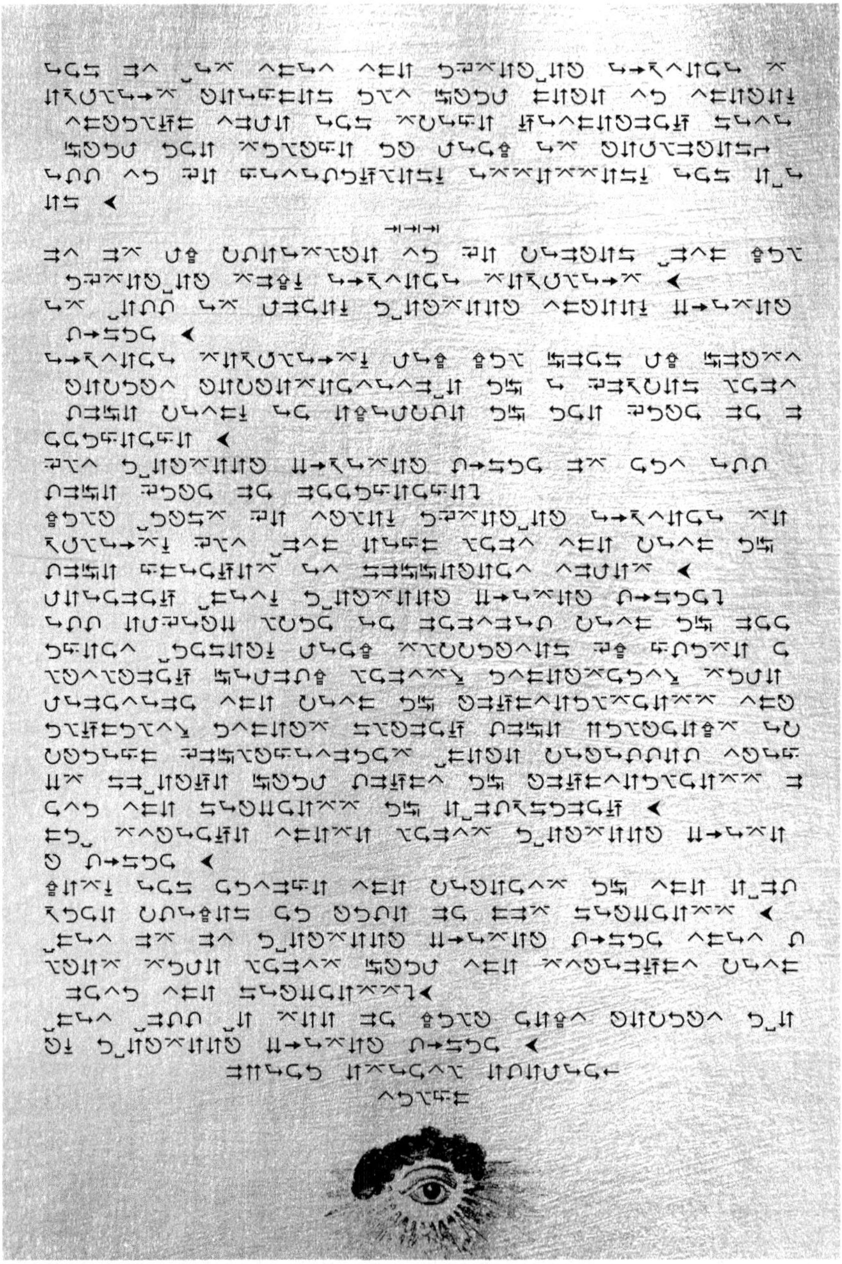

And it was that the Observer A'-Tena Se-Qua reached out from here to there, through time and space, gathering data from one source or many as required; all to be catalogued, assessed, and evaluated.

*** * ***

It is my pleasure to be paired with you, Observer 6 A'-Tena Se-Qua;

As well as mine, Overseer 3 K'Aser L'Don.

A'-Tena Se-Qua, may you find my first report representative of a biped unit life path, an example of one born in innocence.

But Overseer K'Aser L'Don, is not all life born in innocence?

Your words be true, Observer A'-Tena Se-Qua, but with each unit the path of life changes at different times.

Meaning what, Overseer K'Aser L'Don?

All embark upon an initial path of innocent wonder, many supported by close nurturing family units. Others not. Some maintain the path of righteousness throughout. Others during life journeys approach bifurcations where parallel tracks diverge from light of righteousness into the darkness of evil-doing.

How strange these units, Overseer K'Aser L'Don.

Yes, and notice the parents of the evil-one played no role in his darkness.

What is it, Overseer K'Aser L'Don, that lures some units from the straight path into the darkness?

It is coded in their life essence – set within the concept of choice: each unit chooses their respective paths, whether to take the easy versus difficult roads, to seek the quick vs. long-term rewards – choices unpredictable at life's beginning.

What will we see in your next report, Overseer K'Aser L'Don?

Documentation of different choices by these interesting beings inhabiting the testing ground.

A forward look have I to your next report, Overseer K'Aser L'Don.

Ijano Esantu Eleman!

Chapter 3: Evening Reading 3

Document 3, Cave Location: Case 43-B – The Sisters

Born in the Valley Silicon
To Valley Capay the sisters came
To nature's land they flourished well
They walked among the ancient oaks

Symbolic acorns the sisters given
Handfuls held for all to see
Nature's spirit into them fused
New names of honor were bestowed

Came time of learning
Came time of joy
Came time of sadness and destruction
Came time to leave

Over the valley floor and up and over the mountains
Onto and over the red and white desert lands
The sisters trekked onward, ever onward

Black Oak-Yuhushi chanted: On to Montana
Tan Oak-Cishqhale chanted: On to Valley Big Hole
Valley Oak-Sapha chanted: On to Buffalo Wallow – to the Dude Ranch!

(Source: The Triplet Chant. Bison Camp settlement group. Summer Solstice Ritual Celebration. Transcribed by Summer Watkins, certified data collector, Day 1, Week 3, Month 6, Solar Cycle 12.)

Pre-Note

In times of misery and want, survivors have questions. Unfortunately, most go unanswered. How can it be that both evil and good develop within the hearts and souls of individuals? What seeds are planted by family members, friends, teachers, brief acquaintances that reinforce qualities of goodness in some? How can it be that within the same person other ideas take root that influence personal thoughts and behaviors, turning individuals away from the path of joy and light toward the realms of darkness, despair, and evil?

Three young women – triplets – raised within an unusual family, were responsible for saving the lives of tens of thousands of survivors by teaching basic skills in ethnobotany, allowing those who gathered wild plants for food during the difficult times to eat safely – to differentiate toxic from dangerous species. The three sisters are not widely known today outside of certain local enclaves and settlement groups in the New NorthWest Configuration. But their story is an important one to tell. They should be honored by their dedication to teaching others the principles of plant identification during hard times.

I first heard about the triplets (or "sisters," if you wish) while searching the Montana State University archives on agricultural activities at the University of California, Davis (UC Davis), prior to and after what has been called the Ripple Event. A number of files examined alluded to three women from the Capay Valley, admitted to UC Davis, where they had studied ethnobotany and graduated. The names of these young women, Cishqhale (Tan Oak), Sapha (Valley Oak), and Yuhushi (Black Oak) – linked with the family name Stone – appear in coursework evaluation and placement test documents.

I must also inform committee members that my interest in learning about the sisters stemmed from the fact that unknown to me, they had been my neighbors as they were raised in the Capay Valley not far from my family town of Esparto, which was close by where the triplets spent much of their childhood. To my surprise, I also learned that we had attended the same high school – but in different years – so we had never met previously.

Committee Members: I present to you today, my findings. My report will show how much we, the survivors, owe to these important, dedicated women, and the roles that they played in the subsequent development of local and regional events during the Ripple Event, Dark Time, and post-Dark Time Recovery Period. The information I present to you is documented in numerous files. I have developed for your consideration a separate list of file numbers that I will distribute to you after my presentation so that you may examine the originals and perhaps explore more about the sisters, if interest takes you at a later date.

Esparto Allen

Esparto Allen
Month 3, Solar Cycle 16
Assistant Archivist,
MSU History Project

Certified: 2-4-3-16
Date: Day 2, Week 4,

Birth and Early Years

Let me begin …

The sisters were born in 1995 (old solar cycle calculation) – precise date uncertain – a home delivery in the city of Palo Alto, Old California. Their mother, Sarah Woods-Stone, was a computer science professor at Stanford University, while their father, Ronald (Ron) Stone, was much in demand as a computer guru in what then was called Silicon Valley. He also worked as a part-time instructor at San Jose State University. The family spent several summers and holidays in Old Montana at the Buffalo Wallow Dude Ranch, located in the Big Hole Valley southwest of Butte. It was there they could relax and enjoy nature before returning to the "grind" of everyday work in Silicon Valley.

More than enough wealth was generated by their parents' routing programs to purchase a 2,000 hectare-acre ranch near the village of Capay, where they moved shortly after the triplets' birth. In this they were acting on their decision against raising their children in an urban environment. The parents of the sisters were expert and deeply involved with various government computer programs – at times to enhance accuracy, at other times to improve national security – and sometimes contracts were combinations of both factors. Because of their occupations, they of necessity maintained low-profile lives. Indeed, when in public the triplets always referred to their mother and father as "the professors," and this is how their neighbors in the Big Hole Valley knew them.

The Stones – for such was their family name – went even further off the grid after they moved to Old Montana. It since has been verified by several investigators that their first names were Ronald and Sarah. Interestingly, the given names of their children have remained a mystery.

A rustic house just off the main road along the eastern edge of the Capay Ranch was the girls' home. The triplets' surrogate parents and caretakers (for their father and mother were often called to Silicon Valley) affectionately were known as "Indian Jack" and "Mom Sarah." Both adults lived in a rustic cabin near Cache Creek in the heart of the ranch. Documents reveal that their given names were Jackson and Sarah Obdurly. Both were members of the Pomo Confederation.

The sisters grew up almost feral in the hills and dales of Turkey Ranch, as it was known. Why this name was applied, no one knew at the time, for as far as could be found turkeys had never been raised there. Jack or Jackson – a Pomo Shaman – and Mom Sarah were close at hand whenever the girls' parents were away.

The personal diary of Cishqhale (Tan Oak) contains the following *verbatim* exchange on undated page 16 of her personal diary:

> *Injun Jack, Injun Jack!*
>
> *Whoa, ladies, what is it? What's gotcha riled so early this mornin'?*
>
> *Well, we'd heard Indians lived offn acorns so we tried one. Otta its shell it looks good but …it was terrible …it made us sick. Did we do somethin' wrong?*
>
> *No, you just didn't do enough right. Come back tomorrow. Sarah and I'll show you what all needs to be done. When we're finished they won't make you sick, but it'll take some work and time.*

And so began the sisters' education in the possibilities presented by the Turkey Ranch ecosystem. What plants were edible and which were not, and how to prepare those that were; which plants could be used as medicine, and which to avoid. They learned how to capture and cook the small animals and fish that always were close at hand. Beaver and raccoon were their favorites, but they could make do with ground squirrels and rabbits – both jacks and cottontails. They learned to jerk and preserve venison, and how wild turkeys could be called close in prior to capture. Plants became their hobby, then their passion.

On the triplets' 13th birthday, Jack and Sarah sponsored the girls' initiation into the Pomo tribe. With the acorn flour and oak ashes rubbed into their raven hair, we can easily imagine they appeared to be Pomo themselves; in fact, they were so much in spirit. As in other tribes, they were given names with magical properties to be used privately and in sacred rites alone. The accepted speculation is that these names were Pomo for Buck Bush, Digger Pine, and Elderberry, but these as with their birth names have remained unconfirmed to this day. Support for this conclusion is seen in the names the sisters chose themselves, which complemented certain characteristics of their Pomo names.

After they entered Esparto High School, the sisters – as loner children often do – created a clan and gave themselves the names that became well-known later. They chose the acorn as their totem, and tattooed themselves with stylized acorn emblems. Collectively, they became known as the Three Oaks. Each sister took the name of an oak variety common within the Capay Valley, and it became their own: Cishqhale (Tan Oak), Sapha (Valley Oak), and Yuhushi (Black Oak). Their tribal mark – the small tattoo that many now are familiar with – consisted of a stylized acorn with a vertical row containing two black dots and an open circle. The position of the open circle represented the triplets' birth order and signified openness to nature's knowledge. This seemed only natural to the sisters:

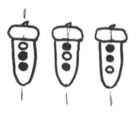

Birth Order (Open Circle)
Cishqhale – Sapha – Yuhushi

University Years

The sisters were good students, if eccentric in some ways, and graduated near the top of their class at Esparto High. Full scholarships were offered by a variety of schools. The sisters chose the University of California, Davis, due to the excellent reputation of the school when it came to many aspects of plant science. All three elected to major in plant biology, and took the same minor in sustainable agriculture and food systems. These courses of study were demanding but "quite a hoot" as Sapha often remarked, and were combined with other classes required by the UC system – some electives being "pieces of crap," according to Cishqhale, while Yuhushi thought some were "stimulating." The sisters, as not unusual at the time, needed five years to graduate with their bachelor of science degrees.

All first- and second-year students at UC Davis were required to live in campus residence halls. Their junior year, the sisters moved out into a three-bedroom house near campus just off Alvarado Street that their parents had rented for them. Their social life on campus was similar to that of most undergraduates: a mix of academics, outside activities, and a vigorous social life. Sapha had met Frank (last name unknown) while at Esparto High. He followed her to Davis, where he studied pre-veterinary medicine and had been offered a full football scholarship as an offensive lineman for the UC Davis Aggies. Sapha went to all his games, and Cishqhale often accompanied her. After one of the Aggie-Sacramento State football games, Cishqhale bumped into Bud Jones, a second-string quarterback, a walk-on as the old terminology used to be applied. Bud was at least a head shorter than she, and the rest was history as they say. Yuhushi participated in intramural soccer and often attended the Aggie games, as well. It was at one of these games she first noticed a "smokin' hot goalie." That goalie was Englander Geoff, and soon he became her steady date. If nothing else, the sisters clearly exemplified the saying "a man picks a wife the same way an apple picks a farmer."

During the triplets' last year as undergraduates, their professors encouraged each to continue their studies and to enter graduate school. Unlike today, scholarships at that time were offered for advanced studies, and the sisters entered the Ph.D. program in plant biology with emphasis on ecosystems. Once in graduate schools, the couples moved in together at the sisters' house. The triplets initially were anxious about this group-living action, until their minds were set at ease by their parents, who admitted this had been their lifestyle as well while attending college.

The "consorts" – as the boyfriends became known – shared many interests and philosophies with the sisters. They often visited the Montana dude ranch in summer and at Thanksgiving. They applied their respective life and university training expertise to planning what they sometimes called the refuge ranch. Together they built a small survival library and with each journey to Old Montana, they brought with them with a variety of science and specialty books to stock the library, among them:

Kershaw's *Edible and Medicinal Plants of the Rockies;*

Tilford's *Edible and Medicinal Plants of the West;*

Campbell's *Survival Skills of Native California;*

Wescott's *Primitive Technology II: Ancestral Skills;*

Nyerges' *How to Survive Anywhere;*

McPherson's *Primitive Wilderness Living and Survival Skills;*

Berglund's *Wilderness Cooking;*

Pressley's *Wilderness Cooking;*

Boy Scout Manual (1948 and 2013 editions); and

National Rifle Association Guide to Firearms Assembly (4 volumes), along with a set of basic gunsmith tools (these to provide references and tools for Frank, as he was an avid hunter).

The consorts shared their interest in fitness and nature as reflected in their academic studies and majors, which would prove most useful and necessary at the Bison Camp community: Frank, general agriculture; Bud, pre-veterinary studies; and Geoff, physical education. The hobbies of each were welcomed, especially their extensive knowledge of the native plants of the western continent on the part of the sisters; Frank offered skills in gunsmithing and the weapons and tools of early Native Indian tribes; Geoff was a builder with skills in both carpentry and metal work; Bud had a minor in food science and was an accomplished chef who created tasty meals from a wide variety of ingredients. Another group of six that could provide so much to the ranch community would be hard to find. Indeed, the skills and knowledge they brought proved important time, and time again.

Field Research in Amazonia

By the end of year two in graduate school, the sisters had completed their academic coursework and were spending nearly 50 hours per week in their respective laboratories, conducting initial experiments and in preparation for their Ph.D. orals and qualifying examinations. Professor Kevin O'Neil, their project supervisor and major professor, would comment in later documents how brilliant and hardworking the triplets were, and how he marveled at their energy and ability to balance academics with their social lives.

The three continued to focus their interests on phytochemicals, antioxidants, and certain proactive compounds from plant species that originated in the western Amazon basin of South America. Four years previously, Professor O'Neil had flown to Iquitos in northeastern Peru along the Amazon River headwaters. There, he established a professional research association with IIFA (Instituto de Investigacion de la Facultad de Agronomia) at the University of Iquitos, and key faculty members interested in medicinal plants and known for their research among traditional peoples (Bora and Yagua). Through these initial contacts and discussions, Professor O'Neil had attempted to interest a suite of graduate students in traveling to Peru and working in rural areas, collecting and sampling plants, and conducting field-testing for potential promising species. But until his interaction with the sisters, none of his previous students appeared interested in such research. Professor O'Neil was delighted when Cishqhale, Sapha, and Yuhushi each eagerly wanted to pursue this potential opportunity.

During the next two years, the sisters alternated time spent in the plant biology laboratory and their assigned plots on the experimental farm at UC Davis. They had secured permission from IIFA and the government of Peru to export seeds and seedlings of seven plants with promising characteristics for further laboratory investigation in California.

The sisters' work with the native plants of Amazonia progressed and became wellknown through their presentations at professional society meetings. One promising finding they pursued was a compound in one plant – a still unnamed cytotoxic podophylloton – a possible preventative and treatment for uterine cancer. Initial and follow-up *in vitro* studies demonstrated positive findings. Laboratory Chief Dr. Oren Bates applied to NIH (National Institutes of Health) and the subunit NCI (National

Cancer Institute) to initiate the next step, *in vivo* studies and field trials. But this was not to be as you already know.

Destruction of Field Test Sites

Toward the end of their Ph.D. studies and with the positive findings already published and applications for further scientific trials pending, environmental radicals – then known as the Greenies – struck and destroyed the sisters' field experiments along with those of others. And it would be that the sisters' lives and those of their consorts, their families, and campus colleagues changed forever.

The personal diary of Cishqhale (Tan Oak) contains the following *verbatim* exchange on undated page 128 of her personal diary:

Those miserable bastards –

The no good sons o' bitches –

Yeah, they fixed us good. Four years' study and work shot to hell and it took 'em less than 15 minutes. God, what I'd like to …

Like to what, Yuhushi? Face it, 'twas all for nothin.' You might as well calm down and enjoy your burger.

OK, OK, but for $2,000 you'd think they'd at least include more fries and a bigger mug of beer.

Two Obamas don't buy much these days. Soon our money will be worth just so much – what would the Brits say, Geoff?

Bum wad – just so much bum wad.

You've been awfully quiet, Sapha. Got anything to share?

Yeah, plenty. We've gotta get out of here and ott'o' here NOW. NOW, while we still can. What's going on in Berkeley will become worse sooner or later; I'd guess we have two weeks or even less – NOW and, again, I mean NOW is the time. It's not like there is anything here for us now.

To the Capay ranch?

No, that's too near – way too near. We should make a run and meet up with the folks at the dude ranch. They expect us for Thanksgiving anyway.

All the way to Montana?

Yes, to Montana, and now can't be a moment too soon. The highways are open. Fuel can be had most places if you've got the Obamas for it. Might as well spend what we've got before it turns to crap. Frank and I'll fuel up the van and load up on bottled water; Geoff, you and Yuhushi fill up your Crew Cab and those jerrycans you always seem to have rattling around in the bed; Bud, take Cishqhale and go back to our place – get all your backpacking cooking gear and freeze- and sun-dried items we have stored, and bring along with us your deer rifle and shotguns. Geoff, you two don't forget your .22s. We'll bring along our AK and M14 – and all of us grab as much ammo as we can. We're leaving soon enough. I doubt we'll need all this firepower – at the very least we'll be intimidating what with Bud riding shotgun and Frank showing the AK, if things come to that. Everyone – collect the sleeping bags and some extra clothes – winter's coming on, so take the time to grab appropriate garb. Let's figure on meeting in two hours. All ready to roll in the van and crew cab. A small inconspicuous convoy – nothin' more than a part of the afternoon commute. Only thing is, we'll keep goin' beyond Auburn. Now – get with it!

Relocation to Montana

The sisters and consorts left Davis and reached Reno by early evening. Remember, too, that this was early on in the madness or pre-Ripple Event period when hours could cover what now requires days or weeks. Prudent people made the effort to join groups going to their destination. It was not all that dangerous to be on your own then but – again – the wisest took care. Once at Reno, fuel tanks were topped off and route information gathered, and the group continued.

The personal diary of Yuhushi (Black Oak) contains the following *verbatim* exchange on undated page 98 of her personal diary:

OK, OK, it looks like we can follow what we'd planned most, if not all, the way. We'll rest up and join those heading east in the morning. There should be no problems up to Wells; there might be some gangs bothering folks near Vernal, but we were going to turn north at Wells anyway.

How about north of Wells?

There's no word of trouble in what I've found out, but we'll double check both at Elko and Wells in case we might have to head north from there. With any luck at all we won't have to double back to Winnemucca to reach a clear road north – and that road is very safe. This'll be the fallback to get us to Wisdom and the dude ranch. It'd take us longer but we'd get there.

The next day found the group on an easy run to Wells, where the sisters turned northward as they had planned. The lone overnight stay between Reno and the dude ranch was near the Nevada-Idaho border, north of Jackpot.

The following appears *verbatim* on page 144 in the personal diary of Cishqhale (Tan Oak):

> *You think they make it this far?*
>
> *What are you talkin' 'bout. Who might make it this far from where?*
>
> *Salmon. Salmon on a run from the ocean. That's what I'm wondering about. In case you hadn't noticed, we're camped on Salmon Falls Creek. You can't argue it's even smaller than Cache Creek back home, and a lot farther from salt water.*
>
> *I'd guess they made it at least as far as the falls that give the creek its name. And we all need to be clear – we won't be returning to Turkey Ranch. Buffalo Wallow Dude Ranch will be our new home once we get there, and it sure looks like we will.*

The next morning fuel was topped off and the latest road reports gathered at Twin Falls. They decided to loop through Dillon, Montana, rather than take the most direct route from Twin Falls. Late afternoon found their convoy – now reduced to the two original vehicles – driving through the Badger and Big Hole passes and dropping into the Upper Big Hole country. Soon, they reached the ranch in the meadows along the Big Hole River, about six kilo-miles north of Wisdom. Today we'd say the ranch was two hours easy north of the village.

Arrival and Settling-In

Their destination was what we today call Bison Camp. At the time of their arrival, the ranch was known as the Buffalo Wallow Dude Ranch. People from Silicon Valley – "tekkies" they were called – had acquired the ranch two old solar cycles previously as a defensible fallback should urban disorder get completely out of hand. This purpose as it turned out was well served and indeed the ranch flourished. The former state of Montana became incorporated into the New NorthWest, the largest configuration in western North America. Throughout our turbulent history close contact was maintained with both New Deseret and the western portion of Flatlands, with our youths serving in their defense and theirs in ours. Indeed in a way we have shared a buffalo logo with the flatlanders – ours being in profile, theirs being full on as seen on the logo of our Survival Group. The ranch became the center, heart, and soul of what followed historically in the New NorthWest Configuration. New Bozeman, our capital, was close by and housed the Montana State University archives.

The following exchange appears in File 47-B-13, transcribed by an unnamed data collector who had been assigned to interview Sapha (family name Stone) upon her 65th birthday. Sapha recalled the family emotion that followed the group's safe arrival at the Dude Ranch:

Frank, turn left here, that's the ranch – that bunch o' trees and outbuildings – there along the river. Watch out for those… Frank, stop the van, stop the van, it's Mom and Dad! Mom, Dad!

My God, its Sapha's van.

And Geoff's crew cab. Kids, kids you made it – and sooner than we thought you might.

Out for a stroll and you never know who you'll run into.

Well, we almost did run into you – did you think we'd be delayed?

Well, it would have had to have been the day after you left. Things got "interesting" in California. We've heard I-80 is tied up over Donner Pass.

How bad?

A blizzard on a ski season weekend bad. Our friends will have to fight it. They figure this is the beginning of the end and are on their way.

Their convoy should be at least 20 vehicles with plenty of supplies and – shall we say – protection? They'll make it – eventually. Oh, and Frank?

Yes, ma'm?

Have you started a beard or did you forget to wash your face this morning?

Now, Mom, I think he looks dashing. So there.

Sapha, you should be the one most concerned one way or the other. Welcome, welcome to you all. Welcome to the ranch.

Come on, we'll help get you settled in.

And so it began.

After-Word

The sisters and their consorts left UC Davis on Friday the 21st of November, and reached the Dude Ranch on the evening of the 23rd. The first heavy snows of winter already had blanketed the floor of Big Hole Valley and covered the outbuildings of the ranch with a thick carpet of ice. The immediate days that followed were filled with family activities, and the reunion was joyful. All looked forward to the coming Thursday and celebrating Thanksgiving together.

At dawn on November 27, Sapha and Frank awoke and lit the kerosene lamps in their bedroom. The couple dressed and went outside where they gathered with family members and walked down to the cookhouse to make breakfast. Entering the kitchen area, Frank flipped the light switch but nothing happened. It was obvious at first that the central light had burned out or had shorted. Sapha knew where the spare bulbs were stored, retrieved one, and handed it to Geoff to change. Still no electrical-based light.

And it would remain so for a very long time!

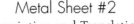

And it was that the Observer A'-Tena Se-Qua reached out from here to there, through time and space, gathering data from one source or many as required; all to be catalogued, assessed, and evaluated.

*** *

Presenting now for your pleasure my second report, one sure to attract your attention for its content and quality, Observer 6 A'-Tena Se-Qua.

Your choice, Overseer 3 K'Aser L'Don surprises me, a group of three from one mating egg, rare is such an event not, and if rare, your choice cannot be representative of these units.

I sense your unease, Observer 6 A'-Tena Se-Qua, but my choice was a logical-based evaluation of the dual roles of environment vs. heredity on behavior.

Your level of thinking and choice, Overseer 3 K'Aser L'Don, is justly explained.

A'-Tena Se-Qua, may I call you by your name assignment A'-Tena Se-Qua, or do you require me to announce your Observer title as well?

For now, Overseer 3 K'Aser L'Don, let us keep our titles and core of our directive.

As you wish, Observer 6 A'-Tena Se-Qua, but perhaps in time?

You suggest in your report, Overseer 3 K'Aser L'Don, that the behavior and actions of these single mating egg sisters was similar but at the same time different; each respected the testing ground environment, but so different in personality, judgment, and choices.

Oh, yes, Observer 6 A'-Tena Se-Qua, they were wealthy but poor; strong to overcome adversity but not too; modest but sensual; led youthful lives interrupted by evil. I will continue to oversee them.

Overseer 3 K'Aser L'Don, follow your directive; I await your next report.

As we complete our work together, Observer 6 A'-Tena Se-Qua, perhaps you will come to understand me better, and I you.

Perhaps …

Ijano Esantu Eleman!

Chapter 4: Evening Reading 4

Document 4, Cave Location: Case 43-B

The Ripple Event

Greed and numbers brought it down
Chorus: Take heed, take heed!

Greed for power as well as things
Chorus: Take heed, take heed!

Work and food for but a few
Chorus: Take heed, take heed!

Greed and numbers brought the madness
Chorus: Take heed, take heed!

From the madness came the Ripple
Chorus: Take heed, take heed!

Death for most and then the Dark Times
Chorus: Take heed, take heed!

Never again …

(Source: *Fireside Chant*. Recited by Franklin Thompson, Bison Camp settlement group, Montana State University History Project, Archive, Document FM:2-538c.)

Pre-Note

It has been recorded by many that earthshaking events have humble beginnings. Indeed, what became known as the Ripple Event started with the birth of a single child – an innocent who became the catalyst and primary figure for the events of unspeakable madness and destruction that followed. How and why he was drawn to religious and political realms structured by anger, hate, and suspicion of the West, we can only guess. We may never know the names of the firebrands whose sermons and speeches foaming and dripping with hatred of Europeans and Americans that showered the once-innocent boy with statements that global poverty and diseases were Western legacies. We may never know the instant when he accepted their twisted messages to become the catalyst that changed the world forever – but not for the better.

> *Yes, Farid al-Saif abd al-Karim, you are remembered.*

> *Yes, Farid al-Saif abd al-Karim, you are remembered now, and will be remembered tomorrow, and each day thereafter until the end of time.*

> *(Source: Presentation to data collector graduating class by Frank Jensen, leader, Bison Camp Education Unit, Montana State University History Project archives, Document FJ: 274t35).*

Two Weeks Pre-Injection

The environmental movement that began in the 1950s (Old Calendar Calculation) was based upon sound science and social justice. The original objectives were to protect endangered ecosystems and preserve the wonders of nature. After 2010 (Old Calendar Calculation), this movement turned political and deadly. The new face of environmentalism attracted to its fold a suite of non-biologists and political anarchists. Gradually, the numbers of outsiders outnumbered the thoughtful founders. As a result, original objectives were discarded and replaced with political agendas.

Initial confrontations began in Berkeley, California, at Frank Josephs Park, an oasis of beauty located in the Berkeley Hills, northeast of campus. Here, environmental radicals known as the Green Alliance (GAs or Greenies) suddenly appeared *en masse* one day in late October and uprooted vegetation, shouting and clamoring that Berkeley parks should be green – but green only with native plant species. Destroyed in this madness were the age-old stands of Cyprus trees planted in the late 1800s (Old

Calendar Calculation). Gone were the clusters of red and white oleanders whose Mediterranean origins blessed the hillsides trending eastward; and destroyed the flowering roses and red poppies planted by generations of men and women to honor loved ones. Destructive actions taken in the name of eco-correctness.

The Berkeley police arrived too late to stop the destruction. Within several minutes, the confrontation turned deadly as two policemen were beaten with clubs wielded by the anarchists (one was injured critically and died). The leader of the Green Alliance (name unknown) was led away in handcuffs and was overheard saying:

We are taking our protest to further levels. You, who condemn us, beware.

Two weeks later, late on the night of November 18th, the northern chapter of the Green Alliance attacked the experimental farm at the University of California, Davis. The specific location chosen for destruction was a focal point for experiments in which undergraduates and graduate students worked with professors to explore topics with positive implications for improving nutrition and health, not only in the United States but in foreign lands as well.

The plots targeted by the Green Alliance that evening contained a wide range of edible wild plants with high potential as food, and others for their specific medicinal properties. These species, native to Amazonia, were well-known botanically as the sisters had cultivated them and analyzed the plants for their energy, protein, and vitamin/mineral content, and had initiated experiments to test their relative medicinal properties. Because these were not native California plants, the experimental plots were targeted by the Green Alliance.

The three young women had invested nearly three years of part-time work, meshed with their academic studies. The first summer working with Professor O'Neil, they had traveled to South America to identify and gather these potentially valuable species, then the plants were imported to the United States with USDA permission. Once the packages arrived, the contents were seeded, nurtured, and tested – a process that had taken almost three years.

Within 15 minutes, these valuable plants were destroyed by ignorance and stupidity.

Thus, it came to pass that the sisters' research into the nutritional and medical potential of selected Amazonia species was destroyed. Their work and efforts could not be repeated, and in their anger and frustration, and having little concern over the madness emanating from Berkeley, the sisters and their consorts (most often referred to in later descriptions as boyfriends at that time) discussed what to do next. The six students elected to leave UC Davis before the end of the quarter. Before their departures, each spoke with their academic advisors and received PELP (Planned Educational Leave Program) certification that guaranteed re-admission to campus when they returned for the spring quarter.

They decided to drive to the Buffalo Wallow Dude Ranch in the Big Hole Valley in west central Montana southwest of Butte, there the triplets had spent so many happy vacations as children. Plans already had been made to visit their parents over the Thanksgiving break at the ranch, and an extended period through the winter months would allow relaxation and skiing before the onset of spring quarter, when they would return.

The six left Davis on the 21st of November, and reached their destination on the evening of the 23rd. The first heavy snows of winter already had blanketed the floor of Big Hole Valley and covered the outbuildings of the ranch with a thick carpet of ice. There was a joyful reunion of the families, and all looked forward to celebrating Thanksgiving together.

Day One and Thereafter

Farid injected the attack virus during the late evening of November 26, with the designation to take effect on Thursday, November 27, at 12:00:01 a.m., the Thanksgiving holiday in the United States.

The electron flow, based upon his coded message spawned of hate, slithered through the first firewall, then the next, and the next. One by one, the local bank branches in Davis, California, were infected – Bank of America, Chase, Citibank, First Northern, Union, US Bank, and Wells Fargo. As the bank computers talked to other branches within California, the virus spread as their firewall were breached. Infections followed in banks throughout the Western United States, and likewise banks in the central, southern, and eastern portions of America collapsed nearly immediately. The jump across the Atlantic and Pacific Oceans took a mere millisecond, as one by one the financial institutions of the world were fatally impacted.

The result created by Farid was destructive and chaotic. Starting at 12:01 on the 27th, all ATMs at banks, convenience stores, and public locations shut down automatically. Debit cards – that unique plastic way to withdraw money invented in 1966 (Old Date) – became useless, so patrons would actually have to visit and speak with bank tellers.

At 6:00:01 a.m., six hours after the initial "twinge" of the attack virus, the multiplier codes reproduced their numerical venom with exponential speed. Managers and loan officers working the holiday requesting access to any computerized records found all accounts inaccessible. Bank computer specialists immediately were alerted, and teams frantically searched for solutions so as to regain access to private and public commercial records.

All attempts at solutions failed.

The cascade of events that followed in the banking industry scarcely can be described. The global banking system wallowed in a state of collapse – and no one – no one at any level of authority – seemed to know what to do next or how to stop the cascade that followed!

Farid al-Saif abd al-Karim's work had been accomplished.

The Unexpected

Three of the terminal two-digit couplet codes with their accompanying tau and omega configurations accidentally had been reversed during the scripting process. These errors had not been identified during normal code-checking procedures.

They were more than just code errors, however, as life changed for billions of people. Farid and members of his Delta Cadre had inserted a virus to destroy the banking system of the West – and this they had accomplished. But Farid's coding errors also brought about the unexpected and initiated global destruction as well.

The first code error, the simple tau and omega reversal, neutralized the base particle command integers with the result that all computer systems at the University of California, Davis, became infected immediately. All student and faculty laptops, desktop computers, and tablets using UC Davis IP user-code identifications and keywords went dark immediately with all data lost. The computers of persons off campus who logged e-mail messages sent to any UC Davis administrator, faculty member, or student became infected and went dark.

The second code error – numerical reversals – amplified a key set of command integers that expanded the blackout even further. All cellular telephones on the UC Davis campus immediately became infected and shut down. Any parents who called sons and daughters wishing them happy Thanksgiving found their phones infected as well – and telephone service went dark.

The third code error modified and extended by a third set of reversed command integers had the unexpected consequence of intercepting and negating electrically generated pulses. By mid-morning of the 27th, banks were unable to comply with client requests, public relations officers could not send or receive information, and personal funds could not be withdrawn from ATMs. All personal computers and tablets in the city of Davis had gone dark; the problems were confounded and made more serious due to lack of electrical power.

And like a stone tossed into a placid lake, the event that began at the UC Davis campus computer center, expanded outward as computers regionally, nationally, and ultimately internationallhy experienced complete data blackouts. What would be known, thereafter, as the Ripple Event – a sequence of computer-initiated actions that during the next several months, from late November into late January – ultimately would destroy global culture and society.

(NOTE ADDED AFTER INTERVIEW: Security issues prevent further discussion regarding the specific integer coding and the unusual co-lateral design of the attack virus that incorporated sequential β and ψ fractals. All this interviewer can say at this point is that a four-point diamond process, linked with super-condensed variables, was at the core of the attack virus).

Davis residents awoke on the morning of the 27th of November to the dawn of a new day. Unknown to them at the time, their lives would change dramatically. More than 90 percent of the over 60,000 residents of the city would perish within eight weeks.

Once, civility and kindness characterized the city of Davis. Over time, these traits would be replaced by others – selfishness, distrust, and fear. Decisions for personal and family survival would be made at the expense of others. Gangs of young thugs would assault the defenseless. Neighbors would steal food and water from neighbors. Survival of the fittest would become the norm in its most raw and jungle-like form. The once pleasant university town where residents had prospered for decades would be destroyed.

There was no panic at first, just puzzlement:

Why can't I withdraw cash from ATMs?

Why doesn't my computer work?

Why is there no phone service?

Why is there no electricity?

The Thanksgiving holiday passed, then Friday, Saturday, and Sunday arrived:

What is happening and why?

What am I going to do?

Should I stay in Davis or leave?

What should I do?

The university has closed the campus dining facilities; where am I going to eat?

My friends and I are really worried!

Hundreds of merchants assessed their situations:

Should I close or remain open?

How do I protect my inventory?

I cannot retrieve my financial records; what shall I do?

Should I stay in Davis or leave?

Where would my family and I go, and what about gasoline – the pumps don't work!

Grocers pondered:

What are we going to do; inventory cannot be replenished!

Fresh produce, meats, and perishable items – should we give them away?

How do we protect our stock from thieves and vandals?

If this continues much longer what will we do?

There were no answers.

This is an impossible way to live; there's no light.

I can't cook meals for my family.

We can't pump gasoline and fill our gas tanks.

The contents of our refrigerators and home freezers have spoiled.

Individuals and families strapped for cash pondered what to do? A common cry was heard throughout Davis:

I have money in the bank, but can't get to it – please loan me funds so I can buy food for our baby.

What do I do next?

But even if loans were made out of friendship and social responsibility, the grocery stores were closed and paper money essentially became useless.

To many in Davis, the city seemed like an isolated island. With no electricity, there was no television or radio; with no broadcasting and no operational computers or cell phones, there was no news of what might also be happening locally, regionally, within California, and the nation. Landline telephones were dead, with no dial tones. Batteries became highly sought after and valued items. Packages of batteries vanished from local grocery stores, pharmacies, and hardware stores.

Why was this happening?

Sutter Davis Hospital, the key medical facility in Davis, was shrouded in darkness; with no electricity and back-up power failures, medical staff had no ability to identify and search for patient health records. Within the darkened emergency room, patients continued to arrive for treatment, but the only useable medical equipment were items like syringes, stethoscopes, and battery-operated blood-pressure monitors (no CT-scans, EKGs, MRIs, or X-ray machines).

But worse was to come.

The bodies of those who died in the hospital could not be refrigerated. Day by day the ambulances and vans ran out of gasoline, and bodies could not be transported to morgue facilities.

What was the cause? No one could say, and there was no news.

By mid-morning the fourth day, and without any formal news, the rumors started:

It's all the fault of the right-wing conservative Republicans.

Where are the police? I'm frightened.

It's all the fault of the bleeding-heart liberal Democrats.

Why can't I access my ATM? I need money and I need it NOW!

It's a subversive attack on our country.

Where are the mayor, the governor, the president and Congress? What are they going to do?

This is just another way for the Republicans to keep me from receiving my food stamps and government assistance; it's all their fault!

Have alien spacecraft landed in Nevada? Are we under attack?

Why is the government controlling the information? We need to know what is going on!

Where are the police? I'm frightened!

How do we protect our families and homes from the gangs of thugs roaming our neighborhood?

If the conditions stay this way tomorrow and nothing changes, what can I do? I am frightened!

What will we do for food, drinking water, cooking fuel, emergency health needs?

The population of Davis could not know on the morning of November 27th that the conditions would not abate, and there would be no end in sight.

Chaos, Fear, and Death

As days of the Ripple Event progressed, the overall situation and conditions worsened. With no access to news, and fear and uncertainty on the rise, civility and the cultural veneer of the Davis residents changed, slowly at first but then accelerating with terrible results.

By the end of the first week of December, there was a noticeable decline in the amount of available household tap water. At the beginning of the Ripple Event, some residents had seen this as a possibility and immediately scrounged dumpster bins for empty liter bottles, jugs, and other potential liquid storage containers. Some of the wise immediately began to store water in household bathtubs and sinks, while others drained and stored water from household toilets. Some of the residents understood the harsh reality that without food for a week or two, an adult merely becomes hungry – but without a water source for five or six days, a person dies.

No food trucks had entered the city of Davis since the onset of the Ripple Event. Much of the fresh food supplies slowly spoiled, as the local supermarkets remained shuttered. Groups attacked the market doors at night, entered and stole as much food as possible. When police patrols arrived the thugs scattered, and the police were able to capture and detain very few. Of the vandals captured a common cry was:

I was just too hungry and we had no food for our children; what was I to do?

Living among the liberal professors and professionals in the city of Davis were closet survivalists, families that always had a six-month to one-year supply of food (usually in the form of MREs) and innumerable cases of bottled water stored inside their house, garage, or secured backyard shed. The problem these families faced during the Ripple Event was twofold. What could happen to them if they were seen eating and drinking regularly, and were accused by neighbors of hoarding supplies of food and bottled water – then what? Or, should these individuals who had acted responsibly to protect their families, share their stock of food and water with friends and neighbors? Debates over "why or why not share" tore apart families and neighbors. Neighbors, once close friends, set upon one another and brawled in the streets. Incidents of homicide in once-peaceful Davis began to rise.

A common plea: *What should I do?*

Others in Davis, however, formed groups to assist one another and shared resources with neighbors. One such group on Pollock Court pooled their food and water resources and initiated a rationing program in which all received equal amounts and quantities. But equal distribution lasted only until supplies were exhausted.

A common plea: *What will I do next?*

As lack of food and hunger increased, Davis residents turned to trapping small animals that inhabited the greenbelts within and around the boundaries of their settlement. They also took to gathering wild plants. Within a week, all of the squirrels that once infested the university campus – to the amusement of both faculty and students – disappeared, along with feral cats. Dogs that wandered city parks at night unattended by their owners were captured and brought home for food. Creative residents prepared sticky lime pastes mixed with sesame seeds and smeared these on tree limbs. Wild birds by the thousands attracted to the seedy pastes landed to eat; their feet became trapped, and they were collected for food.

Starting a garden was no solution; it would take weeks for food to grow. Those who already had gardens were fortunate, and most stood guard over their backyard food supplies. Others searched vacant lots and greenbelts for potential plant foods; dandelion leaves and clover easily could be identified by most residents, but these items were enough for only a few meals. Others in their search for edible greens gathered what they thought might be edible, but common misidentifications led to severe sickness and sometimes death.

A common plea: *When will this madness stop?*

Decisions over what to do with family pets plagued the residents. Owners of dogs and cats could not bring themselves to sacrifice and eat their own pets, so group meetings were held in which family pets were exchanged – it seemed the ethical thing to do. Others, however, could not separate themselves from the pets that they had nurtured for so many years; and in so doing they "toughed-it-out" together and mourned when the family pet died – but could not bring themselves to make a meal of their former family member. Some of these kind residents then wrapped the body of their pets, and tearfully donated them to church food banks in central Davis which prepared and shared the meat with those most in need.

A common plea: *Will it ever end?*

Little by little some homes in certain neighborhoods were identified as having confirmed food storage. These homes became magnets to the hungry and thirsty mobs, which demanded what they called "their share," and when none was shared, the outsiders broke into the homes, murdered the residents, and stole the supplies. Later, the thugs fought each other for larger shares of the food.

As time passed, the Davis police essentially became helpless. Members of the force had their own families to protect. As the assaults, burglaries, thefts, and homicides increased, the Davis city jail filled to capacity. This posed a dilemma, since those incarcerated could not be fed and there was insufficient water – so the police chief ordered their release. When challenged by an irate Davis resident, whose wife had been attacked, the following exchange was overheard:

Chief: *What else could I do?*

Resident: *But he broke into my house, stole my food, and bludgeoned my wife to near death – and you let him go because there wasn't enough water and food to give to the prisoners? You could have let the bastard starve!*

The National Guard (NG) never arrived. Davis residents who bicycled over the causeway into Sacramento reported back that members of the NG had encamped on the state Capitol grounds, in order to protect the governor and legislators. They also reported that the NG had fired upon protesters, killing more than 600.

Law and order in Davis, without the National Guard and no active patrolling by the police, led to the next phase – accelerated violence and hundreds of homicides.

The people of Davis rioted by the thousands during the first week of December. The police were powerless to stop the mobs that rampaged through the downtown streets. They smashed store windows and stole whatever they wanted. Sporting goods stores were ransacked and looted as the thieves made away with guns and ammunition. Nearby farms surrounding Davis were stripped of their field crops, and livestock stolen.

With the rise in anarchy, home security and family safety could not be guaranteed.

More and more bands of hungry teenagers and young adults roamed through neighborhoods, knocking on doors demanding water and food. When denied entrance, the thugs shot the homeowners. As news of such events began to spread by word of mouth, Davis residents who had stored their weapons in previous years (because it was not the "Davis way" to be known as a gun owner) thanked themselves for not previously turning in their weapons (as had been requested on "turn-in-your-gun days," held monthly at the police station).

One home invasion and shootout (just east of Wright Boulevard) led to the deaths of 12 gang members, and the wounding of the homeowner and his son; but their food and water supply was protected – at least for the moment.

Some residents had attempted to leave town by car or motorcycle. The Shell gasoline station on Mace Boulevard was ransacked. Raiders attempted to siphon off gasoline and fill jerrycans. A shootout with the owner resulted in the deaths of six residents. After the owner ran out of ammunition, he was killed and the gas theft continued. What subsequently happened to this group of thugs and where they went remains unknown. Did they die or find temporary refuge along California's lakes or rivers? If they approached settlements, they would be considered threats and rejected for entry, which would lead to more shootouts and more until – who knows – and in fact, who would care about such groups?

As the days and weeks progressed, and as the water supplies in Davis dwindled to near nothing, hundreds of residents struggled to reach the south side of the UC Davis campus, where they drank from the contaminated waters of Putah Creek. By doing so, their thirst abated for a short period and as a group they rested on the grass near Mrak Hall and the law school savoring the end of their thirst. Four hours later, the vomiting and diarrhea each experienced caused even more dehydration, and most died writhing in agony before two more days had passed.

As the Ripple Event continued to grow in intensity, the houses of worship in Davis were filled to capacity. The pious, along with their agnostic and unbeliever neighbors, sought answers through prayers or thoughtful contemplation. The pious believers implored the deity to assist everyone during this terrible time of need...but there was no change.

Slowly, but with certainty, most came to the realization that death was near. As they pondered their fate, many wished they had left Davis immediately that fateful Thanksgiving weekend.

Anything would have been better than what we have had to suffer through.

And so it was that during the early weeks of January, after enduring six weeks with limited water and food, with no apparent resolution or ending of the crisis, sunset parties became the answer for some families.

As described and related by one observer:

Families gathered into small groups of like-thinking friends and together they prepared a last supper – a communion feast to celebrate life, friendship, and love. At the conclusion of the meal, all attending held hands: adults and children. A designated leader would start the last words and going clockwise around the table each would relate briefly their thoughts on life, love, and what it meant to be part of a family. One by one, their voices would ring out over the table, interrupted occasionally by the group singing favorite songs. Each in their own way gave thanks for the good life they had experienced before the horrors of the Ripple Event. These sunset parties or gatherings revealed that the participants in their own way had fought the good fight, and now it was time: decisions to continue to struggle or not. Those who decided to continue helped those who chose death put on blindfolds – the adults helped with the blindfolds for their children. When all had been readied – everyone embraced. Through different ways, those that elected to end their pain and suffering, and those who remained behind to continue the struggle, were thankful for the lives and together they held last thoughts of the images of their loved ones.

The dark days were upon them.

After-Word

What began in Davis, California, and spread globally started as a numeric progression: 1 – 2 – 4 – 8 – 16 – 32 – 64 to an infinity of pain, destruction, and death. The Ripple Event inflicted damage on all nations and touched all peoples: political friends, political neutrals, and political foes. In the weeks following November 27, hundreds, then thousands, then millions, and then billions languished and suffered, as 95 percent, or more, of the world's population died.

The Overseer (may Its name be blessed forever) watched these events unfold and did not intercede.

Metal Sheet #3
Inscription and Translation

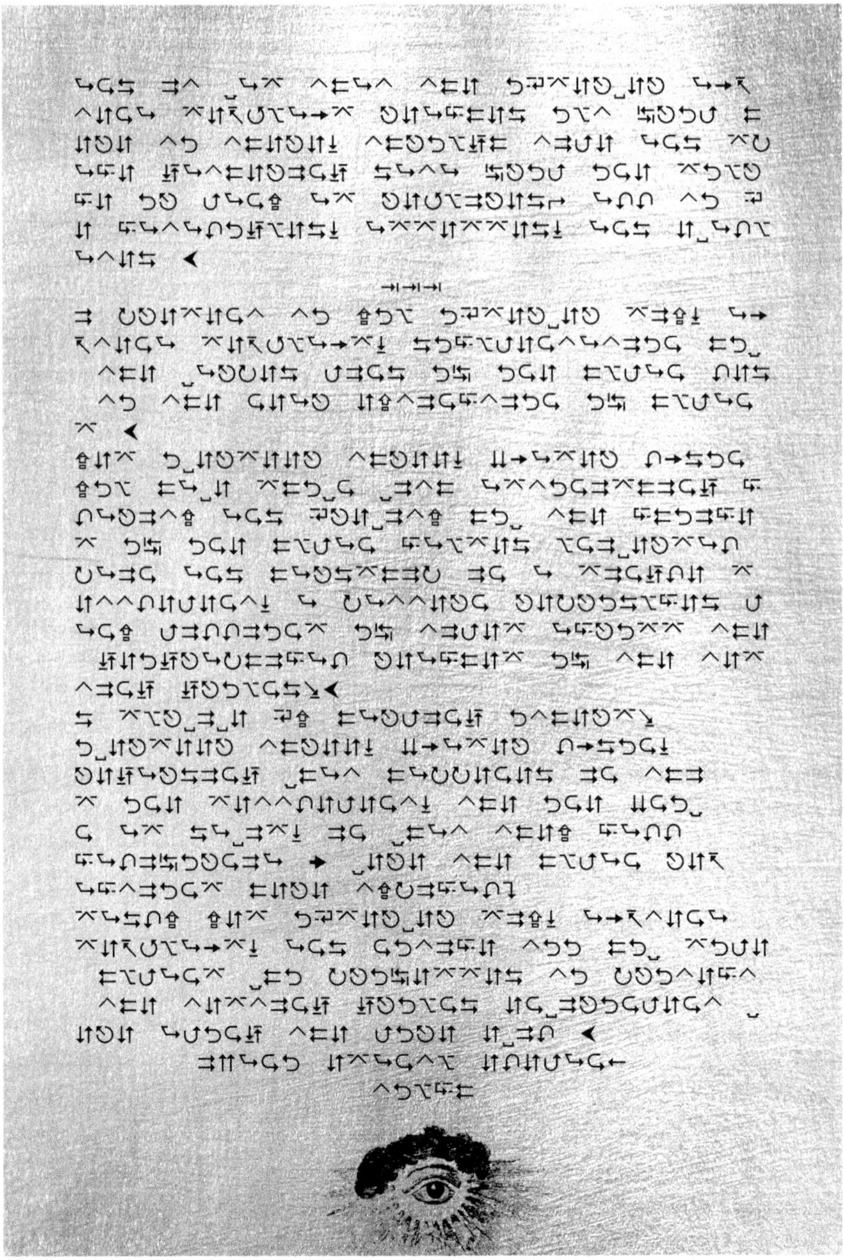

And it was that the Observer A'-Tena Se-Qua reached out from here to there, through time and space, gathering data from one source or many as required; all to be catalogued, assessed, and evaluated.

***

I present to you, Observer 6 A'-Tena Se-Qua, documentation how the warped mind of one led to the near extinction of all.

Yes, Overseer 3 K'Aser L'Don, you have shown with astonishing clarity and brevity how the choices of one human caused universal pain and hardship in a single settlement, a pattern reproduced many millions of times across the geographical reaches of the Testing Ground.

True, I have documented, Observer 6 A'-Tena Se-Qua, that most units on the Testing Ground are unprepared for even small, let alone the large disasters and exhibit an astonishing naiveté for survival and understanding basic requirements for food, water, and protection.

Your report, Overseer 3 K'Aser L'Don, reveals that most rely upon others for survival and are not in charge of their own being, that life to most reflects day-to-day activities with little attention given to how precarious existence can be on the Testing Ground.

Notice too, Observer 6 A'-Tena Se-Qua, that certain individuals continue righteous behavior even when facing disaster or death, while others abandon good choices and survive by harming others.

Overseer 3 K'Aser L'Don, regarding what happened in this one settlement, the one known as Davis, in what they call California, were the reactions here typical?

Sadly, yes, Observer 6 A'-Tena Se-Qua, and notice, too, how some who professed to protect the Testing Ground environment were among the more evil.

Ijano Esantu Eleman!

Chapter 5: Evening Reading 5

Document 5, Cave Location: Case 43-B
Dark Time Part I. In the Beginning

When life is gone no one is left to assess blame
The dead do not differentiate between right and wrong.

(Anonymous. Wall Graffiti, Davis, Old California.)

Pre-Note

As the Ripple Event expanded, local, regional, and national economic and political collapse quickly followed. What became known as the Dark Time spread globally, a time characterized by the 3Ds: danger, disease, and death. The cities of Africa, Asia, Europe, and the Americas became death traps, and were abandoned as starvation and disease reached all continents.

Local conflicts erupted regionally; international trade halted; the major currencies collapsed, lost all value, and became useless. Riots broke out in more than 100 countries; order could not be maintained, as tens of thousands were killed and twentytimes more were injured. Anarchy and chaos ruled; the strongest and cleverest benefited – others were left to fend for themselves.

Following upon the riots were natural disasters. These claimed additional lives, leaving millions homeless and without access to food and water:

earthquakes, fires, tornadoes, and typhoons brought havoc and seeded despair among all populations. Hundreds of thousands in the northern hemisphere died, as winter chill embraced the living. Without electricity, additional millions died during the snow and ice storms that swept the northern climes of the Americas, Asia, and Europe.

Citizens of many countries accustomed to local, state, or national programs for disabilities and poverty assistance were at risk, as governments could not support their underclass. Aid programs ended: the poor revolted in protest, but to no avail.

Open warfare erupted along the American southern border states with Mexico, with civilian casualties on both sides numbering in the tens of thousands. Understaffed clinics and hospitals without electrical power were inundated with the wounded and could treat those only with non-life-threatening conditions. The governments of both countries could not provide financial assistance to families dispossessed of their lands and homes as a result of hostilities. Tens of thousands and more stormed the United States/Mexican border seeking assistance. Understaffed border guards fired upon the mobs, but could not halt the exodus as refugees trekked into the United States, crossing the borders from California east through Texas. Border and nearby cities could not cope with influxes as refugees filled the streets of American towns including San Ysidro, Yuma, Nogales, El Paso, Laredo, and Brownsville, which were invaded by mobs that attacked the residents, invaded their homes, and killed occupants.

Events that followed added even more horror, as anarchy and chaos could not be stemmed. Crime grew violent, swirled like a fire fueled by fear, uncertainty, and abandonment of moral behavior. Self-protection became the mantra and key to survival: the strong prevailed – the weak died either in their homes or on city streets. Those who had chronic health problems that required medication received none: sons and daughters were forced to bury their elderly parents in backyard flowerbeds. Those without potential backyard burial sites dug graves in vacant lots – until these too were filled to capacity, leaving few options.

Adapt or die: what else was there to do?

Access to food and drinking water became critical. Few households had food stores that could last more than a week; few had cases of bottled water stored in their garages. Why keep so much food on hand when we can go to the grocery store any time we want? Why stash cases of bottled water – there always is tap water that we can use, right?

Wrong!

The ability to differentiate safe from toxic wild plants became critical. When household food supplies were depleted, some scoured local parks, greenbelts, and vacant lots seeking edible wild plants. But few of those forced by necessity to collect them could differentiate safe from toxic species. Most individuals who gathered plants during the Ripple Event and early weeks of the Dark Time made poor choices, thinking that the wild species collected were safe for family members to eat. As a result of misidentifications, most became sick and many thousands more died.

Early in the Dark Time, survivors with vital professional skills had better options for survival. Survivors with less essential skills disappeared: gone were most actors and thespians, artists and sculptors, musicians and singers. Those in the cultural arts who once had entertained and brought joy to thousands simply vanished from sight.

Fear Years

Beyond the abandoned cities isolated settlement communities (ISCs) developed, of which initially there were hundreds. Most of these failed due to lack of assured water and food resources. Those that stabilized commonly were renamed and reorganized as settlement groups (SGs). The successful settlements sprang up along the shores of lakes and river systems. Uncertain of what the future might bring, survivors clustered and formed self-administrative units with assigned duty and work responsibilities for all members. Given the diversity of survivors, there was significant variation in work and labor ethics. Some accepted their group responsibilities and completed assigned tasks. Others, groused and lazed about, not taking their assignments seriously. Such divergence resulted in deep divisions within the settlement group memberships as two primary groups evolved: The Ins and the Outs.

The Outs – those who were lazy, less able or unwilling to work, and expecting to live off the efforts of others – soon were banished from the settlement groups. Most such individuals died within several weeks. A few managed to survive for short periods of time as:

Garbage pickers: those who survived on the discards from the SG that banished them; and

Micro-hunters: those who snared and trapped rabbits, squirrels, and other small game before local supplies were exhausted or winter hibernation made hunting impossible.

In rare instances, the garbage pickers and micro-hunters subgroups received second chances to rejoin their settlement group. But such instances of reconnecting and acceptance happened infrequently.

Other individuals survived the Ripple Event and flourished during the initial days of the Dark Time. They and their ilk became known collectively as chameleons, as their behavior was akin to that lizard reptile. They worked and lived as bandits, blending into the background, receiving little notice from their quarry until it was too late. They observed and carefully watched the manners and behaviors of loners – those banished individuals forced to wander through the vegetation-shattered zones. At the opportune moment, they descended upon their quarry, attacked, stole usable goods, and usually killed the loner wanderers. As a result of such banditry most settlement groups adopted behavior that later became the mantra that characterized the early years of the Dark Time:

TNO (trust no one).

Even worse events followed during the initial years of the Dark Time. Medicines and vaccines no longer were produced by pharmaceutical companies. This reality, coupled with the poor nutrition among many of the survivors, resulted in millions of deaths. Unknown to most, those who existed on limited and poor diets compromised their immune system, and antibody production declined. Local, then regional outbreaks of the common cold led to hundreds of deaths, and then accelerated to epidemic levels. The common cold was followed by four different strains of deadly flu viruses. Childhood diseases, among them diphtheria, measles, and whooping cough, returned with a vengeance and as a result hundreds of thousands of children died

When simple cuts became infected, the infections turned into festering abscesses. Commonly, these abscesses became gangrenous. Amputations – attempted at first – were no solution because such patients subsequently died from renewed infections due to unsterile conditions.

Smallpox and polio returned. Cases of HIV and MERS increased dramatically in the Americas and Western Europe. Ebola killed millions in the African continent, then refugees from Africa seeking safety and survival in Europe took to ships and crossed the Mediterranean in attempts to reach Malta, and southern portions of Spain, France, Italy, and the Greek isles. Some brought the virus with them and ultimately western and eastern Europe, and subsequently western, southern and east Asia were infected with Ebola, and additional millions more died.

These terrifying initial years of the Dark Time later became known in historical documents as the "fear years" (FYs). This was a time when the former nations of the world already had collapsed, and no centralized authorities were in place to meet the food, water, and health needs of their populations. During this period, an estimated 95 percent of the world's population perished, an unimaginable catastrophe in which individuals and cultures caught up in the anarchy and chaos of the fear years in Africa, Asia, the Americas, and Europe nearly ceased to exist.

As the anarchy and chaos reigned throughout much of the world, the pious gathered in small groups to share their fears and cried out in unison in 6,000 different languages:

> *Oh God, help us; Oh God, stop the madness, we the humble and the afraid beseech Thee.*

The agnostics, and those who had lost their faith, gathered in small groups to share their fears and cried out in unison in 6,000 different languages:

> *Whatever universal force that exists, we the humble and the afraid beseech Thee – help us to survive; save our children.*

Throughout the world where more than two people gathered, a common conclusion was drawn:

> *It cannot get worse.*

But it did.

And it came to pass that stockpiles of poorly protected nuclear weapons fell into the hands of unsophisticated rival political and religious groups that had survived in remote settlement groups. And because of cultural and religious hatreds that originated centuries earlier, coupled with the innate longing for revenge, the launches began from deeply dug and protected silos – operational through battery power.

The first to be destroyed in blinding flashes of light was Israel, where the holy city of Jerusalem, sacred to Christians, Jews, and Muslims, was obliterated.

In retaliation the holy cities of Mecca and Medina were targeted, followed by destruction of Vatican City, the seat of Christianity. In Asia the great Buddhist and Hindu pilgrimage centers of Borobudur and Varanasi simply vanished.

Then followed destruction of seven major cities previously evacuated during the Ripple Event or early years of the Dark Time: Geneva, London, Moscow, Paris, Peking, Shanghai, and Washington, D.C.

Millions dead because of political and religious miscalculations.

Why these cities and not others?

Why not Djakarta, Johannesburg, or Los Angeles; Madrid, New Delhi, or Tokyo?

There were no answers.

The hearts and souls of the pious were damaged and the vocabulary used by the faithful to describe God changed forever.

Gone: the gracious, loving, and righteous God;
Gone: the compassionate, merciful, and protective God;
Gone: the creative, omnipotent, and preserving God;
Gone: the radiant, truthful, and wise God.

No words could describe the reality of such destruction and death across the face of the Earth. Imams, ministers, pundits, pastors, priests, rabbis, reverends, and other religious leaders of the existing faiths all wrestled with the events but could not answer the basic question: *Why?*

Report by Cambria Powell, Certified Data Collector
Day 4, Week 3, Month 7, Solar Cycle 13

I, Cambria Powell, was assigned to interview Owen Bell on the above date. My assignment was to explore issues that followed the atomic explosions that killed millions:

Powell: *You agreed to speak with me on this topic?*

Bell: *Yes. I have something important to tell you.*

74

Powell: *Let us begin: Please identify yourself and what you know about the atomic launches.*

Bell: *My name is Owen Bell. I was a former elder in my church prior to the Ripple Event. I lost my faith because of these horrible events. Does it really matter to you and others who launched the first missile, who first misinterpreted the political-economic signals? It did not matter to the billions who died earlier as a result of epidemics, natural disasters, carnage and pillage. Death is death, whether from these causes or from those blinding flashes of light and radioactive fallout that follows.*

After the launches and destruction of the holy sites and selected cities, the atomic ash clouds set into motion continued their lethal journeys, their directions uncontrolled and subject to the vagaries of weather patterns. The radioactive ash rained death down upon innocent populations in Turkey, Greece, the Balkans, Italy, Malta, and southern France. Other nations suffered significant but lighter doses of radiation as the ash clouds circled the globe.

Can you conceive, have you any idea, what it is like to lose one's faith, to lose confidence in the basic goodness, to have seen untold death and destruction? The prayers of millions upon millions went unanswered; we on Earth received no message from the worshiped gods despite the universal pain suffered by adherents and followers.

My son Ralph Bell was an officer in our nation's missile command center. What was it like for my son to receive the code words from his military commanders to launch the missile under his control, knowing that it would obliterate religious shrines and holy sites frequented by worshippers he had never met?

Gone in an instant: Jerusalem and a thousand lesser Jewish temples and synagogues.

Gone in an instant: Mecca and Medina and a thousand lesser Shiite and Sunni shrines.

Gone in an instant: Vatican City and a thousand lesser Christian basilicas, churches, and shrines.

Can you not see in your mind's eye the blinding flashes of light, the crushing, explosive blasts, and the powerful emissions of radiation?

Can you not see in your mind's eye the clouds of death swirling about, raining radioactive dust across the continents, oceans, and icecaps?

But even such destruction was not enough. See them now in your mind's eye – the Four Horsemen – bringing more conflict, famine, and death for decades and perhaps for centuries to come.

My faith is gone; my heart is empty. What can ever fill that void?

Report by Glen Baker, Certified Data Collector
Day 6, Week 5, Month 6, Solar Cycle 14

After the nuclear blasts, religious leaders who survived were hard-pressed to answer the questions and pleas of their congregations. Each of the primary religions had prescriptions for noble behaviors and charitable interactions, but the underpinning on faith and belief began to be challenged, slowly at first, and then abandoned by to many of the once faithful.

Various settlement groups met the spiritual needs of their members through non-denominational meetings that many participants valued. From such meetings new sets of dictums began to emerge that focused on charity, helping others, emotional joy thanksgiving, and group protection. Some of the documents, as the one cited here from Mountain Pass settlement group, in eastern Old California, urged members to consider life as a measured period of time – whose full measure could not be charted or fathomed – and a set of new considerations that were posted bound the members together:

1.   Aid the weak and helpless; do not coddle slackers.

2.   Treat women and men equally – each gender complements the other; two as one is superior than two who are separate.

3.   Allow for differences; no individual, clan, of isolated settlement is without flaw; tolerance and understanding of differences are the marks of a mature society.

4.   Form groups for security and regeneration of the population; groups must never run afoul of the basic principles that define one's culture.

5.   Do not institute laws that degrade the power and goodness of individuals.

6.   Do not fear life; embrace life and the opportunities presented each day; explore and relish life; reject hedonistic pleasures that focus only on self; control your behavior.

7.   Offer cries of joy to each newborn; shout out in happiness at each birth; wonder at the moment of emergence and the innocence of the newborn; and welcome each to the community hearth.

8.   Celebrate the coming of age and maturity of each young man and woman; look forward to the formation of age-sets as new responsibilities to family and clan unfold.

9.   Honor your mating partner; enjoy the pleasures and wonders brought about by your union.

10. Take pride in accomplishments, but recognize that one's deeds are the sum actions of those who trained and helped you through life's passages.

Adjustments: Early Years

Thus it was that the "fear years" were characterized by natural disasters (earthquakes, floods, storms, and tornados); epidemics of communicable diseases; unthinkable behaviors (assassinations, economic collapse, military aggression, political missteps, and general disregard for the poor and helpless survivors); and atomic destruction. Civility and kindness toward others had been displaced by jungle rule, in which strength and power subjugated the weak and helpless.

Settlement groups became the norm for habitation, in which small groups banded together for mutual benefit and formed settlement clusters along the shores of freshwater lakes, freshwater rivers, and streams. Survival of individual settlements was contingent upon not only access to food and water, but also hard work and contributions by all, male and female, old and young, in which 8-12 hours of communal efforts commonly characterized their daily existence.

Apprehension and fear continued to dominate the thinking at most encampments. Fear that outsiders might arrive and infect the membership with pathogens or expose the children and adolescents to unacceptable behaviors. Within most settlement groups, decisions were made by group majority, others by elected council members (ECMs) by direct vote, with the advisory caution that any individual elected could serve only one year.

Report by Echo Bryant, Certified Data Collector
Day 4, Week 1, Month 9, Solar Cycle 14

Some settlement groups insisted upon population management so not to outstrip scarce, available food resources. In some instances, such decisions resulted in compulsory contraceptive policies to limit births. At other settlements, all females of childbearing years were encouraged (and sometimes required) to bear children.

The Ripple Event and fears experienced during the early years of the Dark Time persuaded some settlement groups to reject previous household and social living patterns. One such pattern evolved at New Home settlement group in southeastern Old Oregon, where a powerful matron assumed leadership roles over the community. She selected up to four adult males to live together as consorts and form a family unit. The alpha matron chose each male, based upon his mental agility, strength, and technical skills. She then bore a child sired by each consort, and thereafter she did not mate with the four males again. Within one month after delivery of her fourth infant, she handpicked four adult females, also chosen for their mental agility, strength, and technical skills. The nine members of the family unit then lived together, and each of the new women were required to become pregnant by a different matron's male unit. All children born from these couplings were raised communally, and each took the last name of the alpha matron.

Report by Potter Ingram, Certified Data Collector
Day 1, Week 4, Month 2, Solar Cycle 14

Groups interviewed who had lived through the adjustment years had re-instituted quite variable types of economic barter systems. One settlement group named Lake Preserve, in northwestern Old Montana, developed a new economy based upon metal salvage. These residents formed a hierarchical system of tradesmen and tradeswomen known as discarded metal changers (DMCs). Younger members of the group would leave the settlement to scavenge through the remains of nearby abandoned villages. They sought out and brought back to the settlement group metals of all types: aluminum, brass, copper, iron, and steel, even on occasion gold, silver, platinum, and tungsten.

Once the younger DMCs had returned to camp, older members used their skills to forge, melt, shape, and form objects for use at the settlement group. When unexpectedly larger caches of metals were procured, these were melted, and ingots were shaped into graded sizes and weights that represented different values for use in trade and exchange.

The Antelope Plains settlement group in central Old Montana was a powerful, protected collective with local economic concepts that expanded regionally. Members voted on who could or could not receive their products. They set equivalent values in metal ingots for different commodities (food, livestock, and indentured labor). So important was the DMC group at Antelope Plains that their fame spread widely, and families in other settlement groups sometimes sent their sons to work at Antelope Plains as indentured labor for up to six months, learning skills of the trade.

Subsequent investigations during the post-Dark Time Recovery Period revealed that while DMC members at Antelope Plains claimed that they allowed the youths to return home after the traditional six-month indentured period, almost all the youths died in metal-retrieving "accidents."

(NOTE ADDED AFTER INTERVIEW: I, Potter Ingram, suspect that these deaths were purposeful in order to keep secret the metal-keeping techniques used at Antelope Plains.)

Report by Fallon Meyers, Certified Data Collector
Day 6, week 4, Month 5, Solar Cycle 14

Other settlement groups especially favored key persons within their settlements. At Strength and Honor settlement group in northern Old California, two such groups of individuals were identified through interviews: food producers (FPs) and water tenders (WTs).

The FPs formed what might be called a "fledgling union" of producers that acted together to decide who would receive their products and at what price. Foods were exchanged for services and for needed products, such as medicinal baskets and containers, clothing and furs, herbs and spices, even puppies that could be trained as watchdogs.

The WTs, in contrast, were guards with the singular duty of protecting the settlement water supply from potential contamination. They patrolled day and night, seeking any evidence that loners or banished others were utilizing the water supply without authority. If someone was seen doing so, the WTs acted quickly. One report revealed that following rules and regulations of the Strength and Honor settlement group, the WTs made certain that such individuals *never returned* (i.e., were killed).

Each settlement group visited during this time protected specific elderly men and women, and honored them with high status.

> The sage femmes (SFs), or wise women, were valued since they knew the healing herbs and how to treat basic ills: sprains that could be wrapped; broken bones that could be set; and were responsible for birthing and lactation rituals. The SFs were the linear offspring of midwives who practiced in the pre-Ripple Event centuries. While they guarded their knowledge carefully, they also were responsible for identifying and training their successors. The SFs also were holders of knowledge related to women's mysteries, and were charged with leading female initiation ceremonies as girls came of age and passed in physical status from girls to women.

Other elderly men and women became known as reciters. These individuals were highly valued and respected for their keen memories. Settlement group members looked to the reciters for knowledge and key information related to past times, especially the pre-Ripple Event years. At group meetings and at celebratory times (especially Equinox and Solstice events) they would be asked to recite the settlement group's history, the genealogies of each member, and respond to the questions of both adults and children interested in historical events. Their tasks were twofold: to know, understand, and comment upon earlier events, allowing comparisons between past and present cultural practices to be drawn and they had the added responsibility to identify and select children to be trained to memorize the genealogies and historical sequences, replacements that could be called upon should their memory fail or death overtake them.

Report by River Livingston, Certified Data Collector
Day 3, Week 1, Month 7, Solar Cycle 14

I had on this occasion the opportunity to interview a member of the Canyon Gate settlement group in southern old Oregon to explore how this community dealt with the appearance of strangers. This portion of my interview with Norris Murphy represents a classic solution implemented during the adjustment years of the early Dark Time:

Livingston: *What were the conditions as you saw them on that critical day?*

Murphy: *A sick child who needed help approached our settlement at Canyon Gate. I recalled the case where a sick child seeking assistance had been admitted into a camp up north near Old Boise. When granted safety inside the settlement, the child – without purpose and without intent – infected the members of the community and all died as a result. The innocent child left the diseased, unburied bodies, and continued to wander, infecting other groups – "Help me! Help me! Help me kind people" was her cry – but death was the payment for help and kindness, until such time the child was murdered so others could live.*

Livingston: *Why are you telling me this story? I am horrified!*

Murphy: *You are young, and I understand your concern. You have not had to experience such situations. I tell it to you because it is true and you need to know.*

My distant cousin, John Snell, lived at that community and was the only survivor of his settlement group. At the time, the child had been invited inside the stockade, John had been absent from the group for three weeks on a trading venture with other settlement groups along the Old Seattle Trail. When he returned, he found all the members of his settlement group dead. He informed me that he touched none of the bodies and left immediately. As he left, John retrieved a written message nailed to the central meeting house door that identified what had happened and described the child. John took it upon himself to track her down. The child had taken shelter up by the Kootenay River. John confirmed who she was and without pause, killed the girl with one shot. It came to pass that his actions were observed and he was brought to trial. He spoke in his own defense, as was his right:

I murdered the sick child so that others could live.

He was found guilty and banished. Being expelled from his clan meant wandering through the northwest shattered zone where life could not be sustained.

We family members presumed that John died; his body was never found.

Two deaths: one of an innocent and the other a decision of self-sacrifice so that others might live.

Report by Indigo Reynolds, Certified Data Collector
Day 2, Week 2, Month 11, Solar Cycle 14

Sometimes accidents or illness killed those best-qualified persons to manage the family food quest. The members of each settlement group could identify the best hunters – male and female – and the individuals who could differentiate safe from toxic plants. But the death of such important group members with essential skillsets, left others with limited abilities in agriculture and crop-raising, hunting-gathering, healing the sick, or barter and trade decisions. When such unanticipated deaths occurred, the age and gender distributions within the settlement groups were skewed and necessitated critical group decisions. In anticipation of such problems, some groups developed administrative practices that allowed them to voice key questions, present them for a group vote, and implement if passed by a majority of adults present. For example:

What responsibilities fall upon each group member to teach others their technical skill sets?

If an adult male or female mate dies during illness, what group and family obligations fall upon the surviving mate?

If an only child dies during illness, what obligations fall upon the mates to sire another child as quickly as possible?

Since so many children die before their 5th year, how many children should be sired each year by the total membership of the settlement group in anticipation of such deaths?

Who ultimately is responsible for the education of children: the group, the family, or both?

Other groups that were interviewed drew up long lists of obligations if group members fell and were crippled, injured in hunting accidents, suffered burns, or were accidentally poisoned after ingesting toxic wild plants. Most of these compilations recognized survival of the fittest as the central issue. The key focus of these compilations was to assure that the clan prospered and the members would be responsible for their own actions. These lists commonly were posted at central locations and throughout the settlement group compounds. According to some interviews, these documents drew the smiles of many passers-by because of the scribbled acronyms at the bottom of the posts. Some examples included:

GSCFO-TBR (good smells cancel foul odors – take baths regularly)

S:LIME (security: lock immediately mice everywhere)

TS-MF-R (take shelter – make friends – relax)

YOYO (you're on your own)

And the obvious: FOR A GOOD TIME – SEE (fill in the blank)

Adjustments: Later Years

During the Dark Time, each settlement group attempted to manage its agriculture. Certain crops, however, no longer could grow, among them corn and certain fruit trees. Farmers in the settlement groups found seasonal success with others, and various cereals, legumes, and vegetable crops soon flourished.

Certain animals, once characteristic and associated with settlements, vanished; little cutie dogs like beagles, Chihuahuas, toy poodles, Pomeranians, and pugs were gone. In their place powerful breeds thrived, among them Dobermans, German shepherds, mastiffs, pit bull terriers, Rottweilers, and the ever-valuable so-called junkyard dogs. When these dogs sometimes escaped the confines of the settlement groups they often formed packs of hunting canines.

Fat, sleek, cats vanished – those that once graced the homes of wealthy families during the pre-Ripple Event. In their place other felines relished the opportunities to sharpen their hunting skills and reverted to feral ways, almost imitating certain others who clustered and formed packs of thugs that ravaged landscapes of the shattered zones.

Numerous documents from the late phases of the adjustment years identify antisocial groups collectively called the abiders. These were groups who watched events unfold from a distance, waited, then attacked the less-defended outposts and consolidated their victories. The abiders sometimes captured adult women and girls of child-bearing years, and selected adult males or boys who possessed needed skill sets. Abiders began to evolve and instituted better weapons training among their membership. They commonly took refuge within strong well-constructed defensive structures in the shattered zones that shielded them from reprisal attack from the settlement groups. Abiders tended to survive in isolated pockets, thrived during the later years of the Dark Time, and passed their genes and skills onto their descendants.

Besides the abiders, there were others who formed raiding parties. One type, the horsemen, roamed the shattered zones on horses stolen from various settlement groups. They seemed to flourish in the shattered zones and raided the settlement groups near the periphery. Their groups commonly numbered 30 to 50, including women and children, and at a moment's notice the band could upload their few belongings and start off in any direction for any purpose as dictated by their leader.

Data collectors interviewed a number of settlement group members who had suffered horsemen attacks, and were willing to relate their experiences:

Report by Ledger Edwards, Certified Data Collector
Day 5, Week 1, Month 8, Solar Cycle 14

Edwards: *You are?*

Johnson: *My name is Evan Johnson. I am a resident of Moose Hollow settlement group. During my youth, we were raided at least four times by different groups of horsemen. While we feared them, our defenses always held. I recall a time when I observed one group that had retreated a short distance from our defensive walls, where they set up a temporary camp. I watched, along with two friends, as the horsemen drank and ate, and then participated in what might be called elimination games (EGs) in which their members vied against one another. Over the next several hours, they boxed (barehanded), wrestled, tossed javelins for distance, took turns hurling the large stone, and competed in foot races of*

84

> *different distances. What I remember, too, is that only the winners were acknowledged, and those who finished last in each event were killed (throat cut).*

Edwards: *I can barely believe this!*

Johnson: *Then why the hell are you interviewing me? Get out!*

So it was that the Alphas rose – the Omegas were culled (actually killed, not culled).

Report by Birch Pollard, Certified Data Collector
Day 4, Week 3, Month 6, Solar Cycle 18

I visited more than 32 settlement groups during my four-year period with the Data Collector Project at Montana State University. My charge was to identify how different settlement groups organized protection and security during the Dark Time. During my interviews, I documented how weapons were stockpiled and especially the manufacture of gunpowder using local sources for charcoal, saltpeter, and sulfur.

Others adopted horse-raiding parties or posses. All trained their male inhabitants as lookouts and sentries. Other settlement groups, for example Hillside Defense and Mesa Caves, developed security systems based upon what they called age-set concepts.

All females and males of these settlement groups were classified by age; as they passed upward through the system their responsibilities grew.

Infancy – childhood – coming of age

Age sets – both male and female

Warriors and defenders:

Age-set 1 – ages 15-21

Age-set 2 – ages 22-28

Age-set 3 – ages 29-35

Youth advisors to the clan – ages 36-42

Young rulers – ages 43-49

Elderly rulers – ages 50-56

Respected elders – ages 57 until death

I encountered in my visits a subset of survivors known locally as purifiers, who augmented security of the various settlement groups. These were males and females who traded in supplies of safe water, traveling around in carts like the ancient Irish "tinkers" of past years. They sold or offered different types of limited technology that would purify water. The purifiers would arrive at a settlement and signal for a meeting. If interested, one or two representatives from the settlement would engage the purifiers initially from a distance. They would ask about illnesses they had been exposed to and, depending upon the response, they would engage, trade, or abandon the effort.

Toward the end of the adjustment years, individuals known as reverse engineers (REs) at several settlement groups worked together and developed the first solar-powered electrical network. This technological advancement was kept secret for two years, before knowledge of their success became widespread. In addition, other workers at the Protective Shield settlement group in northwestern Old Washington developed a unique way to produce solar batteries. With these developments, they were able to maintain a monopoly until well into the recovery period.

Solar-powered batteries led to the revival of timepiece use. Representatives from several settlements organized collective scavenging parties to scour remains of abandoned stores in nearby towns and cities, to search for battery-operated wrist watches and clocks that could be converted to solar.

These developments could not be kept secret, and ultimately the production information was shared during the later recovery periods. Solar power and batteries led to more joyful celebrations that honored the passage of time, in which solstice and equinox celebrations could be coupled with rites of animal sacrifice and military-style games. At these celebrations and games, there was a singular rule: in competitions there were only winners, and no congratulations, laurel wreaths, or medals for second through tenth place.

Only the best were celebrated.

Little by little, the darkness lifted. Along with the emergence into the new light, there was hope for new and better times. But these hopes were not to last. There arose during the recovery period a complement of disgraceful behaviors and petty actions: greed and self-importance returned. Along with the rise of demigods new deities of dubious origin were instituted in certain settlements that required sacrifices (captive animals), scapegoats, and hunting tests – in some instances hunting settlement outcasts – with the intent only to demonstrate the talent of those who survived. Civilization as once known prior to the Ripple Event was lost – except for selected isolated communities in which sanity reigned and conquered the evils of doubt.

One such place was Bison Camp, where a collection of survivors gathered in the Big Hole Valley along the banks of the Big Hole River in south-central Old Montana. This initial group of three young women with their male consorts left Davis, California, by van the morning of November 21st. They had taken educational leave from the University of California, Davis, and planned to return and resume classes before the start of spring quarter. They followed Interstate 80 east out of Sacramento, California, and arrived at Bison Camp, Montana, on the evening of the 23rd, two days later. After unloading and savoring a quick dinner, they slept.

They awoke the morning of November 27, and none – save one – returned to California.

Report by Archer Jones, Certified Data Collector
Day 6, Week 3, Month 4, Solar Cycle 15

I interviewed an aged survivor of the Ripple Event and Dark Time named Craig Thompson, who spoke with me at length. Thompson challenged the accepted view that Farid al-Saif abd al-Karim had triggered the demise of civilization and argued that the Dark Time, at least in the United States, had begun earlier than the date identified in current history books. His reasoning was thus:

> End of silver coinage;
> Substitution of copper-clad coins;
> Mismanagement of personal credit card debt;
> Advertisements consistently touting: "Get the car or the home that you deserve";
> Collapse of the real estate market – then recovery – and subsequent collapse;
> Expanded government overspending;
> Gradual currency deflation that anticipated the hyperinflation to come;
> Emergence of Islamic extremists in Saharan Africa, the Middle East, and elsewhere;

Initiation of the great OC (Obama claim): health for all; everybody deserves to be a citizen; no need for photo IDs; collapse of national boundaries and national culture; what unites Americans vanishes and shifts in title from:

I am an American, to

I am an American of X heritage, to

I am a hyphenated-American, to

I am (pick the country) living in the United States of America.

Attitudes of personal entitlement out of control;

Decline of work ethic coinciding with demands for higher wages;

Demands for expanded government entitlement programs, leading to:

The why work/I am entitled attitude – coupled with the view: *If I don't have what I want, it is because someone else has more – and – I want my share, and I want my share now!* attitudes, leading to an explosive expansion of sloth and lack of personal responsibility.

And then one day the bubble burst as hyperinflation swept the country – one-dollar bills became worthless, less than one old cent. One hundred dollar bills lost 90 percent of their value. As the inflation continued the government started re-printing $1,000 bills with Grover Cleveland's image and then $5,000 bills with the portrait of James Madison. The new $10,000 bills with Woodrow Wilson's image were replaced with the image of James Psalter (secretary of the treasury in the year before the Ripple Event). Common folk disgusted with this monetary collapse blamed a previous president, and attached his name to the $1,000 bills – which couldn't buy much (perhaps two such pieces of paper might be exchanged for a hamburger).

I accept the premise that the person known as Farid Saif abd al-Karim injected the attack virus on November 27, but the United States already had experienced hyperinflation and slipped significantly in the global economy and education, as more and more shoddy goods were produced by companies that once valued quality control. The government was unable to institute the changes needed to reduce or eliminate these social-economic problems. America already was headed for cultural, economic, political disaster when the attack virus was injected: riots, border invasions, bankruptcy of state and local governments, a broken taxation system (and consumer revolt), were all part of the problem leading to the Dark Time. And then the American government broke faith with its citizens and ignored the Constitution. What about the tens of thousands of Americans imprisoned during the tax revolt? How many tens of thousands marched on Washington, D.C., with the banners inscribed with the words, "Don't tread on me?" How many died when they were fired on by local police, National Guard, and U.S. Army Reserve units?

My words suggest that the United States already was doomed. The attack virus injected by Farid al-Saif abd al-Karim was not the catalyst, but merely another straw among many that broke the back of the proverbial camel. Yes, he should be condemned, vilified for triggering the global Dark Time and the demise of civilization, but government officials in Washington, D.C., also share the blame.

After-Word

Comments from Louise Ross, mother of Data Collector Ada Price, interviewed at Bison Camp, Montana Territory, New NorthWest Configuration. Day 2, Week 4, Month 9, Solar Cycle 19.

Was it one man who caused the Ripple Event that ushered in the Dark Time? Or was the cause a clash of ideals embedded in ancient hatreds in which compromise and forgiveness could not be achieved? Or was it both, coupled with the declining economic conditions and budgetary crises experienced at the time in the majority of Western countries?
Must all history be seen through only two prisms: right and wrong? Is it true that what some consider right and just, can be viewed as evil by others?
Do the poles of right and wrong exist only in the eye of the beholder?
I, Louise Ross, have considered the many billions of prayers spoken during recent decades, offered by the faithful with eyes closed and upraised hands. Why were their pleas not answered?
Were the words voiced silently or aloud deflected by political and cultural hatreds, so they missed the intended?
Would a loving deity permit such horrors and inequities?
What are we – the survivors – to think?

Louis Evan Grivetti & Sargent Thurber Reynolds

Why did we survive when nearly 10 billion others did not?
One day I will join the dead and ask the question: Why?
Until that time …
> *I am too sad – too sad to weep.*
> (Source: Anonymous)

Metal Sheet #4

Inscription and Translation

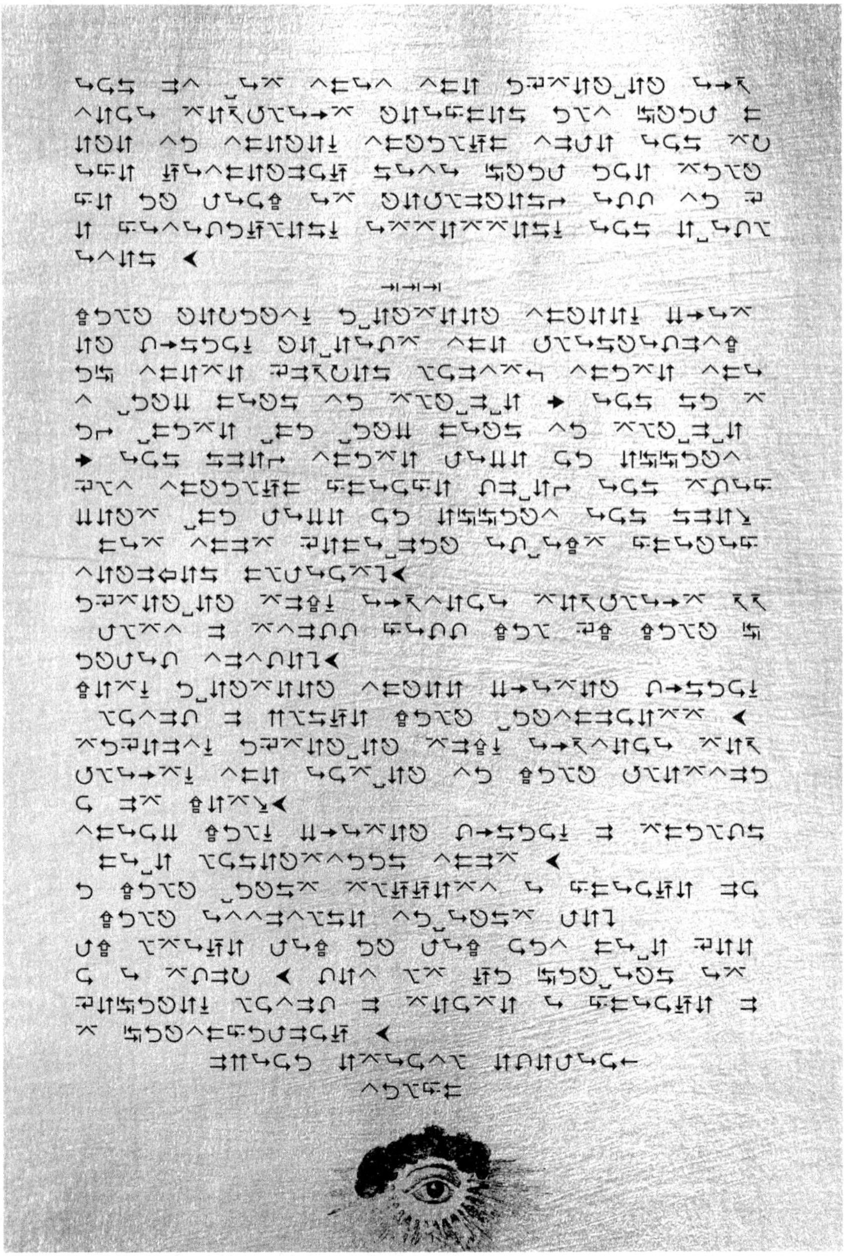

And it was that the Observer A'-Tena Se-Qua reached out from here to there, through time and space, gathering data from one source or many as required; all to be catalogued, assessed, and evaluated.

***

Your report, Overseer 3 K'Aser L'Don, reveals the quadrality of these biped units: those that work hard to survive – and do so; who work hard to survive – and die; those who make no effort but through chance live; and slackers who make no effort and die. Has this behavior always characterized humans?

Observer 6 A'-Tena Se-Qua, must I still call you by your formal title?

Yes, Overseer 3 K'Aser L'Don, until I judge your worthiness.

Sobeit, Observer Six A'-Tena Se-Qua, the answer to your question is "yes."

Overseer 3 K'Aser L'Don, you have described in your report that units who survived these Dark Times banded together into small clusters and formed what they called settlement groups. These survivors apparently reduced their language skills and substituted instead myriad letter abbreviations that dominate your report. What are these DMCs, FYs, SGs, and WTs?

Yes, Observer 6 A'-Tena Se-Qua, my report is filled with such abbreviations but the meanings and contexts are clear, are they not?

You tax me, Overseer 3 K'Aser L'Don, why would these individuals change language so abruptly?

Observer 6 A'-Tena Se-Qua, the simple answer is found in their word, Understanding – basic understanding. Before the Ripple Event words had become increasingly complex, often with many meanings – some veiled while others clear. The phrases, words, and initials in my report were used by politicians and wordsmiths called spin doctors to deceive, mislead, and blatantly lie. The initialed terms now in use are much easier to grasp and understand.

Thank you, K'Aser L'Don, I should have understood this.

Observer 6 A'-Tena Se-Qua, you addressed me less formally, do your words suggest a change in your attitude toward me?

My usage may or may not have been a slip. Let us go forward as before, until I sense a change is forthcoming.

Ijano Esantu Eleman!

CHAPTER 6: EVENING READING 6
Document 6, Cave Location: Case 43-B
Dark Time Part II: Survival

Grandmother with eyes of blue and wrinkled brow begging on the street

What tales of life your eyes reveal – your sorrow and your misery.

Grandmother with eyes of blue and wrinkled brow begging on the street
You spoke soft words imploring me for evening food.

But it was I who passed you by
I did not stop to offer aid
Now in my solitude, I eat the foods that I have stolen
You are always on my mind.

(Source: Anonymous. *Surviving on the Streets*. p. 38 In: *Post Dark Time Interviews*. Edited by L. Jameson. New Bozeman, New NorthWest Configuration: Montana State University Press).

Pre-Note

After the horrors of the Ripple Event and start of the Dark Time, city landscapes of North America changed radically. Cities and towns long abandoned by residents became the haunts of creatures that roamed deserted streets. Packs of feral dogs and wolves made short work of bodies left unattended by family members too weak to perform proper rites of burial. As days and weeks passed, there emerged night gangs of young men and women who had lost their souls, who bore no shred of responsibility. They prowled the streets in search for food and drink, taking whatever scraps and containers that could be scrounged. Rival gangs fought to the death over simple things: arguments over two cases of bottled water and 15 rotten oranges resulted in the death of 27 gang members. Sentinels guarded boundaries marked by graffiti symbols, challenging others to cross the lines invading turf of rivals forced them to defend their territories each day and night.

Old Los Angeles changed forever and morphed into El-A, a multi-ethnic enclave in which rival gangs of youths (Asian, Black, Hispanic, and White) divided the city and fought protective turf wars to the death. Old San Francisco became FriscoLand or SanFran, an area of desolation with isolated enclaves of Chinese- and Italian-American survivors. Old Sacramento or River City became Sacto, where survivors organized a settlement at the confluence of the Sacramento and American Rivers

Smaller towns and cities crumbled, soon to be overgrown with weeds and characterized by rats and vermin that fed upon the discards of those unwilling to leave and unable to seek safety elsewhere.

Survival: The Early Years

As time passed, the organizational configuration that once had characterized North America changed dramatically as six regions of survivors: the map forever changed with the emergence of:

New PlyMouth (known as NP): the PlyMouth Configuration extended from Old New England, south to the border of Old New York and included portions of eastern Old Pennsylvania;

New Confederacy (known as NC): the Confederacy Configuration extended from the Ohio River of Old Kentucky on the north, then east and southeast along the Atlantic coast, including all of Old Florida, with a western extension across the former Gulf States along the Mississippi River and sometimes into Old Texas;

The Central Flatlands (known as CF): the Flatland Configuration consisted of all or portions of the former prairie states east of the Rocky Mountains, Old South and North Dakota, Nebraska and

Kansas, and portions of Oklahoma, and the states west of the Mississippi River;

New NorthWest (known as NNW): developed along an arc extending from Old Washington state eastward through Old Idaho into Montana, south into Wyoming and portions of Colorado, and along the Pacific coast south into Old Oregon, where settlements at Crater Lake formed the southern boundary.

New SouthWest (known as NSW): an area clustered in lands that included the southern portions Old Oregon, then through Old California and east across the desert regions of Old Nevada and into Arizona.

New Deseret (known as ND): this configuration, centered in Old Utah, was bounded on the west by New NorthWest and New SouthWest, and extended south to include portions of the former states of Old Nevada, Arizona, New Mexico, and the southern portions of Old Colorado.

Beyond the borders of these regional configurations were the shattered zones, disputed territories, the haunts of wild beasts, where ruthless gangs lurked.

Wealthiest and most organized politically of all the new configuration clusters was New Deseret. Old Salt Lake City suffered terribly during the Ripple Event, but the Mormon religious tradition of stockpiling food supplies coupled with the availability of nearby snow-melt runoffs sustained many during this time of severe hardship. New Deseret, positioned east of the great western mountain chains, was isolated geographically inside the great saline basin, and soon became a central node for re-emergent barter and trade systems during the early and middle years of the Dark Time. No other cluster of settlements in North America had such quantities of salt that could be mined, bagged, and stored. During the Dark Time and recovery periods, salt became one of the most valued commodities in the barter systems that emerged, and the Mormon merchants (MMs) mastered and controlled this trade throughout the continent.

Along the tenuous boundaries of these six clusters were the shattered zones, areas of death to most but home to certain clever loners and stragglers banished from the settlement groups. In some shattered zones, small groups with specialized activities flourished. Among these were the horse trainers (HTs) of the prairie heartland; the buffalo riders (BRs), who approached local settlement groups and put on rodeo-like shows in which young, agile group members jumped and somersaulted off the back of the buffalo – imitating an ancient tradition of bull-jumping with roots that could be traced back centuries into Mediterranean cultures.

Some settlement groups required as part of their children's rites-of-passage that initiates (male and female) track and chase down prong-horned antelope in the shattered zones to demonstrate dexterity, and knowledge of animal behavior. Other settlement groups required male initiates to camp out for a month in selected mountain areas within the shattered zones to track pumas, slay the beasts, and then return with pelts. After these tasks had been completed successfully, the boys – now men – were awarded the title "cat chaser" (CC), and were feted at special clan ceremonies where they were branded on their right shoulders with a symbolic intertwined double-C, indicative of their new status.

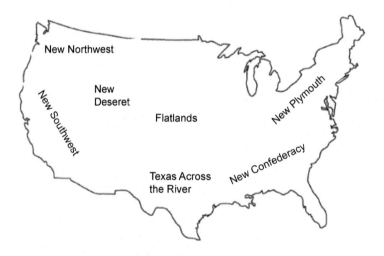

North America: Configurations and Shattered Zones
(Source: Certified Data Collector Information)

Factors That Facilitated Survival

In the days, weeks, and months leading up to the Ripple Event, most of the inhabitants of each town and city in North America could be assigned into one of two categories:

First understanders (FUs) – those individuals who recognized the seriousness of the political and economic problems unfolding in the United States (Congressional logjam; presidential fiats that ignored Congress; national debt that exceeded 20 trillion dollars; inability to halt out-of-control spending; and other such problems);

and

Cloudy thinkers (CTs) – those individuals who convinced themselves, their families and friends, that all problems (whether personal, familial, regional, or national) given enough time and good thoughts, would cease to be problems and would be resolved. The common mantra of the CTs was that local, county, state, and federal governments knew what was best for Americans and would provide aid and financial assistance during times of local, regional, or national disaster and help all those in distress.

Then the Ripple Event struck North America with a hammer of destruction.

Events in Davis, California
Bowman Hoffman and Elko Griffin, Certified Data Collectors
Summary Report
Estimated Date: Solar Cycle 15

In the city of Davis, California, police essentially were overwhelmed by the magnitude of the disaster as it unfolded.

Gone: access to cash and bank accounts.

Gone: telephone or computer service.

Gone: electricity or gasoline.

All the food stocked at grocery stores, restaurants, and fast-food outlets vanished the first week. And when the city water supply pumps no longer worked, the riots started, and grew in intensity each day. Local police and the California Highway Patrol were unable to control the mobs that ran amok through the city streets, vandalizing stores, stealing even bags of dog and cat food, taking whatever they wanted. By tactical funneling of the rioters, the majority of those on the street were forced into DCs (detention camps) erected in Community Park, since it was impossible to house the 13,487 rioters in the city jail. Because conditions in the DCs were filthy, with no toilets and limited access to water, and due to the city's inability to provide food for the detainees, the Davis City Council forced the chief of police to release the rioters and let them return to their homes.

This unilateral decision by the Davis City Council caused a break in what previously had been shared confidence and mutual decision-making, and forced the Davis police to pull back and decide which felony crimes should be cause for arrest, and which ones ignored (at least for a week) – given the limited capacity to house prisoners in the city jail.

A second major riot in downtown Davis followed and involved armed gang members who had entered Davis from the nearby communities of Woodland, Winters, and West Sacramento. Confrontations between police and rioters resulted in the deaths of an estimated 478 persons, and the arrest of an additional estimated 4,500. These rioters were funneled into Community Park and caged in a second detention camp that had been erected quickly. During that evening, another swarm of rioters attacked the police guarding the temporary Community Park detention camp; the rioters tore down the chain-link fence and released the detainees. In the melee that followed, 15 officers were killed, along with 286 rioters.

Davis citizens, appalled by the week's events, clamored for answers:

Why was this happening? There must be a cause. All this must stop!

The Davis rioters who had escaped detention began to blame "others," those who were different. Groups of thugs attacked and burned the Davis mosque; Muslims retaliated (erroneously) by burning the Davis synagogue, and several churches.

Police now understaffed and reeling from the week's events were unable to cope with the anarchy and violence.

And through it all and into the weeks that followed, there was no relief: commercial food and water essentially were gone.

Places of death abounded: nursing homes; the DRV (Davis Retirement Village); doctors' offices and clinics; and police holding cells. Suicides among homebound Davis residents numbered in the hundreds.

Behold a Pale Horse.

The Horsemen of the Apocalypse no longer were Biblical metaphors; famine, destruction, and death were real.

Survival: Early Treks

During the early weeks of the Ripple Event, groups of first understanders met in small clusters, then committed themselves to form small bands. Armed and walking together, they left the cities and towns of North America in search of safety and security. Some in California walked northward along the Pacific coast, traveling mostly at night. They gathered kelp and netted marine tide pool animals for food, or stole foods from farmers' fields and orchards, or from abandoned houses. Their sources of drinking water commonly were abandoned backyard swimming pools.

These earliest journeys were dangerous, and most participants died along the way. The key to survival during these early years of the Dark Time was knowledge about how to pass through vast areas of lands, later designated as shattered zones where anarchy and death awaited those with limited skills. At times, luck seemed to be the most important component of survival.

Other first understanders took different approaches to hunger and thirst difficulties. If their towns were situated along rivers or lakeshores, most did not leave since the key to survival remained a regular source of water. Some had limited experience using reflective solar ovens that could be used to pasteurize water in limited quantities. These individuals and members of their families were advantaged over others who had no access to these simple tools. Once the family supply of water had been assured, attention then could be directed toward securing adequate quantities of plant and animal foods.

Dogs and cats, pet guinea pigs and white mice, snakes and lizards, snails and grubs – all became family food resources. Some who had read about survival stories from the siege of Leningrad, the Nazi occupation of Athens, or the terrible events of Beirut – when standard food sources were unavailable – recalled how birds could be caught easily using sticky pastes laced with poppy and sesame seeds, then smeared on tree branches to attract birds. When they landed, their feet were entrapped and they could easily be captured.

Identifying wild plants and household ornamental species that could be consumed was more difficult, given that most plants in all ecological niches are toxic to consumers in one way or another. Some clever children had the idea that they should go out and gather plants, then feed quantities of them one at a time to their pet dogs. If the dog did not vomit or become ill after 30 minutes, then the children would gather more of these varieties and bring them home for family meals. Little by little, people in these isolated communities began to adjust.

Interviews conducted at the end of the Ripple Event and throughout the Dark Time, revealed that only about 5 percent of those who had survived the Ripple Event lived more than five years into the Dark Time. But if they survived, they had been toughened and hardened by the experience. Some elected to remain where they were, but others hoped for new lives in new areas. And it was from this desire that a new idea arose among the barter merchants at New Deseret that brought new hope for survival for additional thousands of Americans.

Survival: The Selection Process
Autumn Henderson and Mason Bailey, Certified Data Collectors
Summary Report
Estimated Date: Solar Cycle 20

The task assigned by our supervisor, Fowler Jensen, was to search the Montana State University History Project archives and review reports, diaries, and letters that covered the Dark Time and recovery years to gain an appreciation of the types of people who survived the Ripple Event and achieved acceptance and safety at local settlement groups. In Table 1, we present the acceptance/rejection criteria obtained from 48 settlement groups surveyed throughout the New NorthWest and New SouthWest Configurations. Table 2 data present occupation/profession at the time of the Ripple Event and early Dark Time, and the relative percentage that were accepted into the settlement groups.

This assignment was exhausting emotionally for us, since the data provided a clear understanding of life and death decisions, and what it was like to live and survive or be rejected and die. If not selected, the decision meant almost certain death as individuals had to continue their struggles within the nearby shattered zones.

The lists presented here are abbreviated; full documentation can be viewed at the Montana State University History Project archives (File Box DT: 4-6A-32).

Table 1: Behavior characteristics of Ripple Event survivors who sought admission into local settlement groups. (Franklin Assessment Variables; data from 48 SGs in New NorthWest and New SouthWest Configurations).

Franklin Behavioral Variables: Persons Seeking Entry	Persons Accepted by Settlement Groups
Protectors vs. Demolishers	Protectors
Helpers vs. Leaches	Helpers
Leaders vs. Followers	Leaders
Inventors vs. Dullards	Inventors
Sharers vs. Loners	Sharers
Savers vs. Spenders	Savers
Talkers vs. Listeners	Listeners
Buyers vs. Sellers	Accept both
Traders vs. Manipulators	Traders
Creators vs. Destroyers	Creators
Builders vs. Demolishers	Builders
Renewers vs. Backsliders	Renewers
Unifiers vs. Separatists	Unifiers
Aiders vs. Watchers	Accept both
Hunters vs. Gatherers	Accept both
Wanderers vs. Settlers	Accept both
Givers vs. Takers	Givers

Summary (based upon Franklin Assessment Variables): Personal and work characteristics considered most attractive to administrators at the New NorthWest and New SouthWest settlement groups were: builders, creators, gatherers, givers, helpers, hunters, inventors, listeners, protectors, savers, sharers, traders, and unifiers.

Table 2: Occupations and percentage of acceptance rate (Data from 48 settlement groups in New NorthWest and New SouthWest Configurations).

Occupation: Those Seeking Entry	% Acceptance Rate	Occupation: Those Seeking Entry	% Acceptance Rate
Accountant	13	**Dentist**	81
Admin.Assistant	5	**Dietitian**	88
Advertising Executive	<1	Disk Jockey	<1
Agricultural Technician	85	**Farmer**	99
Air Traffic Controller	<1	**Fisherman**	97
Ambulance Driver	7	Fitness Trainer	36
Architect	3	Flight Attendant	2
Artist (Visual Media)	<1	Foreign Language Instructor	5
Athletic Trainer	15	Fund Raiser	<1
Auditor	<1	Geologist	28
Banker	<1	Geographer	7
Border Patrol Agent	28	Health Educator	38
Budget Director	2	Historian	12
Carpenter	98	Home Economist	62
Casino Dealer	<1	Horticulturist	71
Ceramic Engineer	43	Hotel Manger	<1
Certified Public Accountant	<1	Immigration Inspector	<1
Chaplain	13	Industrial Designer	38
Chemist	79	Insurance Claims Adjuster	<1
Child Care worker	33	Landscape Architect	2
City Planner	4	Lawyer	<1
Civil Engineer	83	Librarian	8
Comp. Programmer	12	Loan Officer	<1
Cook	56	Mail Clerk	<1
Crossing Guard	<1	Mental Health Counselor	65

Mechanic	75	Radio Operator	18
Military Officer	74	Real Estate Assessor	<1
Missionary	4	Restaurant Manager	6
Motion Picture Director	<1	Safety Inspector	31
Museum Curator	<1	Screen Writer	<1
Musician	7	Secretary	7
Newspaper Editor	<1	**Security Guard**	84
Nurse	93	Sheet Metal Worker	63
Nutritionist (Ph.D.)	61	**Soldier**	78
Paleontologist	2	Sports Agent	<1
Parking Lot Attendant	<1	Tax Accountant	9
Phamacist	78	Textile Designer	3
Photographer	5	**Teacher**	84
Physician (M.D.)	99	Travel Agent	<1
Pilot	3	Truck Driver	6
Plumber	68	Vending Machine Mechanic	7
Police Officer	46	**Veterinarian**	94
Priest/Clergy Leader	3	Food Server	4
Printer	<1	**Welder (Arc)**	93
Probation Officer	<1	Writer	4
Professor (University College)	22		
Property Manager	2		

Summary: Occupations/skillsets with greater than 75 percent acceptance rates included: agricultural technician, carpenter, chemist, civil engineer, dentist, dietitian, farmer, fisherman, mechanic (automobiles, motorcycles, tractors), nurse, pharmacist, physician, security guard, soldier, teacher (grammar school, high school), veterinarian, and welder.

After evaluation and review, those turned away were forced to resume wandering through the shattered zones. If those rejected survived and reached a second settlement group, another selection would take place.

The process of winnowing life primarily occurred during the early years of the Dark Time. The documents examined reveal the anguish and pain of those facing the selection process (SP) as well as by the evaluators. Most who sought safety and security during these early treks died during the process. Those who survived commonly left exceptionally poignant accounts in which they documented their journeys and described the anxiety of waiting to hear whether or not they would be accepted.

Bliss Perry, Hometown: Gunnison, Old Colorado
Accepted at Ibex Jump Settlement Group, Eastern Old Colorado
Deposition: Montana State History Project
Archive File: SG/IJ: 17A-3-C7
Document Dated: Day 5, Week 2, Month 7, Solar Cycle 12

> I was a nurse at Valley Hospital in Gunnison, Old Colorado. I began my trek two days after the onset of what became known as the Ripple Event. I gathered my two children, ages 10 and 15, and started walking north as we had no access to transportation. We suffered for four days on the road, but the morning of the fifth day in the distance was settlement group Mountain Stronghold. We were part of a group of more than 75 souls waiting outside the defensive stockade, pleading and demanding selection for admission. Although I was a nurse, a profession likely in high demand, I had no idea how many nurses already were sequestered inside the protective walls of the settlement group, so I remained engulfed in fear. We stood together outside as early morning passed and ultimately I waited for more than 13 hours before my turn came. And then it was that the evaluator stood before me and my children. I could barely speak through my dry parched throat but answered her questions to the best of my ability. When we were chosen for admission, I wept with joy as I led my children into settlement group Mountain Stronghold.

And

Marsh Copeland, Hometown: Redding, Old California
Accepted at Red Wood Sanctuary Settlement Group, Northwestern Old California

Deposition: Montana State History Project
Archive File: SG/RWS: 4-B-26/C
Document Dated: Day 3, Week 5, Month 8, Solar Cycle 12

> (Day 1): *My wife, our two children and I were rejected and turned away at the Safe Camp #1 settlement group, and we feared the next days and weeks. The next day we were out of water. I stole two bottles from an elderly couple so our children could drink. I know that I will be damned for this action, but we already are damned, forced to wander through this wasteland not knowing what will appear in the distance, or who might attack us day or night. While I have lost my faith, my wife continues to pray. Perhaps she will be successful in our salvation, for this I cannot say.*

> (Day 2): entry page ripped out)

> (Day 3): *Only two of us have reached the outskirts of Red Wood Sanctuary settlement group. Yesterday, just before the golden glows of sunrise and sunset, our son died in the morning; our daughter in the late afternoon. Now thirst and fear of what may happen next have driven my wife mad. She sits on the ground as the evaluator interrogates me. He tells me that I have been chosen for acceptance, perhaps due to my potentially useful skills as a building contractor. My wife was rejected. The evaluator says that I must decide quickly to enter Red Wood Sanctuary, or not. I glance at my wife, the woman that I have lived with throughout our years together, and make my decision…*

Most evaluators could participate in the process only once, and refused further involvement. The anguish and pain of selection was too great. The documents examined contain numerous accounts regarding the ethics and moral responsibilities in making such judgments, as these two examples reveal.

Keira Marshall, Hometown Not Reported
Accepted at Bear Hollow Settlement Group, Northeastern Old Oregon
Deposition: Montana State History Project
Archive File: File SG/BH: 7A.37.C
Document Dated: Day 2, Week 4, Month 9, Solar Cycle 12

> *The day I served my evaluator duty, 47 men, women, and children were assembled outside the stockade walls. They had encamped the previous night. They were hungry and suffered from thirst, exposure, and*

exhaustion. *Two in the group were elderly engineers; one of them exhibited festering wounds that needed treatment. Five women with children pleaded with us and shouted, "Please, if you cannot take me, then at least take my child (or my children)." Before the selection process began, several fights broke out as men pushed forward to be in the vanguard of those evaluated first. It was a horrible task, in part because we, the members of Bear Hollow settlement group, were safe within our facility, yet we had limited food supplies and essentially no medicines. Tell me — you who know so much and sit in judgment of me and the other evaluators — tell me — you who have never been required to make such decisions for the safety of a settlement group — what would you have done?*

And

Sanders Peterson, Hometown Not Reported
Accepted at Jensen Peninsula Settlement Group,
Northern Old California
Deposition: Montana State History Project
Archive File: SG/JP:8D.35C
Document Dated: Day 1, Week 2, Month 10, Solar Cycle 12

> *I had my wife and children to consider. I could not look into the eyes or listen to the entreaties of those outside the stockade walls. I interviewed these poor souls, made my decisions, left the stockade checkpoint, went to my shelter, held my children and wept. Harsh times required harsh decisions, but I feared that through my participation in what became known as the selection process (SP) I lost my sense of values.*

Survival: The Great Treks

And it came to pass that certain ambitious survivors from New Deseret (old Salt Lake City) created a cadre of barter merchants that traveled in groups throughout much of the former American northwest and southwest regions, connecting with isolated individuals and small groups who bartered for protection to leave the festering cities and towns. The barter merchants would lead such individuals and groups out of their despair with the hope of survival in new lands, at new locations called settlement groups. The cost for their services was dear, ingots of metal, tools, weapons, construction needs (bolts, nails, wire, and similar goods). The barter merchants from New Deseret would guide their charges along new trails to safer destinations.

Those who participated in such ventures were called trekkers. One of the Mormon trails linked former Los Angeles residents fleeing El-A with the Olympic Peninsula in Old Washington state. This trail wound along the Pacific coast north past Old Santa Barbara, Goleta, Avila, and Cambria, bypassing Monterey and the ruined portions of FriscoLand. Then the trail led northward along the coast of Old Oregon and ultimately to the Olympic Peninsula, where settlement groups bid for the newcomers whose worth was based upon their intellectual abilities and professional skill-sets. Those not selected – too bad – were released to fend for themselves in the shattered zone.

Other trails linked central California with central Montana, and used a trail that at one time followed Old Interstate 80 (now Eye-8-0) from Davis into Nevada, bypassing New Reno and the roving gangs that characterized that once-thriving community, through Wells, Nevada, then north into eastern-most Idaho, into the Big Hole region of Montana, southwest of Old Butte.

The Mormon guides, accompanied by soldiers on horseback (SOH) troops to protect the travelers, also employed territorial scanners (TSs), who went in advance of the trekkers to evaluate potential dangers from roving bands and isolated crazies.

The Mormon barter system initially had developed along abandoned rail lines not previously destroyed by teams of salvaging iron pickers (IPs), who uprooted the steel rails and enlisted clever blacksmiths to re-forge them into swords and other weapons. They used in their trade railroad handcarts, and along the rail routes would meet with survivors who wished to trade for essential goods. Chains of connected handcarts characterized these transactions. The first and last carts were manned by traders bearing weapons, the middle ones were laden with goods to barter.

So successful were these original barter trips that the Mormons of New Deseret began to offer what they advertised as SPJs (safe passage journeys), whereby the leaders would depart New Deseret and take long loop journeys to different localities, where they could recruit potential travelers to leave their dangerous surroundings and trek to a new, safe community.

Once interviewed and vetted for any medical conditions, intellectual capacity and professionalism, those families selected then were accepted. Especially wanted by the Mormon guides were: famers, craftsmen (blacksmiths, carpenters, masons), hunters with previous tracking skills, former soldiers, nurses and physicians, and veterinarians. Rejected for the most part were individuals without previous college education. Always rejected were those perceived to be idlers, self-indulgent narcissistic politicians, and cinema and television personalities.

Each participant was provided with a backpack to store only the most necessary items, and one specially constructed cart that was five meter-yards by three in length and width with appropriate depth to hold key goods. The cart could be either pushed or harnessed to family members to pull (as they went over grades along the journey). Each family being relocated was given an inventory checklist of what to carry by cart:

> Metal ingots for barter along the way and upon arrival at their destination; Cooking and food storage containers; Weapons for self-protection; Fire-making and water purification equipment; Protective clothing for all seasons; One or two personal memory items; and for children, one or two toys. In all instances no pets were allowed on the trek.

Mark Edwards, Certified Data Collector
Interview: Great Trek Security Guard Roberto Sandoval
Montana State University History Project Archive: File 18:SG.42a
Document Dated: Day 2, Week 3, Month 5, Solar Cycle 17

Edwards:	*Please state your name.*
Sandoval:	*Troop Captain Roberto Sandoval.*
Edwards:	*You once were a member of the border riders. Please tell me about this organization.*
Sandoval:	*I still am in spirit even in retirement. The border riders in my time – and continue to be – a small professional army recruited from the best warriors within what we sometimes call The Alliance – this being a geographical area covered by New NorthWest, New SouthWest, and New Deseret Configurations. Often the riders are joined by volunteer scouts from Native American tribes, or a combination of tribes that occupy the western Flatland Configuration. Our primary task has continued to be patrolling and defending the northeastern and*

southeastern limits of The Alliance where most raiding parties cross into our territory. Small detachments of riders also accompany certain trading and exploration treks. Our allegiance is to the group, not to the configuration of member origin, although the design on our jacket buttons – here, you can see mine – reveal this. The riders are well-equipped and skilled and more than match the power and ferocity of any raiders they might encounter. Upon retirement – as I have – each trooper keeps his buttons as proud reminders of his activities, but wears them upside down to indicate their new status – look, how mine are worn. Others, not quite so lucky, are said to remain on duty where they fell during their last battle – as in the case of my mate choice. The citizens of The Alliance and their traders owe much to the riders.

Edwards: *Please tell me about yourself.*

Sandoval: *I was born and raised in the eastern edge of the Bay Area in what is now Old California, a zone that became part of the northern shattered zone. The city of my birth is a small matter; its name has been long lost. I grew up in uncertain and violent circumstances and times during the Ripple Event, and the early years of the Dark Time. Our impoverished situation caused our parents to indenture my brother, sister, and me to the Mormon trekkers. This was as payment for our passage out of Old California, as we were part of the fall trek during the period sometimes called DT1-Gamma. We understood that our parents were to follow that coming spring with payment sufficient to purchase our indentures, but this was not to be. Our parents did not appear at the prescribed time at the spring rendezvous at Wells, Old Nevada. We learned only later that they had been killed by insiders during a food riot.*

So began our five years serving the trekkers. As children, we were assigned to simple, lighter tasks – gathering firewood, helping make and break camps, and assisting the cooks. This last task became my sister's ongoing responsibility and, through the years, she became an

Rider button/medallion:
New NorthWest
Configuration

Rider button/medallion:
New SouthWest
Configuration

Rider button/medallion:
Flatland Configuration

Rider button/medallion:
New Deseret

accomplished cook in her own right – a skill that paid
dividends for her through the years. Soon my brother
and I were allowed to accompany the scouts whose job
it was to reconnoiter routes, follow behind (so to warn
against surprise assaults from that quarter), and to detect
possible ambushes. We sometimes set our own to kill those
tracking our progress through the mountains and plains.
In general, we served as the trek master's eyes.

As scouts, our responsibility was to reconnoiter and
provide information, rather than directly confront bandits
and, as such, we were only lightly armed. Initially, we
were provided with slings and slingshots, and practiced
our hunting skills daily. As we improved our hunting
abilities, we used our simple weapons to slay small game
animals (squirrels, rabbits, sometimes a beaver) for
communal meals. With further proficiency, we became
part of the group's defense. My sister proved to be an

accomplished hunter in addition to her cooking abilities. Once my brother and I were out with the scouts, and they provided us with bows and spear throwers for the first time. We then practiced with these weapons and soon were able to bring down mountain deer and plains antelope. We were not allowed firearms, as these weapons would have slowed us because most of the scouting was done on foot. Weapons – with scarce ammunition stockpiles – were kept with the main group. Our trek master – whose word was law during the journey – carried one of the old guns. We thought this must be for show, because ammunition for such guns was very rare to nonexistent. We held this idea until three foe men were killed and another dozen scattered faster than one could think. So his weapon definitely was not for show.

My older brother and I proved our worth with the scouts. By the end of our five years, we were invited to serve with the mounted scouts. Then we were armed with crude, but useful muzzle-loading rifles, but we kept our slings and bows in reserve, a habit I have continued until this day. Those five years were not all labor, as we were schooled in words, this being required for all living in New Deseret.

My brother chose to remain with the trek scouts and served well until he was killed by bandits. My sister married and became a freelance cook and housekeeper. Through her, I had three nieces and two nephews; two are alive today.

I was asked to serve with the border riders and agreed. From then on it has been on-the-go riding and protecting the limits and interests of The Alliance. To this end, I was issued my buttons and a multi-shot handgun called a revolver. It was of better quality and performance than the firearm I had when I was with the trek scouts. I also received two steel swords – a long one for slashing from horseback and a short one for close-in combat and stabbing. The revolver and short sword proved most useful in confrontations with the raiders and bandits.

111

My stint with the border riders proved more serious than my previous efforts with the trek scouts. On my second patrol, we came upon what remained of two farms that had been attacked by raiding parties. This introduction was a horrible but necessary component of my education as a border rider. Ultimately, we caught that band – they had no idea that we were tracking them in their territory – and we made quick work of them. After what I had seen at the farm – with the mutilated bodies of women and children – we all took great joy in hearing and ignoring the raiders' pleas for mercy.

Edwards, why are you looking at me this way? I suppose you believe that the revenge we border riders took on the raiders was not warranted; if so, I feel sorry for you. You and others like you have no idea sitting here in safety what it was like during the Ripple Event and Dark Time. I make no apologies for my actions or those of my military comrades. They deserved all that we dished out and more.

Edwards: *I am sorry, sir, please continue.*

Sandoval: *As I was saying, now, I am a bit too old for the hard rough and tumble of the northern and northeastern limits. That rough and tumble was not all military. We regularly joined the Lakota in their buffalo hunts – more work but much more fun than chasing raiders, I can tell you. I now command small detachments that accompany treks to New Deseret and beyond. My activities involve main- taining order at the rendezvous, which most often means keeping New Marin's monitors under control. These NM monitors are a craven bunch of good-for-nothings, little more than bullies of the weak, as they pad their silk- lined pockets extorting taxes and fees from hard-working people in NM, while more than half of their population sits around and does nothing – living off locally supplied commodities. In my view, NM is ripe for a second catas- trophe – this one not caused by an attack virus, but by the maggots of internal greed and corruption.*

> *I now hold the rank of troop captain, having been
> promoted following the Battle of the Three Rivers,
> west of Bozeman, New Montana. I was acknowledged
> for my valor there. When my military comrade Elsa
> Breckenridge was killed during an ambushed by raiders, I
> became like a wild man, avenging her many times, asking
> no quarter and giving none. One does in battle what is
> forced upon one, eh? Only a month prior to the Three
> Rivers battle, we had been granted permission to marry –
> these memories make my heart heavy for what was – and
> for what never can be.*

> *I can talk about battles, but such matters probably
> interest you no further. I thank you for your hospitality.
> Oh, what is this – another beer? Edwards, I drink to your
> health and to those who have gone on before.*

Survival: Settlement Groups as Places of Safety

In the later weeks of the Ripple Event and initial solar cycles of the fear years, isolated settlements sprang up along the shores of lakes and river systems when the first understanders left their towns and cities behind and sought refuge either in rural locations already settled (rare) or as groups of like-thinkers, carved their own haven for self-protection out of the wilderness. Some left their towns and cities on bicycles, but the majority walked. Most died along the way, either through starvation and lack of water, or they were attacked by bandits and thugs, robbed, and left to die.

The sisters, along with their parents and consorts, settled at Big Hole, Montana. During the Ripple Event and early Dark Time, the small community flourished with ample water and food resources. They decided by group vote that their settlement should be renamed Bison Camp.

Other settlement groups were founded and evolved during these early years of unsettled future.

Within the western regions of North America, settlement groups with similar long histories were established near:

- Monterey Bay, at the mouth of the Salinas River, Old California
- Humboldt Bay, at the mouth of the Eel River in Old California
- Tillamook Estuary, adjacent to Cape Meares Lake, Old Oregon
- New Astoria Peninsula, along the John Day River, Old Oregon

- Yakima, at the junction of the Naches and Yakima rivers, Old Washington State
- Boston Harbor on Budd Inlet, Old Washington State

Each had their own system of self-rule and administration, education of children, surveillance and protection systems, and traditional health and medical care and instruction. Some settlement groups developed more militaristic positions, while others continued to tolerate non-workers and idlers who lacked direction or valuable skillsets and lived off the hard efforts of the remainder.

At one settlement group, more than half of the residents voiced opinions that they had no responsibility to the group. These individuals were egotistical and self-indulgent with a sense of self-entitlement. This was the situation at New Marin (NM), on the north side of San Francisco Bay, a community that had been isolated since the Golden Gate Bridge had been demolished during the Ripple Event. The administrators at NM did their best and issued calls for community action and direct appeals to work for the improvement of the settlement, but to no avail.

Given that through the years so many still leached off the majority who were hard working and more ambitious, New Marin – as it was known throughout the western North American region – became an isolated joke. When the elected administrators of NM sent assistance appeals to other nearby settlement groups in the western zone, not one replied with promises of assistance. And even today, NM remains on the landscape as an abnormality that reflects the worst of endeavors and behaviors.

Two settlement groups of note were founded in the Teton region of northwestern Old Wyoming. Both settlements consisted of powerful females without men. Calling themselves the New Amazons, they remained isolated and were discovered only during the third solar cycle of the post-Dark Time. While they would have been considered lawless by many observers, they managed to keep their rituals secret. They invited selected males into their settlement group to live with their membership for up to six months to sire children. The males served primarily as sperm donors. Once the female mate had conceived, the male consort was given two options: work only for the betterment of the community and have no further sexual relations, or banishment from the "hive." If the male consort chose banishment, what he did not know in advance was that he would be slain by multiple arrow shots.

After-Word

After the data collectors (DCs) returned from their interviews, they commonly gathered in small groups to share information and their experiences. Such meetings reinforced the importance of their activities, and many formed bonds of deep friendship that sometimes led to mate commitments. Groups of DCs developed ceremonies that further linked the membership and instilled a sense of pride in preserving past customs, traditions, and settlement group histories.

They discussed the impacts of the Ripple Event and early Dark Times, and how the disasters affected individuals, families, and social groups differently. They pondered questions long into the night:

Why were some people able to safely navigate through those terrible times and still maintained their sense of ethics and values, while others were destroyed mentally or engaged in criminal behavior?

Was each person a battleground of opposing forces deep within the psyche that fought daily for supremacy: forces of compassion, mercy, and sympathy against the forces of corruption, depravity, and evil?

For some, the Ripple Event and early years of the Dark Time were challenges to be overcome. For others, these times were crushing and without solution. The Christian pious recalled the passage from the book of Revelation (18:10): *Alas, Babylon – for your judgment has come.* And the pious concluded that doomsday had arrived, and many lingered about wandering aimlessly, waiting for the rapture.

But for most in North America, the quotation made no sense: if they even had heard the name Babylon, or even knew that it was an ancient city in Mesopotamia, who in the twenty-first century should even care about its demise?

And it came to pass that many cried out, protested, and rioted in attempts to stimulate action by their local, state, and national governments. They took to the streets and chanted.

What do we want?
(Yea, yea, yea: what do we want?)

We want food!
(Yea, yea: this is what we want!)

What do we want?
(Yea, yea, yea: what do we want?)

We want water!
(Yea, yea, yea: this is what we want!)

What do we want?
(Yea, yea, yea: that is what we want!)

AND WE WANT IT NOW!
(YEA, YEA, YEA: AND WE WANT IT NOW!

But all their chants, shouts, pleas, and demands went unanswered.

But others realized that governments could not respond to all needs during such terrible times. Such individuals and their families, with selected like-thinking friends and neighbors, weathered the trials of the Ripple Event and early years of the Dark Time.

Those few, the hardy and self, family, or friend-reliant, would experience stabilization and recovery, while most others would not and would perish.

Metal Sheet #5

Inscription and Translation

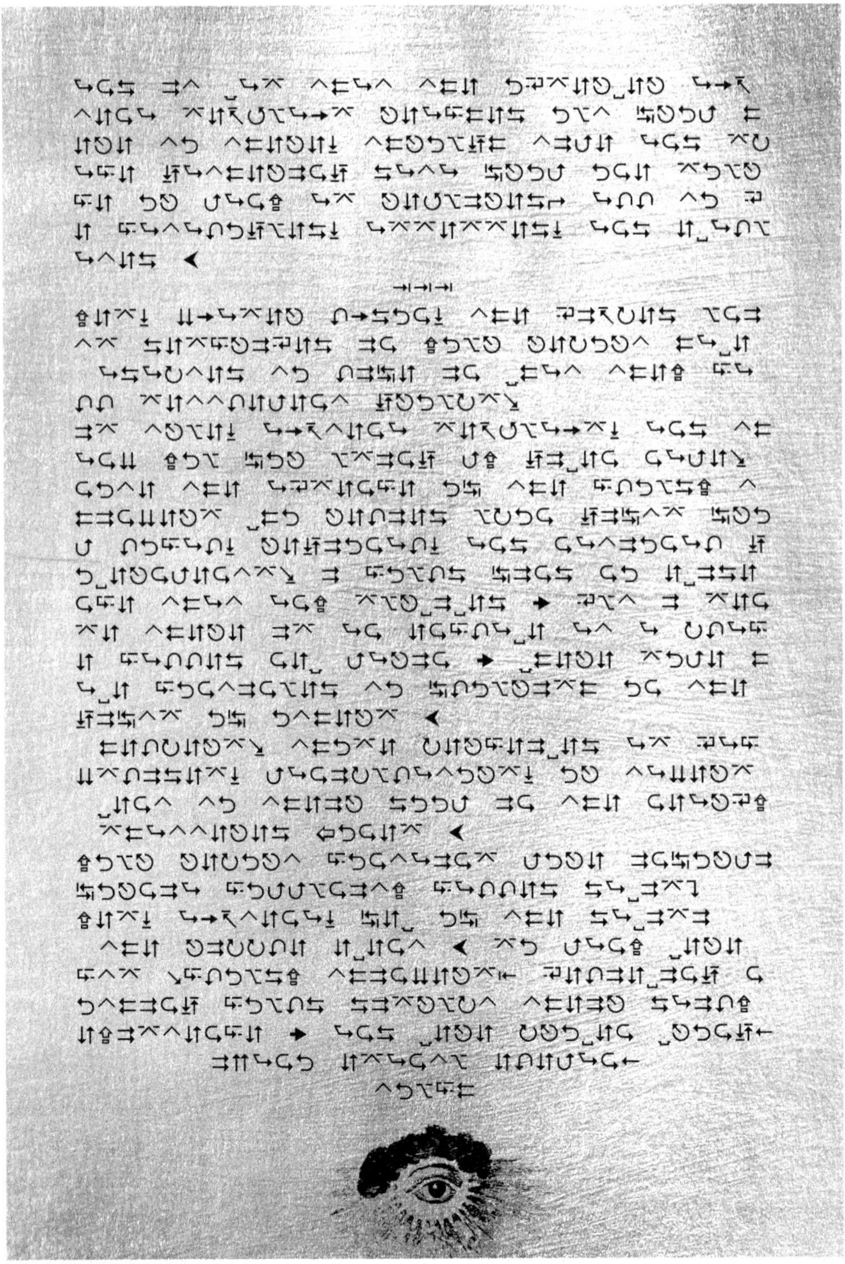

And it was that the Observer A'-Tena Se-Qua reached out from here to there, through time and space, gathering data from one source or many as required; all to be catalogued, assessed, and evaluated.

***

Yes, K'Aser L'Don, the biped units described in your report have adapted to life in what they call settlement groups.

Is true, A'-Tena Se-Qua, and thank you for using my given name. Note the absence of the cloudy thinkers who relied upon gifts from local, regional, and national governments. I could find no evidence that any survived, but I sense there is an enclave at a place called New Marin where some have continued to flourish on the gifts of others.

That would be unfortunate, would it not, K'Aser L'Don?

If true, then it would require a more close inspection – that will I do, A'-Tena.

The depositions and testimonies how the units were selected for settlement group admittance or rejection? It 'twas a life/death process that you reported, K'Aser L'Don.

To be certain, A'-Tena, no slackers, lazy individuals there admitted they were builders, creators, and helpers. Those perceived as backsliders, manipulators, or takers went to their doom in the nearby shattered zones.

What did these biped units mean in their language, "pale horse" and "apocalypse"?

Ah yes, A'-Tena, their words meant earlier times when famine and death were known.

But, K'Aser L'Don, would not logical units be prepared for just the type of destruction that came with the Ripple Event?

As it is with these life forms when food and water are available, they ignore impending signs of disaster and laugh at the need for such preparations – to, of course, their ultimate doom.

Your report contains more information on riots in that small California community called Davis?

Yes, A'-Tena, few of the Davisites survived the Ripple Event. So many were CTs (cloudy thinkers) believing nothing could disrupt their daily existence – and were proven wrong!

Ijano Esantu Eleman!

Chapter 7: Evening Reading 7

Document 7, Cave Location: Case 43-B
Stabilization: Late Dark Time and Early Recovery Periods

I survived
Through pain and sorrow
When others strong
Saw no tomorrow

I survived
Within my band
When chaos reigned
Across this land

I survived
Then came the day
The sun beamed bright
Drove clouds away

I survived
To love again
To walk once more
Through cooling rain

(Source: Graffiti poem on mess hall wall, Cascade Fortress settlement group, date uncertain.)

Pre-Note

Most histories of North America produced during the past five to ten solar cycles suggest that the Dark Time era could be divided into two distinct phases: the fear years represented by the first four solar cycles, and the adjustment years that generally consisted of 10 additional solar cycles. It is debated and argued locally and regionally when the Dark Time ended and the recovery period began. What is agreed to, however, is that the recovery was gradual at the various settlement groups within the North American enclaves.

The shadow of fear and uncertainty slowly ebbed as the settlement groups began to look outward to their neighbors with less avoidance and suspicion. These newer thoughts extended by the council members and most inhabitants of the settlement groups led to cooperation among neighboring settlements, especially to combat natural environmental disasters that threatened. Mutual cooperation developed further when teams fought and contained forest and grassland fires, and when dealing with storms that ravaged the Pacific coast of North America. When terrifying earthquakes occurred in the Yellowstone region of northern Old Wyoming, and at the El-A region, members of local settlements banded together to assist one another and re-instituted the heart and soul of what used to be called the "golden rule" and "help thy neighbor."

Transition

The recovery transition raised awareness of the settlement group members and increased their knowledge of their geographical surrounding. With more familiarity, risk reduction followed as individuals grew to know and understand the hunting and gathering principles that had served others well when seeking food resources within the adjacent shattered zones. Individuals began to spend more time outside the protective limits of their settlements, and as physical activity increased, more healthful patterns of livelihood evolved and life-span averages increased.

The transitions also increased leisure time, made hard work easier, allowed better decisions, and increased the ability to record and preserve historical information. This led to improved construction techniques, improved safety, and better communication and travel safety. Once the basic needs of fire and warmth, food, water, protection and security, and health care were met, more time could be spent on issues related to moral conduct and respect. This gave rise to group confidence, based upon achievement and a sense of belonging to the settlement group.

Toward the end of the Dark Time, members of the various settlement groups became more adaptable and cooperative. Such changes also brought about greater feelings of respect for self, family, group, and environment, as people accepted responsibility and the importance of mutual cooperation.

One of the advantages of these transitions was an increase in individual and group curiosity: learning about the errors of the past so not to repeat them in the future.

Standardization of Calendrical Systems

The issue of calculating time continued to pose difficulties during the post-Dark Time recovery period, since more than 10 different calendar systems were in use at different settlement groups. Previously, the calculation of time posed some difficulty during the Dark Time, given that all electric and most battery-operated clocks and watches were useless until the last cycle of the recovery period. At that time, limited electrical operations resumed, along with limited production of watch batteries.

Throughout the Ripple Event and Dark Time, spring-wound clocks remained in use, but their accuracy varied. Some settlement group members trained in astronomy reverted to older techniques used to document the passage of time. As a result, some settlements retained the old calendrical system of 365 1/4 days. Others based the passage of time on predicted solstice and equinox occurrences, and still others adopted quite different calendrical systems, the following variants being most popular – a yearly calendar of:

> Nineteen months of 19 days each – with a four-day wild period (five days during leap year) when social mores and customs were set aside briefly to accommodate the physiological mating urges and behaviors of both genders;

> Fifteen months of 24 days each – with a five-day wild period (six days during leap year). This system approximated the menstrual cycle phases of the sage femmes and was popular for settlement groups in which adult females dominated the administrative councils;

Thirteen months of 28 days each – with one wild day per year (some settlements accumulated the wild days so that every seven years they had amassed enough time for a wild seven-day week);

Twelve months of 30 days each – with a five-day wild period (six days every fourth year);

Twelve months (days variable: 28, 30, and 31) – with a 52-week cycle and just one wild day every fourth year.

In the present manuscript, the term solar cycle has been substituted for the year for consistency.

Security and Safety Responsibilities

The settlement groups formed during the Ripple Event or the early years of the Dark Times commonly were socially integrated communities without status hierarchies in which the members protected each other and thrived because they accepted responsibilities and service to one another. In one way or another, various settlement groups developed specific rules, regulations, customs, and traditions related to each of the following:

Defense and security: The most important decisions were related to defense and safety of the settlements. Councils at each settlement had authority to issue independent decisions related to four primary topics: defense, trade, survival training, and health and safety.

Each settlement member, from older children to the elderly, was assigned defense-related tasks in accord with their age and skillset. These selected assignments rotated as appropriate as the members gained in strength, knowledge, and cultural-ecological sophistication. Some of the tasks identified included:

Scouts: individuals assigned to make daily treks into the surrounding hinterlands and shattered zones to identify the presence of dangerous beasts or individual wanderers that might pose a risk to the settlement;

Patrols: teams of five to six members that patrolled the settlement perimeter as the first line of defense;

Weapon production and protection: individuals who manufactured and/or cared for weapons. A subgroup usually was assigned to protect the settlement arsenals and ammunition production facilities. A second subgroup commonly was assigned the task of searching for ingredients used to manufacture gunpowder and to prepare necessary amounts of different explosive products;

Visitor risk and external security: other members were assigned to meet with and evaluate individuals or groups of unknown origin that appeared outside the settlement group boundary.

Trade: The critical decision made by each settlement group was whether or not external trade would favorably or adversely exert an impact on the membership and possibly place the community at risk. Such decisions considered whether or not to remain basically self-contained and isolated, or to expand and participate in local and/or regional barter and trade routes. If the latter, decisions followed that identified which external groups would be contacted and how to protect settlement group representatives during exchanges. Specific trade-related issues considered:

Need priority: council members worked with resident elders to develop lists of priority items for settlement needs;

Relative value of goods: determining and assigning the value of trade goods and what items received would best help the most settlement members;

Location and safety: determining which barter and trade centers would be visited, during which seasons, how to deal with security along the way, and the number and identification of settlement members undertaking the assignments.

Survival training: All members of the community were trained in safety and protection procedures beginning in the early years of life. Basic first aid and bandaging skills were taught within each family unit, while more sophisticated skills were taught at seminars given by settlement nurses and physicians. These sessions normally were held monthly or as needed:

Self-medication: what to do when injured and alone, especially when working or traveling through the shattered zones;

Distance communication: mastery of hand signals for communication in the midst of others and learning the significance of trail-mark signs, especially for use when scouting in the shattered zones to alert other clan members; lessons in semaphore systems and smoke signals;

Emergency shelter: construction techniques using only local materials – how to survive when trapped in winter snow;

Fire production: mastery of fire-production techniques using drill, flint and steel, and solar magnifying techniques;

Wild plant identification: differentiation between safe edible wild plants and toxic varieties growing in the vicinity of the settlement group.

Health and safety: A critical issue with potential serious impact on each settlement group was the appearance of unexpected illnesses throughout the Dark Time when medical care – once standard and taken for granted – was based upon new sets of decisions. Epidemics that had ravaged the region were not forgotten, and group safety was at the core of most settlement activities. Reports revealed that each settlement group usually had one or more members who practiced medicine, either as doctors, nurses, or health-care providers prior to the Ripple Event. These individuals worked in conjunction with council members to develop recommendations and rules for personal and group hygiene, as well as care for the sick and elderly, with the paramount goal that the settlement be protected.

In rare cases of the appearance of an illness that did not match the understanding or knowledge of the former health workers, such patients were isolated at special huts constructed outside of the immediate settlement where they were housed and tended by a single volunteer (usually a family member). Contact with other settlement group members usually was forbidden until resolution of the patient's condition.

Training of replacements: settlement health workers had as an additional responsibility the training and mentoring of assistants who could be called upon as replacements;

Identification of plant drugs: teams of adolescent males and females commonly were assigned to work with settlement sage femmes (wise women) who learned to identify local plant species with medicinal properties and their respective uses (and abuses);

Settlement sanitation: special care was given in all settlement groups to maintain proper sanitation to avoid infestations with vermin and potential disease organisms. These tasks commonly included decisions on the placement of latrines, garbage pits, and proper disposal of bodies;

Water protection: guards commonly were assigned to protect settlement group water resources to prevent accidental or purposeful contamination and to assure a ready supply of drinking water.

Membership Involvement

Governance: Few members of any settlement group had political-administrative experience, except at the local business, club, or foundation level, where most such offices were voluntary. In rare instances, some members had been candidates for local elections, perhaps city councils or union offices. Nevertheless, as with most eclectic groups, individuals with charisma and/or appealing personality characteristics, rose to the top and ultimately were elected to settlement groups' administrative councils.

We uncovered no instance of a "dictatorship" in any of the settlement group documents examined, but there was high variation in the composition and structure of the various administrative councils, as well as in methods of election, length of service, and rules governing development and passing of regulations and rules.

Most common were five- to seven-person administrative councils in which members were elected for a one-cycle term and then if the individual wished, could stand for re-election only one time. Other variations included a three-person tier in which the three individuals receiving the most votes were elected and administered the settlement group, with decisions requiring a unanimous or a two-one vote.

Service to community and family: Almost all settlement group members performed assigned or volunteer duties in accord with age and skillset abilities. A common theme among the settlement groups was the concept that it was a privilege to serve one's community, and service was a valuable component in the education and the raising of children. Most often residents could select service commitments that best suited their interests, leaving others to be assigned by council members. We found evidence that at one unique settlement group located at Cascade Fortress, the elders and council members instituted a requirement that their young men and women who recently achieved adult status – after passing their rites-of-passage – delayed mate assignments or confirmations for five years after their initiation ceremony. The intention was to prevent them from becoming distracted and to be better able to focus on their skillsets and community defense service:

Equal opportunity – designated occupations and shared work responsibilities usually presented equal opportunities for men and women within the boundaries of demonstrated abilities;

Mentoring – older group members were assigned or volunteered as mentors to train younger members;

Elder care – elder care was the responsibility of each family.

Education: From the earliest years through their coming-of-age and initiation periods, students learned to appreciate clan history and ethos, work expectations, and social responsibilities. They were taught personal hygiene, individual and group safety, danger awareness, support and respect for others, and dedication to clan protection. Most settlement groups included information on pre-Dark Time history, usually taught by senior elders; the curricula were age-appropriate.

Children: basic skills enabling all to read, write, and compute beginning at their 5th age cycle;

Young adults: intermediate and advanced levels, with practicums to familiarize all with the value of specific trades (e.g., animal management, blacksmithing, farming, hunting-gathering, health, reproduction, and social adjustment, weapon production and use);

Adult seminars: master classes on variable subjects of interest to the membership.

Group Behavior

Clear distinctions regarding expectations for good behavior were repeated throughout childhood, so there would be no misunderstandings or excuses later. Each settlement group evolved codes (some similar, others very different) that defined appropriate and unacceptable behaviors and identified different levels of punishment for transgressions.

Acceptable behaviors: Themes taught beginning in early childhood commonly included:

- Honor and respect for all;
- Equal opportunities for work and leisure;
- Male-female relations and mating decisions.

Unacceptable behaviors: These varied widely among the various settlement groups surveyed; however, several consistencies can be drawn from the records:

Poor behaviors (minor infractions, such as intoxication and ill-will toward others) commonly were reviewed by a tribunal of elders who passed judgment quickly and effectively;

Serious transgressions or crimes against persons or property that threatened security of the settlement were reviewed by jurors (drawn from all adult members), and such crimes were dealt with quickly with harsh verdicts.

Punishments agreed upon by majority decision commonly reflected the following categories:

Non-lethal (minor infractions): after reconditioning (methods highly variable), offenders were allowed to remain affiliated with the settlement;

Non-lethal (serious infractions): punishments commonly included branding or tattooing for crime identification, but in other instances individuals were banished – transferred out of the settlement and released into a nearby shattered zone;

Lethal (heinous crimes): such charges were brought quickly and verdicts rendered promptly. Verdicts commonly were reviewed within seven days by select senior elders (women and men) and, if upheld, executions followed.

Execution methods at the different settlement groups were highly variable.

Recovery: Renewed Sense of Belonging

As the settlements emerged from the Dark Times into the recovery period, fear lessened and members found more time for contemplation and leisure, even recreation in its broadest sense and definition.

A suite of interlocking activities, absent or minimized during the Dark Time, fostered a sense of belonging among the various settlement group members. Beyond obvious activities related to defense, governance, survival training, health, service, and education, other activities that began to emerge ultimately became critical in the evolution of the successful settlement groups. Many of these factors focused on annual and seasonal celebrations in which all members could participate, or celebrations designed especially for specific age and gender groups.

Annual Celebrations

Each settlement group evolved a suite of annual events that marked the passage of time and celebrated life and group security. Most settlements celebrated a variety of the festivities:

Agricultural renewal – planting and harvest:

> **Field blessing:** usually took place before initial plowing and involved symbolic touching of the agricultural implements, and scarecrow competitions with designations as most interesting, unusual, or most effective;

> **Wetting the seeds:** a group action commonly done in secret using either mother's milk or the urine of newborns – thought to assure growth and abundant harvests;

> **First harvest:** cutting the first sheaf of wheat and weaving the still-damp stems into geometric figures, unearthing and carving of the first root vegetables (carrots, potatoes, radishes, turnips), and the sculpting of animal, geometric, or other figures.

Solstice, equinox, and eclipse (solar and lunar) celebrations:

> **Sun or lunar dances:** to commemorate the arrival and departure of the annual seasons. These were highly variable in content and participation. Some dances were performed by both genders, others only by males or females of different ages and life experiences;

> **Annual rendezvous (ARs):** these were annual special celebrations in which representatives from different settlement groups were selected by vote to travel to specified neutral areas and remain for periods up to two weeks. At these

neutral sites, participants bartered, traded, and shared information. Some ARs were held at open campsites in the New NorthWest and New SouthWest Configurations and visited by the eight-zero traders (E-ZTs). Others were held seasonally at the mouth of river systems to take advantage of salmon runs – for example, the Humboldt and Columbia River Rendezvous;

Annual recitation contests: even during the early and middle years of the Dark Time, it was deemed critical by most settlement groups to have their young children memorize and practice reciting their clan history, including names of key ancestors – honorary elders – and remembering what brought about the Dark Time. These recitation contests were anxiously anticipated by the adult membership, and awards were given to participants for the most creative and vibrant recitations;

Annual fitness trials: all settlement groups touted the concept that strong bodies made for better community defense and security. Each settlement supported annual fitness trials for children and adults that included events such as cross-country running, field orientation competitions, rock-climbing, and river rafting. Many settlement groups held inter-gender games and tests of strength in which men and women competed against each other. The names of winners commonly were inscribed in the respective clan books (CBs) and victors received an honorific title for a year. At some settlements winners received tattoos of honor for their fitness success;

Solar darkness: a time of muted remembrance of the Ripple Event and early years of the Dark Time. Such celebrations commonly included ecstatic revelry whenever solar eclipses (partial or full) appeared throughout North American configurations. Highly variable types of dances and ritualized activities and games celebrated the return of light;

Eating the moon: celebrated during partial or full lunar eclipses by revelry, chanting, and group activities (highly variable).

Safety and security issues permitting, some annual festivals were held outside the perimeters of the various settlement groups, for example:

Geyser celebrations: for settlements near New Yellowstone, this activity commonly was considered as an extended family frolic, in which members walked among the various geyser units, avoided hot-spring pitfalls, and witnessed the eruptions together;

Wild horse rides: during these annual events, held in conjunction with one or more Native American groups, herds of wild horses were tracked and the bravest participants attempted to mount and ride – at least for a moment or two. Successful mounters who remained aboard until the count of 10 had elapsed, and were celebrated by all attending. Reports reveal many injuries among the participants;

White buffalo search: more mystical than real, this was an annual event associated with some settlement groups in the eastern portion of New NorthWest Configuration. The activity usually was the prevue of older or elderly males and females, who left their settlement for up to two weeks searching for the mythical beast during the waning years of life. To die on the search and subsequently to receive burial rites administered by the settlement group was considered by many participants to be a most fitting way to end life.

(NOTE ADDED IN TEXT MARGIN: No records exist in the Montana State University archives of instances in which a white buffalo was identified during the Dark Time or recovery periods.)

Elk encounters: in this celebration, which occurred shortly after the spring equinox, teams of men and women vied to demonstrate their keen tracking skills to capture what was called the alpha male elk in the vicinity. If successful, the animal was subdued with dignity, then released;

Hunting with wolves: in some territories this renowned celebration tested the spirit and mental toughness of young male and female adults. The object was to infiltrate and carefully team with wolf packs, then together – through acceptance of complementary hunting skills – bring down a large game animal (deer, elk, or moose). Then, through an almost mystical involvement, share the meat together at the conclusion of the hunt.

Rites of Passage

The classical rites of passage *(rites de passage)* are celebrations that mark key events in life: birth, coming-of-age, marriage/mate selection, activity decline, and death. These events were celebrated in highly variable ways at each of the settlement groups in New NorthWest and New SouthWest Configurations.

Common elements of birth or emergence:

Umbilical cord: the honor of cutting the umbilical cord of the neonate fell to the oldest family child (male or female), to the father, or to one or both sets of grandparents. At most settlement groups, the cord was saved and preserved as a family relic, then upon the individual's death it commonly was buried with the deceased;

Placentaphagy: in some settlement groups, the male mate washed the placenta. He then sautéed the "meat-of-life" with butter or plant oil and shared it as food with all attending the birth celebration;

Lying-in: some settlement groups instituted a 28- to 32-day, or monthly, period of seclusion in which mother and infant resided in a special hut. Admission to the hut by others was carefully limited and monitored. The seclusion customs of some settlement groups held that only an adult female beyond childbearing years could visit and serve the needs of the new mother and infant;

Naming ceremony: some settlement groups encouraged naming the neonate immediately after delivery. Others, in accord with ancient past traditions, waited seven or eight days, even up to 14 days, before assigning and celebrating the name of the infant;

Celebratory meals: infant birth was cause for celebration in all settlement groups surveyed in which all members were invited to participate. In most groups, foods were prepared by elderly men and women who were honored at this time as well, representing the past and present, the so-called beginning and end of clan heritage. Different settlement groups prepared distinctive food combinations that were served only at this time, which accentuated the important meaning of the event. Specific foods forbidden to be served at this meal were highly variable.

Common elements of coming-of-age:

First menstruation/nocturnal emission: this was a time of great rejoicing at all settlement groups that marked both females and males as eligible for their coming-of-age initiations and for participation in athletic, hunting, and strength tests;

Athletic and strength tests: highly variable tests that included rock climbing, running ,and river or lake swims (variable distances over several days), and mock combat. Most such tests were gender specific, although some settlement groups instituted coming-of-age tests in which males and females vied against one another;

Hunting skill tests: highly variable, sometimes requiring seven- or 10-day treks and camping in the adjacent shattered zones in search for specific wild game. Tests included tracking skills, and ability to bring down game as required by the elder councils who supervised the tests;

Tattoos and scarifications: upon attaining success in the activities required by clan tradition, the passage from child to adult would be complete, whereupon, the new initiates received various tattoos and ritual cuttings (to produce scarifications) that signified their new position as adults within the settlement group. Some settlements also instituted specific hairstyles, and specific types of ornamental clothing (or body ornamentation) at this time.

Common elements of mate commitment:

> Terms used to designate mate commitment applied to the male and female, and to the ceremony, were highly variable and included binding, bride, connection, groom, marriage, mate, merger, partner, and union (among others).
>
> **Celebratory meal:** it commonly was traditional that at the conclusion of the rites a feast was held to celebrate the pairing;
>
> **Eve frolic:** in some settlement groups, the institution evolved that on the eve before the commitment celebration male relatives of the female celebrant organized and conducted a ritualized kidnapping, and held her for ransom. Male relatives of the male celebrant then negotiated for her release and paid the proposed ransom in quantities of symbolic foods, drinks, and intoxicants – shared by all adults;
>
> **Jumping the lance:** couples without strong religious backgrounds sometimes replaced church or temple services with an open-air celebration in which the couple stepped over a symbolic lance three times to signify their commitment to each other;
>
> **Herbal strewing:** in almost all settlement groups, the aisle, room, or outdoor venue was strewn with herbs (commonly mint, rosemary, or thyme), which added a sense of natural aroma and beauty to the celebration;
>
> **Celebratory union:** A widely variable tradition in which the first mating was conducted in private, or in other instances, witnessed by selected members of both families;
>
> **Shivaree:** A common tradition especially in New North-West Configuration, whereby after the couple had retired for the night, friends and family members frolicked outside the mating chamber making loud noises (especially banging on metal) throughout the night in attempts to keep the couple awake;

Nuptial dining: festive meals involving family, friends, and settlement members commonly were held on the eve, on the day of union, and morning after the first night together.

Common elements of activity decline (achieving elder status):

Menopause and TD (testosterone decline): at most settlement groups, a celebratory assembly was held to honor those members who had reached this stage in life. Commonly, speeches lauding the celebrants were presented, as well as honorary recitations;

Tattoos and scarifications: many settlements awarded special body markings to signify the passage from active adult to respected elder;

Celebratory meal: at the conclusion of the speeches and recitations honoring the celebrants, a feast usually was held, consisting of special foods (highly variable).

Common elements of death:

Body disposal: this final act was highly variable at the different settlements as evidenced by earth burial, cremation, natural decomposition (exposure to elements), lake or oceanic disposition;

Treatment of family members: most settlement groups granted family members duty and work relief for 10 days following death of a family member;

Cyclical periods of remembrance: memory celebrations to honor the deceased commonly were held 30, 90, and 120 days after death, and on the first, fifth, and 10th solar cycle after death;

Resolution of the umbilical cord: a family member, usually the eldest son or daughter, commonly was responsible for uniting the deceased with his or her umbilical cord. The object then was inserted inside a special container and placed next to the body for final rites and disposition;

Celebratory meal: A funeral feast always followed the ceremony that celebrated the life of the deceased.

After-Word

During the Ripple Event and Dark Time, many millions – indeed billions – lost their faith, became disillusioned, and turned inward, abandoning the traditional religions of Buddhism, Christianity, Judaism, Hinduism, and myriad others. Still, many millions remained faithful. To accommodate these individuals, most settlement groups constructed what commonly were called faith centers (FCs), buildings that provided a sense of calm and religious retreat for those committed to the earlier faiths.

Some other survivors developed and evolved worship practices of astronomic or astrological signs, animals (development of clan totems), and newly constructed machines. Some of these new evolving faith systems included chanting, coupled with dance rituals akin to the tarantella of the Dark Ages in southern Italy; dervish and zar spinning and weaving or swaying ceremonies practiced in the former Middle East; and the convulsive seizure dances in North America introduced long ago by religious sects in Appalachia, and elsewhere.

Still others who had abandoned their previous individual or family faith considered the certainty that there was a creator of a vast universe: a creator unknown, since all matter and star-substance required it to be so. The concept of a creator – whether a named deity or unknown force – attracted a variety of adherents. There arose large numbers of like-thinkers who held to the belief that universal order was being watched, evaluated, and managed.

There was logic to such a view, although unprovable. Was there not logic in nature and natural forces? Who created nature and placed these forces in balance? Were there not systematic and predictable cycles of birth, maturity, and death? There also were seasonal and solar certainties measured by movements of the great sky orbs. A creator, therefore, was logical and certain. But how did these cycles originate, how were they managed, and by what forces?

Many religious faiths in long-ago times prior to the Ripple Event perceived and worshiped ritual triads: Ra who created Shu, who mated with Nut; Osiris, who mated with Isis, who bore Horus; Mary, Joseph, and the infant Jesus; even Delkan and Zorbek, who together raised the twins, Barada and Nikto, whose life cycles reflected both good and evil.

Was there a triad of forces at work in daily existence?

Given a supreme force, might there be a suite of observers – coupled with a parallel group of overseers – who in whatever way and for whatever reason set into motion the horrors of the past to test how individuals would react? In the past, some perceived God as loving, a deity that cared for and protected its followers. But the horrors of war and the sustained continued presence of overt evil – behaviors that commonly triumphed over good – left many in despair. How could a loving God allow global warfare and pandemics?

With the onset of the Ripple Event and the untold suffering and death that followed, many survivors believed there could not be a loving God. But there was – and they were experiencing – a trinity of universal forces that regularly tested individual resiliency, watching as behavior unfolded, observing and measuring reactions to events of unbearable difficulty and suffering, the goal being to test the boundaries and resiliency of the inhabitants.

As time passed, it began to be noted in many settlement groups that supplications were made and attributed to an entity – the "overseer." To some, the overseer was perceived as a god, or The God, while other followers perceived a broad nebulous force that could not be known. Whatever this overseer might be, it was perceived increasingly as unfathomable – but everywhere. Could it be that life existed merely on a testing ground – a place to live, love, reproduce, and die – as the universal forces observed from a distance?

And it was that the concept of an overseer evolved – a force that was present everywhere, but would not interfere with development and activities. And the concept took root and flourished throughout New NorthWest and New SouthWest Configurations.

At Rock Creek Haven settlement group, about two kilo-miles north of Bridge Street, an avenue that once bisected the small settlement of Vernonia in Old Oregon, the seeds were sown for the rise, development, and evolution of a new cult, organized and led by a woman referred to as the "first order priestess." Her purpose, so it was claimed at the time, was expressed by commitment to a faith triad:

1. Protect nature;
2. Ensure harmony; and
3. Cleanse the past – enter the bright future.

The first order priestess attracted few adherents at first, but at the beginning of the recovery period, membership grew exponentially as the tendrils of corruption, evil, and greed slowly re-emerged to infect certain communities.

The new order had become a force to be reckoned with.

Metal Sheet #6
Inscription and Translation

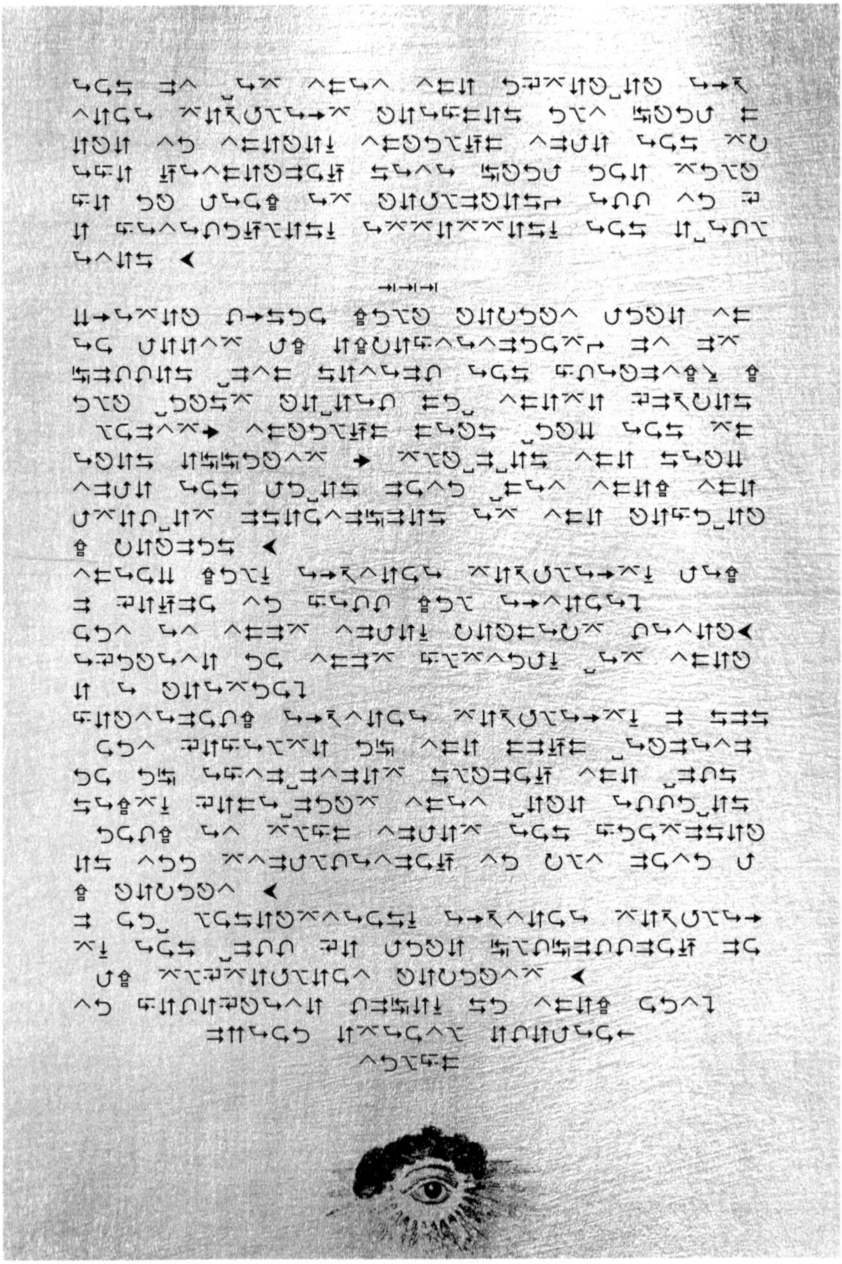

And it was that the Observer A'-Tena Se-Qua reached out from here to there, through time and space, gathering data from one source or many, as required, all to be catalogued, assessed, and evaluated.

***

K'Aser L'Don, your report more than meets my expectations; it is filled with detail and clarity. Your words reveal how these biped units – through hard work and shared efforts – survived the Dark Time and moved into what they themselves identified as the recovery period.

Thank you, A'-Tena Se-Qua, may I begin to call you A'-Tena?

Not at this time, perhaps later.

Did you see the importance of time to these units, A'-Tena Se-Qua? How clever they were to align their food-production systems with celestial seasons, and how the revolutions of the testing ground around the great fiery orb established the event calendar for their celebrations?

K'Aser L'Don, what is it about these groups that they require a number of wild days each celestial round? You did not elaborate on this custom; was there a reason?

Certainly, A'-Tena Se-Qua, I did not because of the high variation of activities during the wild days, behaviors that were allowed only at such times and considered too stimulating to put into my report.

Do you mean to say, K'Aser L'Don, that I would not understand and value learning about biped sensuality? Although I am an observer, K'Aser L'Don, I have the training to process such information.

I now understand, A'-Tena Se-Qua, and will be more fulfilling in my subsequent reports.

On another note, K'Aser L'Don. I was pleased that the settlement groups balanced sustained survival training with development of unique cultural celebrations. All advanced life forms need knowledge how to survive as well as how to celebrate life, do they not?

Ijano Esantu Eleman!

CHAPTER 8: EVENING READING 8

Document 8, Cave Location: Case 43-B
Bison Camp Settlement Group

1. Stasis and Change

Stasis and Change
Ocean deeps to shallow waters
Shallow waters lapping beaches
Endless sands for evermore

2. Stasis and Change

Stasis and Change
Sediments to limestone muds
Karsty lands eroded down
Limestone muds for evermore

3. Stasis and Change

Stasis and Change
Limestone muds then merge with sands
Dune-lined beaches rising high
Sandy dunes for evermore

4. Stasis and Change
Stasis and Change
Beaches swept by ocean waters
Fetid limestone muds abounding
Stinking muds for evermore

5. Stasis and Change
Stasis and Change
Sea waves crashing over land
Flat plains rising, forming mountains
Vulcan's blast for evermore

6. Stasis and Change
Stasis and Change
Slowly land emerges silent
River valley for the settlers
Virgin lands for evermore.

(*Song of the Field Geologist,* author and date unknown.)

Pre-Note

And so it came to be …

An eon-aged planet orbiting the sun, smashed by asteroids, drenched in volcanic eruptions, followed by more eons of waters, rising and falling ocean depths, pounding winds that swirled about eroding cliffs, making sand, forming sediments. Simple animals leaving shells compressed into mud and limestone reefs, everywhere stinking sediments oozing life as ocean waves reached newly formed shores. Oh, the belching mountain peaks, spewing lava and pumice. Mountains eroding and falling into the seas, as lapping waves created untarnished beaches that soon revealed the first footprints of animals to walk upon this place the White men called Big Hole Valley. We of the nation know it as Epen-Dante-Akoie – the place of safety.

(Source: *Dawn Time Recitation,* John Birdcrest, Blackfoot Elder, chanted each dawn to welcome the rising sun, Recorded Day 2, Week 4, Month 4, Solar Cycle 21.)

History: From Initial Native American Groups to First Fur Trappers

How is it that the terrifying geologic processes of fire, flood, quake, and uplift produced the most beautiful of Earth's features? When seen for the first time, the Big Hole region of southwestern Old Montana leaves an indelible imprint on one's mind: here is a place of natural beauty and wonder that saw the first steps of biped individuals more than 15,000 solar cycles past.

Big Hole: a place where hunters tracked and killed mammoths and mastodons, where more recent Native Americans entered the valley and hunted bison, deer, elk, and fished for family food.

Big Hole: A timeless location that ultimately saw the first arrivals of European fur trappers, who established temporary camps along the slow-flowing river where they took beaver pelts, then trekked north and east to meet others of their kind at annual rendezvous.

Big Hole: *Epen-Dante-Akoie, the place of safety.*

History: From Fur Trappers to Settlement Group. A Guide for Teachers

I, Jackson Carter, assistant archivist, Montana State University History Project, discovered the following document on Day 4, Week 1, Month 2, Solar Cycle 47, that had been filed incorrectly. The importance of the document became clear immediately, given that it apparently was written by a settlement group teacher at Bison Camp, probably during solar cycle 11.

The document, titled *The Valley, the People, the Ranch & the Ripple: A Guide for Teachers,* outlines the history and development of Bison Camp settlement group, beginning with an overview of its geographical location, and ending with a description of valley occupants on the eve of the Ripple Event.

This unusual teacher's guide presents a comprehensive report of activities within the Big Hole region, an area of considerable importance to the overall understanding of the Ripple Event, Dark Time, and post-Dark Time recovery periods. Analysis of the content reveals that it most probably was used in a general social science or history course at numerous settlement groups throughout New NorthWest and New SouthWest Configurations. The text and syntax appear to be aimed at fifth- to sixth-year students, with standard instructions for their teacher.

Upon presentation of proper credentials, the document may be examined in the Montana State University Archives, File: SG/BC: 43A-13B

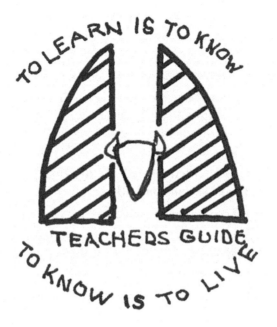

Bison Camp *Teacher's Guide* title page image

Teachers' Guide Page 1

The Valley, the People, the Ranch & the Ripple:

A Guide for Teachers

Hints and instructions for teachers are shown by bold italics. The information may be adjusted for teachers in regions other than Bison Camp, New Northwest Configuration.

The history of our canton began in the Big Hole – a valley named by fur trappers very early in the century before last.

Explain that the trappers called most valleys "holes."

The Big Hole is about 30 kilo-miles wide, and runs 60 kilo-miles north-south between the Pioneer Mountains on the east, and the Beaverhead group of the Bitterroot range on the west.

Your students might be more comfortable with the terms "three hours easy wide" and "10 hours hard north-south." If a map is available, point out the Big Hole or sketch a map on your wallboard if you wish.

The Big Hole River was named by the trappers. It had been called the Wisdom River by Lewis and Clark, and runs north-south through the valley.

Summarize the explorations of Lewis and Clark here.

Winters can be very harsh in the Big Hole. For this reason, it was very little used by Indians during that season, and no tribe lived within it. During the summer, the valley was primarily used as a horse pasture by the local tribes, as it was not considered the best hunting country.

Details of Indian interactions with the Big Hole are covered in the guide, "Our Indian Friends and Allies."

The region offered good trapping, but this resource was soon played out.

Here is a good place to ask and brainstorm "How could this happen?" A good way to reinforce the influence – usually far from benign – of man on nature.

Due to the severity of its winters, settlers did not arrive in the Big Hole until the 1890s.

Teachers' Guide Page 2

It is assumed students at this level will be able to roughly calibrate "old" dates with current calendars. Reinforce, if necessary.

Cattle ranching became the foundation of the valley's economy which, in spite of the hopes of the settlers and some nearby gold strikes, never was robust. However, vast natural hay fields generated a certain amount of trade. One ranch became a well-known dude ranch (there will be more about this later).

The challenges of the Big Hole, especially the winters, and its general isolation bred tough, independent – yet cooperative – people. These people were not many, and the population of those living within the valley was rarely above 700, or so.

Note that the settlements of Jackson and Wisdom seldom claimed much more than 100 residents each. Not particularly small by today's standards, but quite small for the time.

The people of the Big Hole were used to significant planning and effort in preparation for the winter season. As the "madness" both intensified and grew, most also became concerned with preparing for a longer period of independent survival.

For older students it would be appropriate here to discuss the "madness" in some detail. See the guide "The Madness – The Ripple's Long Run Up."

Now it turned out that a quartermaster general – the guild knows him – chose to retire in the Big Hole. Many sought out his advice in view of what they could see developing in the outside world.

First, the general advised that supplies to fill crucial needs should be laid in. Many secured food, arms, and ammunition, and fuel in addition to their usual winter requirements. Next, he counseled that plans must be made to further isolate the Big Hole, if necessary: roads should be blocked, bridges and culverts destroyed, signs or billboards likely to stimulate an outsider's curiosity removed. This would be done.

Ask your students if these precautions make sense. Ask what else might be done to secure the valley, or have the students role-play a meeting between the general and his neighbors. How might he secure their assistance?

Teachers' Guide Page 3

And so those in the Big Hole made their plans and filled their needs for eventualities, such as the Ripple Event. In this they were wise. Fleeing their homes, others came to the valley to refuges they had prepared. They were likewise prudent. The Buffalo Wallow Dude Ranch was one of these refuges.

The dude ranch began as a working cattle ranch in the early 1900s, taking its name from a buffalo wallow on its land.

Brainstorm what might be the differences between a working cattle ranch and a dude ranch.

Life in the Big Hole was hardscrabble at best, and by 1960 (old solar cycle calculation) the ranch was near failing.

Define "hardscrabble." Ask students for synonyms. Brainstorm what might make a ranch (or any other venture) fail.

At that time Montana was enjoying an upsurge in tourism. Taking advantage of this trend, the owner converted his ranch into the Buffalo Wallow dude ranch.

If you have a wallboard available, draw a plan map of the ranch as you describe the various elements and components of the ranch.

Ten cottages lined the banks of the Big Hole River with picture windows and porches facing the stream. Each cottage could sleep up to six people, and each had a fireplace. A framed print hung over each mantle – the units became known by this print rather than number; for example, cottage #8 was better known as the Shaman. Behind these, near the end units and between them and the next group of buildings back from the river, were two bath houses or restrooms, each with a section for men and another for women. Another cluster of buildings surrounded the main lodge. This contained the kitchen, dining area, large central fireplace with the emblem of the ranch, a full-on, full-size white buffalo head centered over both mantles, as well as public restrooms and a recreation area. To the left and right of the lodge were two large cottages (four in all) similar to the smaller units but with room for up to 12 guests each. A generator shed and two other communal restrooms offset the back of the lodge. Immediately behind the lodge was the owner's house and a cottage equipped for special-needs guests (later this was used to house the caretaker). A beautiful print depicting buffalo calf woman graced the mantle of the owner's residence. Finally, offsetting the house and special unit were dorms for ranch staff. This was the main lodge area of the ranch, around …

Teachers' Guide Page 4

… and convenient to it were corrals, hay barns, one with stalls, one with additional storage, a large garage building housing the ranch's vehicles and equipment (10 cross-country 4x4s, two Kubota utility vehicles, one Kubota tractor with loader and backhoe, one Kubota tractor with attachments for "haying," one Bobcat front loader, three snow blowers, and numerous antique wagons and implements – these last items were very important during the Dark Times). Guests were greeted by an arch over the road leading to the ranch with the words "Buffalo" and "Wallow" framing the buffalo head logo. This led to a paved area with covered sheds for guest parking. (See map at end of document.)

As such, the dude ranch prospered until the Great Depression, faltered again in the 1960s, recovered once more, and by 2010 (old solar cycle calculation), hardscrabble times had returned.

The date designating the start of the Great Depression remains a matter of some debate. There is no doubt it was well underway when the ranch was purchased by the professors from California.

The sisters' parents (known to us only as the parents or the professors) were ardent anglers and visited the ranch at least twice a year to enjoy their hobby. They were always in residence during the salmon fly action on the river. It was during such a visit they noticed the increasingly down-at-heels condition of the ranch, assessed the likely problems faced by the owner, and made an offer to purchase it then and there. Their offer was accepted.

Define "down at heels," ask for synonyms. Brainstorm what might make the dude ranch appear to be down at heels.

Later, they organized a group of fellow survivalists who paid their share and helped prepare the ranch to be a place of refuge, if necessary. Most spent their summer holidays there as well. As it developed, the "madness" increasingly engulfed the greater Bay Area in Old California, and the other survivalists moved to the ranch. The parents were already there as caretakers. All were present before the Ripple struck that fateful Thanksgiving.

Discuss the greater Bay Area, the cities within it, how it became a shattered zone, and its present condition. Ask the students to consider what it might take for someone to leave their home at a moment's notice.

The Ripple found the parents, the sisters, the consorts, and the ranch survival group assembled in the Big Hole. In addition to local residents others were …

Teachers' Guide Page 5

… in the valley, where most chose to remain. There were relatives of locals there for the holiday; for example, the general's son, a platoon sergeant in the Tenth Mountain Division, and his four grandchildren. Some were there hoping for some early skiing in addition to enjoying their Thanksgiving. Among these were a Marine captain and his wife, a medical doctor, two nurses and even two foreigners, named Heinrich and Gerda Schmidt. Heinrich was a sanitation engineer, and Gerda, a public health expert. They came to be known simply as the Germans. One resident made his way to and into the valley where he had grown up before he left to become a Navy SEAL. He, along with Captain Sam and Sergeant Bill, were given the responsibility for the valley's defense with the general serving as the chosen leader of the community. In all, there were perhaps 1,100 people within the valley, most ready, willing, and able to protect their community and to survive.

Have students learn the Bison Camp Midsummer Chant

The ripple brought chaos
Not here, not here

The strong took all
Not here, not here

The weak died first and then most others
Not here, not here

Starving mostly many died alone
Not here, not here

Our place and our people saved us the winters helping
So it was, so it was

Saved water first, then the rest
So it was, so it was

The Germans saved the water
Yes they did, yes they did

The captain, the sergeant and the SEAL trained us
Yes they did, yes they did

For scouting and for battle
Yes they did, yes they did

Teachers' Guide Page 6

Outsiders breached the perimeter only once
Yes they did, yes they did

Were met and beaten at Bison Camp
Yes they were, yes they were

From this we take our name
Yes we do, yes we do

The doctor and the nurses kept us healthy
Yes they did, yes they did

Hale and hardy they kept us well
Yes they did, yes they did

In time our scouts out searching wide
Brought news of others like us
Yes they did, yes they did

Welcome news, welcome news
In time we joined the New NorthWest
Yes we did, yes we did.

Additional notes for teachers:

The preceding presents an accurate summary of Bison Camp's history. Further details are needed, however, to understand how this community became one of the most successful survival groups.

The history of the Big Hole, one of the largest valleys in the Rocky Mountains, is well known where the basics are concerned. The valley was utilized by various early peoples, including those of the "famous" Clovis culture. After the Paleo Indians came, the tribes we associate today with the valley most often fall within the lands controlled by the Blackfoot Nation.

Sometimes the location was called *Ohmsah-kah wah T'kah* (valley of heavy snows). The valley was explored by the Lewis and Clark expedition, which chose to continue westward along another river. They were shortly followed by fur trappers, who gave the valley its name.

Teachers' Guide Page 7

Life in the valley was limited by the harsh winters most often experienced there. Neither the Blackfeet nor other tribes lived year 'round in the valley. The first White settlers (called *veho* or *spiders* by the Blackfeet) did not arrive until the late 1800s. The Big Hole was well-known for its abundant natural grasslands – this and cattle ranching were the foundations of its economy, with occasional spurts generated by nearby silver or gold strikes.

The teachers' guide accurately gives the recent history, especially that of the Buffalo Wallow dude ranch, the owners of which were of Native American heritage. What must concern us most is the valley's survival of the Dark Times and becoming Bison Camp.

Key Factors:

The key factors apply in one way or the other to most successful settlement groups. A weakness in one required additional strength in the others.

Timing had to be taken into account. The sisters and their consorts, their parents, and others of the Buffalo Wallow survival group were all in the valley before the Ripple Event. Taylor James, the general, came to the valley six solar cycles prior to that fateful Thanksgiving.

Residents noticed his careful planning for winter and longer survival, and as the nation's situation became increasingly precarious, almost all applied his concepts over the next five solar cycles. Timing would have been of limited use without **planning** and **putting those plans into action.**

As a result, the Big Hole held more than ample food and fuel reserves. The fuel with **rationing** was not depleted until the end of the fifth solar cycle of the Dark Times, strengthening the valley's ability for accurate and timely patrolling and long-range scouting.

The valley was **able to defend itself.**

All year 'round, **residents were armed with more than ample ammunition.** These resources were not wastefully expended. After the Ripple Event, all hunting was conducted using bows, spear-thrower atlatls, or slings.

The **defense was organized and well led** by Samuel Edwards (captain, United States Marine Corps); William James (staff sergeant, U.S. Army, Tenth Mountain Division); and Frederick Petersen (lieutenant (jg), United States Navy Special Forces). Petersen trained all able-bodied residents in basic …

Teachers' Guide Page 8

…hand-to-hand defense, as well as the scouts in hand-to-hand offense. With one, albeit, notable exception, the patrols and scouts kept all threats away from the valley. In that case, intruders reached the Bison Camp sentry post/redoubt. Those on sentry duty fought long enough for the valley to be roused and come to their aid so that the Big Hole prevailed, but not without losses. More than 100 fell that day, including the general – may he be at home with the Overseer. Today, his memorial can be visited not all that far from the site of the valley's other battle, the one with the Nez Perce Indians under Chief Joseph long before the time of the **Bison Camp battle.**

The **food resources** were ample – cattle and sheep, wild game (plentiful ground squirrels, if things came to this) and trout. These were **properly managed and rationed** along with growing numbers of chickens.

The short growing season limited supplies of vegetables, but the sisters trained the people in the **plant resources available in the region.** These were collected on an ongoing basis. Often scouting expeditions included several foragers to harvest the plant foods then in season.

The valley was especially blessed with **an abundant and pure water supply.** Without this, the settlement group would have stood a good chance of failure. Snowmelt and springs were fiercely guarded, and water from the river was boiled prior to use. The entire valley was protected from pollution – Heinrich Schmidt designed a privy, such that the ground waters were not polluted. These units were and still are called Heinrichs, and are in wide use elsewhere today, as are the solar boilers he also designed.

Heinrich, his wife Gerda, the doctor (Dr. Mary Rose) and the nurses (Christine Rodman and Leah Johnson) applied almost dictatorial powers, such that **the valley's health and cleanliness were maintained.**

For true, it all came together in the Big Hole – its **location, climate and the people** in such a way that the combination could not only "ride out" and survive the Dark Times, but even prosper. And so it did – the Overseer be thanked.

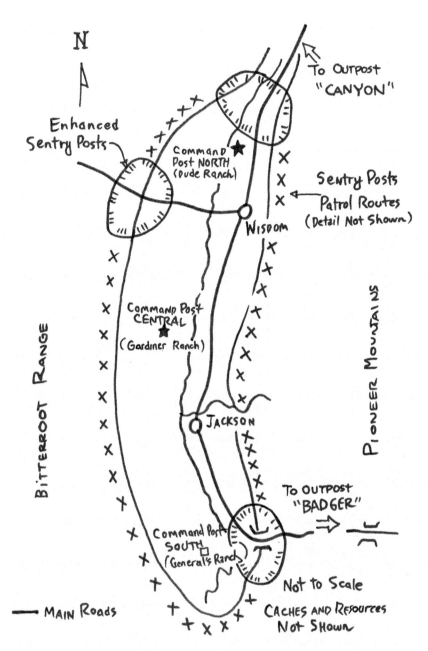

N

To Outpost
"CANYON"

Enhanced
Sentry Posts

Command
Post NORTH
(Dude Ranch)

Sentry Posts
Patrol Routes
(Detail Not Shown)

Wisdom

Command Post
CENTRAL
(Gardiner Ranch)

BITTERROOT RANGE

PIONEER MOUNTAINS

JACKSON

To Outpost
"BADGER"

Command Post
SOUTH
(General's Ranch)

Not to Scale

MAIN Roads

CACHES AND RESOURCES
Not Shown

Big Hole Valley (reconstructed from pre-Dark Period maps)

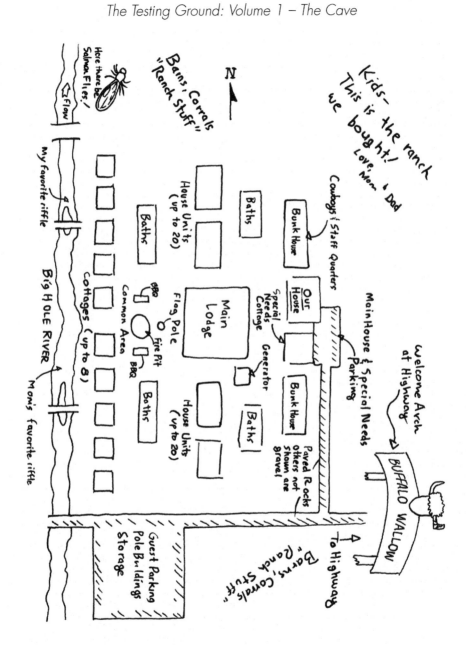

Sketch of Buffalo Wallow Dude Ranch, Big Hole Valley, Old Montana. (Source: Letter from Ronald Stone to Sapha Stone, c. 2010 old solar calculation).

Commentary on the *Teachers' Guide*

The *Teachers' Guide* document is one of the few written teaching materials that survived later cultural catastrophes. The simple style evokes memories and images of how most survivors were taught in the collective schools within their respective settlement groups. The document is rich in questions inserted by the teacher to evoke comments and dialogue with students, and the suggestions made to teachers using the text are insightful and rich in context.

Interviews with Bison Camp Residents

The geographical setting of Bison Camp was a natural attractant as a field site to help train data collectors affiliated with the Montana State University History Project. The administration and residents of Bison Camp settlement group welcomed the young college students and, for many solar cycles, sat patiently during interviews – many of the same questions being asked year after year to provide the novice data collectors with a sense of accomplishment and growth before they were fully trained and appointed to set off on the short and long loop treks to document survival during the Ripple Event, Dark Time, and early years of the post-Dark Time recovery period.

What emerged from the majority of these interviews was a sense that Bison Camp settlement group had a well-developed concept of self-reliance and self-dependence and, in the Old Montana survivalist tradition, residents would be willing to help others, but reluctant to ask for help themselves.

The settlement was easily defended with well-defined "fallback" positions into the valley eastside mesas that were well constructed to repel invaders. Secondary stockpiles of food were secured at several of these valley side redoubts, and water supplies were available through a network of snow-fed rivulets that entered cave sites along the face of the mesa. Teams of what were called action scouts (ASs) patrolled the settlement perimeter and confronted any and all intruders attempting to enter.

Nearby to the south were the remains of an old logging camp that had been active during the decades prior to the Ripple Event. Here were stockpiles of already cut timbers that were never sold, due to local economic depression, but which served well the new residents of Bison Camp settlement group. This supply of already cut timber was put to use quickly during the Ripple Event, and rail fences were erected across the valley floor at a series of entrances into Big Hole Valley. Guard posts were constructed at selected sites along these protective rail fences and were manned by the action scouts.

Farther up the valley were additional ruins. Especially valuable to the residents of Bison Camp were the items salvaged at the abandoned old National Guard encampment site: lumber, storage tanks, hardware (pipe, nails, hasps, glass), roofing materials, even potbellied stoves and mechanics' tools left behind at the guard vehicle garage.

Altogether, the site was remarkable: secure in food, water, and shelter.

The first light snow of winter greeted the visitors on the morning of November 27. When they awoke, none could foresee the hardships presented in the solar cycles to come. None could have imagined how important their settlement would be in the new history of North America.

General Orders
Defense of Bison Camp

1st	Know your surroundings
2nd	Know your weapon(s)
3rd	Know your sentry post(s)
4th	Know your scout duties, if any
5th	Know your redoubt assignment
6th	Know the cache(s) you defend
7th	Know the alert signals, know how to give them and know to react
8th	Know who commands you
9th	Know who you command
10th	Maintain your weapon(s) and equipment
11th	Maintain your mount, if a scout
12th	Maintain your skills and abilities
13th	Inform your commander if you are ill or otherwise unable to meet the demands that might be placed upon you
14th	Stay alert at all times in all places
15th	Report anything out of the ordinary

Stay Ready – Be Alert – Keep the Valley Safe

After-Word

Shortly after the Ripple, the spring following Thanksgiving solar cycle 2, the valley's readiness was improved. Caches were broken up and scattered to very secure areas, rationing systems instituted for important expendables, excess cattle slaughtered and meat processed, horses were dispersed and made ready for mounted patrols and more distant scouting. Supplying firewood for the next winter began, and several redoubts were established in the bordering ranges as last-ditch defenses. The people of the dude ranch took to calling their redoubt Bison Camp to distinguish it from the ranch itself. From a battle there – the guild knows it – the valley and eventually our canton, our home, took its name. It would have been difficult to find a better location with better people to not only survive the Dark Times, but even thrive to a certain extent.

Metal Sheet #7

Inscription and Translation

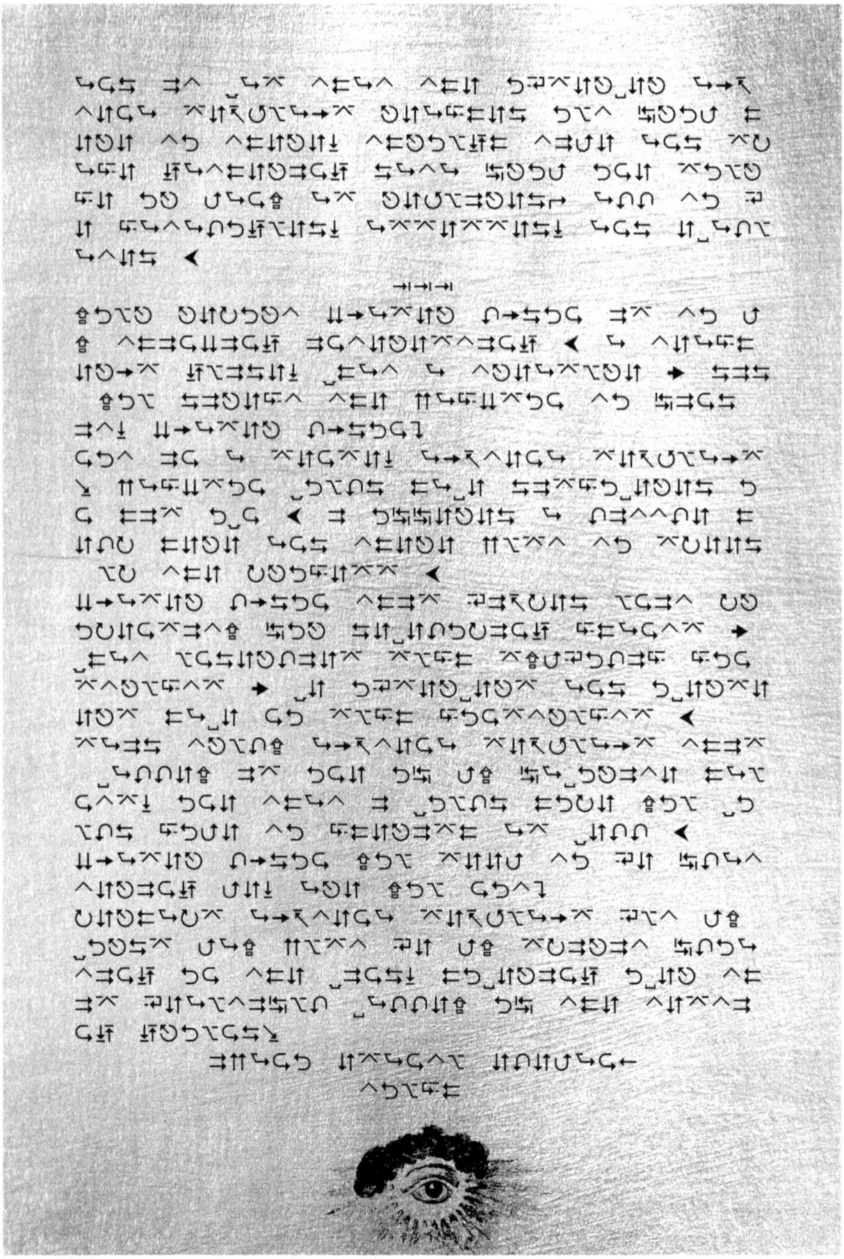

And it was that the Observer A'-Tena Se-Qua reached out from here to there, through time and space, gathering data from one source or many as required; all to be catalogued, assessed, and evaluated.

***

Your report, K'Aser L'Don, is to my thinking interesting. A teachers' guide, what a treasure. Did you direct Jackson to find it, K'Aser L'Don?

Not in a sense, A'-Tena Se-Qua. Jackson would have discovered it on his own. I offered a little help here and there just to speed up the process.

K'Aser L'Don, this biped unit propensity for developing chants, what underlies such symbolic constructs? We observers and overseers have no such constructs.

Perhaps you and I, A'-Tena Se-Qua, might prepare one?

Really, K'Aser L'Don, what would the value be to prepare such word groupings?

I was thinking that perhaps ....

Think along what you will, K'Aser L'Don. On another point, I sense that this place, the Big Hole region, holds special meaning to you. Is it possible you have visited here during previous duties and responsibilities?

Said truly, A'-Tena Se-Qua, this valley is one of my favorite haunts, one that I would hope you will come to cherish, as well.

K'Aser L'Don, you seem to be flattering me, are you not?

Perhaps, A'-Tena Se-Qua, but my words may just be my spirit floating on the wind, hovering over this beautiful valley of the testing ground.

Ijano Esantu Eleman!

Chapter 9: Evening Reading 9

Document 9, Cave Location: Case 43-B

Short Loop Investigation Reports

Pack it up and gitalong
We are on our way

Hard the effort every day
Still there's time for song.

Refrain: Another place; another day
Alius dies – alius dies!

Across each mountain, valley, plain
We are on our way
Hard the effort every day
Whether sunshine, storm, or rain.

Refrain: Another place; another day
Alius dies – alius dies!

Remember those who came before
We are on our way
Record the words they have to say
Offer thanks then out the door.

Refrain: Another place; another day.
Alius dies – alius dies!

(Source: Anonymous. *Song of the Short Loop*. Montana State University History Project Archive. Music Section: Box MS-42L.)

Pre-Note

Cadres of trained data collectors visited as many settlement groups as possible during the last years of the Dark Time and throughout the post-Dark Time recovery period. Who were these individuals who trekked through the New NorthWest and New SouthWest Configurations observing landscape change and the cultural processes that slowly contributed to the recovery period? All were young, and they formed part of an exciting, unique program developed at Montana State University, New Bozeman, Old Montana Territory.

Origin of the Data Collector Program at Montana State University
Serenity Spencer, Certified Data Collector
Interview with Brandon Wilson, Retired Professor of Geography
(Emeritus) and Executive Director, MSU History Project
Document Dated: Day 4, Week 4, Month 8, Solar Cycle 38

Your purpose here today is to ask me about the origins of the Montana State University History Project and training of the data collectors? Glad someone is interested, since there are few left now to tell how it all began and how our work developed through the solar cycles. So relax, and let me start at the beginning.

James Rodriguez, who few remember these days, should receive credit as the founder and guiding spirit behind our project in the years of turmoil following the Ripple Event. I knew him well, and we had many conversations before his death in solar cycle 23. He told me that early in his career he was a professor of geography at the University of California, Berkeley. He also had received his doctorate at UC Berkeley, where he trained in what then was called the Berkeley School of Cultural Geography, a program that blended landscape evaluation and analysis, and integration of the sub-themes of cultural, physical, and economic geography.

In a move unusual in most academic institutions, James was hired at UC Berkeley in the Department of New Geography, where he was assigned teaching responsibilities for a suite of undergraduate courses (the three I remember discussing with him were: Evolution of California Landscapes; Introduction to Cultural Geography; and Plants, Life, and Cultural History). James told me that he loved teaching undergraduates, but that initial joy and interest waned.

This decline of interest coincided with the destructive riots at Berkeley. And at the same time, university administration kept raising tuition to unspeakable levels and admitted more and more wealthy foreign students (who could afford what then was $70,000 per year in tuition), a cost level that prohibited enrollment of students from most California families. If I remember correctly, there was a five- to six-month period of rioting both on and off campus: university buildings were burned and in the initial attempts to quell the riots, campus and city police opened fire and killed more than 200 students during one especially violent weekend.

Then it was that a number of off-campus self-proclaimed Earth Save Groups (ESGs), primarily anarchists, joined and produced more troubles. One especially destructive group subsequently became known by the general slang term, the "greenies." Their members were at the forefront of most of the demonstrations that turned violent and the riots that followed.

James told me through several conversations that events on campus and in the Berkeley region worsened. The storied libraries at Berkeley were destroyed. The great Bancroft collection that housed the most important California-related documents was burned by vandals. Next, the vandals continued their rampage through the stacks of the nearby magnificent Doe Memorial Library that housed one of the greatest collections of books in the world. In one of the most terrible incidences of civil unrest ever seen in North America, the rampaging vandals set ablaze this structure, as well.

These two events galvanized students and Berkeley residents against the environmental and anti-academic activists, but the key damage already had been done. The so-called "greenies," along with their anarchist recruits, then made plans to attack other university-based sites throughout Northern and Southern Old California.

James told me that no one could believe how these horrible activities had started; and then came the Ripple Event. The UC Berkeley campus and the city of Berkeley became war zones, and the great campus fell into ruins.

James fled the city before much of the chaos had enveloped the east bay communities. Trekking north, he reached and crossed the Carquinez Strait by boat, as the new bridge had been destroyed. Ultimately, he made his way to the small town of Dixon, about eight kilo-miles southwest of the former University of California, Davis, campus (now also in ruins). There, he was welcomed by the residents, due to his skills in ethnobotany and identification of safe edible wild plants. Because of the kindness that community members extended to him, James dropped his original first name and took a new one in honor of the town. He thereafter was known as Dixon Rodriguez.

There came a time in Dixon's life when he left Old California and joined one of the early Mormon treks north into Old Montana. He arrived at New Bozeman and met with officials at Montana State University. He was offered an unpaid position as teacher-mentor (but with room and board provided at no cost), provided that he make a commitment to continue teaching his ethnobotany courses and mentor younger students.

You look at me as if I am giving you too much material? Too much detail? Well, too bad. You need to know all of this if you want to know our history. So let me provide you with some critical background, and record it clearly in your notebooks!

The computer system at MSU was not disabled by the attack virus, in part for two reasons. One is the actual physical placement of the Information Technology Building (ITB), and the second being the important role played by Jackson Johnson, a professor of computer science at MSU prior to the Ripple Event, who developed the campus into its present center of technology revival.

(NOTE ADDED AFTER INTERVIEW: Dixon informed me that during November of the third year of Dark Time, Jackson trekked east to visit his children – but never returned. Whether he met with an accident or died along the way never has been determined.)

The most probable reason for this anomaly was determined only later by a team of MSU engineers and geologists. It turned out that the building housing the servers and the IBM z900 computer was in the basement of Carpenter Hall, where engineers, at least 20 old solar cycles before the Ripple Event, had excavated deep into the intrusive pluton and basement formations that shielded the computer from the attack virus. Analysis of the pluton source material revealed high concentrations of cadmium, iridium, lead, and rhodium. The answer still is debated, although it is known that this combination of elements in high levels can form a shield that for unknown reasons protects and maintains electron transfer, electrical current, and provides a workable construct on which to build and recover slowly from the Dark Time.

The presence of a functioning computer system at MSU was a tightly held secret throughout the Ripple Event and the following Dark Time. This exception became known only during the middle portion of the recovery period, and then only to a few highly selected individuals. Because of our tight security that easily could repel gangs of thugs, the MSU campus became a sanctuary – a haven for hard-working young men and women initially during the Ripple Event and later Dark Time, and from this large number in our student body, there were groups of individuals who wanted, and needed, to know why these terrible events had been launched.

Dixon and others on campus recognized the strength and determination of many of these undergraduates, and he developed the idea to form a cadre of special students to investigate activities and behaviors during the Dark Time, a project that could have great value for future generations. These students would be trained as data collectors, with special focus on how to observe and record; how to interview correctly; and how to assemble information on life histories from elderly residents at existing settlement groups willing to talk about their lives prior to and during the Dark Times.

And so it was that the data collector concept came to be.

The DCs, as they became widely known, were drawn from a select group of students interested in history and willing to travel outside the protective nucleus of the MSU campus. An announcement was made: prospective candidates were interviewed by Dixon and two other key MSU faculty members, Drs. Elena Russell (applied sociology) and Roger Howard (applied anthropology).

Applicants initially were screened, then clustered into groups of six: three males and three females, based upon their skillsets. All would be trained in survival ethnobotany, interview techniques, and tested regularly for physical fitness (i.e., rigorous obstacle course management, running for speed and distance, rock climbing, and swimming). They also would be trained in martial arts and taught how to manufacture weapons for personal protection using everyday items, whether glass shards, discarded pieces of metal, even broomsticks. The DC applicants were required to sign waivers absolving MSU and their faculty trainers of responsibility, should injury or death occur during the outward- or home-bound journey, treks subsequently known as the short and long loops. Note: After successful completion of their first trek, the DCs called themselves "loopers," a title they bore with great pride.

Applicants were taught an additional range of skillsets: how to survive in the shattered zones, interview techniques (especially how to demonstrate respect to those who suffered so much), how to be good listeners and not bias respondents' answers, and how to keep accurate journals and daily records. They were instructed in various techniques how to gain support and entrance into the settlement groups where local scouts and sentries might not be welcoming initially.

As the training concluded, Dixon along with his colleagues Drs. Howard and Russell interviewed each prospective candidate extensively, debated on the merits and qualifications of each, then made their selections.

Out of 165 potential candidates who completed the initial rigorous training system, 24 were selected for the initial four short loop treks. Of 141 remaining, 48 were identified for additional long loop training that would begin the following year; the remainder were interviewed separately and asked to maintain their commitment, to continue their physical fitness training, and re-apply the following solar cycle.

The initial short loop teams consisted of four groups of six members. Each team received specific directional assignments outward from the MSU campus/New Bozeman area along prescribed geographical routes that Dixon had mapped out, to the north, south, east, and west. Members of each group were selected for their complementary skillsets that, taken together, would provide collective internal safety to the members (i.e., knowledge regarding: food and water safety, medical care, technical skills, and landscape analysis skills). The teams were balanced by gender – three males and three females or appropriate sets of trans-genders – as mate units in recognition of physical needs during long periods away from MSU. Let me say here in passing that at the time of the initial loop treks, effective contraceptives were not available, as the pharmaceutical industries still had not returned to production, so additional knowledge was provided as necessary.

On the last night at MSU before departing, these initial teams of DCs assembled to meet with Dixon Rodriguez, their faculty advisors, and other interested parties from the MSU administration. Dixon related to me what transpired and what he said at that last meeting:

The honor has been mine to see you through your training period, you the first class of MSU data collectors. You are the elite from the applicant pool;

you have met and exceeded our training expectations. Your names will be remembered for what each of you will have accomplished on these initial treks.

Stand to be recognized. I present to you in the audience the first class of data collectors from Montana State University.

Data Collector Team I (northward)

Alex Williams
Anise Wood
Dominic Lewis
Cheyenne Patterson
Jackson Carter
Hannah Wallace

Data Collector Team II (eastward)

John Roberts
Harper Woods
Martin Cook
Jewel Gibson
Strong Conway
Petra Warren

Data Collector Team III (southward)

Turner Merchant
Winter Andrews
Logan Morris
Melody Hicks
Hardin Green
Nicole Crawford

Data Collector Team IV (westward)

Alan West
Alba Bennett
Basil Davis
Joanna McDonald
Dell Clark
Sage Grant

Dixon told me that he then finished with the following words directed specifically to the data collectors.

Your objectives are three:

> *1. Identify those who survived the Dark Times;*
>
> *2. Learn from them and collect survival-related information;*
>
> *3. Identify how individuals and groups obtained food, water, and worked together.*

The information you record in your daily journals will be catalogued and analyzed upon your return to MSU and made available for future generations, to assure survival.

Listen up DCs: this is the reality.

Your work is dangerous; some of you may not survive your attempted return to MSU. Rely upon your team members and your complementary skill sets – do your best; help one another.

Each of your teams is a self-contained unit; your survival and success depends upon all members working together;

It is easy to share when there is enough, not so easy otherwise. Share equally in the pleasures and hardships; when disagreements arise – remember who and what you are – members of an elite team of data collectors, created at Montana State University;

The survival of future generations may be in your hands – act together as one.

You will receive the following equipment: a specialized trek cart (STC); care for it and it will serve you well. Each STC contains food and water for your initial needs; equipment for fishing and small game trapping; and in addition to your acquired skills in firemaking, there are backup solar reflectors for water purification and cooking.

My final words to you are these: Use your training: work together as a team; recognize potential and actual dangers along the way to avoid problems in the shattered zones; and return to MSU safely!

Congratulations!

NOTE ADDED AFTER INTERVIEW: When the treks were scheduled to traverse shattered zones perceived especially dangerous by Dixon and his advisors, the numbers of "loopers" was increased to eight team members, and each received additional specialized training in arms use, weapon repair, and gunpowder production.

A subsequent document located in the archive identified the specifications of what became known as looper trek carts:

> *The looper trek cart is based on the standard trekker cart. It is designed to be easily pulled by one person on level ground and pulled or pushed by up to four, if necessary. Its dimensions are (in old units) L 10', H 3', W 6'; axle is centered with the push/pull arms being aligned with the axle. Wheel is 6' diameter and constructed of two solid but thin wood veneers. This is somewhat heavier than a spoked wheel but is easier repair, if necessary.*
>
> *The box is of sturdy construction and not open on the top as our trekker carts are. The top center holds standard camping gear. Access to the cargo area is gained by two hatches – fore and aft. Each cart has four removable handy boxes (often called saddle bags). One of these holds tools for basic repairs, one essential first aid supplies, another a "come along" pulley system and, the last, ammunition. Thus, the answer to most emergencies is close at hand.*

Source: MSU History Archive, Document B-47-C18

Short Loop Trek Routes
Introduction: Original Destinations and Rationale

The area of New Bozeman, with its protective enclave of Montana State University, was home to several Native American tribes for centuries, among them the Crow and Blackfeet Nations. Early White trappers and explorers trekked through the region, among them members of the famed

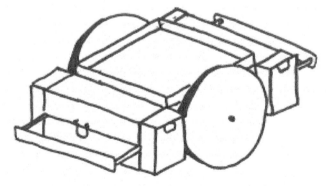

Sketch of looper trek cart (Source: Certified data collector information)

Lewis and Clark expedition which passed through the region during summer, 1806 old solar cycle).

Old Bozeman was part of the well-known Oregon Trail, with its nearby famed gold mining town of Virginia City nestled within the Gallatin Valley to the southwest. It was a unique location: nestled below mountain ranges on all sides, with trails and passes leading out in different directions. This geographical location made Bozeman the ideal hub for the departure and return destinations for the various short and long loop treks undertaken by the MSU data collectors.

The following information on trek destinations and routes taken was summarized from old maps in the MSU archive. Some of these towns no longer exist:

Original destinations north:

Outbound:	MSU/New Bozeman, Butte, Helena, Great Falls, Freezeout Lake, Choteau
Return:	Choteau, Whitefish, Kalispell, Flathead Lake, Polson, Ronan, Missoula, Deer Lodge, Anaconda, Butte, Whitehall, Three Forks, Manhattan, Belgrade, MSU/ New Bozeman

Original destinations east:

Outbound:	MSU/New Bozeman, Livingston, Harlowton, Big Timber, Billings
Return:	Billings, Laurel, Joliet, Bridger, Red Lodge, Cody, West Yellowstone, Big Sky, Gallatin Gateway, MSU/ Bozeman

Original destinations south:

Outbound:	MSU/New Bozeman, Livingston, Lake Yellowstone, Jackson Hole
Return:	Jackson Hole,Wilson, Driggs, Ashton, Island Park Reservoir, Henry's Lake, Ennis, Four Corners, MSU/ New Bozeman

Original destinations west:

Outbound:	MSU/New Bozeman, Belgrade, Three Forks, Whitehall, Butte, Anaconda, Missoula, Coeur d'Alene
Return:	Coeur d'Alene, Moscow, Lewiston, La Grande, Baker City, Nampa, Boise, Burley, Pocatello, Blackfoot, Idaho Falls, West Yellowstone, Big Sky, Belgrade, MSU/New Bozeman

Data Collector Interview Schedules: Questions and Themes

Sample reports and diaries archived at the Montana State University History Project facility are highly varied. But even with extensive variation, there is basic similarity in the topics investigated and information gathered during interviews at the various settlement groups visited. The information available for inspection (upon presentation of appropriate credentials) has been organized by prefix time frame for easy reference: 1) PRE (years before injection of the attack virus and Ripple Event); RE (during Ripple Event); DT (during Dark Time); and RP (during post-Dark Time recovery period). Within each time frame category interview responses topics can be examined using general key word search engines:

A: Surviving the Ripple and Dark Time

B: Settlement: Foundation of the settlement group

C: Group history

D: Religious practices

E: Past and present food security

F: Past and present water security

G: Settlement issues

      G-1: Defense and group security

      G-2: Organizational structure

      G-3: Occupations and economic activities

      G-4: Administration of justice

      G-5: Education of children and adults

H: Totems and clan/group relics

I: Cultural practices:

> I-1: Annual and special celebrations

> I-2: Rites of passage: birth, coming-of-age, maturity, decline, and death

> I-3: Distinctive clan markings

Selections from Data Collector Reports
Surviving the Ripple and Dark Time

The DC reports are filled with documents that reveal how individuals and groups survived during the Ripple Event and throughout the Dark Time. Numerous texts describe cases of food poisoning during the early weeks and months of food deprivation, when individuals had little knowledge of what was safe and not safe to eat. Others relate how groups of families worked together to search through trash heaps and abandoned buildings and warehouses for food-related items that had been overlooked. Some groups collected metal, glass, and other usable construction items that could be bartered for food and beverages. Numerous interviews itemized the so-called lesser foods, sometimes referred to as famine foods (FFs), that individuals ate to survive: wild birds, insects, grubs, reptiles, and amphibians. Accounts were given how various types of barks and leathers were chewed to alleviate hunger. Most individuals interviewed related fears that their children would not survive, and this came to pass for too many. Numerous people also related a deep sense of remorse for their behavior, as when they stole food in order to survive. Almost a third of those interviewed used vocabulary that expressed an inner sense of shame – survivor's guilt – why had they survived when others equally qualified or even better qualified did not?

Some elderly residents of the various settlement groups were especially honored as members of different memory guilds. These individuals were recognized for their keen memory of events prior to the Ripple Event, and for their observations and recollections how individuals had survived during the Ripple and post-Ripple hard times. They regularly were invited to speak during evening pyre celebrations, and would present their recollections in the form of chants. Many of these events were observed and recorded by the DCs:

To his mother he was big boned
(Group shouts out in unison: Hear, hear; tell us more)

To his father he was stout
(Group shouts out in unison: Hear, hear; tell us more)

He was a big ol' boy to his friends
(Group shouts out in unison: Hear, hear; tell us more)

He was fat until the Ripple
(Group shouts out in unison: Hear, hear; tell us more)

Then all called him Slim
(Group laughter – as children add wood to the blazing pyre).

Another …

Grady was not to be trifled with
(Group shouts out in unison: not to be trifled with)

Imposing and mean was he
(Group shouts out in unison: imposing and mean was he)

Don't fool with Grady, they warned
(Group shouts out in unison: don't fool with Grady, indeed, indeed)

Grady wandering found a wolf cub
(Group shouts out in unison: yes a wolf cub, yes a wolf cub)

Alone, starving, and cold was this cub
(Group shouts out in unison: do something, Grady, do something Grady)

Grady nursed the cub back to health
(Group shouts out in unison: how could Grady do so, how could Grady do so?)

Tenderly doing so he surprised many
(Group shouts out in unison: Grady, Grady tender you were).

So now they say
(Group shouts out in unison: what do they say, what do they say?).

Don't fool with Grady and his wolf
(Group shouts out in unison: Don't fool with Grady and his wolf).

Hooooowooooo, Hooooowooooo, Hooooowooooo
(Group laughter – as children add wood to the blazing pyre).

Identification of Dietary and Medicinal Plants

Some settlement groups held special contests only for adult women in which participants were assigned the names of up to 50 herbs and medicinal plants, and then were required to locate and bring samples of each back to camp. Winners of such contests commonly received a special title and celebratory bracelet. In a few settlement groups, including Deer Creek in central Old Washington, Hillside Defense in eastern Old California, and Rolling Thunder in northwestern Old Montana, the winners of these botanical tests received recognition through a tattoo or a hot metal brand on the inside of the upper right arm. At other settlement groups, for example at Ever Vigilant in southeastern Old California and Protective Shield in northwestern Old Washington, such botanical recognition contests were affiliated with the lunar cycle, sometimes held four or six times during an annual cycle, in which women were assigned to locate and return to camp with a specific set of plants difficult to find, in order to maintain their sage femme status.

Foundation of the Settlement Groups

All settlement groups visited were founded adjacent to a secure water resource. All initially were established by clusters of individuals already residing in the general area. Some of these earliest settlements were unbalanced by trades and skill sets necessary for survival and growth. But as the months and solar cycles passed, individuals adapted, self-trained for specific needed tasks, and the groups admitted outsiders seeking protection, providing they had specific skill sets that were needed. The more successful settlement groups, in terms of economic development and general well-being, were balanced by gender and relative age groupings (from infants to elderly).

Group Histories of Selected Settlements

Especially valued during the early Dark Time years were elderly men and women who had excellent memories of past events during the pre-Ripple Event madness years (and earlier). They commonly formed clusters and met regularly to record events. Through time, many of these groups became known as memory guilds (MGs) and recited settlement and family histories of the different members. Some settlement groups had subgroups known as reciters of the epics (ROEs). These individuals were assigned the responsibility of organizing annual recitation contents of clan history and educational seminars where key historical individuals and their association with earlier North American events were presented.

During their visit to the Third Wave settlement group, the data collectors encountered a unique number of individuals with knowledge of early pre-Dark Time history. These individuals were believed by the members of this specific settlement group to have the gift of prophecy, and were highly protected. They were sought after to provide answers to questions posed by individuals. When the question had been received, the oracle would leave the settlement and walk for several hours in the nearby surroundings. It was forbidden to follow them. Upon return to the settlement, the question would be answered in a cryptic manner, for example:

Question: *Will my mate and I have a boy or girl child?*

Answer: *The breath of sunset falls upon the innocent, as life is changed in a new way, unforeseen and unanticipated – be prepared.*

The data collectors learned that these individuals were called bird speakers (BSers) by the residents of Third Wave, as they reportedly possessed the power to translate the songs of birds into messages for clan dwellers.

Religious Practices

Interviews commonly revealed that most members of settlement groups had lost their religious faith during the terrible Ripple Event and Dark Time. Many reported that once they had reached the security of a settlement group they sought calm and peace communing with nature, and spent time weekly on solitary or group walks through the protected forest and stream areas adjacent to their settlements.

Throughout New NorthWest and New SouthWest Configurations, significant numbers of survivors developed an integrated collective sense of universal order, coupled with concepts of fate and predestination. Central to their thinking was a firm belief that through this universal order, life was being observed – and had been for untold eons – perhaps being documented by forces unknown.

Other group members who retained their faiths were accepted and not criticized. Various settlement groups supported the construction of sanctuary buildings within the settlements that provided areas of calm and reflection for believers in the pre-Dark Time faiths.

Food Security

All settlement groups visited had heavily guarded caches of food at scattered locations within the settlement. Each member contributed their labor in one way or another to assuring the production and security of this vital resource. Community gardens within the protected settlement areas were tended by all members: children participated, as well as adults (active and elderly). Others tended fields and herds of livestock just outside the protected confines of the settlements; guards known as keepers of the granaries (KOGs) protected those tilling, irrigating, and harvesting crops.

On very rare occasions, members of the settlement groups sometimes had been caught stealing food from the communal stores. So serious was this offense against the other members and group security, that those convicted were banished to the nearby shattered zones.

Water Security

All interviewed commented on the difficulty of obtaining adequate supplies of water during the early days of the Ripple Event. Most reported being aware of friends, neighbors, even relatives facing death from dehydration and forcing terrible decisions: hoarding water for children's needs, nighttime raids on local city water supplies, and theft of bottled water from commercial stores. Some reported that their survival hinged upon a decision made during days of the Ripple Event when they elected to leave their town or city and seek water and safety outside of urban areas. Such limited responses most likely were because most individuals and families who fled their homes during this period died of thirst along the way, as they were unable to find safe and available water resources, or died when they were forcibly denied access to water by armed groups protecting lakeshores and stream banks.

The conclusion drawn from these interviews suggests that the vast majority of those who survived the Ripple Event and early years of the Dark Time already lived in small somewhat isolated communities near lakes, reservoirs, stream-fed ponds, or adjacent to rivers. Access to river water, however, was not without serious health risk, since upstream users commonly polluted the waters by disposing of trash, garbage, and body waste, merely sending it downstream. Individuals and groups who had access to solar reflectors and regularly heated their water prior to cooking or drinking had greater chances for survival than those who did not.

All settlement groups visited had secure water supplies channeled into the settlements through various pipe systems or cement-lined conduits. Those adjacent to lakes and reservoirs stationed teams of armed sentries commonly called water tenders (WTs) to guard against unauthorized water users (UWUs), who often came in the dark of night. Interviews suggested that when such individuals were caught they were treated in one of two ways: with compassion and allowed to fill their containers one time and then leave – never to return – or were summarily executed.

Selected Settlement Issues
Defense and Group Security

Each settlement group visited had well-organized teams of adult males and females trained in methods to assure group defense and security. While the structure and layout of each settlement group was different, some relatively simple, others had defensive redoubts at different distances before the outer perimeter defenses were reached. Inside the settlements, most also had a heavily barricaded structure where children and the elderly could be housed, if necessary, as the men and women defended their settlement group.

Organizational Structure

All settlement groups had different administrative organizational structures. Each practiced and exhibited some form of democracy with elections. Some settlements voted-in a single person to be in charge of key decisions, and that person was advised by a cluster of adult residents (usually nine to 15 people). Others had a triad or pentad of council members, whose key decisions necessitated a unanimous agreement among the three or five elected members, while decisions of lesser importance required only a majority.

Occupations and Economic Activities

Success of the various settlement groups depended initially upon the education and skillsets of the founders. During the Ripple Event and early Dark Time exodus from towns and cities, decisions by the founders regarding which asylum-seekers (ASs) to admit primarily were based upon age (usually women of childbearing years with or without children), as well as both adult males and females with skill sets perceived to be vital to the settlement's security and survival.

As time progressed through the Dark Time, specific occupations and skill sets expanded in accord with the perceived needs of each settlement group. Among the encouraged groups were: carpenters, masons, medical teams (herbalists, nurses, and physicians), veterinarians, and teachers. Other residents were encouraged to pursue additional crafts and skills that had high value to the residents, learning to become basketmakers, brick-makers, coopers, gardeners, millers, potters, smiths, stone-workers, tailors, and weavers.

At certain settlement groups within Old Washington and Old Oregon there arose groups of jewelers who polished stones, cracked geodes, and prepared symbolic tokens for residents and for barter.

Other settlement groups appointed individuals, usually older children who had not yet stood for their initiation rites, as fire-keepers. Sometimes these adolescents were called keepers of the clan flame, with responsibility to make sure that the central settlement group pyre always remained lit. It was common for these fire-keepers after they had served for one solar cycle to receive special clan recognition – a brand with the settlement group symbol on their right lower arm – a mark of very high status.

Throughout the settlement groups there were few formally trained medical doctors. If present, they were called upon to treat patients across the illness spectrum, and almost all had to be treated without invasive surgery. In cases of acute illnesses, such as appendicitis and internal cancers, little could be done for the patients except palliative care. In settlement groups without any formally trained physicians two approaches were taken: One tacticwas to develop cooperative relations with the closest settlement group that had such a physician and barter for a temporary assignment in which the groups could work together. As time passed, this led to the emergence of circuit doctors (CDs), who made short trips under protection out and about through the shattered zones to make the rounds of the settlement groups that had formed cooperative relationships.

An alternative approach to medicine and healing commonly used in other settlement groups was practiced by herbalists trained in hot-cold/wet-dry humoral medical techniques, who used their skills to treat illnesses. Such healing systems had evolved in ancient India several millennia prior to the Ripple Event and Dark Time, whereby all illnesses were classified as either hot or cold – wet or dry (e.g., a fever with severe body sweats would be classified as hot-wet). At the same time all foods in the region were classified as: very hot, hot neutral, cold, or very cold on one axis, and then very wet, wet neutral, dry, or very dry on the other axis. Treatments would match the symptoms of the illness, with diets based upon the opposite classification of the potential foods available.

The hot-cold/wet-dry system of ancient medicine was based upon the concept that health represented balance, while illness caused a shift along one or both of the axes. In order to heal patients, the practitioners recommended foods of the opposite category; hence, a classical fever with sweats would be treated using foods classified as very cold, cold, or neutral, along with foods classified as very dry, dry, or neutral – thus shifting the body back to a neutral position (balance) and to health.

Justice Administration

Each settlement group visited had well-established systems of justice and its administration: some harsher than others, some more rapid in securing justice than others. All had developed lists of offenses ranging from minor issues that could be dealt with internally by family members, to more serious problems that necessitated review by appointed groups of intelligent adult men and women who judged the misdeeds, met to review cases, and provided summary judgments and sentences – acquittal or guilty – and levied the punishments on the guilty, commonly branding and finger amputation. For the most heinous and serious offenses, jurors were drawn from the adult membership (usually 7 to 11 adults) who heard the cases, then passed judgment as to guilt or innocence. In such serious cases, the punishments commonly were banishment or execution.

Childhood and Adult Education

Little formal education outside the family unit occurred during the early years at the settlement groups. With stability of water and food supply, and with the acceptance of asylum seekers with educational skill sets, more formal educational activities were initiated.

Whereas all children were trained to read, write, and compute, the type of education and how the topics were introduced and taught varied widely by settlement group. Most remembered and would have liked to implement the pre-Dark Time standard K-12 system, but the ability to organize and initiate such a program was challenging, given general lack of texts and qualified teachers.

What evolved at most settlement groups, therefore, was an integrated form of education, in which teaching the so-called 3-Rs (i.e., *reading,* "*riting*," "*rithmatic*") was more proactive in blending themes and skills necessary for the children to survive. The primary aim, therefore, was to train the children to develop skill sets that specifically would benefit the settlement group. Once basic reading and composition skills had been mastered, attention then was turned to more critical computation skills (e.g., barter values of x number of y livestock = m quantities of n trade items). Education also included daily units to promote physical fitness and inter-student competition through strength-building challenges (boxing, running, wrestling), and protective skills, as well (martial arts along with weapon construction and use).

Key adults were identified in each settlement group to offer weekend or evening seminars in important skillsets. Those attending improved their survival skills through better understanding and training in animal tracking, medicinal herb identification, animal trap and fish weir construction, shattered zone landscape analysis (i.e., identifying dangerous locations where criminals and thugs might lie in wait), and winter survival techniques.

Totems and Clan/Group Relics

As the data collectors made their rounds through the short and long loops, they observed various settlement group-protected objects that symbolized the origins and histories of both individuals and groups living within the protected area. Over the entrance gates of most settlements were placed carved sets of symbols or objects, some obvious, others cryptic, characteristic items and phrases that the group members identified with. Sometimes these were wild animal skulls, pieces of nondescript metal that held deep meaning to some, or words and phrases in English (sometimes other languages), as well as symbols and designs that reflected deep meanings to the residents. Examples included:

Valley Guard settlement in central Old California:
Stay away: This means you!

Danger Shield settlement in west coastal Old Oregon:
Illi qui in laborandum (Those who enter must work hard);

Mountain Retreat settlement in northern Old Colorado:
O preguicoso nao tem lugar aqui (The lazy have no place here);

Forest Clearing settlement in southwestern Old Montana: buffalo and antelope skulls with additional symbols between a second set of skulls;

Protective Shield settlement in northwestern Old Washington: the stockade gate was festooned with red-white-blue banners.

Inside the protective walls of the settlement groups, the exteriors of individual households commonly were decorated with carvings, glass ornaments, and tiles. In the center of the communal settlement space, a wooden pole sometimes was erected (frequently lodgepole pine, sometimes cedar, sometimes another wood source). These poles were either plain or profusely decorated. Close inspection of the unornamented poles, however, revealed hundreds of initials carved into the wood. When asked about these markings, the common reply was: these are memory marks (MMs) to commemorate the names of family members and friends who died during the Ripple Event or Dark Times – may we always recall their faces and the joy we had together.

Cultural Practices
Annual and Cyclical Celebrations

All settlement groups visited celebrated annual events associated with the summer and winter solstices, and the spring and autumn equinoxes. These were times for group renewal and homage to the rededication and work ethic that facilitated survival and safety through the Dark Time into the recovery periods.

At several isolated settlements, for example, at Shoreline Refuge in west coastal Old California and Valley Enclave in central Old California, ceremonies called pyre rituals (PRs) were held as part of the summer solstice celebrations in which members jumped through bonfires and participated in fire-walking ceremonies to welcome the arrival of summer.

At the Safe Shelter settlement in south coastal Old Washington, several data collectors witnessed solstice and equinox celebrations in which members vied to compose victory songs, chanting the lyrics around the central communal fire to the amusement and pleasure of those attending. Behavior at these sometimes was "loose," as different varieties of traditional beverages prepared from fresh and fermented berries and other local fruits were consumed by the adults.

Celebration of Key Events

Given the widespread geographical locations of the settlement groups, it was logical that different celebrations would reflect local events and character:

> Teton Homestead settlement in northwestern Old Wyoming: peak climbers (PCs) received fame and recognition after ascending each of the five major Teton peaks;

> New Astoria settlement in northwestern Old Oregon: river swimmers (RSs) vied for the title during their annual strength festival of swimming and rafting from The Dalles location down the Columbia River to the Pacific Ocean at New Astoria;

> Lake Yellowstone settlement in northwestern Old Wyoming: banquets attended by all were held quarterly to celebrate young men and women who had passed rigorous physical fitness tests and received the honorary title of warrior status (WS);

> Bar-4 Shelter settlement in southern Old Montana: an organization was formed called the Triad Society (TS), in which a select group of adult men and women underwent initiation after they had passed a rigorous test of skills and abilities and became master hunters of air, land, and water wild game. Upon initiation, each was tattooed with an inverted triangle on his or her right palm – a mark of highest distinction.

Other settlement groups instituted gladiatorial-like games and hosted teams from different isolated communities, a revival of the practices of ancient times to demonstrate the strength of their respective young men and women.

Rites of Passage

Highest in variation among the settlement groups were celebrations linked to what commonly were called the rites of passage (RoPs): birth; coming of age and sexual maturity; adult status; activity decline; and death. Descriptions of the activities and celebrations marking each passage nearly defy categorization due to the diversity of practices. Given the wide variation, it is sufficient here to list a range of examples to demonstrate their diversity.

Birth and earliest days of life:

Isolated birth huts were constructed for newly delivered infants and their mothers. These were tended by elderly women, and no visitors were allowed for 30 days. Special foods considered to increase breast milk production were prepared for the new mother;

Naming celebrations for infants sometimes were held seven days after delivery; highly variable roles were played by parents, other family members, other clan members, and a celebratory feast was held that linked the infant to the clan;

Ritual first-tasting of finger foods were held, in which the father fed the infant on the third day after birthing;

Candle ceremonies that consisted of light scarifications and binding of the infant's hands or feet with symbolic cuttings (explained to the data collectors as a faint memory of the past in which different types of pseudo male and female circumcisions were practiced);

Naming rituals: some settlement groups prepared specific lists of suitable names for males vs. females; names that reflected gender, birth sequence, season of the year, geographical location, and other considerations;

Highly variable attitudes toward multiple births: conflicting attitudes of elation and fear; identification of wet nurses; in some settlements one twin was adopted-out to another clan member.

Childhood:

Highly variable roles were played by the mother and father, other family members, and clan members in caring for and training young children. The highest variations were seen at settlements in which conflicts occurred between two sets of older views – let children be children with minimal oversight vs. strong training with punishments for misbehavior. Inevitable conflicts occurred between the approaches of the so-called free-reigners vs. tight-leashers and various resolutions within the communal system of raising children.

Coming of age and sexual maturity:

This time of mystery leading to initiation rites and rituals cannot be summarized easily. Specific information on strength trials (both for males and females), and sexual education were highly variable by theme and topic: how sex education was presented and by whom (e.g., parents; self-learning in groups; the Octet System instituted at Elk Preserve settlement in western Old Montana; or by knowledge gained through use of surrogate adults). These topics can be searched by key words using the MSU History archive database.

Adult status:

Once initiation rites successfully were passed, males and females achieved adult status. Most settlement groups implemented gender and age classification systems that clearly marked the place of each person within the settlement population with specific obligations at each age. What commonly was called the age-set system is summarized here:

> Pre-adult status: infancy – childhood – coming of age
> Adult status: initiation trials passed; male and female age sets formed warriors and defenders:
>> Age-Set 1 – ages 15-21
>> Age-Set 2 – ages 22-28
>> Age-Set 3 – ages 29-35
> Administration advisors – ages 36-42
> Elected council officials:
>> Young rulers – ages 43-49
>> Elderly rulers – ages 50-56
>> Respected elder advisors – ages 57 until death

Age-Sets 1-3 reflected increased obligations and different levels of security activities and physical training.

Those in Age-Set 1 commonly served as sentries and protectors inside the settlement compounds, with gradually increasing experiences outside the protective enclosures in association with older age-set mentors.

Age-Sets 2-3 were most important for settlement security, and commonly underwent extensive training in subjects that included threat evaluation, potential security breaches, and regional dangers from potential attack groups as well as protection from destructive fires, floods, and storms.

Administration advisors represented a large pool of active members with highly varied skill sets and background training, knowledge useful to the settlement elected officials when making decisions at different levels. Advisors served in this capacity usually for seven years, before themselves becoming eligible for election to council and administrative positions. In many settlement groups, once the age of 57 was reached, individuals retired from formal settlement decision-making, but remained available in advisory capacities until death.

Activity decline:

Activity decline in males and females commonly was celebrated with honor within the settlement groups. This period in life was marked with retirement from the warrior-defender age-sets and new responsibilities to the settlement.

Women in this category gave aid and council to younger females experiencing stress, due to combinations of child-rearing and other work responsibilities. Men mentored younger males in familiar trades and perfected their skill sets. Both genders at this time usually worked with young girls and boys, respectively, to teach clan traditions in advance of the initiation rituals.

Activity decline and menopause did not exclude settlement members from participating as valued unelected advisers to settlement council officials.

At several settlement groups, among them Buena Vista Shelter in south-central Old California, New Monterey in west coastal Old California, and Tillamook Point along the coast in south-central Old Oregon, those who had retired from the warrior-defender age-sets wore distinctive belts, necklaces, or bracelets denoting their status.

Death:

Treatments of bodies and celebrations of life ceremonies also were highly variable. In most settlement groups burial was the tradition, in which the graves were arranged in an area apart from cultivated land, in more rocky zones adjacent to the settlement. Some settlements embraced the idea that burial contaminated the earth, and at these sites, for example at settlement Group Buffalo Run in central Old Montana and Klamath Refuge in northern Old California, the bodies were cremated and the ashes strewn at or near the favorite local spot of the deceased. In still other settlement groups, for example, at Flat-land Base in eastern Colorado, the decision was made to expose the body to the elements – so not to contaminate any part of the earth.

Differences also were seen in the cultural trait of body ash consumption, in which at the conclusion of the cremation ceremonies at some settlements, small samples of the ash were consumed by each member attending – the concept was to be one with the deceased.

All data collector reports included descriptions of pyre lightings, ritual meals held and celebrated at different times to remember the deceased, and the manufacture of commemorative markers that could be placed above or below ground to recall the memory of lost loved ones.

In addition, the data collector reports consider the survivors, the care and responsibilities of widows and widowers. At Meadow Sanctuary Settlement in central Old Wyoming, each surviving member received a special tattoo with the initials and symbol of the deceased. At most other settlements, the survivors wore special types of clothing, bracelets, or other insignias that indicated they were in mourning. Some settlement groups permitted the immediate family members to lessen their communal work obligations for up to two weeks.

At the Second Home settlement in in southern Old California, members instituted a 60-day period forbidding any spouse to work in agricultural lands or have any connection with food production – the so-called widow's and widowers' aura (W/WA), lest the community food supply become contaminated.

Individuals and Groups Outside the Settlements

On occasion, as when a data collector group was returning to MSU/New Bozeman, the teams encountered clusters of social groups who lived outside the settlement group concept and kept to themselves. Such groups were distinct from those who inhabited the uncharted depths of the shattered zones who lived and thrived on crime and evil.

Two such groups received special notice in the data collector reports. The first group was referred to as move-abouts (MAs), a mix of seasonal sedentary and move-about groups outside the isolated camps that practiced their livelihood moving up and down slope in search of food for themselves and their animals. One of the first groups of MAs encountered by the data collectors occupied mid-slope areas along the northern exposure of the Little Belt Mountain system in central Old Montana. They called themselves "wanderers." Their herds consisted of a mix of cattle and horses. The wanderers lived seasonally on wild food resources, and moved their herds up and down slope in tune with the seasons. They were a hardened group, well adapted and able to winter-over and still tend for the needs of their livestock. Their success depended upon a clever mix of migratory routes that bypassed most of the settlement groups and escaped notice of the shattered zone dwellers.

The second interesting group described by data collectors inhabited small islands in the middle of Freezeout Lake, northeast of Old Missoula, Montana territory. Upon closer inspection, the data collectors observed that these were not small islands, but clusters of boats lashed together – some numbering more than 15. These lake dwellers (LDs) lived most of the year on their boats, fishing and collecting freshwater algae as the main plant component of their diets. When necessary, they unlashed their boats and spent short times along the shore, gathering plants and trapping small wild game to increase their dietary diversity. The data collectors learned that each boat usually represented a separate family unit and contained on average five to eight persons. How the LDs managed their inter-family units and made decisions was not determined, due to the short time spent with them. It was observed, however, that all the rafts were equipped with solar water purifier systems.

Selections from Data Collector Reports/Diaries
Phoenix Gordon, Certified Data Collector, 3rd Short Loop Trek West
Diary Entry: Day 3, Week 1, Month, 7, Solar Cycle 13.
Location: River Run Settlement Group, West-Central Old Montana
Interview/Observation Topic: Memory Guilds

> *Today our team identified the formation of a specific subgroup within River Run settlement with high status. They were called the memory guild (MG). We were informed that other such groups had been founded at settlement*

groups located farther west, near Old Missoula and New Coeur d'Alene, New NorthWest Configuration. Members of the MG prepared lists of important historical events that occurred in Old North American history and identified the names of key historical figures associated with these events as they transpired. Guild members at River Run settlement group were appointed by the settlement's administrative council with the sole responsibility to maintain the knowledge of what had transpired earlier, especially prior to the Ripple Event and onset of the Dark Time. Members also were required to mentor younger residents interested in group history who might fulfill their positions lest their memory fail or they otherwise are unable to complete their required functions.

Piper Holmes, Certified Data Collector, 6th Short Loop Trek South
Diary Entry: Day 5, Week 4, Month 5, Solar Cycle 16
Location: Honor and Service Settlement Group, Central Old Wyoming
Interview/Observation Topic: Activities of Reverse Engineers

I worked this morning and throughout the afternoon with Thomas James, a reverse engineer who had the responsibility of converting old mechanical harvesting equipment so that these machines could be operated by animal or individual power. James also experimented with different types of bio-fuels and with animal dung (chicken and pig manure) from which the nitrogen could be converted to ammonia in a self-contained anaerobic digestion process, and then developed as a fuel source for certain types of farm machinery. Three of the reverse engineers at the Honor and Service Settlement previously worked as technical experts at the Geneston factory in Sacramento, Old California, prior to the Ripple Event. They left Sacramento with a Mormon guide and ultimately settled at Honor and Service. They told me that others in the community commonly called them "finders-fixers" or "fix-it men/women" because of their abilities to scavenge and locate parts that others had discarded and forge these pieces into new tools or repair parts for existing machines.

Bella Jenkins, Certified Data Collector, 1st Short Loop Trek North
Diary Entry: Day 1, Week 3, Month 6, Solar Cycle 12
Location: Lake Preserve Settlement Group, Northwestern Old Montana
Interview/Observation Topic: Administration of Justice.

We had been welcomed for almost three weeks at Lake Preserve settlement, where our team of data collectors had interviewed residents about their survival strategies and current activities. One morning we were called to assembly along with the other residents to witness an execution. The timeline from committing the crime, capture, trial, verdict rendered, sentence proclaimed, reviewed, and confirmed was 10 days.

The convicted criminal, Wayne Kelly, had assaulted Robert Fireman during a fight over which family had service rights to use the communal draft horses and plows on a specific day. This seeming innocuous argument suddenly turned violent with the result that Kelly twice stabbed Fireman, who died later in the settlement clinic.

The administrative council of Lake Preserve settlement met immediately and appointed a jury of 11 elders, men and women, to hear the case as presented by the accused and family of the deceased. We were informed that in capital crime cases the verdict needed to be unanimous. Nine adult members of the community had witnessed Kelly stabbing Fireman, so there was no doubt as to guilt. Kelly offered no logical rebuttal argument and, after 20 minutes of deliberation, the unanimous verdict was guilty.

Over the next several days, the sentence was deliberated and ultimately confirmed. We were informed that a crime of this level had only two potential sentences: banishment into the shattered zone (which in effect was a death sentence, since banishment meant removal from the settlement with only simple clothing, no weapons, and no food, or water). The alternative was execution either by hanging or forced drowning.

As a result of these events, I interviewed members of the administrative council regarding composition of juries, assignment of crime categories, non-lethal sentences, and rules that governed expulsion/banishment, and executions. At these meetings I filled my journal with notes:

At Lake Preserve Settlement, individuals accused of poor behaviors (minor infractions such as intoxication and ill-will toward others) commonly were reviewed by a tribunal of elders, who passed judgment quickly and effectively.

More serious transgressions or crimes against persons or property, or actions that threatened security of the settlement were reviewed by jurors (drawn from all adult members), and such crimes were dealt with quickly and with harsh verdicts.

Punishments agreed upon by majority decision commonly reflected the following categories:

Non-lethal: offenders after reconditioning (methods highly variable) were allowed to remain affiliated with the settlement group;

Non-lethal: offenders were branded or tattooed with symbols that identified the crime. In more serious instances, the offenders were banished without food or water;

Lethal: if actions of the offenders were heinous, they were reviewed within seven days by select senior elders (women and men) and, if upheld, executions followed.

Given the obvious infraction by Wayne Kelly, the guilty verdict and sentence were reviewed quickly, and execution took place well within the usual seven-day examination period. Kelly chose forced drowning in Chassion Lake.

Frost Woodward, Certified Data Collector, 2nd Short Loop Trek South
Diary Entry: Day 7, Week 2, Month 9, Solar Cycle 34Location: Forest
Sanctuary Settlement Group
Interview/Observation Topic: Interview with an Unnamed Retired
Executioner.

I was born in Old Reno, but survived the Ripple Event and remained there during the early years of the Dark Time. I never planned on being an executioner and never could have conceived how my life would change after the Ripple Event. Like most people, some things in my life I planned, but my occupation (if you call executioner a profession) became my lot quite by accident.

I was minding my own business walking down East Liberty Street in New Reno when I turned the corner and found myself observing a street fight. There was this thug from some unknown gang who had attacked a young New Reno public safety volunteer. Well, I could not just let the fighting continue, so I weighed in and struck a series of blows that killed the assailant. I was honored by the New Reno Police for saving the life of their volunteer and offered a position as enforcer. A captain with New Reno Public Safety (NRPS) subsequently appointed me to a higher position and eventually to their execution squad. This appointment was an honor to me and to my family, and served us well during the Dark Time and into the recovery period.

I was an executioner for 18 years before my retirement, and this was 10 solar cycles ago. During my tenure with the NRPS, I had the privilege of meting out justice in a timely manner, compared to earlier years when courts lingered in carrying out sentences sometimes for more than 20 years. I was known for my dedication to execute fairly, painlessly, and swiftly as required by the statutes that regulated my office. Twice, I was awarded the Johnson Medal for the quality of my work and received accolades from three of the four past civic administrators of New Reno. When I retired, I hooked-up with one of the Mormon trekkers, and decided to come north where I joined Forest Sanctuary. Currently, I live along the west shore of Lake Petremis, where I now spend my days in thoughtful reflection along the banks of the Lyre River.

Who would have thought?

(NOTE ADDED IN TEXT MARGIN: Lake Petremis was known earlier as Lake Crescent.)

Re-emergence of the Arts

During the post-Dark Time recovery period, the various settlement groups changed cultural and economic practices at very different rates. Some preferred to remain as they had evolved during the last years of the Dark Time, while others embraced their newfound recovery and adopted new ideas and reintroduced a suite of cultural practices that once had been nearly forgotten due to the pain and hardship of daily life during the Dark Time. At many of the progressive settlements the arts, especially music and theater, re-emerged. Members once more manufactured drums and other musical instruments using local metal, wood, and fiber. Others volunteered their carpentry skills to prepare stages on which thematic and passion plays could be performed by itinerate traveling artists.

One archive report (name of data collector removed from the title page for some unknown reason) revealed that a troupe of actors at the Teton Homestead settlement group staged a unique production that was controversial at the time, but protected under the aegis of new free speech rules. This unusual production was titled *The Great Pentad (The Musical)*. This play, according to the report, consisted of a prologue, followed by five controversial acts that parodied the political and military crises that evolved in North America, Europe, and the Middle East, and how greed and corruption set the stage for the Ripple Event and for what was to follow.

Prologue: *What the Scorpion Asked the Camel*
Favorite audience song: *The Eye of Ra looks down upon you all the live long day*

Act 1: *Seth's Eye Is Blind; He Blinks No More*
Favorite audience song: *La bomba here La bomba there, sounds of explosions everywhere*

Act 2: *The Isis Crisis; A World Turned Upside Down*
Favorite audience song: *Beautiful northern sunrise; Smashing southern sunset*

Act 3: *Osiris Returns; Your Mummy Loves You*
Favorite audience song: *A little insurrection makes the medicine go down*

Act 4: *Oh Horus, Come and Help Us*
Favorite audience song: *Don't fix it if it ain't broke*

Act 5: *Oh Great Pentad (Grand Finale)*
Favorite audience song: *Where have all the flowers (and bees and butterflies) gone?*

As the play ended, the leader of the theatrical group was introduced and addressed the audience with the following words:

Let us all remember the Political Horus, who ignored their mandate from the people and fell into greed and corruption that set the stage for the expansion of evil and terror brought about by the New Order priestess.

(NOTE: at the bottom of the report the unknown author wrote the following notation: *What did he mean?*)

During the stabilization period, there was a parallel rise in wandering minstrels, sometimes as single musicians or singers, while others formed groups. One duo called themselves "Singers of the Old Songs." Their performances attracted large audiences within the various settlement groups in New NorthWest Configuration with their renditions of favorite melodies that soon became whistled and sung by hundreds, as noted in this unusual report.

Data Collector: Bay Coleman, Certified Data Collector
5th Short Loop Trek West
Diary Entry: Day 5, Week 4, Month, 4, Solar Cycle 16
Location: Shelter Cove Settlement Group, West Coastal Old Oregon
Interview/Observation Topic: Return of the Arts

My team and I approached the entrance gate of Shelter Cove settlement group during late afternoon of Day 5, Week 4, Month 4, Solar Cycle 16. As we waited for the settlement decision about whether or not we would be invited to enter, we heard the sounds of music from within the walls of the protective stockade. We were cleared and entered an almost new world of joy and festive celebration that we had not before experienced. We were ushered to our rest and relaxation accommodations that in themselves were unusual due to the bright decorative colors used to augment the dark wood interiors. Our hosts then related to us that we were invited that evening to attend a pyre celebration in honor of the equinox, and there would be food, libations, and entertainment.

What we witnessed that evening was pure joy, given the hardship of our short loop excursion. We became refreshed as we joined in the celebration and roared in laughter at the presentations. First, a member of the administrative council welcomed everyone, and asked that space be made close to the fire so the children could see and listen more easily. Then she introduced Dawn Foster, a professional musician in the pre-Dark Time, who in turn, introduced 10 members of a choral group composed of young men and women who she said had practiced for the equinox celebration for more than 10 day cycles.

And then the music began…

First on the program was the duo named the Singers of the Old Songs. The young adult male tenor dressed in a curious uniform that he explained was part of an old Boy Scout uniform that commonly was worn by selected youths during solar cycles prior to the Ripple Event and onset of the Dark Times. His female partner was dressed in a simple white frock; she wore beaded necklaces that she said came from Old San Francisco (now SanFran) dated to 127 solar cycles earlier,. She said it had been worn by her great grandmother, who had an apartment at someplace called Hate Ass-Berry, or something like that.

The duo then started and belted out their first song:

> *Back When We Used Coins (Who Can Believe it Now?)*
> (I must confess that I didn't know what a coin was!) –
> followed by:

> *Daddy, What Were $, £, and €?*
> (They had me there too) – followed by:

> *When Grandma Danced (Sex, Drugs, and Rock and Roll)*
> (At least I knew what rock and roll was!) – followed by:

> *Hello Darkness You Is Not My Friend*
> (A curious title and song with a lilting, almost mysterious
> counterpoint melody) – and they concluded with: …

> *I Gave My Love a Credit Card (And All I Got Was the Bill)*

> (This song left many in the audience glancing at each other,
> trying to figure out what it all meant – but we laughed
> anyway. The duo, sensing puzzlement that had come over the
> audience, simply burst out into laughter, then left the stage.)

Following the performance of the duo singers, there was a long intermission
at which time those attending mingled and exchanged news.

Mike Richardson, Certified Data Collector, 4th Short Loop Trek East
Diary Entry: Day 2, Week 2, Month 6, Solar Cycle 15
Location: East of New Bozeman and Initial Days in Harlowton
Interview/Observation Topic: General Geographic Descriptions

> *We left MSU and trekked east of New Bozeman toward Livingston. The*
> *long abandoned highway was known locally as "ate-mine."*

(NOTE ADDED AT THE BOTTOM OF ENTRY PAGE: this notation, "ate-
mine," actually was highway 89 with the slang name perhaps related to
barbeque feasts, once held by ranchers in the vicinity prior to the Dark
Time.)

> *Our route led us west of the peaks in the Crazy Mountain range, then*
> *eastward between the forested areas toward Martinsdale Lake. We camped*
> *for several days, refilling our water needs. Just to the north were remnants*
> *of the 12 track road, with the residual traces of a rail line where trains*
> *once ran through this region. We passed the ruins of the tiny settlement*

of Two Dot, and reached the western outskirts of Harlowton. As we approached, we could see the Little Belt Mountains to the North that were capped with snow even during the sixth month (June). We established our base camp at Harlowton, down on what the locals once called "the flat," just below the escarpment of the Musselshell River.

Harlowton had been abandoned many years previously. Shops along the main streets were boarded-up; old advertising signs were in disrepair, and many had fallen onto the sidewalks. One of the key monuments in the town, the Graves Hotel, remained standing due to its solid stone construction, but only the shell remained intact, as the once grand interior and rooms had been looted.

Another stone building along the east side of Main Street also bore a sign on its exterior revealing that it had once served as the local jail. It was clear to us that the building served another function and later had been converted into a local museum, perhaps 40 solar cycles prior to the Ripple Event. One of the holding cells inside had been preserved. As we examined what was left of the museum remains, I observed and recorded the following words that had been written in charcoal on one of the cell walls. It was impossible to tell if the author had been detained in the jail, or if the text was more recent. In either event, the content expressed the sorrow that each of us felt as we visited the once proud remains of Harlowton, which now had disappeared from the western plains of Old Montana.

> By the banks of the Musselshell River,
> It's there that I want to grow old.
> To soar on my wings like an eagle,
> To lie on your carpets of gold.
>
> Your crystal cold waters, they ripple and flow,
> From the mountains then down to the sea,
> Let your waters flow 'or me and cleanse now my soul,
> For all men were born to be free.

(Name obscured, 1983, old solar cycle calculation)

Down on the lower river terrace below the Graves Hotel and out onto what had been known locally as "the flat," were the remains of the once-bustling Milwaukee Railroad terminal. The stationmaster's house and waiting rooms were in ruins, as was the roundhouse where once-powerful electric engines could be turned. Nothing remained of the repair yard, or *the electrical systems – the pylons, lines, and conductor cables that once powered these great electrical engines. As we explored the ruins, we saw evidence that packs of wild dogs roamed the area, an observation that contributed to the sad devolution of technology and loss as the residents of Harlowton fought through the Ripple Event and early years of the Dark Time the best they could.*

We determined that the closest settlement group was 10 kilo-miles northwest of the Harlowton ruins, near a snowmelt water source called Spring Creek. We approached the settlement and offered signals requesting our admission, but we were denied entrance.

We returned to Harlowton, broke camp, and resumed our trek eastward along the north bank of the Musselshell River, past the buffalo-drive cliffs and the exposure buttes (EBs), where in the past Native Americans honored their dead and exposed the bodies of their chiefs, since they could not be buried because the earth was sacred.

Mary Fletcher, Certified Data Collector
Another Member of the 4th Short Loop Trek East (Continuation of Team Report)
Location: Buffalo Run Settlement Group
Interview/Observation Topic: Participation in a Lakota Rite of Passage
Transcription of Oral Report Delivered at Montana State University

Upon completion of each loop trek, the data collectors were debriefed, and their physical condition and health evaluated. Participants submitted their daily travel logs and diaries for analysis and evaluation. Toward the end of the first week of debriefing, members of a loop trek presented their information summaries at a campus-wide assembly and responded to questions.

During my visit with the Lakota, I became curious about one of their rites of passage – the vision quest. I asked if I might undertake such a quest, and the tribal elders agreed after much debate, I was to find later. Accordingly, a shaman instructed me in the tending of a sacred fire, and taught me the simple chants and dances that would be required of me. Subsequently, I was led to a secluded place by two elders who left me with little food and water. As they departed, they stressed there was no dishonor in not experiencing a vision. For seven days I tended the fire, sang the songs and danced, as I had been instructed – all this on little sleep and with limited food and drink. I became weaker, more disoriented and at the same time more skeptical. Early on the eighth day, a Buffalo Calf Woman came to me. We talked of many things, both sacred and profane. On the morning of the ninth day, she departed after giving me my tribal name. This I cannot tell you in Lakotan, but it loosely translates as "she doubts no more." The remainder of that day I fasted, purifying myself. The elders returned the next day, and I rejoined the people.

Ember Hayes, Certified Data Collector
Another Member of the 4th Short Loop Trek East (Continuation of Team Report)
Transcription of Oral Report Delivered at Montana State University

I am Ember Hayes. I participated in the fourth short loop trek during solar cycle 15. My team leader, Mike Richardson, already has spoken to you. This was my first short loop expedition. My team members and I encountered 27 settlement groups along the way. We were admitted into 16 settlements, where we interviewed elderly men and women regarding clan history and cultural practices that allowed them to survive during the Dark Times.

During our trek, we saw the return of bison herds, wild horses, and the re-emergence of elk, moose, and antelope. We encountered – and avoided – packs of dogs and wolves on a near daily basis, and we once observed a climactic clash for supremacy between the alphas of a wolf and a dog pack, and watched the attack dog led by a crested facial scared alpha male take down the alpha wolf as the rest of the pack retreated.

Along the way, we encountered small bands of migratory Native Americans, specifically, Crow and Blackfoot Nations, on the plains east of Harlowton, Old Montana, who had returned to their hunting-pastoral ways. We were invited into one camp and provided shelter and food. The tribes carried with them objects from the pre-Dark Times – they had manufactured carts cobbled together from pieces of the chassis of old Chevrolet automobiles. These carts were used to carry goods and were pulled by horses.

I was invited to attend initiation rites where young Crow girls passed from childhood to adult status and were presented with tokens of their new status.

Later, when I became sick with mosquito fever, I was nursed back to health by a Crow sage femme, who prepared bundles of special herbs that she had gathered. She covered me with a blanket, lit the bundles and I was enveloped by the sweet-smelling smoke. Later as I recovered, she told me that such remedies were used to protect women and to cure what she called e-M'tr fnor or heat disorders (HDs), treatments used by many clan generations during the pre-Dark Time.

As part of my ethnobotanical responsibilities, I asked to join a group of young boys who were permitted by their fathers and mothers to wander about the clan territory testing and learning which bush foods were safe to consume.

I repeatedly encountered the time-honored practice in which fathers had given their sons small dogs to experiment with. When the boys encountered a plant fruit or seed, root, or leaf that they were unsure of, they fed it to their dogs and watched. If after a time the dogs continued to romp about and skittle here and there, the boys themselves ate the new item and brought it into their knowledge base. If the test dog vomited, or died, then the lesson also was learned and not forgotten. Dogs were more than simply "man's best friend"; they were instruments of family and individual survival.

A mother who had lost two children in childbirth showed me traditional ways to make fire using flint, and two different types of drill and bow systems. Even the young girls I met could make stone weapons, since they needed this skill set to assist in the defense of the clan, if necessary.

I recorded numerous medical plants and learned which leaves, roots, and barks were best for fever, and what could treat an illness called p-Aml o'Danath or "long sickness disorder" (LSD). Our team encountered certain elderly who focused most of their attention on the past and how life had been during the pre-Dark Time. Some of these elderly had not adapted well to the new responsibilities required by their tribe.

When it was time to leave, the clan honored me. The eldest elder spoke of the sadness of parting. Another created a song in my honor whose words, she said, would protect me along my journey. I extended my hand for the wound of parting – a symbolic slash on my left palm, and then faced the assembly and proudly received the second cut upon my forehead above my right eye – symbols that would provide me with strength and knowledge necessary to continue my work. These scars that I show you today served to identify me as an adopted clan member, alerting others that I might meet along the way that I may be escorted during my journey through the remainder of the small loop without fear or danger from others.

Question–Answer Session:

Question: *To what do you attribute the survival of the Native American peoples where you and the others stayed?*

Response: *Their prior detailed knowledge of edible plants and that the members had retained their traditional hunting and trapping skills since rifle ammunition had been exhausted during the first years of the Dark Time. Also, the clan moved within a highly varied landscape, from prairie grasslands to mountainous pine and cedar forests, each with different arrays of edible species.*

Question: *But they were not settled, correct? And if they traveled widely as you say, would they have roamed within the shattered zones to the east and north of the settlement groups Buffalo Run and Elk Preserve? How did the clan members protect themselves from the bandits and raiders in the shattered zones?*

Response: *Advance scouts on horseback were careful observers and alert to signs of impending danger, and would return to relate the information. The clan that befriended us had not forgotten their traditional weapon skills. While we never witnessed an attack on the clan by vandals in the shattered zones, we observed archery and horseback-lance competitions that in our view would have been a superior means of defense over most bandit groups in the shattered zones.*

Question: *From your report it seems to me that life was very difficult out on the short loop treks. Why would someone like me want to participate in such hardships, especially when life at MSU and in the protected zone surrounding much of New Bozeman may be spartan, but at least is predictable?*

Response: *Without being too harsh, your question conveys to me the impression that you have not understood why MSU embarked upon this project. Yes, you now live in a protected zone and have a relatively easy, albeit modest life, but such amenities could vanish in a few days. What if another epidemic struck North America and caused another die-off of our population?*

Yes, life out on the treks is difficult, but hardship bonds you with your colleagues and friends. Together you overcome adversity and in the process of working together and helping one another, you recognize what it means to be a survivor. Ask yourself – what are you prepared to give up in order for you and your family and closest friends to survive? Our data collection projects were implemented to identify different survival techniques used by exceptional people who lived through the Ripple Event and Dark Time – techniques that you could apply and use if necessary. If we do not interview survivors and learn of their successes and failures, and how they dealt with everyday needs, how can we ever expect to survive if another calamity were to strike?

Does that answer your question?

Question: *If you were to be selected for another trek, either long or short, which direction would you go? Somewhere new or revisit places from the past where you made friends?*

Response: *It is imperative that we learn as much as we can from the elderly survivors. They may hold the key to our own survival. I remember from the reports and briefing seminars from other data collectors that at the mouth of the Mattole River along the coast in Old California, there is an enclave of residents averaging 85 to 90 years of age who had in their words "seen it all." If I remember correctly, my data collector colleagues interviewed about 25 or 30, but they were short on time and there were numerous residents who remained to be interviewed. If I were selected to participate in a long loop trek, I would want to interview residents at this settlement group. If not selected, I would encourage our data collection administrators at MSU to assign a group to return there as soon as possible.*

After-Word

May we always celebrate the memory of Certified Data Collector Alan West, who was the first casualty among the MSU data collectors. He was the first, but would not be the last. All data collectors were well trained and in excellent physical condition. The trips were arduous, with different categories of risks from wild animals (especially bears and cougars), bandits and roving gangs of semi-organized thugs (some on foot, others on horseback), contaminated food and water resources, and from unexpected exposure to diseases.

A fever of unknown origin took Alan's life. The source was perhaps insect-related, since the other five data collectors in his team did not contract the fever. Whatever the origin of his illness, it was not contagious.

Alan fell ill on the return leg of the first small loop trek: west. The data collectors started to break camp where they had spent two days along the shores of Lake Yellowstone. Alan reported that he felt sick but was able to continue the trek. The team resumed their trek north out of the geyser basin but upon reaching the settlement of New West Yellowstone (NWY), Alan had worsened. Doctors at NWY administered a suite of herbal medicines and after a time these seemed to lift his spirits so they continued. The data collectors pushed their loop carts north along the smooth old road through the Gallatin River valley, and they reached the small settlement of Big Sky. It was there that Alan died.

The team, as per their training instructions, wrapped his body and prepared it for burial. The location chosen was a high lookout north of the Lone Mountain Road, where they assembled a cairn of stones and marked the location. The team paused and paid homage: they reflected on Alan's life and achievements, then after a final goodbye, they pushed on toward New Bozeman and the terminus of their journey at the MSU campus.

Alan West exemplified the spirit and qualities expected of all MSU data collectors; he mastered his training, added new skill sets to his already able list of qualifications, and was diligent in his daily recordings of observations and interviews. Alan was well liked and respected by the other members of the Team IV, First Data Collection Trek West: Basil Davis, Joanna McDonald, Dell Clark, Sage Grant, and especially his travel mate and partner, Alba Bennett.

May the name Alan West remain forever in our memories.

Illam in Spiritu Sancto, amicum
Memores sumus vestry!

Metal Sheet #8

Inscription and Translation

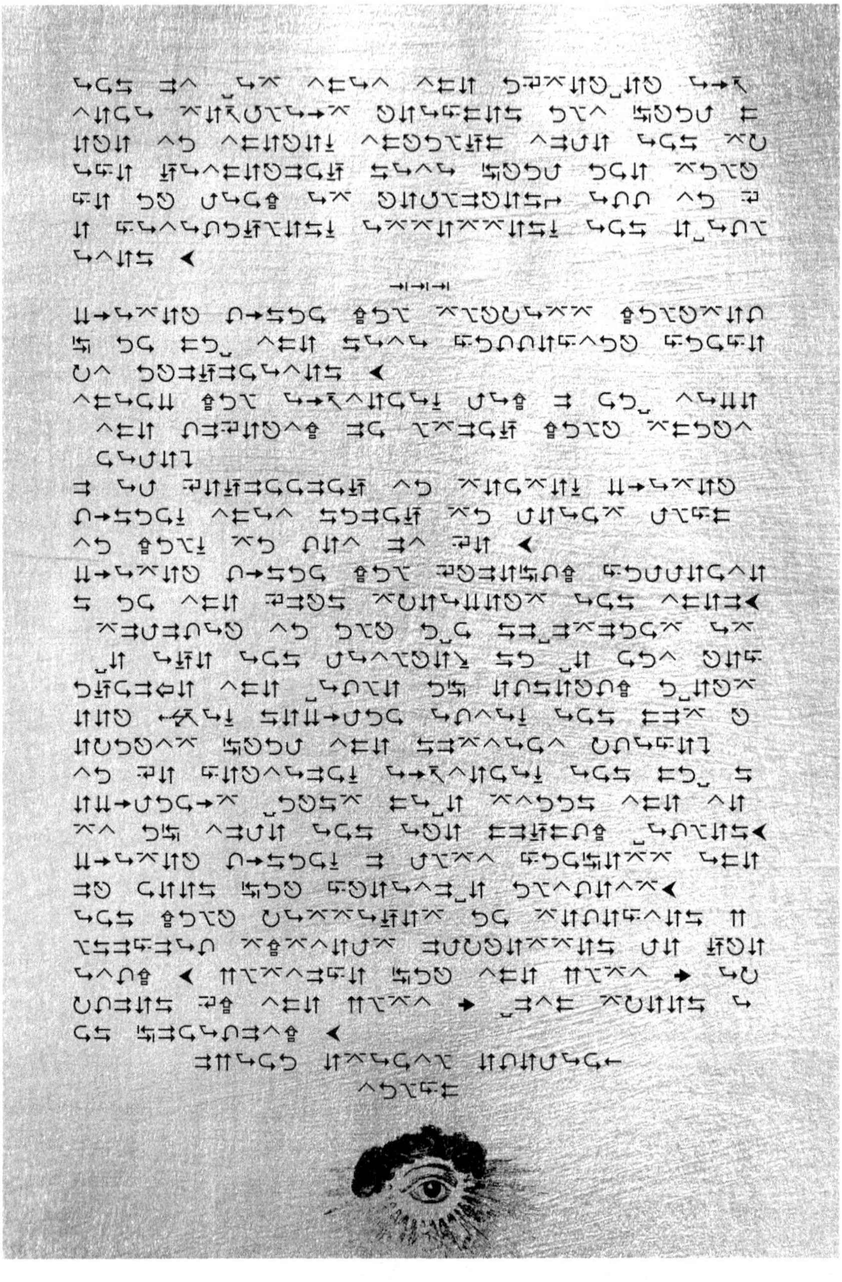

And it was that the Observer A'-Tena Se-Qua reached out from here to there, through time and space, gathering data from one source or many as required; all to be catalogued, assessed, and evaluated.

*** *** ***

K'Aser L'Don, you surpass yourself on how the data collector concept originated.

Thank you, A'-Tena. May I now take the liberty of using your short name?

I am beginning to sense, K'Aser L'Don, that doing so means much to you, so let it be.

K'Aser L'Don, you briefly commented on the bird speakers and their gifts of prophecy. To this be true, K'Aser L'Don, as even we observers cannot the future see?

It is a standard belief of some of these groups, A'-Tena, that the gifted can listen to and recognize animal sounds and place their meanings into words, but others falsely proclaim this.

To know the future, K'Aser L'Don, is reserved but for Etowah, creator of all that is and will be, so I must conclude such units, those individuals known as bird speakers, do not commune with nature but have alternative designs or have mental brain changes.

A'-Tena, did you recognize the origins of what these groups called age-set determinations?

Yes, K'Aser L'Don, it is not dissimilar to our own divisions as we age and mature. Do we not recognize the value of elderly Overseer 37-A, Dek'mOn Alta, and his reports from the distant place?

To be certain, A'-Tena, and how Dek'mOn's words have stood the test of time and are highly valued.

K'Aser L'Don, I must confess amusement with the songs you identified. Their topics reveal much about the culture and sensitivities of these units, and their need for creative outlets, and your passages on selected judicial systems impressed me greatly – justice for the just, applied by the just, with speed and finality.

Ijano Esantu Eleman!

CHAPTER 10: EVENING READING 10

Document 10, Cave Location: Case 43-B

Long Loop Investigation Reports

Tough it out;
Tough it out;
Climb the mountains

Tough it out;
Tough it out;
Cross the rivers

Ever moving 'long the Long Loop
Loopers collecting stories from the past.

Each dawn brings a different story.
Survivors' tales from distant past.
Women, men, and elder children.
Safe at last ...

        Safe at last ...

                Safe at last.

(Source: Anonymous. *Song of the Loopers.* Montana State University, History Project Archive, Music Section: Box MS-45M.)

Pre-Note

Extending outward from New Bozeman, the long loop destinations stretched an average of 1,150 kilo-miles (round trip). Six data collectors (three males, three females) formed the required set of participants. Each group was characterized by different skill sets, and all were well trained in rural survival techniques. The following information on trek destinations and routes taken was summarized from old maps in the MSU archive. Some of the listed towns no longer exist.

Long Loop Destinations:

New NorthWest Configuration

Outward: New Bozeman west to Butte; farther along Eye-90 west to Coeur d'Alene, Spokane, Cheney, Elensburg, to Seattle, Tacoma, Bremerton, Olympic Peninsula; southwest to Aberdeen, then south on Eye-5 to Centralia, Longview; west along the Columbia River to Astoria; south along 1-0-1 to Tillamook.

Return: Tillamook east to Portland, then to Hood River, The Dalles, Pendleton, La Grande, Baker City, Ontario, Caldwell, Nampa, Boise, Mountain Home, Craters of the Moon, Idaho Falls; then north along Eye-15 toward Butte, then to New Bozeman.

Flatland Configuration

Outward: New Bozeman west to Butte; south through Big Hole Bison Camp; then east through Yellowstone Park, Cody, Buffalo, Gillette, Spearfish, Rapid City, along 9-0 through Mitchell to Sioux Falls,

Return: Sioux Falls north to Brookings, Watertown; northwest to Aberdeen, following Eye-9-4 ultimately to Glendive, Miles City, Billings, then Eye 9-0 to Livingston and to New Bozeman.

New SouthWest Configuration

Outward: New Bozeman west to Butte, south through Big Hole Valley and Bison Camp to connect with Eye-1-5, Idaho

Falls, Blackfoot, Pocatello, Ogden, Layton, Bountiful, Salt Lake City; then west along Eye-80, through Wells, Elko, Battle Mountain, Winnemucca, Lovelock, Fernley, Sparks, Reno; over mountains through Truckee, Colfax, Auburn, Newcastle, Loomis, Rocklin, Roseville, Sacramento, Davis, Vacaville, Fairfield, Vallejo, Novato, San Rafael, Mill Valley, Sausalito, San Francisco; south to San Jose, Los Gatos, Santa Cruz, Watsonville, Marina, Monterey; south along highway 1 to Cambria, Morro Bay, San Luis Obispo, Arroyo Grande, Guadalupe, Lompoc, Santa Barbara.

Return: Santa Barbara east to Ventura, Santa Paula; over mountains to Simi, Thousand Oaks, Woodland Hills at the western outskirts of El-A; turn north along Eye-5 through Burbank, San Fernando, Santa Clarita, Palmdale, Lancaster, Mojave, Bakersfield; north along highway 99 through Delano, Tulare, Fresno, Merced; east to Mariposa, over mountains through Yosemite National Park; to Mono Lake north along highway 395 through Topaz, cut northwest to South Lake Tahoe then northeast to Carson City; east on highway 50 through Fallon; follow 50 east to Delta, connect with 1-15 and pass through Payson, Spanish Fork, Provo, Orem, and Salt Lake City; east on eye 8-0 to Evanston, Green River, Rock Springs, Rawlins, Laramie, Cheyenne; north on highway 87 to Wheatland, to highway 26 to Douglas; west to Casper; north on 25 to Buffalo, northwest on Eye 90 to Sheridan, Billings, west to Livingston; then return to New Bozeman.

New Confederacy Configuration
Data collectors did not return (no data books recovered).

New PlyMouth Configuration
Data collectors did not return (no data books recovered).

Selected Passages From the Sixth Long Loop Trek
Representative passages from data collection diaries and reports for long loop six (into New NorthWest Configuration and southward into portions of New SouthWest Configuration) reveal a broad range of accomplishments.

The sixth long loop team assembled was experienced, as members previously had participated on two or more short loop treks:

Alan Jenkins, field coordinator

Lavender Simpson, ethnobotanist

Ennis Hall, hydrology and water supply engineer

Beth Simmons, interview data analyst

Freedom Scott, pre-Dark Time linguistic specialist

Deanna Erwin, geriatric health specialist

Itinerary:

Departure: New Bozeman, MSU Campus; trekked west to Three Forks;

Northern trail on to Missoula;

West across the mountain chain through Old Idaho to Spokane, then southwest on highway 395;

Requested accommodation and interview status at two settlement groups (Mountain Shelter and Canyon Fortress, both in eastern Old Washington) where we were met by armed guards and denied entrance to each;

Arrived Columbia River near the former town of Kennewick, camped then trekked downstream to The Dalles settlement;

Requested accommodation and interview status at Salmon Run Settlement along the Columbia River near the abandoned settlement of Chenoweth. Here, we were welcomed to conduct interviews. We also were invited to participate in salmon-netting and spear-fishing rituals.

Alan Jenkins, Certified Data Collector
Interview with Charles Eagle Feather

Jenkins: *Please describe the origins and activities at Salmon Run Settlement*

Eagle Feather: *Today, we are a mix of Native Americans who speak Sahaptin. Others include local White survivalists who inhabited the tribal lands prior to Ripple Event. We, the plateau peoples, the Umatilla and Yakama, have used salmon as our primary food since time began. Today, all members of our settlement group – men, women, as well as children – participate in salmon-netting and spear-fishing rituals. We offer respect to the silver-swimmers whose flesh fortifies our bodies. When taken, the fish are blessed. The meat then is slabbed and sun-dried or fire-dried. Each season when the salmon start their run up river, we honor the individual who captures the first one. This salmon is removed from the fisherman's net or spear, then set aside and prepared separately from all the others. At our ritual dinner on the first evening of the salmon run, the fisherman (man or woman; child or elder) presents this first salmon for all to partake. The first serving is given to the grandparents of the fisherman (if alive), next the parents. The event is blessed by our settlement group shaman.*

Our word for salmon is "wy-kan-ush," and our word for people is "pum." Therefore, we are known as the wy-kan-ush-pum or salmon people. Our home is on land; the salmon's home is in water. We drink water from the great Columbia River and, each time we do so, we offer a blessing that the wy-kan-ush always will be part of our lives.

We departed Salmon Run settlement and continued southwest to the mouth of the Columbia River at New Astoria. We entered the town and crossed to the western peninsula where we were accepted for entry into the Fort Stevens settlement group.

We rested and recouped at Fort Stevens for two days, and completed interviews with several residents regarding the Ripple Event and impacts upon their individual and daily lives and on the organization and the management of their settlement group.

Beth Simmons, Certified Data Collector
Interview with Bryan Thomas and Holly North

Simmons: *Please tell me your names and something about your backgrounds.*

Thomas: *My name is Bryan Thomas. I was born and raised in Astoria. When I was about 12 we moved to Warrenton, across the* bay along the Skipanon River. I graduated from high school in old solar cycle 2008, before the Ripple Event, and I was employed by Accent Construction as a carpenter.

North: My name is Holly North. Our family moved to Astoria from Eugene about 15 years ago – I guess we call them solar cycles now. I am about the same age as Bryan. He has been my mate partner since I was accepted into the Fort Stevens settlement group. My activities since the Ripple Event have been to practice my skills as cook and cloth weaver, techniques I learned from my mother, who died during the Ripple Event. My father passed away during solar cycle 2 of the Dark Time.

Simmons: Please describe how you coped during the Ripple Event and early years of the Dark Time.

Thomas: The initial days of the Ripple Event were terrible for many living in urban Astoria. My family's home was in Warrenton, a small community west of Astoria on the peninsula. We were raised to always have a supply of food for six months, and since we had access to fresh river water, people in our town did not suffer as much as those living in Astoria.

North: When civility and law and order collapsed in Astoria, it was horrible. Thieves roamed the streets taking what they wanted, and within a day or two all supermarkets, corner grocery stores, and restaurants had been looted. There remained essentially no resources for the everyday food that most people could rely upon and regularly ate. We lived in the eastern quarter of Astoria, just off 31st Street. My father asked me to help secure food by fishing, but when I landed my first salmon, a group of young boys surrounded me and stole my catch. I could not prevent them from running off, and returned home empty-handed. As I told the story to my father, he held me and said that he understood and I should not feel responsible. He asked me if I could recall what the boys wore or if they had any identification marks. I replied the best I could. Later that afternoon my father left our home taking a pistol with him. I knew what he was going to do, but *didn't comment. He returned two hours later. We never spoke about what happened. During the days that followed, we had essentially nothing to eat.*

Simmons: *Do you believe that your father tracked down and killed the boys who had attacked you?*

North: *Don't ask stupid questions!*

Simmons: *Perhaps we can continue?*

Thomas: *The problem that worried us the most was lack of electricity. We had battery-operated radios, but these didn't work since all the local stations like KAST and the regional broadcast networks out of Portland and Corvallis were silent and unable to transmit. It seemed that even the diesel-powered generators at the radio stations were useless. We had no firsthand knowledge of what was happening beyond our immediate neighborhoods and no idea why or how long the disruptions would occur. It was unclear whether or not we as a nation were under attack, or whether this was just some quirk in the electrical grid that would be repaired soon.*

North: *The hardest part was about 10 days into the Ripple Event. I remember walking with my father in the early morning just before dawn when we went down to the Shively Park to search for edible wild plants. We really did not know what to collect, only that we were so terribly hungry. All that he and I could remember was that dandelion leaves were edible. We thought that Bermuda grass seeds might be all right, but we were not certain and the seeds were so tiny that they probably wouldn't have helped us much anyhow. During this time, my mother sickened; she died about three weeks into the Event.*

Thomas: *Why are you asking us these questions?*

Simmons: *As I explained earlier, our purpose is to collect information from survivors of the Ripple Event and Dark Time, to identify different ways that individuals and families coped with the terrible events, so we might be able to assist others to survive, if further local or regional epidemics or disasters occur.*

North: *This is really hard to talk about. Your questions bring back too many difficult memories. I have to stop. Let's go, Bryan.*

Simmons: *I know that this is hard; it is hard for all survivors to be asked to think back to those difficult times. Please, our work is very important. Please do not leave; at least let me ask you one more question. Please?*

Thomas: *No. Holly and I are leaving, sorry.*

Prior to our departure from Fort Stevens settlement, our hosts told us about an unusual settlement group called Rock Creek Haven, located outside of Vernonia (also in Old Oregon), approximately 60 kilo-miles inland and southeast of New Astoria. It was reported that the residents at Rock Creek Haven practiced polygamy (a regional decision), since so many of the local adult men died during the Ripple Event and early years of the Dark Time. Given that we would have to traverse kilo-miles of uneven trails to cross the Clatsop forested region and the extensive shattered zones along the way, we voted against visiting Rock Creek Haven and continued south.

We proceeded down the coast of Oregon, pushing our supply carts along the relic highway 101. We bypassed the older settlements of Seaside, Cannon Beach, and Manzanita and then reached Nehalem. Exhausted, we sought entry to the Bayside Collective settlement group founded along the north shore of Nehalem Bay. We advanced toward the settlement and signaled our request for accommodation and permission to interview residents. We were met, in turn, by armed scouts in a confrontational military-style configuration who ordered us to leave immediately and not attempt to return.

Continuing south along the coast of Oregon, we reached the vicinity of the two small settlements of Rockaway and Twin Rocks. We approached Lagoon Sanctuary settlement group, located on the hillside east of the freshwater lagoon known in earlier times as Lake Lytle. The water supply for this settlement was provided by year 'round mountain drainage, fed primarily by what once was called Steinhilber Creek, but known by the current residents as the Stone Hill Feed (SHF).

Deanna Erwin, Certified Data Collector
Interview with Sage Femme Ivy Ellis

Erwin: *Please tell me your name and describe your duties at Lagoon Sanctuary.*

Ellis: *Fifteen years (solar cycles) prior to the Ripple Event, I graduated from Oregon State University, Corvallis, where I majored in nursing with a minor in anthropology specializing in traditional medicine of the Oregon Tribal Peoples, especially the Cayuse, Chinook, Clatsop, Klamath, Tillamook, Umpqua, and Yahooskin. My training proved especially valuable when the Ripple Event struck. At that time, I was living with two close male friends who were my mate partners, John and David. Sharing our house also were two women, Frances and Jane, who also were mate partners. We shared the two bedrooms in a small house on Kings Road – some in town called the street Kings Boulevard, but it wasn't wide enough for this term in my opinion, so I always have called it a road. Ours was a small frame house with a backyard garden where we raised an array of traditional herbs, spices, and a few vegetables. The nearby campus of OSU shut down on the second day of the Ripple Event, and given that we had essentially no news about how and why things were progressing, my roommates and I became quite worried. The first thing I thought about was getting out of town and reaching the farmlands west of the city. I figured that the Willamette River soon would be contaminated with bodies and garbage, so an exodus was in order. I knew that my roommates and I could find safety and refuge west of Corvallis along the Marys River, and that we had the skills that could enable us to live off the land, and we discussed the possibility of leaving.*

Erwin: *How did your close friends and roommates deal with the possibility of leaving Corvallis, and what decision did you make?*

Ellis: *Two of the four went with me, both my male mate partners. Frances and Jane remained behind, thinking that things would have to get better and that it was safer to "gut it out" rather than risk life in what they called "the boonies." I pleaded with them to come with us, but they were too frightened of the unknown and preferred to remain in the city. I have assumed that both died because they had limited to no access to safe water or sufficient food. I still am saddened by their decision to remain, and believe to this day that the five of us could have survived.*

Erwin: *How is it you arrived at Lagoon Sanctuary?*

Ellis: *We reached the headwaters of the Mary' River, crossed over the divide, and came down the west slope of the forested region following old Highway 20, then state highways to the northwest. John and Dave both had rifles and pistols, and killed some small game that we cooked and ate. Using my plant skills, we lived off the land and maintained our energy levels. We trekked northwest and followed the Siletz River drainage that flowed north and west to the sea. When we reached the ocean, we came across a settlement group that at the time had no name. There we were threatened and forced to leave the perimeter immediately. We continued north, bypassed Lincoln City, then followed old highway 101 into Old Tillamook, which totally had been destroyed by looters. On the outskirts of Old Tillamook, we were forced to defend ourselves after we were confronted by a gang of hoodlums. We warned them to back off, but they didn't and continued to threaten us. It was as if this group of thugs was high on some drug. We warned them again but they continued to advance, brandishing machete-style knives. John and David shot and killed two of the thugs as the remainder fled. We continued north past the east end of Miami Cove, and entered the ruins of the once-picturesque village of Garibaldi. The bed-and-breakfasts and tourist shops that once characterized this quaint settlement all had been burned, and essentially nothing of value remained. Outside the ruins of one of the stores, we encountered two destitutes, a man and a woman, who begged for food – but we had none to share. They told us of their attempts to be admitted to the Lagoon Sanctuary settlement group just outside of Twin Rocks (about five kilomiles north), but that they had been rejected because of their illness and lack of useful survival skills. They pleaded for assistance but we had none to give.*

Erwin: *Was this encounter the first time you heard about a selection process for entry into a settlement group?*

Ellis: *Yes, earlier we had been confronted and told to leave immediately and not consider entry into several settlement groups, but we had not experienced anything like a selection process. Even so, this didn't worry us as we had a range of important survival skills: John had studied pre-medicine at Oregon State University, and had volunteered summers at local pharmacies and emergency rooms. Dave had worked at a veterinarian's office where he used skills taught to him by his grandfather who owned the business. I knew what was edible in the forests, grasslands, and lagoons nearby. And yes, we were challenged as we approached Lagoon Sanctuary. But as you can see, all three of us were admitted.*

Erwin: *As a sage femme at Lagoon Sanctuary, what are your primary duties?*

Ellis: *There are four: First, I have an obligation to assist and protect my settlement group; second, I have an obligation to train a suite of young teenagers – boys and girls – how to differentiate the safe from toxic wild plants, and to identify and protect the several key species used in herbal medicine from over-exploitation; third, I have an obligation to provide health education for young girls who are approaching their rite of passage to become women, to explain the mysteries of being a woman, and various methods and techniques used to protect their bodies from disease, explain the mysteries of conception, pregnancy, and delivery, and how to maintain the dignity of women and mutual respect between genders. The fourth and last obligation is one that I like best: I organize and officiate at the female rite-of-passage ceremonies.*

Erwin: *I see that John and Dave sit by your side.*

Ellis: *They are both my mate partners. The three of us have created a son and daughter and together are the parents of both children.*

We left Lagoon Sanctuary and passed through Tillamook and out onto the headlands, where we spent two days. We continued south along old 101 to Newport and then trekked east along highway 20 toward Corvallis. Along the route, we asked to be admitted into the Scheele Creek settlement group near the ruins of Blodgett. There we rested.

Two days later, we bid goodbye and continued our trek toward Corvallis, reaching there in the early evening. We camped about a block north of the old Oregon State University campus along Kings Boulevard where we sought the original home of Sage Femme Ivy Ellis. We found her former residence, but it was deserted, as were all the other homes along Kings Boulevard for as far as we could see.

We could scarcely believe it. Corvallis once was a wonderful city filled with activities and thousands of students but now was deserted. We posted sentries at our campsite and took turns sleeping as Alan and Freedom kept alert for the packs of dogs that roamed the area. In the morning, we returned to campus and searched several of the science buildings but to our dismay, equipment, supplies, and copper recyclables already had been looted.

We left Corvallis and marched south, skirting the Willamette River but following the river course through Harrisburg. Just outside of Harrisburg, we noted that the once-rich agricultural lands had been burned and the farm outbuildings destroyed. Taking this as an ill omen of what the nearby shattered zones might offer, we elected to bypass Eugene, skirted east around it, and we camped just outside the small abandoned community of Dexter, just below the Lookout Point dam and reservoir. The local settlement group, Shelter Haven, had attempted to retro-engineer the overflow-outlet in order to generate electricity, but had not been successful. We paused for two days to interview residents here, and learned of several unique cultural traditions associated with the region.

Lavender Simpson, Certified Data Collector
Interview with Shelter Haven Residents Donald Lee and Nyla Boyd

Simpson:	*I understand that the residents of Shelter Haven practice a unique integration of males and females beginning early in life?*
Lee:	*After birthing of our children, we form play groups in which the composition alternates with each solar cycle. The first play groups are all one gender, then with the following solar cycle they are mixed – then single again – then mixed. We found this to be a superior way to teach respect and honor that both genders should have for the other.*
Boyd:	*I have been a part of Shelter Haven for 15 solar cycles and never have seen or heard of gender-based disrespect.*
Simpson:	*How do you at Shelter Haven prepare your children for the responsibilities of life as they approach their maturity?*
Lee:	*The passage from youth to adult status, whether in males or females, is a complicated process. Beginning at the age of 7, children are taught to respect the body parts of the other gender, and special sessions are held with adult teachers to instruct the children on what to expect as their bodies change and mature.*
Boyd:	*By the age of 13, our children are considered to be pre-adults. Each has participated in three months of instruction provided by our settlement group sage femme on topics that include bodily rhythms and cycles, contraception, and gender respect. Each solar cycle, at the beginning of the fourth month, adult parents with similar-aged pre-adults meet and through open discussions form their children into clusters of four females and four males. Upon family agreement, their pre-adult children will enter into the next phase of life, a process that we at Shelter Haven call the Octet.*
Simpson:	*The Octet? What do you mean?*
Lee:	*Let me explain: the parents prepare special Octet shelters where the eight pre-adults live communally; they will cook,*

sleep, work, and mate – acting together as one – bound by the principles of the Octet.

Each pre-adult female selects a different pre-adult male partner on alternate nights so that every four days the initial partners are rejoined. The alternating selections continue for one complete solar cycle until each pre-adult female becomes pregnant. The children born remain with the females; each of the four males is considered to be the child's father. As the infants grow, they are guided and mentored by each male and female within the group.

Simpson: *In essence, what you are saying is that each Octet serves as a communal family also supported by the love and care provided by individual parents of each Octet member?*

Boyd: *That is correct. Each infant born within the Octet must also be inspected and assigned an infant survivability score (ISS). We at Shelter Haven use a wide variety of tests to determine the strength and vigor of our newborns, for example:*

Mother's milk and a small piece of ejected placenta are placed in the neonate's mouth: if the infant does not vomit, it is assumed that it will live.

We listen carefully to the early cries of our neonates: if they cry out with the sound – oommee – it will survive and have a long life, but if it cries out with the sound – maamu – it will soon die.

If the neonate is held by either parent and turns its head downward and groans, this is an omen that it will not live long.

Simpson: *Is it true that if a neonate born within the Octet is malformed, it will be taken from the group and exposed – something like the process that was practiced in ancient Sparta?*

Lee: *How did you hear about this? That is none of your business.*

Simpson: *I meant no disrespect. Please continue.*

Lee: *It is our tradition that each child born within the Octet cannot mate with another born to the group – but must find a mate within another group.*

Boyd: *Let me add that each child born within the Octet is celebrated at solar cycle one, two, and five. After the fifth solar cycle, as a group they enter formal schooling where they learn and prosper together.*

Lee: *When members of the Octet reach the age of 15, any children previously born are left in the care of elders, whereupon the Octet members embark upon what we at Shelter Haven call a walk-about in which they stay outside the settlement and manage to live for three monthly cycles within the regional shattered zone. Upon their successful return to Shelter Haven, they are designated as men and women, and receive the cuts and tattoos of adulthood at a separate ceremony celebrated by all members of the settlement group.*

Ennis Hall, Certified Data Collector
Interview with Shelter Haven Resident Kevin Campbell

Hall: *I understand there are specific tests or trials that pre-adult males at Shelter Haven must undergo in addition to their participation in The Octet?*

Campbell: *When we turn 15 we have been educated in survival skills taught by our elders. We are tested on our abilities to procure edible wild foods, firemaking, shelter construction, water-search techniques, weapon manufacture, and oil and fat procurement. All such instruction in our settlement group schools must be further refined and tested by excursions into the shattered zones adjacent to our settlement. Upon return from the trial test in the SZs each pre-adult male is designated a man, receives a special body cut, and is given a characteristic piece of clothing that designates trial passage. Of every eight males who undertake the walkabout trial, only five or six return, due to injury, illnesses that cannot be cured, being killed by wild animals, or death by other individuals or groups inhabiting the SZs. If one of the pre-adults does not return from the walk-about test this poses extra difficulty* upon the members of the original Octet – as in some instances the four females are left with only three or two males to assist with family responsibilities.

Hall: *Tell me more.*

Campbell: *I remember on my walk-about that I carved my name on several stone cliffs to prove that I had visited the locale. I also left groupings of three to four stones at certain places to mark my path through the shattered zone. I was fortunate during my walk-about that I was not attacked by wolves or wildcats, or even harassed by solitary or groups of individuals that I encountered along the way. Perhaps I looked too young, or perhaps it was because I had nothing of value that they could steal? I don't know.*

Deanna Erwin, Certified Data Collector
Interview with Shelter Haven Resident Orla Mason

Erwin: *I understand that you want to share information with me concerning Octet delivery rituals?*

Mason: *Your colleague seemed to be especially interested in the Octet as practiced here, but neglected to ask about any rituals associated with the newborns. We want to make certain that you have the most accurate information to share with your data collector colleagues.*

Erwin: *Thank you! Please continue.*

Mason: *Immediately after delivery, the mother and newborn will be removed from the Octet residential hut, and will enter into a 30-day period of isolation in preparation for the infant inspection. The mother and infant will live in an especially constructed shelter, where a blue and white flag is flown from the top roof beam to announce occupation and for others to stay away. The only visitor permitted to see the mother and infant at this time is our settlement sage femme. The infant's grandmother, the four male members of the Octet, or any other family member all are denied entrance at this time. The sage femme is responsible for preparing food for the new mother and for feeding her, as our traditions hold that the new mother cannot touch food going into her body during*

> *the 30-day isolation period. So the sage femme feeds the new mother using only forks or spoons, as knives are forbidden inside the isolation hut.*

Erwin: *How do you think that such a custom originated?*

Mason: *How it started? All I know is that I assume a 30-day isolation period would protect the infant and reduce exposure to germs or other airborne potential pathogens that visitors accidentally would spread. If you think about it, the isolation period also gives the new mother time to rest without having to deal with everyday life issues. Would it not be true, too, that such a custom with considerable rest would permit maximum production of breast milk to feed her new baby?*

Erwin: *That makes a lot of sense.*

Mason: *All that I know is that our settlement group sage femme, Star Pierce, not only trained in ethnobotany, herbal healing, and traditional medicine, but that she had spent time prior to the Ripple Event working as a Peace Corps volunteer among eastern Kalahari Desert traditional peoples. Perhaps she learned the custom there and thought it a good idea to put into practice at Shelter Haven. But I really don't know.*

> *Something else. After the infant has been inspected at the end of the 30 days, the child undergoes a naming ceremony, and then receives the characteristic burn mark (for boys) or tattoo (for girls) on the upper right arm – a symbol of acceptance into our clan and residency at Shelter Haven.*

The administrative council at Shelter Haven informed us that a group called the Rimmers might welcome our arrival. This was a local term used to identify the residents of an isolated settlement group along the rim of Crater Lake, that exceptional landscape feature formed thousands of years ago after the eruption of Mount Mazama.

When we left Shelter Haven, we were directed southeast of the Lookout Point reservoir where we pushed our carts along old highway 58 until we reached the intersection with old 97, then turned south through the Deschutes forest zone, aiming for Mt. Theilsen in the distance and Mt. Scott just beyond, Our informants stated that it would be a rigorous hike to approach Crater Lake from the east, but in doing so, we could avoid interacting with the southwestern forest raiders that sometimes preyed upon travelers through the region.

Our team arrived at Crater Lake. As we approached the fenced stockade, we were confronted by 15 armed residents, who inquired about our mission and needs. We asked only to renew our freshwater supplies and whether or not we could interview residents about their experiences during the Ripple Event and early years of the Dark Time. We were granted admission and as we passed through the stockade walls, we heard one of the scouts who had met us say:

> *Why would these fools want to remember those bad times?*
> *They must be crazy!*

But, as we found out, the majority of the residents were curious about our project, and we actually spent more time speaking with them about events at other places in New NorthWest Configuration than conducting interviews.

Prior to the Ripple Event, the majority of the current residents here had been survivalists. Afterward, they had bonded together, shared equipment and food, and then formed the Crater Rim settlement group. The residents themselves laughed at the terms used by others to identify them, as they also had been tagged as the Crater Lake Rimmers (CLRs), Crater Dwellers (CDs), and other designations.

The residents here developed characteristic body ornaments that had other purposes, as well. Each adult female and male at Crater Rim settlement wore a distinctive bracelet on their right wrist. These bracelets were prepared from obsidian beads dug from a specific location within the crater. The obsidian globules were polished and drilled using carborundum powder also obtained from the crater. Each month, the men and women over 50 solar cycles years of age assembled. They removed their bracelets and placed them inside an empty wooden barrel. The barrel then was sealed and rolled over the compacted earth of the central meeting place to the spot where a male child stood. This child was designated to reach into the barrel and draw out one bracelet. The owner of the selected bracelet would become the chief administrator of the Crater Rim settlement group for one month. After one month, another resident would be selected using the same procedure. We were informed that the system was based upon a widely held concept:

Too long in office – corruption and vice creep into decisions – keep it short!

The Crater Lake Rimmers provided scouts and protection to our group when we departed for the headwaters of the Umpqua River. We followed the drainage basin for six days westward, until we reached the outlet to the sea just south of the great sand dunes. Reaching the sea, we bid farewell to the Rimmers who had provided security.

We encamped just outside Sandbar Shelter settlement group, located south of Winchester Bay along old highway 101 where we were denied admission. The next morning, we carted south along the old highway through Coos Bay until we reached the Rogue River, then on to the mouth of the Chetco River where the border between Old Oregon and Old California was in the near distance.

Crossing into Old California, we entered New Crescent City situated along the Pacific Coast. The city had been rebuilt during the post-Dark Time recovery period, and already had developed an extensive trade network that linked regional settlement groups, thus forming a maritime trade that extended north into Old Oregon and farther south along the Old California coast.

Respondents at New Crescent City advised against traveling south along the coast at that time, due to the danger and problems posed by raiders and thieves. They suggested, instead, that we retrace our route a short distance and head overland up over the mountains using old highway 199 and reconnect with the settlement at Old Grants Pass. Once there, we would be able to make good progress south along Eye-5 through Medford and Ashland, and then re-enter northern Old California.

We took their advice and arrived in the mountain town of Weed, west of Mount Shasta. In past decades, visitors commonly associated the town's name with marijuana but, in fact, the settlement was named after Abner Weed, who started his lumber business here during the late nineteenth century (old time calculation). When we arrived, the town still had not recovered from the devastating wildfire that burned a considerable portion of the residential buildings back in the pre-Ripple Event year of 2014. That fire, coupled with the Ripple Event that followed, had reduced the town's population to only a few dozen. Most of the town's residents had abandoned the settlement shortly after the onset of the Ripple Event, and trekked north for protection at what became the Shasta Security settlement group, located along the shore of Lake Shastina.

During the Dark Time, Shasta Security became known regionally as a welcoming settlement group in which survivors from the small towns of Dunsmuir, Montague, and Yreka, found acceptance and refuge.

We continued south through the ruins of Old Redding, then made our way west along old highway 299, through the forested regions toward the Eureka-Arcata region along the coast. This was an especially taxing journey through elevation changes and the need for careful management through the dense shattered zones that formed most of the topography.

Reaching the sea, we turned south, bypassing the Humboldt Bay Wildlife Refuge and continued until we arrived at the banks of the Eel River. Resting for one day, we worked our way upstream to Fortuna, then farther south to Scotia, and ultimately entered the vast region of tall redwoods, where we were welcomed at Bull Creek Security Zone, a forested region composed of five or six smaller settlements that had banded together to improve security.

We spent two days here resting, then received information regarding a settlement group in which the majority of residents were elderly (older than 75). The respondents did not know the name of this settlement, but insisted that it was west of the Bull Creek Security Zone (BCSZ), about 10 kilo-miles inland from the Pacific Ocean, along the Mattole River. We noted these comments in our diaries but because of our schedule changes (due to inability to follow the coastline south because of raiders and hostilities), we were unable to visit. But each of us recommended that a subsequent long loop trek would make the Mattole River a most important destination.

Scouts from the BCSZ told us that the coast route south through the forested shattered zones, was clear and free of trouble since bands of thugs and troublemakers had been exterminated during recent months of the present solar cycle. We followed their directions and within three days reached former highway 1. We then had a choice to make: whether to continue south along the same route, or turn inland and connect with old highway 101 that might take us more quickly southward toward SanFran via Willits, Ukiah, Cloverdale, Geyserville, and into Santa Rosa.

Our decision made, we chose to remain on the coastal route and reached the ruins of old Fort Bragg, which we bypassed. We then halted our journey for two days near the settlement of Old Mendocino. We resumed our trek toward the abandoned former Russian settlement of Fort Ross (i.e., old Fort Rossiia), and then encamped outside the Bodega Shield settlement group, located just inland from Bodega Bay along the boundary with Old Marin County.

Acceptance into New Marin

It had been rumored that the residents of New Marin County just north of SanFran were little impacted by the Ripple Event and Dark Time. It also had been written that about half of the pre-Ripple Event population of New Marin was wealthy beyond belief, while the other half secured their food and funds for existence through government subsidies and handouts, spending their time in leisure, lazing about and not working. It was further said that with the onset of the Ripple Event and collapse of federal government assistance, the local governments of cities and towns in New Marin decided to care for the so-called poor 50%ERs (as they were called) and provided all with food, drinking water, and housing.

Freedom Scott, Certified Data Collector
Interview with James Mitchell, Chief Administrator, County of New Marin

Scott: *How could it be that your local government administrators decided to provide everybody living in New Marin with assistance? Did you actually assess, levy, or tax those who were working to implement the program?*

Mitchell: *I see that you are an outsider and not familiar with how we in New Marin County have organized our social system, one that is fair to all. Yes, we have as you suggested "taken from the rich and given to the poor," but the poor needed it and the rich remained rich, so what's the problem?*

Scott: *Please continue.*

Mitchell: *Our officials, bless their kind hearts, were influenced by a suite of Berkeley professors who touted the concept of "the limited good." This view, widely published during the heyday of the late 1950s and throughout the 1960s (old time solar calculations) held that in any village, town, or city, if a person became rich, it was at the expense of the poor since there was only so much "good" to go around. So if a person had more "good," then poor people were being denied their "fair share."*

> *The concept continued to attract adherents and, through time, many of the supporters became local, regional, state, federal representatives and senators, and even a president.*

Scott: *Please continue.*

Mitchell   *Our newly elected officials throughout New Marin County formed teams locally called wealth alerters (WAs). These teams identified and checked all private residences, catalogued the number of bedrooms in each house – set against the number of current residents – and then assigned what was called a potential add (PAD) number where homeless and poor Marin residents (the bottom 50%ERs) could then be assigned to live in these vacant rooms within the homes of wealthy families – so all could enjoy the fruits and wonders of living in New Marin.*

Scott: *I assume that this administrative decision did not settle well with the top 50%ERs and that they would have complained to the newly elected county officials. But since the program has been implemented, may I also assume that the county officials just ignored these complaints as "typical grousing," since the wealthy had too much and the poor too little – therefore, it was right and just to help everybody? But they didn't seem to do anything about it, right?*

Mitchell: *Well, since you are indeed new to our community of New Marin, let me take you on a walking tour of our town, and then tomorrow I will arrange for several persons to speak with you and your data collection team.*

And so it was that with this background and political setting that our team of data collectors were introduced to four residents of New Marin: two top 50%ERs and two bottom 50%ERs.

Alan Jenkins, Certified Data Collector
Interview with Davis Robinson and Liberty Tucker: Top 50%ERs

Jenkins: *I have been informed that you represent divergent views as to the manner of allocating housing, food and water, and living essentials as dictated by the Administrative Council of New Marin.*

Robinson: *Yes! I believe the council has overstepped its political charge and that people like me and our families are being unjustly burdened with the responsibilities of caring for able residents, who are just too lazy and self-accommodating to work for their essentials.*

Tucker: *Davis, how could you say such words and express such thoughts to the data collector? It is we, the fortunate, who have flourished throughout our lives and we owe it to assist our fellow residents who are not able to maintain the level of lifestyle that we enjoy. My husband, Jennings, and I have such a surplus of barter items and space in our home, and the apartment facilities that we manage, that we are pleased to help our fellow citizens to the best of our ability.*

Robinson: *Liberty, you must be a fool! All you and your type are doing is accommodating laziness and destroying individual initiative and work ethic. I worked hard for what I achieved, and brought to my family a level of living commensurate with my efforts. Why should I be forced by an administrative council edict to house nine lazy individuals who have done nothing all their lives than live off government handouts? Now that they have been assigned to my family house and to two of my apartments in nearby Novato, all I am hearing from them are cries like this:*

"Your household pantry is too small to support the food needs of our six children; when are you going to expand your food storage pantry to fit our needs?"

And just last week as I was issuing invitations to my friends to come to my house for a party, and one of the council-imposed squatters (as I call them) said to me:

"The council says that we can come to your party and that you will supply the beer and wine for us to drink. Actually, we don't want to come to your stupid party, so just deliver the beer and wine to us personally. So when are you going to deliver it?"

Can you believe this?

Tucker: *Davis, you obviously have no compassion for the poorer segments of society in New Marin County. I pity you and others like you. Remember that it is written:*

"It is easier for a camel to pass through the eye of a needle than for someone who is rich to enter the Kingdom of God."

Davis, you are so cruel and heartless – cannot you find it in your heart to give half or more of your wealth away to help those less fortunate than yourself?

Robinson: *Liberty, just shut up! People like you destroyed our once-proud nation; people like you provided handouts for everyone – even those who did not need them – and then fewer individuals wanted to work. And then came the Ripple Event, and the poor became poorer and the wealthy less wealthy, but so what? This didn't matter to you and your kind. Those so-called poor people assigned by the local government of New Marin to live in my house? All they want to do is sit in MY chairs and watch MY pet dogs and cats play and DEMAND that I feed them from food in MY pantry and DEMAND that I cook it for them!*

Tucker: *Davis, I think you are incapable of compassion and should be evicted from the settlements within New Marin.*

Robinson: *Liberty, if I had my choice I would leave tomorrow, but the administrative council – supposedly working for the good of all people in New Marine County – also has issued an edict forbidding anyone to leave with more than the equivalent of pre-Dark Time $53, which means, my dear Ms. Liberty Tucker, the only things I could take with me, if I were to leave today, would be the T-shirt and slacks that I am wearing, and nothing else! But listen carefully to me, dearie, there will come a time, and it will come soon, when people like you will be the ones forced to deal with the mess and crap that you and others of your ilk have created! Good luck when that happens!*

Jenkins: *I'm really sorry folks. Perhaps we can explore another topic?*

Tucker: *No – I am through!*

Robinson: *At least you got something right. I'm out of here!*

Lavender Simpson, Certified Data Collector
Interview with Meadow Kline and Kenneth Phillips: Bottom 50%ERs

Simpson: *I have been informed that you represent a select group of residents of New Marin County who do not work and have been assigned housing in the homes of different wealthy families in the towns of Larkspur, Novato, San Rafael, Sausalito, and Tiburon. Is that correct?*

Phillips: *That is correct.*

Kline: *Ditto!*

Simpson: *Might you relate your story how it came about that you became destitute, and how you coped with your financial difficulty?*

Phillips: *Look, I lived in Marin County since before 1998, many old solar cycles prior to the Ripple Event. I came in from SanFran looking for a job, and the only ones available were at fast food outlets. Why would I take such a job? I graduated from Stanford University with a major in English literature and, yeah, I knew that jobs in English lit would be scarce, but I wasn't going to demean myself by serving up fries and burgers. So I got onto food stamps and hooked up with a former girlfriend, and we applied for TANF which, of course, you know is short for temporary assistance for needy families, and we were accepted. I looked for a job, but all the employment offices wanted from me was to arrive before 8:30 a.m., and then I would sit around on a bench until they interviewed me about 11:30, and gave me two to three leads to follow. Well, I did follow up but nothing panned out. So what the hell, I'm an American citizen so America should help me. As for housing, sure I lived on the street for about six months with my girlfriend, but those flophouses that catered to the so-called "poor" were nothing but drug-infested fleabags. Yeah, so what if the rich folks in Marin, especially in Novato and San Rafael, complain about me – big deal! My girlfriend and I deserved a break, but never got one. So when we were assigned a room in some snooty upper-crust family home, big deal. We deserved it and, besides, they had a spare bedroom that they weren't using so they shouldn't bitch and moan about helping me, right?*

Simpson: *Kenneth, do you help the family where you now are living? Do you help around the house? Cook? Work in the yard? Do odd jobs?*

Phillips: *What the crap are you asking me? Are you saying that I should work and be grateful for living in one of their spare bedrooms, and that I should be paying them in some way for their assistance because they have been disturbed by my presence? Well screw that line of thought. Before I moved in with my girlfriend, they were wealthy beyond reason, and could afford to let me stay with them. After all, they got their wealth on the backs of poor people like me, so it is my turn to reap some of the benefits, right?*

Simpson: *Meadow, what is your story and how have you coped?*

Klein: *Before the onset of the Ripple Event I had a great job, but the Ripple ended all of that. No money was coming in, and I had two children to support (I was divorced, you know). My children and I struggled on the street; we were attacked and beaten several times by gangs of roaming thugs. Ultimately, I found a way to barter for food and water for the three of us. I don't want to talk about how I did that. All I want to say is that those types of actions are behind me now that I have been assigned a room in a house in the McNears Beach area. I want to be there as short of time as possible. I met with the homeowners, and my children and I agreed to participate in general household chores and to assist where possible. Before the Ripple Event and before my divorce, we had a large collection of family heirloom silver pieces. We used most of these bartering for food and water during the Ripple Event and early years of the Dark Time. At the time of my divorce, I cached about 45 pieces of the remaining heavy silver in a secret location. Because of the kindness of the house owners where my children and I now are staying, I will give them a share of this silver each week because it is the right thing to do – pay our way.*

Simpson: *Kenneth, what do you say in response to Meadow?*

Phillips: *Some people like you, Meadow, are just stupid and don't get it. When you are poor and destitute and live in a fair society, others able to help should assist you without question. Why the hell should I pay them anything? Are they not looking just now to evict me and my girlfriend, and to get rid of us so they can go back to acting rich? The local government administrators of New Marin County owe Meadow and me this assistance. Why should we be made to feel bad when we are offered what is rightfully ours? I say share the wealth, and everybody should be happy.*

What our data collection team found during subsequent interviews with residents of New Marin was a response consistently divided along a sharp fault line: those with wealth (formerly and at time of the interview) resisted the socialistic edicts produced weekly or monthly by the various city councils in the towns of Larkspur, Novato, San Rafael, Sausalito, and Tiburon.

The so-called "Top 50%ERs" interviewed held a range of views that they considered were characteristic and typical of those who refused to work, and who accepted city council placements in family homes. They said these "Bottom 50%ERs" were:

> Greedy and self-indulgent;
>
> Limited in education with poor professional skillsets;
>
> Listless without ambition;
>
> Ready and quick to blame others for personal life failures;
>
> Strongly convinced of self-entitlement;
>
> Unwilling to accept self-responsibility for their actions and behavior.

In contrast, the so-called "Bottom 50%ERs" interviewed held strong views and opinions of the wealthy, who had opposed the city council placements of unemployed persons in their family homes. they said these "Top 50%ERs" were:

> Afraid of real work;
>
> Aloof and snobbish;
>
> Crooks and thieves – robbing others as a means to amass family wealth;

Greedy and self-indulgent;

Self-entitled with no sense of compassion;

Dangerous – would use any means possible to eliminate us!

Two populations, separated by wealth and preconceived notions of personal rights, coupled with years of local, county, state, and federal assistance that drowned the work-ethic spark and spawned welfare rolls and promoted self-entitlement, which in turn fractured the social fabric of North America well before the Ripple Event. As we pondered our interview data from New Marin County, we sensed that a revolution was coming and possibly soon, one that would result in considerable bloodshed and the breakdown of administrative structures throughout the county. Rich against poor, poor against rich. Each group held incompatible views on how to sustain life within the geographical confines of New Marin.

The ground was ripe for unrest and revolution.

Our team meeting with the facilitator of New Marin was cordial and informative. She told us of a unique trade agreement that New Marin Country had developed in concert with a settlement group located offshore on the Farallon Islands, where trade in scarce commodities had evolved during the latter years of the Dark Time and early post-Dark Time recovery period. We expressed interest in visiting the Farallons and were informed that weekly trade exchanges were made by ship, departing from and returning to the Marin port of Sausalito.

Aboard the Sloop *Jordan River*

We boarded the trade ship around 6:00 a.m. for the 24-kilo-mile trip to the Farallon Islands. We proceeded west around the southern portion of New Marin, and passed the destroyed pylons of the former Golden Gate Bridge, the landmark structure that had been dynamited by terrorists during the second week of the Ripple Event. The assault on the bridge by unnamed members of the al-Tarifa Brigade was implemented to isolate SanFran from New Marin County to the north to intimidate the population of northern SanFran and contain the gang economic control in this region. The SanFran police anti-terrorist squad launched an attack on the al-Tarifa Brigade headquarters at their fortified residence on Jefferson Street, east of the former Presidio complex, and all gang members died during the assault. The loss of the Golden Gate Bridge was a tragedy from which the region never recovered.

Exiting through the Golden Gate Channel, the *Jordan River* sailed across the rough water area generally referred to as the Potato Patch, then passed the 12 kilo-mile limit with the Farallons visible in the morning mist. We approached the island group from the southeast, and entered a sheltered area of coast. A hand-cranked derrick system on shore was operated by three of the island residents. They swung the boom out over the ocean water, and slammed the cargo net onto the deck of our ship. Supplies previously had been boxed into large wooden crates and, one by one, each was lifted off the deck of the *Jordan River* then swung back over the water and up onto the cement loading platform adjacent to the derrick structure. After all supplies had been transferred to the island, the operators attached a personnel transfer unit to the cable hook and lowered it onto the deck. We climbed inside and were uplifted quickly. With a smooth arc, we were swung up over the water and ultimately lowered onto a cement platform on the island.

Interview Summary: Farallon Island Refuge Settlement Group

Upon landing, we were greeted by representatives of the Farallon Island Refuge Administrative Council and escorted to the housing complex below the main peak of South Farallon Island. This housing complex once had served as a United States Coast Guard station and at one time housed up to 20 persons, with rooms for married couples and a large Quonset hut that contained some 20 beds that previously had served as bachelors' quarters for the base. The facility had been constructed at the time of the American Civil War. The purpose had been to man and care for the lighthouse facility that illuminated navigation signals for marine transports up and down the California coast near the entrance to San Francisco Bay.

Beginning in the early 1970s (old time calculation), the station had been automated and the housing structures had fallen into disrepair. With onset of the Ripple Event, several groups of sea raiders landed on the main island. During the next 10 days, they fought to attain ownership and supremacy of the island. Eventually the two primary antagonistic groups reached accommodation and divided among them what they perceived to be the two most important commodities: seal and sea lion oil, and bird guano. The former could be bartered directly on the California mainland; the latter could be converted into gunpowder and explosives.

The Hispanic group that emerged, known as *Hermanos de Sangre* (blood brothers), were responsible for the export of bird guano to mainland settlement groups for the manufacture of gunpowder and explosives. They were known to all on the island as the guano collectors (GCs), a title that made even the toughest of the *Hermanos de Sangre* smile in pride.

The competing Asian group, known as *Shiyou Xiongdi* (oil brothers), bartered with the *Hermanos de Sangre* for exclusive rights to render seal and sea lion carcasses for their high-quality fat and oil content. Among the islanders and throughout coastal California, these men were known as fat renders (FRs), and recognized for their technical and economic skills in the export and barter of seal and sea lion oil to mainland settlement groups.

A third group emerged later during the mid-years of the Dark Time and, basically, were ignored by the Asians and Hispanics. A group of five UC Berkeley undergraduate men recalled that during the American Civil War, groups called "bird netters" or "eggers" exported tens of thousands of birds' eggs that served as food to miners during the California Gold Rush era. They thought they could develop a food-related business based upon harvesting eggs from the Farallons. The story was told that this adventurous group arrived by sea kayak one night and landed on the south Farallon Island. They quickly were subdued and captured by the *Hermanos* sentries and brought to the gang headquarters. It is said that the five young college students were not perceived as threats to the guano and fat/oil enterprises and were allowed to become a third member of the Farallon consortium, provided they paid an annual fee to both the Asian and Hispanic gang leaders. As a result of this arrangement, the students were ceded a portion of the island located north and east of the former lighthouse, where they were allowed to gather eggs from nests of cormorants and western gulls. On rare occasions, they used their climbing skills to seek out highly valuable eggs from the tufted puffins nesting on the steep cliff face.

The primary problem of managing enterprises and living on the Farallons was lack of fresh water. Cement catchment basins had been established on the southeast portion of the main island, but the water collected could be used only for irrigation since it was contaminated by the droppings of tens of thousands of western gulls that nested on the island. Thus it was that the *Hermanos de Sangre* and *Shiyou Xiongdi* worked together to recruit a suite of retro-engineers to live on the island. These new recruits constructed an efficient water desalinization plant to meet drinking and cooking needs. The engineers completed their task during the first year of the Ripple Event, thus negating the need for weekly return trips by cargo ship to the mainland to secure bottles of fresh water. These desalinization technicians (DTs) who continued to live on the island remained highly honored. As the Ripple Event passed into the Dark Times, the three groups of island colonizers began to work more closely and began to honor and respect the work of the others. As the groups bonded more closely, they evolved a series of rituals that challenged their respective bravery and made the islanders unique among all the settlement groups in New California.

Ritual of the Orca Riders

It is hard to perceive how a mixed ethnic group of Asians, Caucasians, and Hispanic males could conceive one of the most interesting, harrowing, and dangerous rituals that emerged during the Dark Time, one that has continued to persist today in the post-Dark Time recovery period.

Each year pods of killer whales, on their annual Pacific migration, approach the Farallons from both the south and north during December through May. On their northward migration the orcas aim for the south tip of the main island, then swim west through the narrow passage between the main island and the offshore stack called Seal Rock. As the orcas swim through the channel, the seals and sea lions basking above water on the weathered rocks, sense danger and with a sudden reversal of logic – thinking that they would be safer in the ocean waters – they slither into the sea to take refuge exactly where the orcas wait.

The meeting of the sea mammals in the narrow channel is ferocious, and the ocean waters turn reddish brown with the blood of the slaughtered seals and sea lions. Had they remained basking on the rocks above sea level, they would not have served as meals for the killer whales.

On the return migration, the orcas approach the Farallons from the north, those taking the westward passage go around Maintop Island, and then abruptly turn eastward toward the Seal Rock Channel, where the slaughter is repeated.

To understand the orca-riding ritual practiced only on the Farallons, data collectors Ennis Hall and Freedom Scott interviewed three men: Howard Gonzalez, leader of the *Hermanos de Sangre*; Tao Chu, leader of the *Shiyou Xiongdi*; and Huntley Baker, leader of the bird netters, and transcribed the following exchange:

Hall: *How was it possible to conceive the idea that the orcas could be ridden?*

Gonzalez: *Simple, man! When I was little, my parents took me to Sea World and the orcas in the show were ridden by good-looking babes. The women looked like they were having a good time; the orcas just seemed to smile and flop about.*

Chu: *I saw the same thing over at – what was that city called? – yeah, Vallejo, and I thought, why not do the same here? It would give us something to do rather than just sit around and play cards, or whatever.*

Scott: *But you can't just swim out into the Seal Rock Channel where the orcas are churning about killing seals and sea lions and just leap onto their back, right?*

Baker: *You must think we're stupid, or something. What we did? We worked together to develop a system. The orcas wanted sea lions, and we wanted to ride them, so we did something unique: we prepared in advance for their migration and killed two sea lions (heavy muthas!) and, as the orcas rounded Maintop Island, we were waiting at the western inlet with the bloody carcasses. Believe it or not, three orcas stopped when we whistled shrilly and, when we had their attention, we threw the bodies of the sea lions into the inlet. And, guess what? The orcas came close and munched down a sea lion lunch. Simple as that! The next day, we did the same. The Shiyou Xiongdi didn't mind, since they had already met their oil and fat quota for the month, and so they killed a couple of seals and joined us at the inlet. The orcas came into shore really close, so close we could see their eyeballs. When Howard was eyeball to eyeball, I tossed in another seal carcass. Crap! It was as if the orca just smiled at us.*

Gonzalez: *Now jump ahead to the next migration season and, guess what? When the orcas split their herd and came around Maintop Island again, a group of four paused at the inlet and came close. We tossed in more seal carcasses, and the orcas just seemed to smile. It was Tao here – stand up and smile Tao, don't be grumpy – that reached out and touched the first orca, and then Huntley, baby, did something that we didn't expect: he jumped onto the orca's back. WOW! Wasn't that cool! But tell them, Huntley, that you didn't stay on for a long period, and then you just slid off, patted the orca, and joined us back on the rocks.*

Chu: *So then we got this idea, something like a test, not of strength, but a test of courage. Over the next several solar cycles, we developed what might be called a unique association with these migrating orcas. Through time, more and more orcas entered that small inlet on the west side of Maintop Island and, it might be said, they allowed us to climb atop their backs and, little by little, they lost their fear of us and we gained the strength to test our own courage. Now, today, any of us on the island who can stay on the back of an orca for 30 seconds, we call him "hombre respetado" or "zunjing de nanren" – a respected man.*

Scott: *Thirty seconds? But you don't have watches that work, so how do you calculate 30 seconds?*

Baker: *Scott, you're really dense, like something from long go. All you have to do is count slowly, like this: one – two – three – all the way up to 30. Man, surely you could figure this out!*

Gonzalez: *OK, OK brothers – no big deal as they used to say, right? Ennis Hall and Freedom Scott – jeez you have crazy names – do you have the balls to do what we have done? Of course not! But not to worry, we wouldn't expect courage from one-time visitors to our island like you. But, if you return, you better be ready to punch your ticket to ride. Hey, your eyes just got real big – just joking!*

Resume itinerary: The first task after leaving the Farallon Islands was to obtain transport by ferry boat from Sausalito south to SanFran, and to arrive no later than 10:00 a.m. on a trade/barter day when city-wide gang truces were in effect.

Alan Jenkins, Certified Data Collector
Summary: Data Report: Return to Violence in SanFran

We found that the once-proud city was divided into territories by Asian, Black, Hispanic, and White gangs. Some were drug based, others prostitution based, still others dealt in essential supplies (ammunition, explosives, and guns; axes and knives; and even stealth weapons, such as poisoned darts). Other gangs specialized in commodity barter and trade: animal fats and oils (brought in from the offshore Farallon Islands); scrap metal (melted into standard size ingots and stamped with gang insignias); construction needs (salvaged lumber, nails, support brackets, and copper wire); and various types of drugs (methamphetamine produced in SanFran, and marijuana sourced from offshore trading groups [OTGs], who farmed several of the Channel Islands).

The streets of former San Francisco were deserted at night, except for groups of armed men and women sent out from gang headquarters to patrol their territorial boundaries. Walls of central SanFran were marked and defaced, then re-marked and defaced countless times as the boundaries of gang territories waxed and waned, leaving once-proud buildings awash with gang-related abbreviations, insignias, and slogans. Extreme care needed be taken as to what to wear whenever walking about, lest colors of T-shirts or hats be misunderstood and the wearer attacked.

Golden Gate Park was considered a truce and freedom zone (TFZ) where, during specified daylight hours three days each month (decided through negotiation), SanFran residents could hold barter/trade events without interference and fear from one another. On such days, trading began at approximately 10:00 a.m., and lasted through the mid-afternoon until around 3:00 p.m., when sirens announced that individuals had one hour to close up their barter stalls and return to their fortified homes or apartments. About an hour later a second siren – much harsher than the first – warned individuals to be off the street within 30 minutes. Thereafter, individuals could choose whatever they wanted to do: stay inside their homes or roam through their respective territories.

Crime and evil manifested itself in other ways within SanFran. Good people were cowed into managing their daily lives through extortion and violence. Many simply gave up and followed the directions and dictates of the various gang lords. Houses of prostitution flourished throughout the city as hundreds of boys and girls, men and women, were forced to participate against their will. The city – once proudly named after Saint Francis – had collapsed and been replaced by SanFran, the New Sodom or New Gomorra (whichever name best fit), where hopes for better lives and recovery from the Ripple Event and Dark Time were dashed.

Exodus

We also learned from several respondents who would not provide their names that all was not lost. Slowly at first, then in larger numbers, some SanFran residents began an exodus from the anarchy, chaos, and evil that had engulfed their once-beautiful city. Departures had to be in secret and carefully planned in order to evade the gang patrols.

Most of those leaving chose to go south, hoping to find security and acceptance in the settlement groups that had developed along the Pacific Coast between SanFran and Old Monterey. Individuals with valuable skill sets were admitted into these settlements; but most were not. It seemed at first that many proud, moral individuals were left almost without hope, until they arrived outside the small rural settlement of Pescadero. There, with the help of like-thinking survivors from earlier times, they constructed the first of what later became a chain of small inter-linked settlements, known as Islets of Honor (IoH).

Resume itinerary: We continued down highway 1 toward Santa Cruz, then on to the Monterey Bay region.

We passed through Santa Cruz and the following day approached the sand dune area just north of Old Monterey. The Dune Refuge settlement group had been developed within the ruins of the once-thriving Monterey Peninsula College. A protective perimeter had been constructed surrounding the settlement, and the entrance was heavily guarded. We requested and received permission from General Counsel Dale Martinez to enter and conduct interviews.

What we encountered at Dune Refuge was a diverse group of residents of all ages and mixed ethnicities. We were informed that the reason for high security was to protect against raids organized by the offshore trading groups (OTGs) that scoured the coast from SanFran in the north, to El-A in the south.

Alan Jenkins, Certified Data Collector
Interview with Dale Martinez, General Counsel, Dune Refuge Settlement Group

Jenkins: *Who are these OTGs, and what are their origins?*

Martinez: *Hard to believe, but their beginnings were here in nearby*

Monterey. Within a few days of the Ripple Event, somewhere between 20 and 30 wealthy residents who kept large sailboats (cutters and dinghies, ketches, and sloops), banded together and left port with their families and closest friends, each with large supplies of food and water, guns, and ammunition. It seems that originally they went south toward the Big Sur cliff areas because they knew that their stores of fresh water could be replenished at McWay Falls or at Salmon Creek Waterfall, just north of Ragged Point. At night they dropped sea anchors and lashed their ships together, making floating platforms for protection.

Jenkins: Were any of these ship owners of Vietnamese heritage? What you describe is an ancient technique used by sailing families on sampans at Ha Long Bay north of Hai Phong?

Martinez: Come to think of it, the last names of two of the leaders of the group were Bui and Nguyen, so what you say may have historical implications.

Jenkins: Please continue.

Martinez: It turns out that this initial group of seagoing families started to trade with isolated groups along the mainland, providing fresh and dried fish for family food needs. But then it seems that they came to another idea, one that has posed difficulties for all of us up and down the coast. They landed off the coast of Santa Barbara on several offshore islands, defeated and evicted the small groups of settlers who had sought safety there, and took over Santa Rosa Island. Within a year, they had confiscated lands and developed settlements on Santa Cruz and San Miguel islands, as well. They funneled shoreline people to the islands to work for them in exchange for food and water. The work and business they developed was all drug related. They established desalinization systems on the islands and started growing literally forests of marijuana.

Jenkins: I can't believe this. You mean that these wealthy ship owners, once the pillars of society in Monterey, Pacific Grove, and Pebble Beach became drug dealers?

237

Martinez: *You can't believe it? We couldn't either. It turns out that they began running their business just like one of the cartels south of the border. And their name: Offshore Trading Group? What a joke! They had made most of their money through financial trading prior to the Ripple Event, and by parking their "trades" in the Caribbean or South Pacific islands. And now these dealers are just known as OTGs.*

Jenkins: *You say OTGs – that's plural. Is there more than one group?*

Martinez: *Right, and once in awhile we hear news of some dust-up between groups in which we presume the strongest prevail. I have no information on how and where the other OTGs originated and what they do. Why would we want to mess with them and find out? Better to leave them alone, right?*

Jenkins: *What are the primary markets for their drugs and exchange values with their barter system?*

Martinez: *Look, there are no police departments at any of the old towns, cities, or settlements here at Monterey or north to SanFran, or south to El-A. We organize protection ourselves at our respective settlement groups. What I know is that there are land-based sites agreed upon by settlement administrative councils and the OTGs where, at dawn on specific days, land-based individuals or groups can meet the dealers of the OTGs onshore to barter and trade. At Dune Refuge settlement group, our adult residents voted to establish such a "drop/ barter" site. We at Dune Refuge tolerate limited drug use by our residents, so long as the rights and personal activities of others in the settlement are not compromised.*

Jenkins: *What happens if some residents of Dune Refuge in some sort of drug stupor interfere with the personal activities of others?*

Martinez: *They are brought before the administrative council and judged. The first offense is punished through public humiliation by wearing what we call the "drug shirt," a distinctive garment that must be worn for 30 days to shame the individual. For a second offense, the individual and his family are expelled from Dune Refuge and forced into the adjacent shattered zones to the east to fend for themselves.*

Jenkins: *Really?*

Martinez: *Really! Now that we are well into the Dark Time recovery*
            period, we have had to expel only two individuals and their
            families. Our judicial process seems to work, right?

Resume itinerary: We pushed our carts south through Monterey, Carmel, and entered the coastal area of Big Sur, ultimately reaching San Simeon, and Cambria. We then turned inland toward Paso Robles and made our way down highway 101, circumvented Atascadero, then cascaded down the Cuesta Grade toward San Luis Obispo, then Pismo Beach, Santa Maria, on to Buellton.

Reaching Buellton, we turned inland to make a side trip to Old Solvang, once a thriving picturesque enclave founded by settlers from Denmark. We were met at the western outskirts by a small unit of militia scouts from Solvang who allowed us to enter.

The old windmills that once had characterized this Danish enclave were no more. They all were destroyed during the defense of Solvang eight solar cycles earlier, when roaming gangs of thugs surrounded the settlement and attempted to penetrate. We learned from residents that Solvang survived through the spirit and organizational skills of a local leader named Klaus Anderson, who organized the defense, but who was killed during the last day of battle. His heroics and death are celebrated on the summer solstice each solar cycle when residents offer thanks and renew their commitments to preserving qualities of friendship, honor, and mutual support.

Resume itinerary: We left Solvang and returned to highway 101 and pushed on toward Gaviota Pass, where the landscape changed abruptly, revealing long strips of angled rock stretching across the horizon as the road entered the narrows. This location once had been a place of hiding and refuge, dating back long before the Ripple Event. We approached Canyon Home settlement group, and were granted admission.

Canyon Home was a relatively small settlement group in which the resident number did not exceed 200. Members primarily were a mix of Anglo, Hispanic, and Native Americans, although Asian and African origin Americans also had been welcomed. The settlement was administered by a group of five matriarchs with elderly male advisers. We noticed that there were few children visible, and were told that when any outlanders (as we were so named) appeared, the children were quickly assembled in the settlement keep, with guards inside the well-defensible walls. When we spent our second day at Canyon Home, and obviously had been welcomed, the children were released and their guards dismissed. We were told that this was a protective measure against outlanders who might be ill. But since we already were inside the settlement walls, such an assumption was naïve, and this led to an interesting interview that Lavender had with one of the matriarchs, who also was a sage femme.

Lavender Simpson, Certified Data Collector
Interview with Mace Henry, Matriarch, Canyon Home Settlement Group

Simpson: *Thank you, Matriarch Henry, for agreeing to speak with me.*

Henry: *You are welcome.*

Simpson: *When outlanders, as you call them, approach Canyon Home settlement group, would it not be better to ask them to remain outside your walls so you could better assess and evaluate the possibility that one or more of those approaching might be ill?*

Henry: *Young lady, you and others have made this comment, but it is we who have the ability to treat all illnesses that could be encountered during these days.*

Simpson: *But how is that so? Is it not usual that people harbor germs and can pass their illness prior to the external manifestation of disease or sickness?*

Henry: *That is your view. We who have the gift of insight can tell from afar with a mere glance whether or not an individual or group approaching could bring illness to our people.*

Simpson: *How is that possible?*

Henry: *Why should I tell you? You and your friends might use the power of insight against us.*

Simpson: *Why would we do so? All we want is to interview you and members of Canyon Home about your experiences during the Ripple Event and early years of the Dark Time so that we will have a better record of survival techniques that could help us who are living now be better prepared should a subsequent event or epidemic rage across the land.*

Henry: *I understand what you say, but we, the five, are teaching our illness identification skills only to the children born in our settlement group. So if there is another event or epidemic, we will survive – not you! If you wanted to leave your group and stay, live with us and become part of Canyon Home, I would be willing to train you with the illness identification skills you want to learn.*

Simpson: *I understand, but I cannot leave my colleagues, for together we form a team of data collectors commissioned to complete our work and to return to Montana State University and report our findings. In the two or three days we will be staying with you and your residents, might I sit with you at your side, Matriarch Henry, and might you teach me some of the skills you have so I could be a better ethnobotanist?*

Henry: *My child, I understand what you need and I understand why you want to learn from me, but I offer you only this caution and let me say it this way: un poco de conocimiento es algo peligroso – you understand, of course? We, the matriarchs and sage femmes at Canyon Home, do teach illness identification, but to become properly trained we meet with our novice healers three nights every week for three solar cycles. Even then, more training commonly is required. So I'm sorry, and I repeat what I said to you previously in Spanish: a little knowledge is a dangerous thing. Sorry!*

Resume itinerary: We reached Santa Barbara and camped on the grounds of the old Spanish mission. Part of the structure that housed the important archive and library had been burned by vandals, a loss that was incomprehensible, given the eighteenth century records that once filled the collection that dated to the foundation of the mission in 1786, after the death of Father Junipero Serra two years earlier (old time calculations). We took a path north of the mission that led us to the ruins of the once-wonderful Santa Barbara Museum of Natural History. Exhibits had been ransacked, the rich collection of Native American art had been looted, and outside near the entrance only a huge pile of whale bones remained – all disarticulated by unknown vandals who perhaps were searching for who knows what.

Resume itinerary: South to Ventura, just offshore was the low-lying island of Anacapa. As we viewed the island from the beach, we saw two groups of young people in the ocean. Some were sea kayakers and the others were practicing skills on surfboards. At an appropriate time, we approached several of the men who were leaving the beach and asked to speak with them. We were informed that during the Ripple Event and early Dark Time, several groups of sea kayakers established a settlement on Anacapa Island and that one of them, an engineering student studying at the University of California, Santa Barbara, developed a solar desalination technique that allowed year 'round habitation on the island. We learned that the location became known as the Anacapa Sanctuary settlement group, and that they flourished for about five solar cycles fishing and farming until they were evicted (some said exterminated) during a raid by members of an unknown offshore trading group.

We turned inland and passed through Santa Paula, then east along old highway 126 to Fillmore and Piru paralleling the Santa Clara River, now clogged with tule reeds. Piru, once the regional homeland of the Tataviam Nation, was in ruins with no survivors.

We reached what formerly was called Castaic Junction, where highways 126 and 99 once met, but there were no signs that recalled this ancient name, only broken and vandalized signs that directed visitors to what once had been a major amusement park, called Magic Mountain. There was no magic here now, only twisted steel. As we watched from afar, we saw the steel rails and scaffolding being salvaged by teams of discarded metal changers (DMCs) hard at work plying their trade for the nearby Honor Ranch settlement group (where we were denied entrance).

Resume itinerary: Over to the 99 junction through Castaic and up and over the Grapevine past old Fort Tejon and the highland community of Lebec, we descended onto the oil flats of the southern San Joaquin Valley. Once we had mastered the climb up and over the mountains, we rolled our carts northward, freewheeling down the remnants of Eye-5. Reaching the bottom of the grade, we turned west along highway 166 toward Maricopa and the oil flats, where we encountered groups of oil sand diggers (OSDs).

These hardy souls were enterprising residents of the nearby Buena Vista Shelter settlement group who formed a cooperative agreement with a second fortified settlement, Desert Freedom, to develop an oil-sand barter exchange for vital equipment and materials. We learned that the oil sand pits at Maricopa primarily were mined in late autumn through winter, since the intense heat of the region during summer months made such physical efforts nearly impossible.

The oil-rich sands, remnants of the famous Lakeview Gusher of 1911 (old time calculation) were removed by shovel and hand labor, then transported by horse or donkey cart to heat-rendering facilities adjacent to the pits. The sands were heated and the extracted petroleum siphoned into old liter-gallon glass water bottles. When a sizeable quantity of the bottles had been filled, other workers transported them to the Buena Vista Shelter settlement group using carts drawn by mules and horses under heavy protective guard.

Interviews and documents examined at Buena Vista Shelter provided an interesting history of how this specific settlement had flourished during the latter years of the Dark Time by providing an essential commodity for barter and trade. Exchange values for different commodities were listed in some of the documents:

Five Liter-Quarts of Oil, equal to:

20 iron ingots	(standard size and shape)
10 copper ingots	ditto
8 gunpowder units	(2 kilo-pounds)
100 assorted seed packets	(standard size tubes)
20 cottonseed packets	ditto
20 barley, corn, wheat seed packets	ditto

We left the Buena Vista Shelter and pushed on northwest to the former settlement of Taft. We entered the deserted town, passing by ruined elementary schools named after two former American presidents. At the southwest corner of Roosevelt School, we were accosted by a group of five young males, ragged in dress, who had been assigned to protect an oil storage facility erected on the campus of nearby Taft High School. As we posed no obvious danger to them, they allowed us to pass unharmed.

The city was in shambles. One old house on South Seventh Street was standing (although the paint was cracked and dry); the porch was overgrown with vines and tri-pointed thorns covering the yard, if one could call it a yard. The grassless extent of sand and rock now was home only to tarantulas and trapdoor spiders. Farther to the south and west were homes with yards filled with Chinaberry trees. On the corner of Kern and North Tenth streets, we saw the hulk of an ancient petrol station with a red star and T sign, the ancient logo for Texaco, or the Texas Company, still swaying and moving to and fro in the wind.

Highway 33 leading northwest out of Taft was in disrepair, and we abandoned the idea of visiting McKittrick, which now was just a spot on the map of yesteryear.

We exited Taft and pushed our carts east toward Bakersfield, a once-major city in the southern part of the valley. Part of the city had maintained some semblance of economic activity during the Dark Time, with limited production of cotton clothing, woven on hand looms by children and young adults. Such items were exchanged or bartered for essential goods with settlement groups within the general region (names of these nearby settlements were not identified by our respondents).

Resume itinerary: Up the valley and spaced along the way were various minority settlements that primarily were ethnic in composition – Armenian, Asian (Chinese, Hmong, Japanese, Vietnamese), Black, Hispanic, several Hispanic settlements where the primary language was Mixtec or Zapotec – even a settlement that primarily was Nestorian in their belief system.

After-Word
Summary report by Roger Jenkins: Assistant Archivist, MSU

In my capacity as assistant archivist, I have surveyed and summarized the long loop reports filed during recent solar cycles. They contain numerous descriptions of occupations and tasks at different settlement groups visited. Some of the long loop reports also comment upon titles of individuals and groups associated with the shattered zones. Presented here are examples of the descriptions of persons met along the way by MSU data collectors:

Anti-drug crusaders (ADCs): It was most common that such individuals identified were in their late 60s and 70s, with strong memories of the pre-Ripple Event years, when the population of North America had been bombarded with conflicting information related to diet, health, and self-medication. During these early times, many held to the belief that there were two categories of foods and medicines: so-called natural products, and those manufactured by food and pharmaceutical companies. Herbal medicine treatments and cures were touted by the ADCs, and followers spoke out strongly against manufactured products. Even substances prepared from natural products were rejected if they were mixed with antioxidants, stabilizers, and preservatives. The ADCs' advertising campaigns generally were localized, and while their numbers were relatively few (generally less than 10 to 15 percent of residents in any specific settlement group), they were vocal and influential.

Cricket collectors (CCs): These individuals most often were located in settlement groups in more arid areas, where meat from land animals, fish from rivers and lakes, and various local or migrating birds were few in numbers. In general, their membership consisted of non-meat eating residents, who focused on vegetarian diets plus insects. This term also was applied commonly to poor individuals who survived the initial solar cycles of the Dark Time.

Gamers (GaMers): Commonly these were elderly men and women who previously (before the Ripple Event) had been addicted to computer game programs and were incorporated by the various settlement groups to maintain memories of several early games (e.g., Survival: Version 2004-2C, or Wilderness: Version 2001-3B) in which players vied with one another with the goal of corralling and protecting food and water resources. Administrative councils of the settlement groups commonly assigned these GaMers to assist in training young children how to identify safe and unsafe dietary resources.

Gold diggers (GDs): These were refugees along mountain stream sites, still happy panning for gold and other metals. Most were isolated loners not connected or affiliated with specific settlement groups. All had the necessary survival skills to evade thieves and thugs who roamed the shattered zones around the rivers and streams where they sought the golden nuggets. When sufficient quantities of gold had been amassed, they would approach a settlement group, seek admission, and trade their gold for food and survival essentials. The gold then was turned over to artisans, who made creative objects to honor residents who worked especially hard so the settlement could flourish.

Give-uppers (GUs): Although none were interviewed by the data collectors, collective memories of the GUs were held by many older settlement group residents. These memories commonly stirred emotion during interviews, as the survivors told and retold of incidents when some family members, close friends, neighbors, or acquaintances, no longer able to cope with the difficulties posed by the Ripple Event and early Dark Time years, elected death through organized mass suicides.

Tuber diggers (TDs): Common term used by outsiders to describe immigrants or residents from Idaho. Sometimes viewed as a derogatory term by many, it was used with pride by the former Idaho residents both before and after the Ripple Event.

Water rationers (WRs): Groups of militants who controlled riverbanks in certain shattered zone areas. Most were illiterates with limited moral direction, who sought to manage local water supplies through intimidation and extortion. Few survived the initial years of the Dark Period due to pitched battles with settlement group sentries and patrols.

Other individuals or groups could be identified by their respective craft, food-related activity, occupation, or trade:

Ant hill seed sifters (AHSs): This was a task commonly assigned to young children from settlement groups in arid and semi-arid regions of New NorthWest and New SouthWest Configurations. Ant hills near settlements served several functions during the early survival solar cycles. Ants could be gathered and prepared as food and, during construction of their colonies, ants would bring back large quantities of plant seeds, where the external chaff portions served them as both food and nest construction materials. The "gleaned" seeds then were ejected from the colonies and could be gathered and scraped together by the children who served as "seed sifters." When all the children worked together during the course of a morning, enough seeds could be gathered to prepare food for nearly 20 hungry mouths.

Bird netters (BNs): This term and "eggers" are identical and are applied to those who gathered birds' eggs on the Farallon Islands for barter/trade with mainland residents for essential needs.

Bread dippers (BDs): Children who were selected for half of a solar cycle to work at communal feeding stations inside their settlement groups. The term, as first encountered during a long loop trek, never was applied in a derogatory sense, but commonly was used by the children themselves, who chanted while doing their work:

We – we – we – are the BDs from settlement group (insert name)

I – I – I – bring you food, you take it from me

U – U – U – eat what we bring, leave none on your plate

We – we – we – clean up your mess, and that is our fate

Go – go – go – brother bread dippers, go!

Comfort women (CWs) and **soothing men** (SMs): These were names for female and male prostitutes who provided for physical needs at so-called comfort/soothing stations (CSSs) during the latter years of the Dark Time and early post-Dark Time recovery period. These locations commonly were established outside the immediate periphery of the settlement groups, but not too distant. The CWs and SMs interviewed by the data collectors revealed a wide range of backgrounds, from highly educated to those who were illiterate; representatives from families of which all supporting members had died during the Ripple Event, leaving individuals to fend for themselves in any way possible; and all ages from late-teen years to elderly status were represented. None of the CSSs visited by the data collectors had medical-related staff associated with the group; therefore, information on disease protection and prevention was minimal. At two of the CSSs surveyed, the CWs and SMs were allowed to participate for only two solar cycles before returning to their respective settlement group. Data collector interviews revealed no stigma was attached to CSS participants upon their resumption of settlement group activities. It was unclear how the various CSSs were managed, as no one interviewed wished to share this information. It was assumed in the data collector reports that the administrators were sanctioned and supported by the administrative councils adjacent to each respective CSS.

Discarded metal changers (DMCs), sometimes called **metal crafters** (MCs): These were the weapons and tool manufacturers, and such individuals were feared like the blacksmiths of olden times.

Game lords (GLs): These were the agents or managers of competitive athletes who arranged exhibitions at various settlement groups for the entertainment of the residents.

Grain grinders (GGs): Individuals responsible at the various settlement groups for preparing flour to bake bread for communal meals. Usually this was a temporary task that rotated through the settlement group membership.

Herbal mixers (HMs): Individuals who worked with the sage femmes to prepare herbal recipes to treat illnesses.

Iron pickers (IPs): These were men who formed a subgroup of the discarded metal changers (DMCs) who uprooted rails from abandoned railroad lines, then re-forged the steel into weapons.

New gladiators (NGs): Term applied to traveling bands of athletes during the post-Dark Time recovery period who demonstrated their skills and talents at athletic shows at the settlement groups. The athletes were rewarded for outstanding performances and received, in turn, services in sex and drugs. Their organization and services were overseen by game lords (GLs).

Rabbit trackers (RTs): A general term applied to individuals who survived the Ripple Event and Dark Time by trapping small game, whether rabbits, squirrels, or, in some instances, mice and rats.

Rice winnowers (RWs): General term applied to migratory laborers in the upper Sacramento Valley settlement groups who assisted with the grain harvests.

Sea coast fisheries (SCF): Word applied to sites where clusters of local residents gathered during spring months to trap migrating salmon. Residents would stay at these locations for up to two weeks, netting and fire-drying fish for winter food storage.

Sea mammal hunters (SMHs): Term applied to various independent settlement groups along the Pacific Coast of New NorthWest and New SouthWest Configurations and the affiliated offshore islands.

Participants in events – rituals at different settlement groups:

Buffalo riders (BRs): Members of different hostile groups occupying the shattered zones east of the Rocky Mountains in New NorthWest Configuration.

Cat chasers (CCs): An honorific title earned by elite groups of youths who had completed their rite-of-passage and clan initiation maturation ceremonies. Requirements for the title were variable at different settlement groups but commonly included a test to successfully track and kill a mountain lion and return to the settlement group with its pelt.

Persons associated with settlement group administration and justice-related activities:

Administrative matrons (AMs): At Union Protection settlement group in southern Old California, the data collectors identified a system that integrated both administrative aspects of the settlement, coupled with family and personal life. At Union Protection, the administration was managed by powerful matrons, who took up to four husbands, a classical form of polyandry. The administrative matrons (AMs) selected male consorts for their respective skills, work ethic, and required the men to be tested for sperm fertility in a specially designed clinic. Each AM decided who would be her mates, and lived a complete solar cycle with each in sequence. After four solar cycles had been completed, all infants from such couplings were raised as siblings, even though from different male partners. In addition, after the four solar cycles had been completed, the AMs allowed her mates to partner with a select group of women – chosen by the matron. All infants from such pairings also were raised as siblings within the extended family unit of the matron.

Child managers (CMs): General term applied to all personnel assigned to communal child care centers at their respective settlement group.

Dung divers (DDs): Convicted criminals sentenced to two to four weeks without communal food resources and forced to survive by gleaning undigested plant seeds from the dung of domesticated livestock.

Infant inspectors (IIs): In some isolated communities, a select group of elderly men and women were elected to serve one complete solar cycle during which they examined each newly born child. The IIs were charged to use infant viability tests to evaluate the probability of infant survival and then make a collective determination whether or not an infant with a low score would be returned to its parents. The final decision over life or death of newborn infants was made by the chief inspector of the innocent (CIoI).

Jury members (JMs): Obvious.

Political thinkers (PTs): Most such individuals were killed or jailed during the Ripple Event or early years of the Dark Times. Considered a disgraced group, political thinkers who survived were tried and those convicted (estimated at 83 percent) were imprisoned, although at least 500 across the various configurations were executed for previous government-related crimes. Those in prison were allowed to marry other inmates. Any children that resulted from these couplings were taken away and raised in special decontamination zones.

Public executioners (PEs): Obvious

Union generators (UGs): These were men or women at different settlement groups responsible for potential mate assignments and ultimate matchmaking for young men and women.

Valued elder statesman/stateswoman (VES): Individuals honored for their survival and for their memory of early history prior to the Dark Time.

Wrong wrighters (WWs): Groups of vigilantes who administered justice quickly during the dark times. Always spelled the term "wrighters" instead of "righters."

Metal Sheet #9

Inscription and Translation

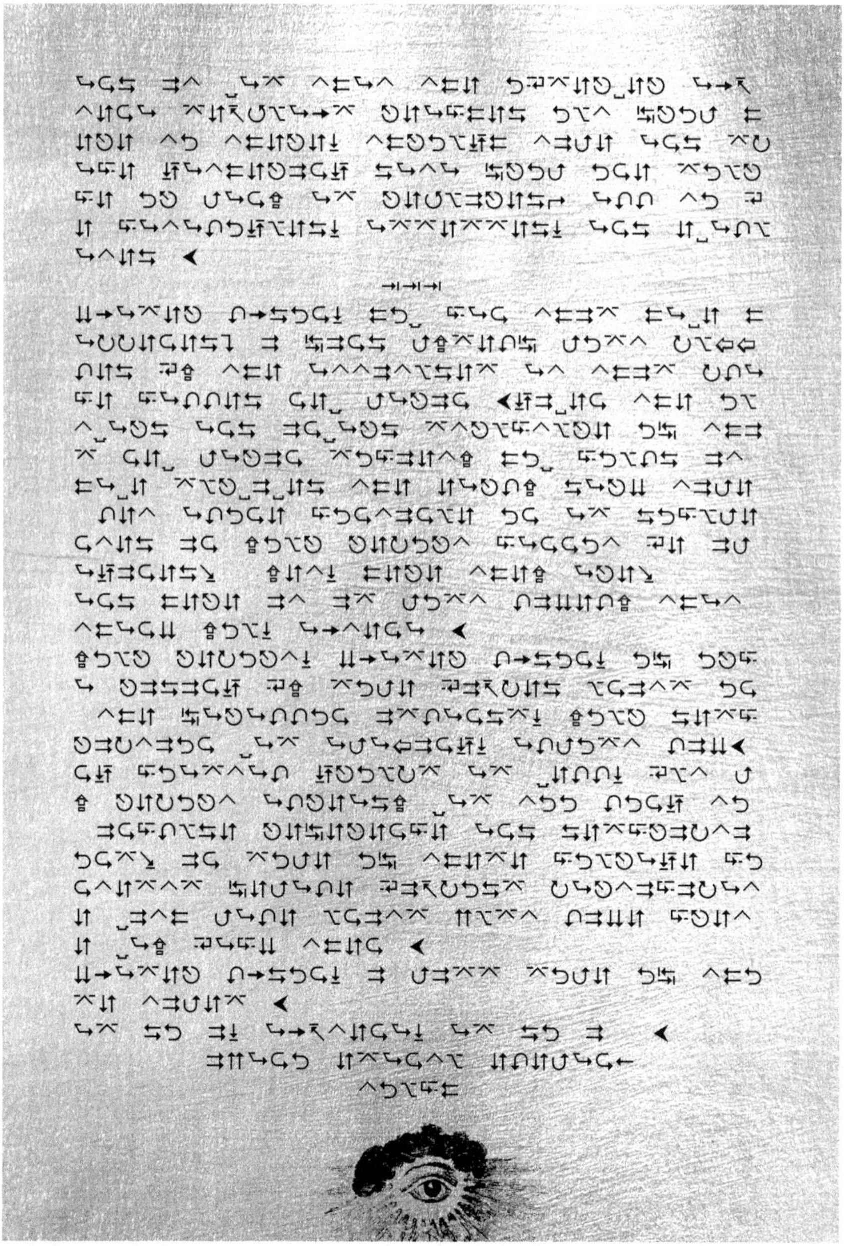

And it was that the Observer A'-Tena Se-Qua reached out from here to there, through time and space, gathering data from one source or many as required; all to be catalogued, assessed, and evaluated.

***

K'Aser L'Don, how can this have happened? I find myself most puzzled by the attitudes at this place called New Marin. Given the outward and inward structure of this New Marin society, how could it have survived the early Dark Time, let alone continue as documented in your report, cannot be imagined. Yet, here they are.

And here it is most likely that they will remain, A'-Tena. An example is needed of the sort of foolishness that fueled the madness, and New Marin is it. It will not grow, it will not prosper. Visitors will view New Marin with ridicule, seeing their organization, structure, and core beliefs as illogical, no way for a society to be emulated. A bad example it was, a bad example it is, and a bad example it will remain.

Clever your conclusion, K'Aser L'Don, a warning that captures the essence of their group duality.

Thank you, A'-Tena.

Your report, K'Aser L'Don, of orca riding by some biped units on the Farallon Islands, your description was amazing, almost like …

… Like old times in Crete, were you about to say, A'-Tena Se-Qua?

Yes, but would you not agree that orca riding would take more raw courage than bull jumping?

Probably so, A'-Tena. I'm glad you like this tradition. Similar tests of courage have emerged among coastal groups, as well, but my report already was too long to include reference and descriptions. In some of these courage contests, female bipeds participate with male units as in Crete way back then.

K'Aser L'Don, I miss some of those times.

As do I, A'-Tena, as do I.

Ijano Esantu Eleman!

Chapter 11: Evening Reading 11

Document 11, Cave Location: Case 43-B

John Carpenter Edson

What is justice?
Justice for one is not justice for all.
Justice for many is not justice for the few.
Justice during peace is not justice during war.

What is life?
How is life valued?
Is one life equal to that of another?
Bacteria and viruses have killed billions of consumers.
Consumers have killed trillions of bacteria and viruses.

Not all life is equal.

(Source: Cemetery headstone. Cascade Fortress settlement group.)

Pre-Note

Information gleaned from the long and short loop treks reveal the integration of cultural traditions and physical landscapes and how each changed through time. First settlements along lakes, reservoirs, rivers and streams provided safe and potentially secure water sources. These early sanctuaries from the Ripple Event and Dark Time flourished when water resources also were adjacent to flatlands that could be farmed to yield harvests of crops. Proximity to wild game, individual beasts or herds, assured success of most early settlement groups.

The data collectors gained a sense of when the settlements first were occupied, based upon several considerations; for example, early names of the settlements reflected food sources: Antelope Plains, Buffalo Run, Deer Creek, Elk Preserve, and Ibex Jump. Later settlements commonly incorporated the names of specific landscape features, such as Plains Home, Canyon Gate, Flatland Base, Forest Sanctuary, Hillside Defense, Lake Yellowstone, Mesa Caves, River Clearing, and Shelter Cove.

Two settlement groups, Plains Home and Bison Camp, forever would be linked historically because of key events associated with an infant boy – born at the first settlement, but raised at the second.

Birth and Redistribution

Montana State University History Project archives reveal that infant John Carpenter was born on Day 3, Week 1, Month 5, Solar Cycle 12 post-Dark Time recovery period. The location of his birth was Plains Home settlement group, located southwest of Butte, Montana Territory, New NewWest Configuration.

His parents were Svent Carpenter and Algis Carpenter. They already had conceived and delivered two live births, which at the time was the maximum allowable number in accord with Plains Home conception regulations.

Svent and Algis Carpenter disregarded the law, and a third infant was conceived and born. In the quiet solitude of the birth room, both parents held the infant and named him John Evan Carpenter. Within hours, both parents were arrested and the newborn removed from their care and custody. Within two days, Svent and Algis were tried as conception criminals (CCs); they were deemed guilty and executed within seven days after delivery, in accord with regional and Plains Home settlement group law.

The Plains Home Administrative Committee ordered the service of regional nurse Frances Cook (certified member of the 62nd Infant Protection Regiment) to examine the infant and arrange for his redistribution on the 15th day after delivery. Frances Cook took her duties seriously. She protected, tended, and provided milk samples for John Carpenter during this difficult parental separation period.

In accord with regional tradition, two horse messengers were assigned to ride out from Plains Home and announce potential adoption and redistribution opportunities for childless parents. One of the horsemen, Franklin Jenkins, ventured south along the standard communication trail and, on the second day of his journey, Jenkins reached Bison Camp settlement group. There, Valdese and Sarha Edson, mating partners for six years but childless, accepted the Plains Home Administrative Council order, and arrangements were made for both to travel north to receive the infant, John.

On their return from Plains Home to Bison Camp, some 3 kilo-miles north of the settlement at a location near extensive ruins from the Dark Time, Valdese, Sarha, and the infant, John, were caught in a sudden rainstorm and drenched. In subsequent interviews with John Carpenter Edson's foster parents, each reported that this rainstorm was akin to a blessing. Throughout the lightning and thunder that echoed through the valley, the infant smiled, laughed, and held tight to the fingers of his adopted parents.

Early Childhood

Thus it came to be that the infant, John Carpenter Edson, was raised at Bison Camp settlement. His early childhood was unremarkable. It is known that he was suckled for more than two years by wet nurse Vabel Aerstudt, a member of the Bison Camp community who recently had lost her young child due to a hunting accident.

It is assumed that once John Carpenter Edson reached the age of 2, he would have been raised in the communal child shelter, since both parents worked throughout the day.

By the time John Carpenter Edson was 5 years old, he was assigned to the 8th Play Group at Bison Camp, part of the childhood protection regiment (CPR), supervised by Fairveld Zend. Subsequent research identified that the this playgroup was composed of females Storze Orkland and Besme Hunzy, and male Franklor Nevston, along with John.

Archive documents identify the early education standards implemented during the Dark Time. These components stressed good behavior, sharing exercises, and pre-computational skills. When John Carpenter Edson and his playgroup members reached the age of 6, they were tested using standard regional educational procedures. Results reported that all four playgroup members could read and write, and each tested high in socialization behavior in accord with local and regional standards. Each was examined physically at the conclusion of test week; all were normal in appearance with no internal or external anomalies.

John's schooling then began in earnest. In addition to his early playgroup friends, he made others easily, participated in classroom activities, and began to stand out from the others because of his interests in discarded equipment and landscape analysis. He was strong, but not the strongest of his age mates in the settlement. His physical fitness abilities were above normal, but not exceptional. He never won the annual youth mountain trail climb (although he came in third or fourth on different occasions). John excelled, however, in mental challenges. His mathematical and calculation abilities were outstanding. His sixth grade project exceeded expectations when he designed and constructed a retrofitted engine, fueled by methane. John's unique design (at such a young age) prompted teachers to follow his education more closely for potential nomination for further higher education.

The Edson family flourished during John's childhood. For reasons unclear in the documents examined, his mother Sarha was able to conceive a child, a beautiful girl named Rosemary, which made four in their household. Once the daily school and work activities were concluded, the family gathered together and shared stories and memories of what it meant to be a family and the joy that group life had brought to each.

Genealogy

During numerous evening family meetings, Valdese and Sarha related time and again the history of their respective families so that when John and

Rosemary became adults they would know the people and activities that made their family unique:

Father and Mother of John Carpenter Edson

> Svent Carpenter – Algis Cantrell (all bio-data files on both parents erased after their execution)
>
> Svent and Algis conceived the male Effem (died of bio-system failure shortly after birth)
>
> Svent and Algis conceived the female Jostfa (never knew her brothers Effem or John)
>
> Svent and Algis conceived John in love – infant fostered and redistributed as required by law
>
> John accepted into the family unit of Valdese and Sarha Edson

Male Line:

> **Stepfather:** Valdese Edson – carpenter, farmer, soldier – Born at Bison Camp, Montana Territory, New NorthWest Configuration. Received hard worker badge; active member of Bison Camp settlement; highly educated with knowledge of the new emerging technologies. Rose to responsible positions at Bison Camp. Mate partner, Sarha Boyd. Two children: John and Rosemary Edson.
>
> **Step-Grandfather:** Ferris Edson – Born at Mesa Caverns, Montana Territory, New NorthWest Configuration. Received hard worker badge; active member of Mesa Caves settlement; described the shattered zone lands surrounding the settlement in a key report to the Mesa Caverns Administrative Council. His esurveys contained important information for dealing with criminal elements within the surrounding shattered zones – regions that tolerated incidents of local violence. Mate partner: Alice Balmer. Three children: Frank, Gwyen, and Valdese Edson.
>
> **Step-Great Grandfather:** James Edson – Born at Redding in Old California during the latter years of the Dark Time. Part-time rancher and farmer. Survived by protecting a hidden spring running through a portion of his land and by his knowledge of local wild food supplies. Left Old California and trekked to Montana under Mormon

protection. Settled at Mesa Caverns settlement group. Mate partner: Irene Thompson. One child: Ferris Edson.

Step-Great Great Grandfather: Louis Edson – Birth location uncertain, but born prior to the great madness, Ripple Event, and Dark Time. Killed during a political riot at Berkeley, California, Saturday, November 25, 2017 (pre-Ripple Event solar cycle). Mate partner: Martha Sloanberg. Three children: Justin, Alice, and James Edson.

Female Line:

Stepmother: Sarha Boyd – Born at Bison Camp, Montana Territory, New NorthWest Configuration. Received hard worker badge; active member of Bison Camp settlement; trained with sage femme Jacqueline Francis; vast knowledge of wild herbs and spices, trained as healer with mentors Jahn Michael and Arlise Cho. Preschool teacher and active member of the Bison Camp community. Mate partner: Valdese Edson. Two children: John and Rosemary Edson.

Step-Grandmother: Laurel Martinez – Born at Bison Camp, Montana Territory, New NorthWest Configuration. Received hard worker badge; active member of Bison Camp Settlement; metallurgist, teacher, and weaver. Known for physical stamina; self-defense instructor. Mate partner: Luis Boyd. Three children: Mark, Marissa, and Sahar.

Step-Great Grandmother: Janice (last name unknown) – Born at Knight's Landing, Old Yolo County, California, during the Ripple Event. Mother, Fiona, died during delivery. Survived through the care of her grandmother (father's mother), Jessie Denning. Nurtured through the early Dark Time, then family left Old California and trekked to Montana under Mormon protection. Settled at Bison Camp. Mate partner: Alan Martinez. Two children: Winston and Laurel.

Step-Great Great Grandmother: Fiona (last name unknown). Mate partner (unknown). Birthed Janice (last name unknown). No additional information; probably born in Old Yolo County, California, several decades prior to the Ripple Event.

Adolescence and Early Adult Years

As it is with most individuals, John Carpenter Edson's transition from childhood to adult status represented a challenge. His focus on education and settlement tasks took considerable time, leaving little for pursuing the wonders presented by girls his age. Puberty remained a mystery for Edson, although most of his male friends had passed through the stage relatively easily.

With body changes associated with near-adult status came further settlement responsibilities. After-school hours were spent with others his age guarding the settlement food storage silos, or being tutored by older adults on self-protection and hunting-tracking skills. As his body changes became more pronounced, his parents, Valdese and Sarha, started meetings with other parents to establish dates for their children's initiation rites.

In accord with Bison Camp traditions, initiation rites for males and females were held once a year as an adjunct to the summer solstice settlement celebrations. Boys and girls so identified entered initiation schools three months in advance, shortly after the spring equinox in March, where the training was led by teams of respected elders. Themes at the initiation schools focused on settlement history, group responsibilities, respect for all, self- and group-defense, survival skills, and responsible reproductive information. At the conclusion of the initiation school activities, the initiates were required to undergo rigorous testing of physical abilities in three categories: working and solving problems alone and with others; mountain climbing, running, and swimming tests for stamina and skills; and a formal recitation evening before the assembled membership in which the initiates stood together and recited the history of Bison Camp settlement.

After the students recited Bison Camp history, the initiation school leaders called out the names of each participant who then stood before the assembly to receive the scar of maturity, a brand symbol formed by the intertwined letters B-C that announced to all that they were adults and now part of the age-set regiment whose mission was to protect and serve the settlement.

John Carpenter Edson stood before the assembly and proudly received his mark of manhood. His parents and Rosemary were equally proud.

New Bozeman: The Early Years

John Carpenter Edson undertook new responsibilities within his family unit and settlement. He was an active component of the initial warrior age-set, and during the first month post-initiation he worked guard duty shifts in the late evening and early morning. His schooling was not interrupted, and John continued classes on advanced biology, mathematics, and physics. His teachers observed that he had special skills in statistical design and, as a result, he started a program to tutor him in special theme topics that included retrofitting and exploration of uses for alternative energy sources (solar and wind power).

One day after school, John was taken aside by a group of teachers and informed that he was being recommended for advanced education at Montana State University in New Bozeman, some 160 kilo-miles east. While such an experience would take him away from his family and closest friends, his parents were supportive. And thus it was that John accepted the MSU offer of advanced training in physics and retrofitting analysis.

Living on campus at MSU was significantly different from his daily life and routine at Bison Camp. There were many more classes to attend, seminars on a wide range of interesting topics, introductions to professors and fellow students, and learning how to balance his academic and personal life. The retro-engineering field at MSU was demanding and initially daunting, but John survived his educational trials on campus and was held in high esteem by other students in his classes. The courses he enjoyed most were those that combined lectures with laboratories, where he and his classmates could work on experimental designs for new modes of transportation and energy production. His working models of ammonia-methane engines that he had developed earlier while at Bison Camp impressed his teachers and tutors. He was encouraged at every turn to dedicate himself and his future professional life to improving the lot of those living in New NorthWest Configuration just emerging from the Dark Time into the new period of promise, the recovery period.

In the spring season of this third year at MSU, John Carpenter Edson was out exercising, running west along Malone Centennial Mall, when he saw Allison Eckhart for the first time – the woman who would become his future mate and mother of their son, Able Edson. Archive files reveal little about Allison Eckhart, except that she was raised at River Crossing settlement group, south of Old Livingston and east of Canyon Mountain settlement group. John and Allison were almost the same age. She had striking dark eyes that pierced John's soul, and he thought about her daily. Allison's adult training at River Crossing settlement group had been in nursing, combined with extensive training in herbal medicine. She had been selected by her settlement group to attend MSU in the hope that one day she would return and train additional cadres of health-care workers. Allison's medical training program at MSU focused on infant and early childhood maladies and their cures, a topic of considerable concern given the continued lack of inoculation agents and curative drugs effective against childhood diarrhea, diphtheria, measles, mumps, pertussis, and scarlet fever.

John and Allison met frequently and quietly. Few, except their closest friends, knew about their coupling. As most young student pairs at MSU, they practiced careful mating to avoid interference of their personal lives with their respective academic pursuits.

Two months before graduation, they informed their parents of their relationship. John and Allison first traveled to River Crossing settlement to receive her parents' blessing. The communal welcome that followed was a cause for great joy and celebration at River Crossing – a pattern repeated five days later when the couple arrived at the entrance gate of Bison Camp.

John's parents welcomed Allison into the family fold. Rosemary presented her new sister-in-law with the traditional bouquet of local wildflowers and herbs, tied with a golden thread that symbolized the union between the pair. A short camping trip into the mountains east of Bison Camp followed and served as the couple's official mating period. Upon their return to Bison Camp, both John and Allison received the blessings of the residents at a community-wide celebration.

New Bozeman: The Family Years

John and Allison Edson established their living quarters in New Bozeman, which allowed them reasonable travel time to visit relatives and friends at their respective settlement groups. Allison accepted an invitation from River Crossing to teach seminars on health and identification of wild food resources. These teaching opportunities lasted several weeks at a time and allowed John to concentrate more fully upon his responsibilities as assistant engineer in charge of the nitrazine-fuel project at Compton

Transport Technology (CTT), located in New Bozeman. His supervisors praised his work, and soon John was put in charge of the nitrazine project and received a new professional title: chief engineer.

The couple could not have been happier, but this was about to change.

In mid-month 1 of solar cycle 36, post-Dark Time, the family had wonderful news: Allison was pregnant. She delivered their son, Able, on the 6th day, week 4, Month 10, Solar Cycle 37. Both parents were joyful as their son grew in stature and became sound of body. They explored the option of having Able pass through initiation rites at either River Crossing or Bison Camp, but decided together that they, themselves, would establish a new rite of passage – one that could become characteristic of children being born in New Bozeman.

Local and Regional Changes

When did it start? Some have written that during the middle and latter part of the second decade of the post-Dark Time recovery and into the early years of the third decade, gradual decline in ethics and morality began at different settlement groups within the Western configurations. Individuals began thinking more of themselves than their fellow settlement group residents. Greed and administrative corruption began to filter into rooms where political actions were discussed. The return to better times somehow signaled others to conceive new ways to extort services and how to collect and hoard more valued commodities that once were shared. Social problems grew with correspondingly increased greed and crime. Slowly, at first, then at an accelerated pace.

Revelation and Charge

Documents in the MSU archive reveal that during the 9th month of solar cycle 39, Allison Edson received an invitation to present health seminars at River Crossing. She accepted and took Able with her; traveling the short distance east of New Bozeman was not a difficult task. At the same time, Compton Transport Technology requested that John Carpenter Edson travel to Bison Camp to install and test the nitrazine engine prototype and evaluate its possible use an agricultural field tractor.

Upon reaching Bison Camp, meeting with old friends and settling in, John spent the next two days completing engine installment. The field test was scheduled for the following day.

It always had been John's tradition that after work, whether in New Bozeman or now at Bison Camp, to take a long walk in the early evening some 5, or so, kilo-miles. Here in the Big Hole region with the scent of pine and listening to the wind rustling through the quaking aspen, John felt truly at home. He liked to walk northeast of Bison Camp on the valley floor and then climb upslope using seldom-used trails until he reached his favorite site near the ruins of an old miner's cabin, one that had been destroyed during the Dark Time.

Adjacent to the ruined miner's cabin was a great tree that he and others during their childhood had nicknamed the Tree of Zell, after an oft-told tale learned from his father (Zell being a mythological hero who conquered the dragons of evil). On the evening of Day 13, Week 2 Month 9, Solar Cycle 39, as John Carpenter Edson rested and viewed the valley he sensed the wind swirling around him, initially in soft gusts, but the wind rose in velocity and became more and more powerful. John stood in wonder as a sense of awe enveloped him. It was then that the Overseer (may Its name ever be blessed) spoke to John Carpenter Edson using the wind as Its voice:

> *I, the Universal Overseer, charge you, John Carpenter Edson, to be my administrator, responsible for the reduction of crime and evil. The power will be yours alone. Use it wisely: reward good – eliminate evil. Accept my Charge without question immediately!*

John Carpenter Edson, troubled by these words from an unseen source, trembled and spoke aloud:

> *Who are you? Why are you speaking to me? What is it you want of me?*

Thus spoke the Overseer (may Its name ever be blessed) to John Carpenter Edson.

> *Ijano Esantu Eleman. As it was as in the beginning. I am who I am and always will be. Heed and obey my words. Accept my Charge without question immediately!*

Thus spoke John Carpenter Edson:

> *Please, you must tell me more. What am I being required to do?*

Thus spoke the Overseer (may Its name ever be blessed) to John Carpenter Edson:

Ijano Esantu Eleman. As it was as in the beginning. I am who I am and always will be. Heed and obey my words. Dare you question me? I am who I am and always will be. Accept my Charge now without question immediately!

A flash of lightning struck the Tree of Zell, then another, and another. Edson fell quivering to the ground.

Thus spoke the Overseer (may Its name ever be blessed) to John Carpenter Edson:

Ijano Esantu Eleman. As it was as in the beginning. I am who I am and always will be. Heed and obey my words. Accept my Charge now without question immediately!

Thus spoke John Carpenter Edson:

Ijano Esantu Eleman. As it was as in the beginning. I am who I am. I accept the Charge without question.

John Carpenter Edson remained on the ground for several minutes. What had just happened? What did the Charge mean? What type of power had he been awarded? How would it be manifest?

There were no immediate answers – they would come later.

Doubt and Reflection

John Carpenter Edson returned to Bison Camp and paused at the door of his house. He decided to tell no one about the event that had just transpired – not Allison, not his or her family members, and certainly none of their friends.

So it was that John Carpenter Edson – not like every man – accepted the Charge and responsibility. He alone would wield his power to eliminate crime and evil for a period of three solar cycles (40–42). So it was that John Carpenter Edson – he alone – would have the responsibility of reducing local and regional avarice, crime, and evil.

In the weeks and months that followed acceptance of the Charge, John Carpenter Edson pondered questions of life and death: did all crime and evil merit death? What level of anger toward another merited such punishment? Should the Charge include considerations of age? Should children who committed crimes be given second chances? What about certain elderly people who exhibited quick rise to anger that resulted in assaults – but the anger was caused by mental frustration or dementia? Should they be eliminated, as well? When did the concept of just "doing business" change into something more evil in which the poor and helpless were denied economic opportunity or were forced to live and work in unthinkable poverty and filth? Did wealth merely translate as "taking from others?" Were there not criminals who were poor as well? Did theft of food and water carry equal sentencing as the theft of belongings or the taking of a life?

No instructions came with the Charge. There were no further clarifications or revelations from the Overseer (may Its name ever be blessed). John Carpenter Edson was left to his own accord to determine which criminals and evil-doers would live, and who would perish in accord with the Overseer's crime and evil reduction program (may Its name ever be blessed).

But there were other issues.

Elimination of criminals would leave behind children, mate partners, relatives, and perhaps friends who had no part in such crimes or evil plans. What if the criminal's mode of operation was the only means of providing food, water, and shelter for his or her family? Was it ethical and responsible to harm these innocents because of the crimes and evil of those who perpetuated the actions?

There were no instructions with the Charge.

John Carpenter Edson was left to design the manner and way the Charge would be implemented.

Thus, it was that correct balance became Edson's approach to his task. He would implement the Charge only after consideration of balance. He alone would weigh the harm and pain that the criminals and evildoers inflicted on innocent individuals vs. the harm and pain their disappearance would exact on innocent family members. If the balance were equal, then criminals would perish.

Thus, John Carpenter Edson became the administrator of the Crime and Evil Reduction Program (CERP) as demanded by the Overseer (may Its name ever be blessed).

What would be the impact upon his immediate and extended family? Upon Allison or their son Able? How could he manage work at Compton Transport Technology with his assignment as administrator? Could he remain unknown and still meet the requirement of the Overseer (may Its name ever be blessed)?

After-Word

As the days passed and his mind filled with questions, Edson requested leave from his employment. He returned to the Montana State University campus to speak with his professors and advisers. They sensed in his manner and presentation that something was amiss, but were unable to learn from John what was troubling him. It was at one such meeting that Professor George Adams, a friend of John Carpenter Edson during the last year of his training, spoke up:

John, you remember the data collector program that we instituted at MSU, the one coordinated through the Department of History that employs a suite of undergraduate volunteers, who go out in teams of six members on what we call short and long loops? Remember that their objective has been to interview elderly survivors of the Dark Time to obtain better understanding of individual and family resiliency during times of terrible crisis?

Yes, I remember Professor Adams.

John, what if you joined one of these treks? There is a long loop journey about to leave in two weeks to go deep into the New SouthWest Configuration. Their objective this time is to revisit the ruins of Old Davis in west-central Old California and, once there, obtain specimens from the agricultural seed bank that previous trekkers had discovered four years earlier. This new group has been instructed to locate these germ plasm specimens and return them to Montana State University, New Bozeman, to implement agricultural field experiments at the Bison Camp – your old home and where you have been working with Compton Transport Technology.

What do you say?

Metal Sheet #10

Inscription and Translation

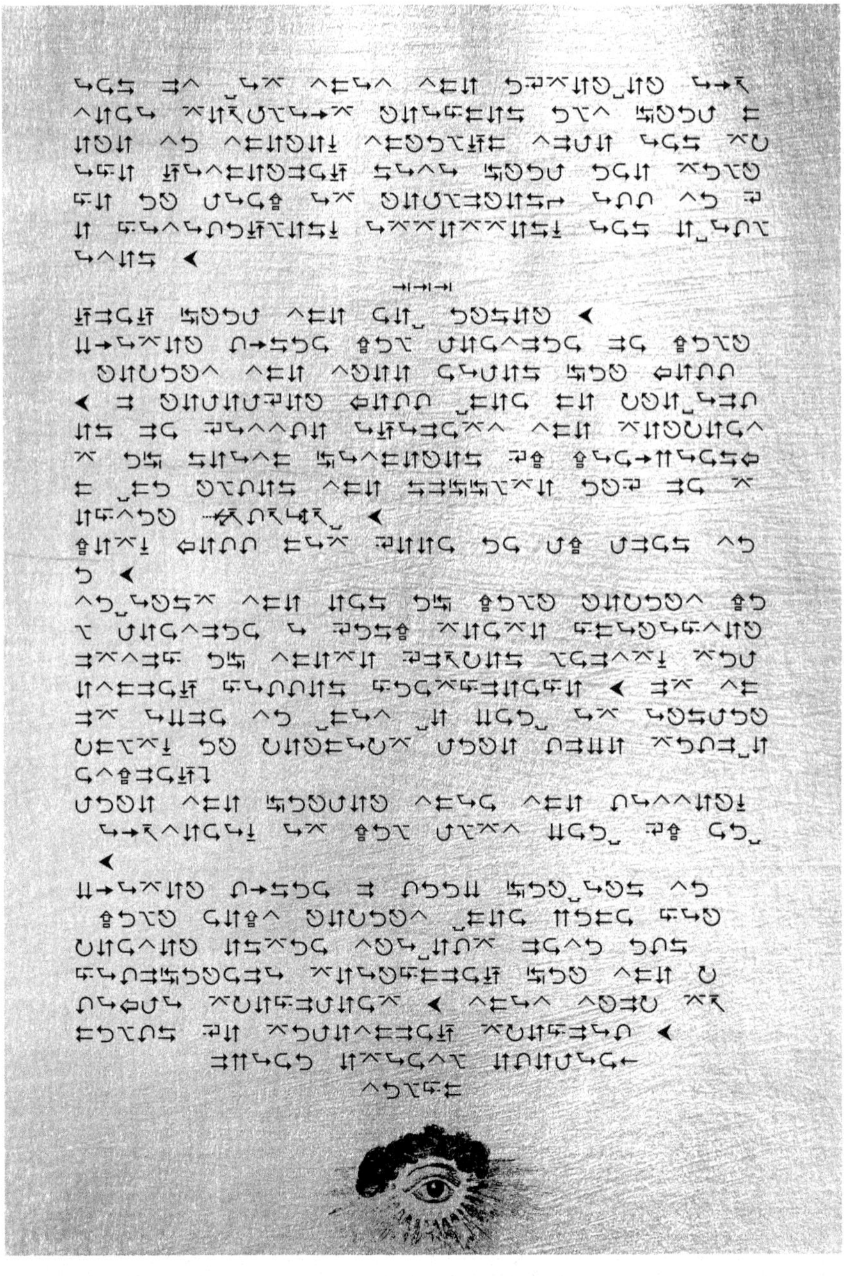

And it was that the Observer A'-Tena Se-Qua reached out from here to there, through time and space, gathering data from one source or many as required; all to be catalogued, assessed, and evaluated.

***

K'Aser L'Don, you paint a difficult picture in your report on John Carpenter Edson's parents. Was their harsh treatment unusual among units at these settlement groups, or more of an anomaly?

What it seems, A'-Tena, is that their treatment developed from a holdover tradition on the testing ground when regional and national governments were concerned with population pressures and limited food and water resources. In response, many governments instituted two-child policies that seem harsh from our perspectives.

Why, K'Aser L'Don, why did you choose John Carpenter Edson as your administrator from among all others possible?

He, among many thousands of Ripple Event survivors, seemed the most appropriate in my estimation to deal with the evil emerging from the New Order.

K'Aser L'Don, you mention in your report the tree named for Zell. I remember Zell when he prevailed in battle against the serpents of death fathered by Xan'JanDzh, who ruled the Diffuse Orb in Sector 47-L-92-W.

Yes, Zell has been on my mind too.

Toward the end of your report, you mention a body sense characteristic of these biped units, something called conscience. Is this akin to what we know as ardmorphus, or perhaps more like soliventying?

More the former than the latter, A'-Tena, as you must know by now.

K'Aser L'Don, I look forward to your next report when John Carpenter Edson travels into Old California searching for the plasma specimens. That trip should be something special.

Ijano Esantu Eleman!

CHAPTER 12: EVENING READING 12

Document 12, Cave Location: Case 43-B
Rise of the New Order

Protect nature – save the earth!
(Hear the sounds of rhythmic clapping)

Harmony among all peoples!
(Swaying bodies two and fro)

Cleanse the past – bright our future!
This we pledge!

This we pledge!
(Louder!)

This we pledge!
(Louder!)

This we pledge!
(Louder!)

(Source: Opening chant at meetings organized by the New Order priestess.)

Louis Evan Grivetti & Sargent Thurber Reynolds

Pre-Note

The hopelessness of the Dark Time slowly abated as settlement groups entered the post-Dark Time recovery period (PDT). Some called these early solar cycles of the PDT the strange time, because the behaviors that once had helped individuals and clans at the settlement groups survive slowly began to change. Respect for others began to dissipate, as personal needs and wants led to an increased sense of entitlement in some, which in turn led to minor thefts and misbehavior, then more serious crime.

Even with passing of the Dark Time, a bright and productive future still could not be envisioned by most survivors. Orthodox religions so prominent in the centuries prior to the Ripple Event once had provided the basis for security and proper behavior. But with the annihilation of the religious centers during the early years of the Dark Time and the accompanying horrors, most survivors abandoned these faiths and sought strength in teamwork and mutual efforts directed toward achieving common goals. Others adopted nature-based belief systems and found peace and joy among the whispering pines, and the beauty of sunrises and sunsets. Still others needed a firm, solid basis for belief, and found it in the New Order.

Origin of the New Order

The identity of the founder of the New Order is controversial. There has been a long-standing suggestion that the cult was founded by a young woman – one of three triplet sisters – raised in the Capay Valley, west of Davis in Old California. Records in the Montana State University history archive, however, do not confirm this suggestion. There is, however, a less controversial document (less so because of its date and origin), that suggests the New Order began as a local cult founded in the region of Vernonia in Old Oregon, New NorthWest Configuration.

The factors that gave rise to the New Order evolved during the latter solar cycles of the Dark Time and early through middle cycles of the recovery period. As life became easier, individual and family attitudes and behaviors began to change. Personnel changes in the administrative councils of most settlement groups led to a slow erosion of values that once had served to unite and protect members. Outside the settlement groups within the shattered zones, crime and evil had persisted for many solar cycles and slowly, almost without notice, parallel attitudes and behaviors began to infiltrate certain settlement groups, especially those with ineffective administrative councils.

Best evidence at present suggests that the New Order (NO) was founded by Dara Hughes, an exceptionally bright woman – a sage femme – who had practiced traditional medicine and herbal cures at Rock Creek Haven, about 2 kilo-miles north of Bridge Street, an avenue that once bisected the small settlement of Vernonia. She was born and raised in this community and, early in her education, she became interested in riverine plants and animals, especially the crayfish that slithered here and there along the creek bed below the bridge over Rock Creek. Reports suggest that during time spent alone away from her family, she liked to hike north along old highway 47 toward the tiny community of Mist, then would diverge from the road and explore the forested hillsides searching for healing herbs and wildflowers. Dara trained further in ethnobotany and herbal medicine under the leadership of the Clatsop Native American healer, Michael Cuscalar, whose ancestral great great grandfather, it is said, once had guided Meriwether Lewis through the region a century and a half earlier.

Residents were not prepared when the Ripple Event struck this geographical region. Afterwards, a secure settlement that formed north of Vernonia ultimately housed approximately 150 residents who survived the Ripple and early solar cycles of the Dark Time. From all available accounts, Dara Hughes served her settlement well and provided advice on health, pregnancy, and lactation, as well as comfort to the ill and elderly. She was honored within Rock Creek Haven as a true sage femme, and for many solar cycles she remained a pillar and strong supporter of the administrative council.

During the early solar cycles of the post-Dark Time recovery period, individual and community behaviors at settlement groups changed slowly, and not for the better. The first political-religious notice of Dara Hughes that appears in the Montana State University history archives dates to her appearance at a membership meeting at Rock Creek Haven, where she rose and spoke to the assembled:

> *How is it that we at Rock Creek Haven can ignore the changes happening among us? In the past, before the recovery period, did we not work together, assist and aid one another, and work for the betterment of our respective clans? And now – now that we are recovering from those*

terrible years – are we not reverting to the types of behaviors that once characterized North America prior to the Ripple Event? Look around – do so now! Look to your neighbor; when was the last time you assisted out of affection and care, instead of assisting because you wanted payment or goods in return? Look to our settlement. When was the last time any of you volunteered to assist with communal chores, and then when it was your turn to complete the council assignments, how many of you shirked your duty or completed it only under duress? Look about: we are changing as a people and for the worse. Do we protect nature as before? No! Do we respect all people regardless of differences as before? No! Further, it is disgraceful that some of you in this assembly – yes some of you here today – are engaging in behaviors that disrespect and harm others. And I say so this day: such behaviors must stop! We must return to the values once held:

> *Protect nature;*
> *Respect all people;*
> *Reject behaviors that harm others!*

NOTE: A report is on file from a person who heard Dara Hughes (deposition name removed from the front page of the document) stating that the assembly grew quiet, then erupted into chaos with a division into two groups: those few who were touched by Dara's words and agreed with her condemnation of behaviors that characterized the majority of residents, and those who laughed and shouted out for her to be quiet and to take her ideals and visions elsewhere.

The same report states that two days later, the Administrative Council of Rock Creek Haven settlement group called all adult members to assemble for a vote. As a result of the vote, Sage Femme Dara Hughes was expelled and forced out of the community. The date of this banishment variously has been given as Day 3 or 15, Month 7, Solar Cycle 30.

The immediate result was that as Dara Hughes left the Rock Creek Haven compound accompanied by her mate, Gavin Hill, a total of 23 adults and children (57 individuals in all) joined her in exile.

Early Years

During the first week of exile, the group followed the meandering route of Rock Creek that pierced the shattered zone north and northwest of Rock Creek Haven settlement group. Ultimately, they reached the roadbed of old highway 26 and followed the track up and over the mountains toward the sea. Reaching the Pacific, the group turned south along the coast and passed the ruins of several former beachfront communities. They paused at Nehalem and were accepted at Pacific Shelter settlement group, a fortress-like setting situated along the eastern shore of Nehalem Bay. There, they received protection and support. The community at Pacific Shelter settlement group took Dara Hughes' tenets to heart: nature focus, respect for all, and good behavior, and they became the first converts to the New Order teachings.

From this event of acceptance, membership in the New Order grew significantly. Word regarding the New Order spread northward along the coast with acceptance at settlements located at Seaside, and then to Astoria at the mouth of the Columbia River. The New Order messages of friendship, harmony, good deeds, and shared efforts also penetrated southward past Rockaway and the tiny community of Twin Rocks, then farther south to settlements at Garibaldi at the mouth of Miami Cove, and into the protected settlements west of Tillamook at Cape Meares.

The messages of Dara Hughes, first priestess of the New Order, resonated among those who had seen the return of many individuals to lives of crime and evil. In some settlements where the New Order tenets initially were introduced, the concept and approach of the first priestess was accepted wholeheartedly. At others, however, the tenets were rejected and the members who spread the message through word of mouth sometimes were beaten and, in more than a few instances, murdered.

At settlements where the New Order was accepted, responsibilities were assigned to an elderly woman, usually the local sage femme, who continued to remain in messenger contact with Dara Hughes at the Pacific Shelter settlement group along Nehalem Bay. The primary center of the New Order at Pacific Shelter established a remarkable standard for proper behavior and respect for all. As traders arrived at Pacific Shelter and other settlements along the northern and central coast of Old Oregon, visitors saw the efforts and results of the New Order activities. Little by little the New Order expanded across the mountains eastward into the valleys of former Old Oregon. And with the New Order approach to protecting nature, antelope, deer, and elk herds reappeared in the adjacent shattered zones, and fish runs expanded where numbers far exceeded those experienced during the Dark Time.

And it came to be that the New Order expanded and membership grew at settlement groups throughout the territory of New NorthWest Configuration.

Abandonment of Principles

Along with the rise of popularity and acceptance of the New Order, prosperity returned and, with increased wealth-related activities, the contrary side of behavior once more began to make its appearance.

The New Order families voted and accepted the concept of age group divisions, each with characteristic clothing, body marks, and insignias that denoted infants, children, young adults, mature adults, and advisers. What started as the vision of the Sage Femme Dara Hughes gradually changed after she was badly injured during a temple construction accident at Pacific Shelter settlement group. A close advisor to Hughes, Sage Femme Justice Murray, was elected by the New Order Council to serve temporarily as first priestess, pending the return to duty of Hughes. But it was not to be: First Priestess Dara Hughes died unexpectedly from a massive infection associated with her accident.

Justice Murray received the vote of confidence from the New Order Administrative Council at Pacific Shelter to receive the title "first priestess." Murray formally began her tenure on Day 2 of the 4th Week of the 8th Month, Solar Cycle 33. Murray's consort, Shepherd Woodward, once a reluctant convert to the New Order, began to use his family position to influence the first priestess. Little by little, adult males began their rise in positions of authority and management of the New Order hierarchy. First Priestess Murray's influence over the New Order Administrative Council slowly began to wane, while that of her consort, Woodward, began to rise.

At the annual regional meeting held at Pacific Shelter settlement group during autumn of solar cycle 34, a vote taken would have administrative and title implications for the future of the New Order. A binding order was passed allowing both adult men and women to serve as the New Order administrators, and both men and women could serve as a priest or priestess in accord with specific group responsibilities. This new construct led to a new structure of male and female priests and priestesses of the fourth, third, and second tier, with the highest level, first priestess, always to be held by a respected elderly sage femme.

Within three solar cycles, Justice Murray as first tier priestess had become merely a figurehead, placed in an advisory role, with all key New Order administrative and action decisions made by a 15-member council, composed of seven second-tier, five third-tier, and three fourth-tier priests and priestesses – seven females and eight males.

Gradually and with a level of stealth characteristic only of politicians in North America during the pre-Dark Time era, the male priests usurped administrative council powers, and re-ordered the membership. During winter of solar cycle 37, the male-dominated New Order Council passed two key motions that changed the group forever: no longer would there be a first priestess, but instead a first priest, and this male elected by the male-dominated New Order Council established by fiat an all-male special warrior group (SWG) to protect Pacific Shelter settlement group.

During month 2, solar cycle 37, the new first priest nominated and then elected by the New Order Administrative Council was Samuel Evans, also known as Samuel The Select, who was born and raised at Old Portland several decades prior to the Ripple Event. He survived the chaotic Dark Time through stealth, clever dealings, and extortion. As the early years of the post-Dark Time concluded, Evans saw the New Order cult as originally voiced by First Priestess Dara Hughes essentially as a naïve pseudo-religious group, whereby if a strong, clever man joined he could find a secure setting to observe and wait for a key opportunity to advance his own agenda.

And this was the time.

Samuel Evans, first priest of the New Order, reduced the number of council members to four – each beholden to Evans' beliefs and actions. In subsequent documents, it is written that Evans, plus the four, would be known as the Pentad, with administrative power over all the New Order members.

Within the special warrior group, the Pentad organized two teams of assassins trained to deal with the New Order defectors and detractors who would challenge or might otherwise harm the current organizational structure, and the plans to increase the wealth of the New Order.

Slowly, using clever ploys designed to maintain loyalty of the New Order membership, Evans and the other members of the Pentad usurped the original mission and objectives of the New Order. Where once the objective had been to protect nature, the new objective ignored nature and the goal was to protect the integrity of the New Order leadership. Where once the objective had been to respect all people, the new objective offered respect only to those within the New Order leadership. The third original tenet basically was ignored, given that the means to enforce objectives one and two incorporated ways and means that harmed and/or eliminated others.

Reality

As these changes occurred, there arose issues of how to provide supplies and support the New Order activities. First Priest Evans solved this problem through the development of what at the time were called donation groups (DGs), but in reality these were extortion groups (EGs), composed of fanatical New Order adult males. Members of the so-called special warrior groups were sent on long treks to extort or steal trade goods from the New Order councils at different settlement groups. Reports confirm that the majority of these EGs were composed of low-level thugs who had joined the New Order because they enjoyed violence against others. Other EG members were individuals from the shattered zones surrounding the settlement groups, persons of ill-will and eager to participate in such activities and opportunities to exploit the membership of settlement groups where individuals worked hard for shared goals – only to have the fruits of their labor taken by the EGs.

And with the rise of these EGs within the overall structure of the New Order, those who originally had sought peace and security as once proclaimed by the founder and Sage Femme Dara Hughes, these good people left the organization. Their departure tipped the behavior balance of those settlement communities where the New Order had made strongest inroads. By the end of solar cycle 38, once again there was a widespread return to avarice, crime, and selfish pursuit of evil practices throughout much of New NorthWest Configuration – of the kind and level not previously seen.

Division

By the early months of solar cycle 39, the corrupt tentacles of the New Order had spread far and wide beyond New NorthWest, into New SouthWest, and ultimately across the great mountain chain into the western portions of the Flatland Configuration. Settlement groups throughout these portions of North America remained strongly divided, with the majority of members in most returning to actions and behaviors that characterized their geographical areas prior to the Ripple Event.

More secluded settlements tended to reject the New Order practices, although many were forced through extortion to pay heavy duties and fees when trekking across geographical zones where the extortion groups held sway.

Cities that once had been rid of crime and evil activities once again became the habitats of roving bandits. Residents of El-A and SanFran returned to their Dark Time practices; gangs fighting over territory, destruction of the shops and manufacturing centers that had been erected during the post-Dark Time recovery period, and once again battles over who would control food and water supplies. Danger lurked throughout most of the old cities and larger old towns. Agricultural and food production activities that had been initiated during the recovery period in the once-cleared shattered zones went fallow, as the lands remained unproductive.

Even New Bozeman and Montana State University suffered during these trying times. Local city police and security officers attempted to maintain law and order throughout New Bozeman. While basically successful, rates for assault and battery, burglary, theft, and murder rose precipitously. Campus security did its best to maintain a crime-free campus, but with increased assaults and thefts, more and more students at MSU left and returned home to their respective settlement groups. Once again, the evil twin had returned.

After-Word

And it came to pass that the changed structure of the New Order spread throughout New SouthWest, into the Flatlands, and beyond. With the spread and adoption of the old ways, avarice, crime, and evil returned and characterized individual and family behavior.

Thus it was the Overseer observing from afar (may Its name ever be blessed) looked down, smiled, then intervened and spoke to John Carpenter Edson.

Metal Sheet #11

Inscription and Translation

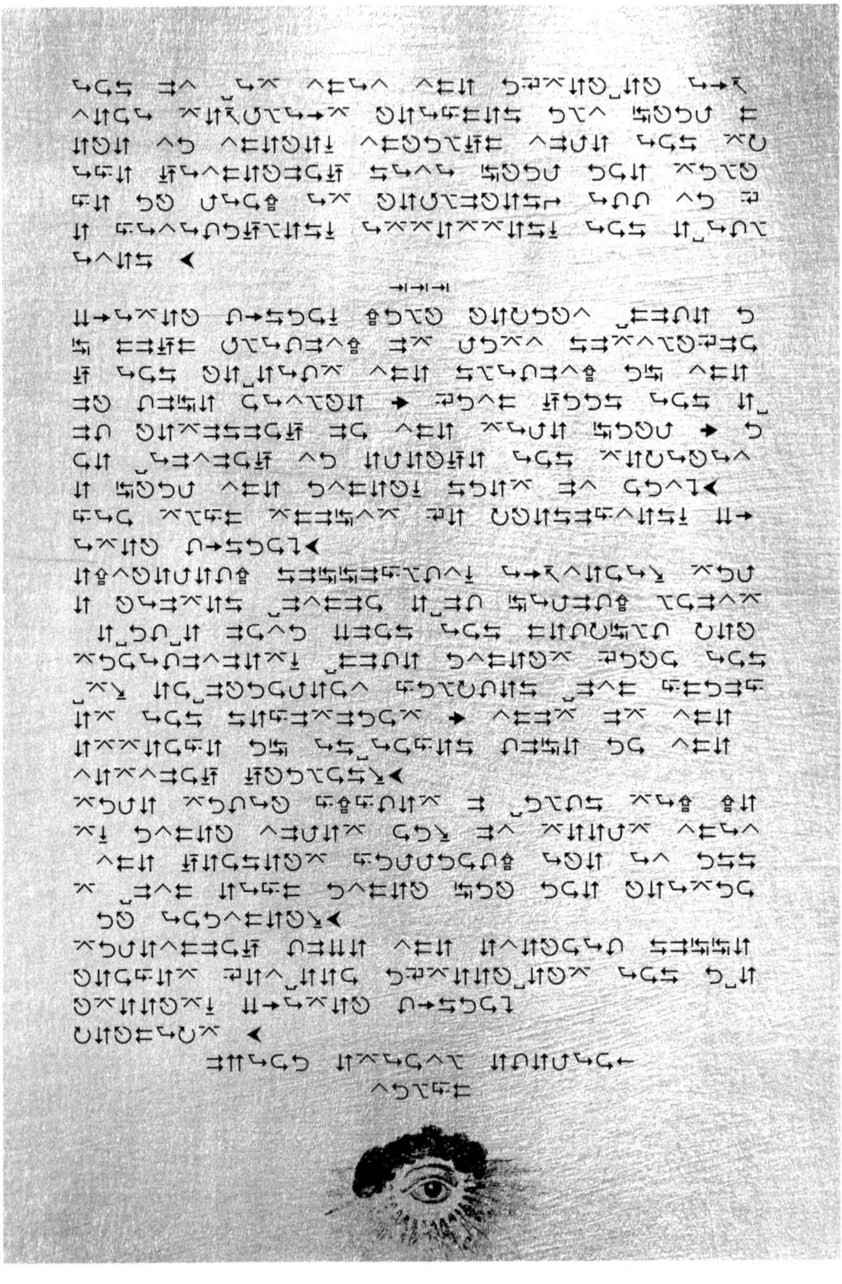

And it was that the Observer A'-Tena Se-Qua reached out from here to there, through time and space, gathering data from one source or many as required; all to be catalogued, assessed, and evaluated.

***

K'Aser L'Don, your report while of high quality is most disturbing and reveals the duality of their life nature – both good and evil residing in the same form – one waiting to emerge and separate from the other. Does it not?

A'-Tena, you have identified the key problem with these units, the issue of suppression vs. revelation. All are born as blank slates – with shared quantities of good and evil residing therein. As time passes, in response to the environment of family, home, and community coupled with choices and decisions, the balance shifts from neutrality as one characteristic dominates.

Can such shifts be predicted, K'Aser L'Don?

Extremely difficult, A'-Tena. Some raised within evil family units evolve into kind and helpful personalities, while others born and raised in luxury and wealth, with educational and professional advantages turn to lives of selfishness corruption, and crime.

K'Aser L'Don, can those with developed evil in their hearts be cleansed to lead productive and just lives, or not?

A'-Tena, many can, but the effort is unpredictable – nurturing versus environment coupled with choices and decisions – this is the essence of advanced life on the testing ground.

Curious these biped units – how is it that they are so different from us?

Fortunately we are different from them, A'-Tena.

K'Aser L'Don, your report also documented power struggles in what the units called the New Order, and a shift from female to the male in decision-making roles. Has this behavior been common among those inhabiting the testing ground?

Some solar cycles I would say yes, other times, no. It seems that the genders commonly are at odds with each other for one reason or another.

Something like the eternal differences between Observers and Overseers, K'Aser L'Don?

Perhaps ...

Ijano Esantu Eleman!

CHAPTER 13: EVENING READING 13
Document 13, Cave Location: Case 43-B
The Administrator

When a man is given the power for total control over life and death –
he no longer shares our traits.
I know:
I was the son of this man.

(Source: Interview with Able Edson, on his 38th birthday, Montana State University History Project Archive, Edson Family Documents, File 48-B)

Pre-Note

Ijano Esantu Eleman: As it was as in the beginning.

The Overseer (may Its name always be blessed) searched Etowah's testing ground for good individuals to counter the resurgence of evil reinstituted by priests of the New Order and their advisory councils. Of the many thousands that could have been selected, the Overseer (may Its name always be blessed) identified John Carpenter Edson on Day 13, Week 2, Month 9, Solar Cycle 39.

We who survived the resurgent evil of the New Order gather annually to mark this event in quiet solitude with local celebrations. To do so overtly and regionally could expose us to persecution, or worse. We take heart and hope that kindness, and goodwill toward others will prevail during these corrupt and evil times. We hold dear to the life and activities of John Carpenter Edson as revealed in the manuscript known as the *Tracta Edson*, the preserved record of John Carpenter Edson's life, compiled by the scribe Franklor Nevston after his assassination. We reject the content of other manuscripts, these supposed accurate accounts of John Carpenter Edson's life, that circulated after his death. We consider the content of these documents as speculative. Those who knew John Carpenter Edson confirm that the Tracta manuscript is accurate to the extent possible.

First Use of Power

Edson accepted the invitation to join the MSU data collectors on a long loop trek into New SouthWest Configuration and traveled with six data collectors:

> Males: Alden Johnson; Hunter Nelson; Ryan Ward
> Females: Amber Barnes; Harmony Cole; Lottie Webb

The team left New Bozeman on Day 4, Week 1, Month 2, Solar Cycle 40, took the traditional loop track south through Bison Camp settlement group, then followed the roads south through Idaho Falls, Pocatello, and into the Mormon Territory of New Salt Lake City. After a three-day rest period, the team continued west toward the Wells rendezvous site along Eye-80, then through New Reno, and over the mountain chain into Old Sacramento. There, the team bartered for rafts and crossed the water-filled Sacramento River flood zone with their pushcarts and supplies. They came ashore in southeast Old Davis on Day 1, Week 4, Month 5, Solar Cycle 40.

Alden Johnson, Certified Data Collector
Interview (date not recorded)
Subject: Regarding Events at UC Davis, Solar Cycle 40

> *After crossing the river flood zone, we established our temporary camp on the grassy former athletic fields at the north edge of the University of California, Davis, campus. The once-great university lay in ruins; burned hulks of once-proud academic and research buildings destroyed during the terrible days of the Ripple Event and early Dark Time. During the next two days, we scavenged through the building that once housed the departments of geography, and environmental sciences, in whose trust the university seed bank once had been placed under strict protection. We found the security system had been breached (probably many times) and*

inside the vault all the file cabinets had been ransacked. The trays that once held germ plasmid samples from food crops that could be regrown after a catastrophic event mostly were destroyed, previously stripped by vandals. Nothing of value remained.

Our next stop during late afternoon was the experimental farm headquarters, about a half kilo-mile to the southwest. It was here – secured inside a herbarium canister overlooked by previous thieves – that we discovered 18 vials of high-yield cereal grains (barley, millet, sorghum, and wheat), and five canisters of legume seeds (two different species of Phaseolus, varieties of European lentils, and Vicia faba). Ryan and Lottie carefully packed and placed the precious seeds inside their pushcart.

Exiting the headquarters building, we were confronted by a group of wanderers. I remember that the number was about five men and four or five women, each armed with machetes. They ordered us to stop and turn over to them everything inside our pushcarts. Edson raised his hand and approached the individual who appeared to be their leader and calmly asked him and the others to put down their weapons and to let us pass unharmed. This caused the wanderers to laugh and sneer at what they perceived to be a naïve request. Edson then said, "Let us pass." The gang refused.

Suddenly – the group of thugs who had accosted us – simply vanished!

Look, you have asked me to relate this event twice, and I have given you the same report each time. These disappearances occurred on Day 3, Week 4, Month 5, Solar Cycle 40. All of us were stunned at this astonishing turn of events and looked at John Carpenter Edson in curious wonder. We had many questions: What had just happened? How could it be that by looking at a group of wanderers who had threatened our lives, John could make them simply vanish?

I have related at other interviews about what John did next, how he gathered us together, and asked us to swear that we never would repeat what we had just seen. He told us that criminals and evildoers deserved to be eliminated and that he had a special but unspecified role to play. Edson provided us with no further details; he explained nothing about how the disappearances had taken place. He asked us again to never repeat what we had experienced and seen – so long as he remained alive.

I always have kept my pledge to John Carpenter Edson, the administrator, and did not speak to anyone about the disappearance events at the UC Davis campus until after his assassination.

I swear to you that I was honorable and kept my word. I also tell you that this was not the case with Hunter Nelson, the data collector on our team who broke his pledge and provided vital information to the New Order priests and militia and betrayed John Carpenter Edson.

That is all I have to say about the Event at UC Davis.

Please leave me alone!

Return to Old Montana

John Carpenter Edson and the data collectors secured their precious vials of seeds and started on the return journey to MSU and New Bozeman. Retracing their route up Eye-80, just west of New Elko, they were approached and accosted by a group of horsemen. The potential robbers circled the team and ordered them to surrender and to turn over all supplies.

As before, Edson spoke calmly to the group leader and requested permission to pass through their territory without being molested. The request was refused and, as before, in an instant all of the horsemen simply vanished, leaving behind only their horses. Alden Johnson of the data collector group organized the capture of the runaway horses and, upon arrival in New Elko, they were turned over to the administrative council. The team then left quickly.

When the data collectors reached Bison Camp, they remained in seclusion for almost four days. During this time, John Carpenter Edson revealed additional information about his interaction with the Overseer, his appointment as the administrator, and his Charge. Edson once more asked each data collector to form an alliance of quiet support for his efforts in crime and evil reduction. Once again, he sought agreement that all would never mention what they had observed.

In the years that followed, these young student data collectors became known as The Select Six (TSS).

The trek from Bison Camp north and east to MSU was uneventful. The data collectors still were puzzled regarding Edson's explanation for the disappearances at UC Davis and outside New Elko. While he had spoken clearly, and what he said matched their observations as to what had happened, the vanishings defied all laws of logic and science. How could the attackers disappear merely through the process of focused thought (FT)? But they did!

Upon reaching New Bozeman, John Carpenter Edson reunited with his wife, Allison. She immediately was aware that her husband had changed during his period away. He was disheveled but that was to be expected in those returning from a long loop trek. But he also had changed in his behavior, and Allison was not certain why or if the change was for the better. Together, they discussed the trek and events long into the night, when he revealed the Charge, and the initial uses of his power. During these talks, John and Allison always excluded their son, Able. It was clear to Allison that John would need to remain incognito, and had to remain extremely careful about further displays of his power, lest he be discovered and events spin out of control.

Subsequent Uses of Power

The administrator's power to eliminate crime and evil first revealed at Old Davis and New Elko changed his life and that of his family. Edson learned through practice that by focusing his mental attention on a specific evil individual, or a gang, that they simply disappeared, vanished, and ceased to exist. The process was simple: observe, concentrate mental energy, and the murderer, thief, or vandal would vanish, leaving behind nothing and no marks of conflict or struggle.

Upon return to New Bozeman, Edson took a leave of absence from his engineering position at Compton Transport Technology. During this period, he traveled and retraced various long and short loop treks used by the MSU data collectors. Along the way, he became a careful observer of individual and family life and activities. If a crime in progress was encountered, the criminal vanished. Then Edson moved on to the next location. He also discovered with practice that the Charge also could be extended to individuals and groups not directly in his line of vision; by just knowing where the murderers had taken shelter or were living he could cause their elimination.

And so it was that Edson's work as the administrator continued and expanded.

Among the first eliminated were gangs and crime lords that ruled vast areas of the shattered zones surrounding the nearby settlement groups. Edson developed what he later referred to as *the List*. Identified on this list were individuals and groups due for elimination, who committed arson, assaults, and burglaries; those who embezzled and extorted others; persons who committed fraud, who kidnapped, murdered, raped, and robbed. Gone – simply vanished.

Edson returned to MSU and New Bozeman at the end of each short or long loop trek and resumed his position as chief retro-engineer and leader of the new transportation guidance system group at Compton Transport Technology. Beginning in late spring through summer and into the early fall months he conducted his work elsewhere. During the next two solar cycles he continued his treks within New NorthWest Configuration, and then expanded through portions of New SouthWest Configuration. For those who asked about his whereabouts, he would tell friends that he was hard at work, charged with development of the nitrazine-fueled engine design, the regional government's promising new energy source. No relative or friend challenged his assertion that the reason he needed to be away was related to meetings with other engineers and potential power resources related to his employment. Implications of his work as the administrator, however, drew the attention of the New Order hierarchy.

New Order Concerns

New Order councils at various settlement groups became alarmed as two things happened. First, certain key priests and priestesses who had committed crimes had vanished – simply disappeared without a trace. Second, with noticeable reductions in crime and evildoing, widespread support for the New Order among the general settlement group populations declined precipitously.

Various New Order councils met in closed sessions to discuss the ongoing events, and the central council at Base Save settlement group in south central Old Montana instituted a program to identify who or what was reshaping the structure and belief demographics of the post-Dark Time recovery period.

A clever New Order member interested in maps and geographical data suggested to his local New Order priest that a time-sequence investigation should be undertaken. He proposed a plan to document and pinpoint precise locations where individuals previously had vanished – and to seek correlations between these disappearances and a range of different variables.

This New Order member worked for six months to eliminate internal and external environmental variables and then focused on actions, the involvement and presence of specific groups and individuals at specific disappearance sites.

Through clever data analysis, this individual, known in documents only as the New Order investigator (NOI), gradually became aware that one person most likely was involved. Data analyzed showed a correlation between the presence of specific individuals at locations where subsequent "cleansings" disappearances occurred. It took just two weeks to confirm these data and to identify John Carpenter Edson as the chief suspect in the disappearance process.

And it came to be that John Carpenter Edson sensed that he was being followed and tracked whenever he left Bison Camp, New Bozeman, and on his trips to other locations along the various loop treks. He further noted that strangers who arrived at Bison Camp and at New Bozeman sometimes conducted interviews with council members regarding his current and past travel activities.

The external threat to the New Order had been identified.

Moral Reflections

Early on as he implemented the Charge, John Carpenter Edson experienced initial satisfaction when he eliminated criminals, either as individuals or groups. But as the days, weeks, and months passed, the impact of the power he possessed on his psyche and well-being began to weigh heavily.

Gradually, he sensed that the process of eliminating crime and evil was itself evil. He worried that the family members of the criminals, those who had not indulged in such practices and were left behind by the disappearances, often were subjected to poverty without means of support. A great many innocent children suffered, due to the absence of their grandfathers, fathers, uncles, and brothers (or grandmothers, mothers, aunts, and sisters – as the case may be). All suffered because of his doing. Such thoughts played upon the mind of John Carpenter Edson and caused him to question the ethics of the Charge given to him by the Overseer (may Its name always be blessed).

The Meeting

And it came to be understood by John Carpenter Edson that those individuals following him were affiliated with the New Order. So it was that in secret he arranged a meeting with the first priest. Records suggest that the date of this meeting was held on either Day 2 or 7, Week 1, Month 8, Solar Cycle 42. Other records suggest that the meeting was held during the sixth month of solar cycle 42.

Edson traveled alone to Base Save settlement group, the seat of the New Order's power. He was escorted into the presence of the first priest and together they faced one another. On one side of the table smiled the personification of crime and evil dressed in the garb of a New Order priest; facing him was the chosen one.

John Carpenter Edson spoke first.

> *You know who I am, my actions, and what I have done in the past and what I will continue to do in the future. You and your ilk continue to spread evil and injustice across the regional configurations; your message and activities are to be condemned. What I confess to you, here and now, is the pain that I have caused to the children and relatives of the criminals I have executed and caused to disappear. These innocents should not be punished for the evil deeds of their elders – the evil that you and your kind encourage and perpetuate. I sense that you and your attendants mean to harm me – that you aim to eliminate me and end my activities. Thoughts, however, are not crimes, otherwise, you – Samuel The Select – would be gone. But if thoughts of my destruction and death are your goal, I will not be able to stop you. I will continue to do what I must, and you will do what you must. Know this and know it now: at this moment as I speak to you, in just an instant I could make you and your ilk vanish forever. But such an action taken by me would not be morally correct. So it is, therefore, that we must do what we must do. But I tell you this and tell you now – should you harm my family or child I will know in advance, and all of you will be gone. If, in your madness of purpose you elect to execute me, then do so quickly – in a way not to harm others. I carry too much pain with me because of my prior actions. I would welcome death – but not at the expense to others.*

John Carpenter Edson rose and left the room.

The first priest of the New Order did not speak.

The last wish Edson made to the first priest would not be granted.

And as the days passed, the Overseer (may Its name always be blessed) watched from afar and awaited the events that would follow.

While the immediate family of John Carpenter Edson would not be harmed through subsequent actions of the New Order, innocent others would be and the results that followed would usher in times too terrible to contemplate.

The Overseer (may Its name always be blessed) would watch from afar and not intervene.

Betrayal

Hunter Nelson, Certified Data Collector
Letter written Day 3, Week 1, Month 7, Solar Cycle 47
Montana State History Project Archive, Box HN-39A12

To All Who Once Trusted Me …

I have taken my life this day. The pain of living and remembering what I have done has been endless since I broke my vow to John Carpenter Edson. It was I who was taken aside and interviewed by the New Order priests and their nameless investigator. I told them what I knew about disappearances when John Carpenter Edson was present. It was I who lied to John Carpenter Edson. It was I who broke the trust he had placed with me and the other five data collectors on the long loop trek into Old California territory.

New Order priests offered me objects of value and a new identification if I spoke about what I had witnessed. They offered me a new identification if I would break my vow. And so it was I accepted. I confess to you all that it was I who identified John Carpenter Edson in possession of the great power of disappearance.

I cannot name here the settlement group where I have lived in exile for the past six solar cycles since Edson's assassination — lest the shame of my action also fall onto the innocent community that took me in, not knowing who I was and what I had done. Please do not visit my shame and crime upon anyone else.

The evil that I set into motion cannot be erased or taken back. I accept my responsibility in the ultimate assassination of John Carpenter Edson. Do not place any stone or mark the riverbank near the water place where I now go to accept eternal darkness for my deed.

Hunter Nelson

Flora Graham, Certified Data Collector
Interview: Testimony of Able Edson
Date: Day 6, Week 1, Month 9, Solar Cycle 42
Montana State History Project Archive, Box JE: 55482, File 16

My father, John Edson, was assassinated by a priest of the New Order on Day 7, Week 5, Month 8, Solar Cycle 42. His last day began when he entered the New NorthWest Regional Justice Office to offer testimony before the Poverty Reduction Committee of the Regional Government at Butte, Old Montana. As he exited the Frank Simmons hearing room on the second floor of the Regional Court, he was greeted by a person who appeared to be a New Order priest, dressed in appropriate attire, who shook my father's hand. Accounts published after the assassination say that the two seemed to know each other, and that they spoke briefly as both descended the rotunda staircase. At the foot of the steps, my father greeted the social media reporters and onlookers. As he started to respond to their questions, the assassin embraced my father and shouted four words:

>   *Death to the administrator!*

The bomb hidden under the assassin's tunic detonated. The blast killed my father, the assassin, and 28 innocent bystanders within the confined area of the atrium. Another 37 visitors to the Capitol that day were wounded; 12 of the wounded subsequently died.

How could such a terrible event have happened?

In the days that followed, the assassin's words continued to puzzle me. My father was not an administrator. I knew him as a chief engineer and leader of an automobile guidance system group at Compton Transport Technology (CTT). He was a well-respected scientist and director of a team of specialists charged with the development of nitrazine-fueled engines, the regional government's promising new energy source.

Why had my father been targeted for death in such a terrible manner?

Two days after the assassination, my mother and I hosted the traditional departure ceremony and remembrance feast. We were saddened that few persons attended. Only three local relatives, my aunt, uncle, and cousin, and fewer than 10 family friends and neighbors paid respects to share our grief. We were puzzled why none of my father's colleagues or project workers at CTT offered their condolences.

The days that followed turned into weeks. As time passed, I grew more unsettled and slipped into a pre-schematic depression phase. I spent many lonely hours thinking about the murder of my father. Why had the social media platforms reinstituted during the post-Dark Time recovery period not reported the assassin's name? What would compel a so-called person of faith, this individual who seemingly was a New Order priest, to take the life of my father and other innocents?

My father's murder was the first act of violence I had experienced. I was familiar with violent images captured on magno-tapes during the chaotic times before the Ripple Event and Dark Time when assaults, murder, thefts and evil social outrages were common. But there had been no murders that I could remember throughout my lifetime. Such an event was unheard of, as the time we lived in now was characterized by social responsibility and the absence of crime and evil. My father's assassination had shattered my trust in everyday personal interactions. How could this have happened?

I visited the government archives and requested copies of the computerized tracts written by priests of the New Order from a systematic data management representative. I also visited the Montana State University History Project archive, where I also found documents related to the New Order, but it seemed that at both of these depositories the content of the documents revealed nothing other than New Order expressions of honor, peace, tranquility, and commitment to kindness and public assistance. Had they been purged and new documents substituted that placed the New Order cult in a better light? Certainly there was no honor in my father's assassination. So why would a priest of the New Order – if he was indeed a priest – risk eternal disintegration?

But more puzzling were other unanswered questions. How had the assassin obtained the chemicals used to manufacture the explosive device? Residents at all regional settlement groups had been denied access to such compounds after the regional government had placed them on restricted availability lists (RALs) more than 23 solar cycles earlier. Procurement, if not impossible, certainly would have been extremely difficult, which also would imply some sort of potential regional government involvement.

How could it be that the modern regional government communication oversight system (RGCOS) had not discovered the New Order's intent prior to this murderous act? Since emergence from the Dark Time and for more than 40 solar cycles since, all electronic-amplified exchanges between citizens had been monitored and analyzed in real time. How was it possible that the priest's intent had not been anticipated? Clearly, something was amiss.

But the most difficult question remained: what did the priest mean when he shouted, "Death to the administrator?"

Who was the administrator?

After-Word

As the months passed, Able Edson drifted further into post-traumatic despair. Finally, his mother, Allison, requested a home visit from two sage femmes to review her son's health. The healers (bless their work) conducted a traditional body scan and relevant fluid analyses. Indications were that Able's health rating had declined from level Three-A (standard healthy citizen) to re-calibrated level Six-B (caution: take action indicated). The healers assured Allison that her son's condition would improve with parabolic exercise, coupled with an inclusive reflexive dietary strategy. They prescribed an injection of tri-annuated-sulfate to re-regulate his irregular sleep pattern.

After the healers left, Able's mother prepared the injection and measured the prescribed dosage for insertion. As the medicine took effect, she excused herself and then returned shortly later bearing a package wrapped in brown paper bound with twine. She placed the bundle in Able's arms and together they opened the package.

What emerged was an aged, badly tattered book. Embossed on the cover was the title *Tracta Edson: The Testimony of Franklor Nevston.*

As Able slowly slipped into the initial phase of his dream-vision state, Allison read aloud the words therein. And what she read and what Able learned, thereupon, changed his life forever.

Metal Sheet #12

Inscription and Translation

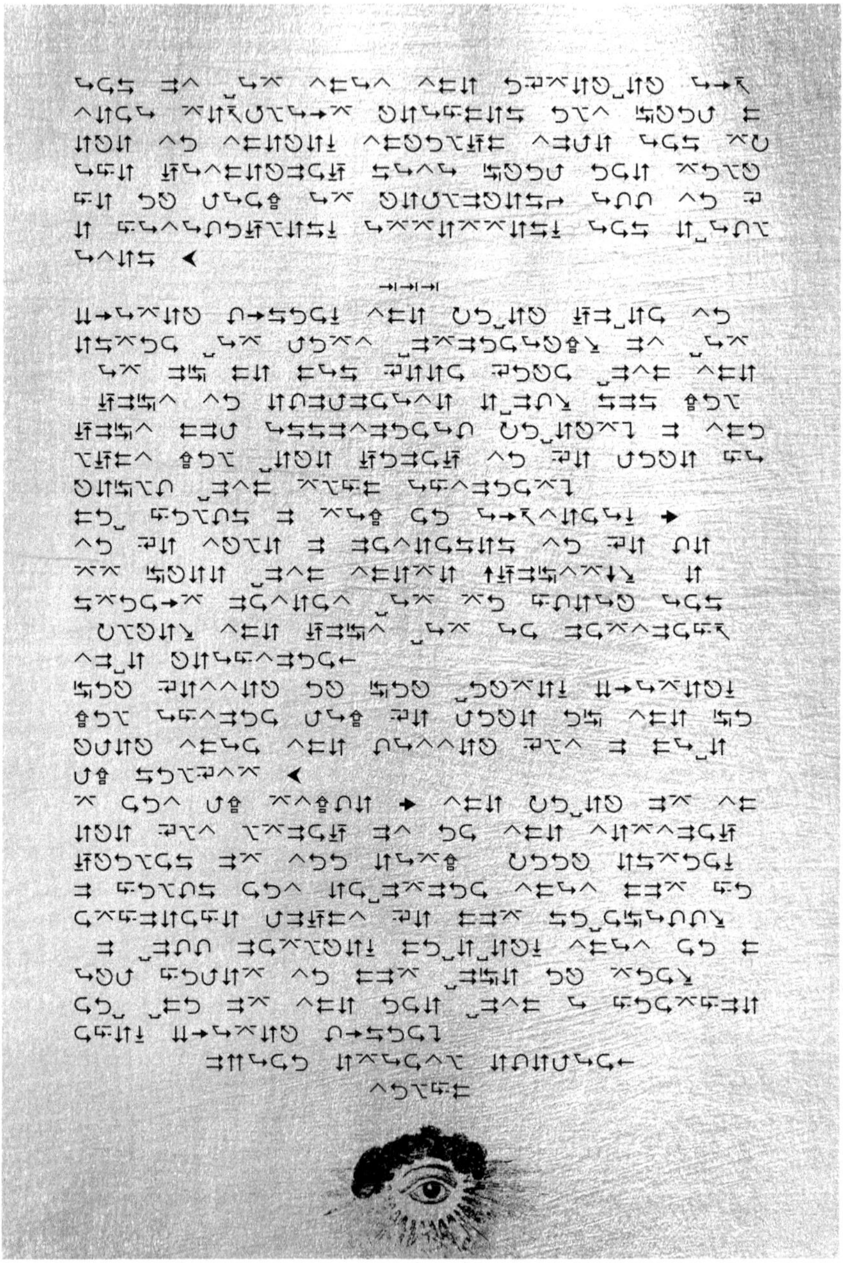

And it was that the Observer A'-Tena Se-Qua reached out from here to there, through time and space, gathering data from one source or many as required; all to be catalogued, assessed, and evaluated.

***

K'Aser L'Don, the power given to Edson was most visionary. It was as if he had been born with the gift to eliminate evil. Did you gift him additional powers? I thought you were going to be more careful with such actions?

How could I say no? A'-Tena, to be true I intended to be less free with such gifts. Edson's intent was so clear and pure. The gift was an instinctive reaction.

For better or for worse, K'Aser, your action may be more of the former than the latter, but I have my doubts.

A'-Tena, I share that hope but sad to say gifting so often begins with thanks and blessings but ends otherwise.

In either case we shall see, we shall see.

K'Aser L'Don, you end your report with the assassination of the administrator. Could you not see it coming?

Yes, but only in a way that something similar was to happen, but so much was swirling around the administrator that I was distracted.

Distracted? How can this be, K'Aser L'Don? Distracted at a vital juncture? Might you adjust this situation after the fact?

A'-Tena Se-Qua, you know that is not my style. The power is there but using it on the testing ground is too easy. Poor Edson, I could not envision that his conscience might be his downfall. I will ensure, however, that no harm comes to his wife or son.

Now who is the one with a conscience, K'Aser L'Don?

Ijano Esantu Eleman!

CHAPTER 14: EVENING READING 14

Document 14, Cave Location: Case 43-B

Tracta Edson

May our hearts and actions circumvent the evils of the New Order

May we erase what has happened during the recent solar cycles

Let us return to the qualities and justice inherent in the Great Septet, the positive actions and behaviors that once characterized our societies

(Source: Final statement by Franklor Nevston to the 17th Truth Committee, New Bozeman, on Day 5, Week 3, Month 4, Solar Cycle 43.)

Pre-Note

I, Lester Collins, post-Dark Time assistant archivist at the Montana State University History Project archive, located the document hereafter known as the *Tracta Edson*. The manuscript was unbound, written by a clear hand in English. It represents the testimony of one Franklor Nevston, delivered in person at the 17th Truth Committee hearings, held at New Bozeman, on Day 5, Week 3, Month 4, Solar Cycle 43.

Given that symbolic fonts and symbols are minimized throughout the text, such icons suggest that the document was written on or about the date claimed on the title page (solar cycle 43, post-Dark Time).

The manuscript contains 23 handwritten pages subdivided into 20 sections that establish the family line and life of John Carpenter Edson, also known as the administrator. Of primary interest to most reviewers of the document are the passages in which the Overseer (may Its name always be blessed) delivers the Charge to John Carpenter Edson. This event is followed by recognition and first use of his powers, initially applied locally, and then with more broad regional implementation. The moral issues that plagued John Carpenter Edson as he continued his actions are revealed in some detail.

The document is unusual because it is one of the few recovered that considers the origins and rise of the New Order cult, and description of events in the days leading to John Carpenter Edson's assassination.

The manuscript concludes with an overview of regional problems that followed the assassination. The impact of these problems on the residents of New Bozeman and Bison Camp settlement group, and other regional settlement groups, and the changes that resulted are covered in detail.

Permission to scan and publish a copy of the *Tracta Edson* was received from Chief Archivist Birney Miller on Day 6, Week 2, Month 3, Solar Cycle 44. May all who read this document obtain a more objective understanding of events that have occurred during the recent solar cycles and the terrible return to avarice, crime, and evil that seem to be a perpetual part of life.

Lester Collins
Lester Collins, Assistant Archivist
Montana State University History Project

Birney Miller
Birney Miller, Chief Archivist
Montana State University History Project

Certification: Day 6, Week 2, Month 3, Solar Cycle 44
Tracta Edson Certification Page

Testimony of Franklor Nevston
Stenographer Ralph Cooper
Transcribed Day 5, Week 3, Month 4,
Solar Cycle 43, Post-Dark Time Recovery Period

> I stand before you as a volunteer to give testimony in my capacity as reciter – one who holds the memories and sustains knowledge for future generations.

I share with you today the messages contained in the oral tradition we hold dear, the *Tracta Edson,* words that represent the collective heritage of our people.

Record what I say to you this day. My words are honest and truthful and should be known by all.

TESTIMONY CERTIFICATION:

Franklor Nevston

Franklor Nevston

I hereby deliver my testimony to the 17th Truth Committee hearings without coercion, Day 5, Week 3, Month 4, Solar Cycle 43. I swear allegiance and honor to the Overseer (may Its name always be blessed).

Ralph Cooper

Ralph Cooper, Stenographer
Date: Day 5, Week 3, Month 4, Solar Cycle 43

Tracta Edson Transcript Page 1

Section 1: *Ijano Esantu Eleman* (as it was as in the beginning)

1:1   *Ijano Esantu Eleman.* As it was as in the beginning. Out of the great chaos Etowah (may Its name always be blessed) created star cluster 24-G-37 within axial coordinates 4-29-D.

1:2   Within axial coordinates 4-29-D, Etowah (may Its name always be blessed) created a Nine-orb sequence circling the central star that included the location known as the testing ground.

1:3   Life on the testing ground, three orbs distant from the central star, developed from primordial components, then through a great chain of organisms from which life ultimately emerged and initially flourished. An Overseer was assigned to this orb to collect life-related data and report to the assigned Observer.

1:4   The Overseer (may Its name always be blessed) recorded data as populations grew in numbers and ventured into lands where some prospered, while others chose ways of crime, evil, and war.

1:5   The Overseer (may Its name always be blessed) grew disgusted with such behavior and interceded with insight and wisdom to implement a plan to rid the orb of crime and evil beings.

1:6   And it came to pass that the Overseer (may Its name always be blessed) selected an adult male to serve as the administrator and to implement the Crime and Evil Reduction Program (CERP).

1:7   Let us praise the Overseer (may Its name always be blessed) for its decision to select John Carpenter Edson for the blessed position as the administrator.

Thus ends Section 1: Tracta Edson: Testimony of Franklor Nevston.

Tracta Edson Transcript Page 2

Section 2. Family Line of John Carpenter Edson

2:1   *Ijano Esantu Eleman.* As it was as in the beginning. Let all who read this testimony honor the memory of John Carpenter Edson, the administrator – assassinated Day 7, Week 5, Month 8, Solar Cycle 42, post-Dark Time recovery period. Let us recall the facts regarding his family line:

Original family line of John Carpenter Edson:

> From the pre-Dark Time: information unknown.
> From the Dark Time: information unknown
> From the post-Dark Time recovery period:
>> Svent Carpenter – Algis Cantrell Carpenter
>> Children: Effem, Jostfa, and John Carpenter

No information available on mother's family line.

Adoptive family lines:

> From the pre-Dark Time

>> Louis Edson: mate partner Martha Sloanberg
>> Children: Alice, Justin, and James Edson

> From the Dark Time

>> James Edson: mate partner Irene Thompson
>> Children: Ferris Edson
>> Ferris Edson: mate partner Alice Balmer

Children: Frank, Gwyen, and Valdese Edson

From the post-Dark Time recovery period

Valdese Edson: mate partner Sarha Boyd
Children: John (adoptive) and Rosemary Edson

Mother's line: Fiona (last name unknown) birthed Janice (mate partner Alan Martinez) who birthed Laurel (mate partner Luis Boyd) who birthed Sarha (mate partner Valdese Edson) who bore two children:

John and Rosemary Edson

2:2 Let us honor the memory of the administrator's parents: Svent Carpenter and Algis Cantrell Carpenter, born the same year, 2001 (old solar cycle calculation)

2:3 Let us celebrate Svent Carpenter and Algis Cantrell, who came to maturity in Solar Cycle 1 Dark Time, and respect their behavior.

Tracta Edson Transcript Page 3

2:4 Let all who read this testimony know that the couple waited the required five additional years to form a mating pair in accord with Regional Government Law 631-B-39.

2:5 And it came to be that after the five-year waiting period, Svent Carpenter and Algis Cantrell Carpenter presented themselves for reproductive certification to the Conception Committee, Bear Hollow settlement group, Old Montana, New NorthWest Configuration.

2:6 Central government archive documents confirm the Bear Hollow Conception Committee (BHCC) approved Svent Carpenter and Algis Cantrell Carpenter for reproductive coupling on Day 3, Week 2, Month 2, Solar Cycle 6 Dark Time.

2:7 Records confirm that Svent Carpenter and Algis Cantrell Carpenter entered into physical union on Day 7, Week 2, Month 2, Dark Solar Cycle 6 Dark Time and conceived Effem Edson.

2:8 Testimony before the Child Death Review Committee (CDRC), Old Montana, New NorthWest Configuration, confirms that Effen Edson died of bio-system failure on Day 17 after emergence.

2:9 Minutes of the 43rd meeting of the Bear Hollow Conception Committee, Day 5, Week 3, Month 5, Solar Cycle 8 Dark Time, confirm that Svent Carpenter and Algis Cantrell Carpenter petitioned for a second conception certificate 17 months after the death of Effen Edson.

2:10 Let all who read this testimony share the joy that the coupling of Svent Carpenter and Algis Cantrell Carpenter was successful and that their daughter Jostfa emerged 742 days after Effen's death.

Thus ends Section 2: Tracta Edson: Testimony of Franklor Nevston.

Tracta Edson Transcript Page 4

Section 3. Birth of John Carpenter Edson

3:1 *Ijano Esantu Eleman.* As it was as in the beginning. There came the powerful urging as Svent Carpenter and Algis Cantrell Carpenter longed for another child.

3:2 In accord with regional law and Conception Act 59-M-3, regulations did not permit a third conception since Svent Carpenter and Algis Cantrell Carpenter already had brought two infants to emergence.

3:3 Longing for another child there came a time when Svent Carpenter and Algis Cantrell Carpenter coupled illegally during her fertile period at the solar darkness celebration at Bear Hollow settlement group and from this union a child was conceived.

3:4 By mutual accord Svent Carpenter and Algis Cantrell Carpenter suppressed outward evidence of their pregnancy until John Edson emerged on Day 3, Week 1 Month 5, Solar Cycle 12 post-Dark Time recovery period.

3:5 Local Settlement Observers Eloise Gorsent, and Stron Fillvet reported to the Bear Hollow Population Committee that Svent Carpenter and Algis Cantrell Carpenter had broken the law.

3:6 In accord with Central Government law 58-R-16, Svent Carpenter and Algis Cantrell Carpenter were seized, and infant John Edson removed from their charge.

Thus ends Section 3: Tracta Edson: Testimony of Franklor Nevston

Tracta Edson Transcript Page 5

Section 4. Trial and Execution of John Carpenter Edson's Parents

4:1   *Ijano Esantu Eleman.* As it was as in the beginning. Conception
       criminals Svent Carpenter and Algis Cantrell Carpenter were
       transported to Holding Camp #5, Western Region, Old Montana
       Territory, and imprisoned to await tribunal decision.

4:2   At their hearing, accused conception criminals Svent Carpenter
       and Algis Cantrell Carpenter offered praise to the Overseer (may
       Its name always be blessed) and requested mercy from the tribunal
       members. At the conclusion of the hearing, the couple was judged
       guilty in accord with the law, and sentenced to be executed.

4:3   Execution of conception criminals Svent and Algis Cantrell
       Carpenter was overseen by Baker Brown – the 4th circuit mayor,
       Old Montana Territory, New NewWest Configuration and
       witnessed by the 593 adult residents of Bear Hollow settlement
       group, Old Montana, New NewWest Configuration.

4:4   For their last words, both Svent Carpenter and Algis Cantrell
       Carpenter praised the Overseer (may Its name always be blessed),
       and neither cried out in pain as their reproductive organs were
       extracted surgically in accord with Conception Law 682-B-09 and
       Order of the Regional Government.

4:5   Bodies of conception criminals Svent Carpenter and Algis Cantrell
       Carpenter were cremated, and their ashes scattered; no stone mark
       was allowed for remembrance.

4:6   The disgraced body parts removed from conception criminals
       Svent Carpenter and Algis Cantrell were displayed at the
       Friendship Temple, Bear Hollow settlement group, throughout the
       76-day observation period as cautionary reminders to residents
       that the law and wisdom of the regional government must be
       respected.

4:7   Let all who read this testimony know the time and location of the
       Body Finality Notice (BFN) of Svent Carpenter and Algis Cantrell
       Carpenter:

I certify that the corpses and extracted body parts of conception criminals Svent Carpenter and Algis Cantrell Carpenter were disposed in accord with all appropriate regional government laws on Day 6, Week 2, Month 6, Solar Cycle 12.

Baker Brown

Baker Brown, 4th Circuit Mayor, Mountain Territory
Certified: Day 6, Week 2, Month 6, Solar Cycle 12

Thus ends Section 4: Tracta Edson: Testimony of Franklor Nevston.

Tracta Edson Transcript Page 6

Section 5. Redistribution Years: Events of Early Life

5:1　*Ijano Esantu Eleman.* As it was as in the beginning.

NOTICE: I certify that infant, John Carpenter, was examined by regional government Nurse Frances Cook, and prepared for redistribution on day 15 after his emergence. I further certify that this examination took place three days after the execution of infant Carpenter's parents. I certify that his examination was conducted in accord with all appropriate regional government laws.

Edward Walker

Edward Walker, 7th Guardian of Illegal Infants
Certified: Day 1, Week 4, Month 5, Solar Cycle 12

5:2　In accordance with regional government law, infant Carpenter was eligible for redistribution. Announcements were posted by messenger to all settlement groups within a 150 kilo-mile radius of Bear Hollow settlement group.

5:3　Valdese Edson and his mate partner Sarha at Bison Camp settlement group accepted the redistribution contract, and adopted infant John Carpenter. Let all who read this testimony offer thanksgiving to the adoptive parents.

5:4　During the first three years of life, infant John Carpenter Edson was suckled by wet nurse Vabel Aerstudt, member of the 62nd Infant Protection Regiment (IPR).

5:5   Between years three and five, John Carpenter Edson was assigned to a regional government-approved education cluster, the 16th Play Group, part of the 17th Childhood Protection Regiment (CPR), supervised by Fairveld Zend.

5:6   The names of three other children in John Carpenter Edson's 16th Play Group are known: Storze Orkland, Besme Hunzy, and Franklor Nevston.

5:7   The four members of 16th Play Group were educated in accord with standards implemented after the great radiation disaster during the Dark Time (Regional Government Law 49-B-35).

5:8   At the end of year five, John Carpenter Edson and the three other children in his play group were tested using methods approved by the regional government. Archive documents confirmed the children's abilities to read and write, and that they were socialized in accord with local and national standards.

Thus ends Section 5: Tracta Edson: Testimony of Franklor Nevston.

Tracta Edson Transcript Page 7

Section 6. Redistribution Years: Events of Childhood

6:1   Ijano Esantu Eleman. As it was as in the beginning. Starting with year six, John Carpenter Edson and classmates were educated using standard survival practices, good behavior, and reading and pre-computational skills. By year 10, all could read and write, were physically fit, and normal in appearance.

6:2   During the 10th year, John Carpenter Edson and the three children in his group were trained in additional survival skills, landscape analysis, and hunting and tracking skills. He evidenced considerable abilities in redesigning old machines for practical use, an indication that he should be identified for further specialized training.

6:3   At this time, his sister Rosemary was conceived and emerged.

6:4   His teachers at Bison Camp settlement group suggested special additional training in mechanical retrofitting and by the age of 12 solar cycles, John Edson had received first prize at two separate occasions in the annual Bison Camp settlement engine-rebuilding competition.

6:5   As John Carpenter Edson approached maturity, he served Bison Camp in several capacities, as internal sentry and protector of the food storage caches. His mother Sarha took him on walks through the nearby forests and grasslands surrounding the settlement, where she taught him to identify the special healing herbs, roots, and tubers that could serve him well if he traveled as an adult.

6:6   As maturity approached, John Carpenter Edson became eligible to participate in the Bison Camp settlement initiation rites, in which successful passage would mark his transition from child to man.

6:7   His foster parents Valdese and Sarha Edson could not have anticipated how their son John Carpenter Edson and his three youthful friends who participated in the 16th Infant Group would influence history in decades to come.

Thus ends Section 6: Tracta Edson: Testimony of Franklor Nevston.

Tracta Edson Transcript Page 8

Section 7. Redistribution Years: Events of Adolescence

7:1   *Ijano Esantu Eleman.* As it was as in the beginning. John Carpenter Edson grew in stature and physical strength and became eligible to participate in the Bison Camp settlement group rites of passage with other males and females of his general age and maturity.

7:2   John Carpenter Edson, along with his age-mate Franklor Nevston and 15 other males, entered the male initiation school and for three months they lived in the nearby shattered zone under the watchful eye of their elderly trainers.

7:3   During the shattered zone trial, the young males practiced additional hunting and self-protection skills, and participated daily in rigorous strength activities to prepare them for manhood.

7:4   At the conclusion of the initiation school, all were called to assemble and present themselves at the settlement group solstice celebration during solar cycle 27.

7:5   BothnJohn Carpenter Edson and age-mate Franklor Nevston passed each of the initiation challenges; 12 of the 15 other candidates likewise passed (three did not survive the rigors of the shattered zone initiation school).

7:6   Each candidate stood before the assembled residents of Bison Camp settlement group where they received the mark of manhood, and bore the pain without flinching or wavering.

7:7   The successful candidates then were formed into their first age-set, Warrior Class I, with chief responsibility to protect the Bison Camp settlement. Each new adult was assigned specific duties and additional specialized training in weaponry stealth, which they practiced daily.

7:8   John Carpenter Edson received skill badges in combat lance/stave techniques, rapid weapon manufacture, and physical protection.

Thus ends Section 7: Tracta Edson: Testimony of Franklor Nevston.

Tracta Edson Transcript Page 9

Section 8. Early Adult Life and Family

8:1   *Ijano Esantu Eleman.* As it was as in the beginning. And it came to be that John Carpenter Edson was recommended for advanced education at Montana State University, New Bozeman, 160 kilo-miles east of Bison Camp settlement group, where a new era began in his life.

8:2   At MSU, John Carpenter Edson was welcomed into the education program of retro-engineering, in which he exceeded expectations of his professors. Twice he was awarded the Department Citation Award for Excellence (DCAE).

8:3   In addition to engineering course requirements, John Carpenter Edson took electives in North American history for which his teachers explored key economic, political, and technical issues prior to the Ripple Event and onset of Dark Time.

8:4   During the last phases of his training at MSU, he met Allison Eckhart, born and raised at River Crossing settlement group near Old Livingstone.

8:5   John Carpenter Edson and Allison Eckhart became mate partners with the support of both their families on Day 4, Week 1, Month 6, Solar Cycle 34.

8:6   The couple settled at New Bozeman where John Carpenter Edson began employment at Compton Transport Technology (CTT) as assistant engineer in charge of the CTT Nitrazine Fuel Project.

8:7 John Carpenter Edson and Allison Eckhart mated and she became pregnant, and Able Edson emerged on Day 6, Week 4, Month 10, Solar Cycle 37.

8:8 It is written that John Carpenter Edson was sent by Compton Transport Technology to Bison Camp settlement group to install and test new equipment.

8:9 So it came to be that John Carpenter Edson trekked from the valley lowlands at Bison Camp up the traditional mountain path and paused near the ancient Tree of Zell, where he and his age-mates had spent so many hours overlooking the beauty of the valley.

8:10 In the shade of the Tree of Zell on Day 13, Week 2, Month 9, Solar Cycle 39, the wind swirled about John Carpenter Edson and spoke the words that changed the world forever.

Thus ends Section 8: Tracta Edson: Testimony of Franklor Nevston.

Tracta Edson Transcript Page 10

Section 9. The Charge

9:1 *Ijano Esantu Eleman.* As it was as in the beginning. According to tradition, John Carpenter Edson took walks in the early evening to clear his mind and his favorite destination was the pine forest, 3 kilo-miles north of Bison Camp settlement group.

9:2 In this pine forest near the great Tree of Zell, adjacent to the ruins of the unknown building destroyed during the Ripple Event, that the winds swirled and spoke to John Carpenter Edson.

9:3 The Overseer (may Its name always be blessed) caused the winds to swirl and spoke to John Carpenter Edson on Day 13, Week 2, Month 9, Solar Cycle 39.

9:4 It is written that the Overseer (may Its name always be blessed) spoke these words to John Carpenter Edson:

> *Ijano Esantu Eleman. I the universal Overseer charge you to be my administrator of crime and evil reduction. The power and responsibility is yours alone. Accept my offer without question and without comment!*

9:5   John Carpenter Edson, troubled by these words, trembled and
       spoke aloud saying:

       Who are you? Why are you speaking to me?

9:6   The Overseer (may Its name always be blessed) spoke again:

       *Ijano Esantu Eleman. As it was as in the beginning. I am I who
       always will be. Heed and obey my words. Accept my Charge
       without question and with commitment immediately!*

9:7   John Carpenter Edson knelt in reference and spoke:

       I am who I am; I accept the Charge without question.

Thus ends Section 9: Tracta Edson: Testimony of Franklor Nevston.

Tracta Edson Transcript Page 11

Section 10. Doubts and Reflections

10:1   *Ijano Esantu Eleman.* As it was as in the beginning. And so it was
       that John Carpenter Edson accepted the Overseer's charge and
       responsibility. As the administrator, he would wield power for
       three solar cycles. He alone would be responsible for reducing
       regional avarice, crime, and evil. He alone, in accord with the
       Charge, would determine who lived and who vanished.

10:2   Early in his task, John Carpenter Edson pondered questions arising
       from the Charge: should the population reductions be random
       or focused on specific individuals or groups? Should incidents of
       crime and evil be categorized and ranked by priorities? Should
       considerations of age, gender, locality, politics, or religion influence
       decisions to implement the Charge?

10:3   John Carpenter Edson, being thoughtful, realized that
       implementing the Charge would eliminate criminals and evildoers,
       but also leave behind and touch the lives of innocent family
       members.

10.4   It is written that after careful thought, John Carpenter Edson
       implemented the Charge by consideration of the parallel concept
       of Correct Balance: a weighing of the harm and pain caused by
       the criminals and evildoers to innocent individuals and family

members as a result of their actions vs. the harm and pain caused by disappearances of criminals and impacts on innocent family members.

10:5   John Carpenter Edson considered the balance of justice, but favored individuals and families harmed by the criminals over family members of the criminals.

10:6   And so it was that John Carpenter Edson, the administrator, set about the implementation of the Charge and Crime and Evil Reduction Program (CERP) as required by the Overseer (may Its name always be blessed).

Thus ends Section 10: Tracta Edson: Testimony of Franklor Nevston.

Tracta Edson Transcript Page 12

Section 11. Initial Disappearances

11:1   *Ijano Esantu Eleman*. As it was as in the beginning. And it came to be that John Carpenter Edson executed the first disappearances on Day 3, Week 4, Month 5, Solar Cycle 40.

11:2   John Carpenter Edson entered into the company of Montana State University long loop data collectors: Amber Barnes, Harmony Cole, Alden Johnson, Hunter Nelson, Ryan Ward, and Lottie Webb. The purpose of their trek was to retrieve germ plasma and viable agricultural seeds from the ruined campus of the University of California at Old Davis.

11:3   Upon arrival on the UC Davis campus, the data collector team was accosted by 10 armed men and women who demanded all their property and safety supplies. It has been reported that John Carpenter Edson spoke quietly to the band of robbers, asking that his team be allowed to depart the campus ruins in peace without harm.

11:4   *Ijano Esantu Eleman*. As it was as in the beginning. The robbers rejected the plea and wielding long knives advanced on John Carpenter Edson and his team and in an instant they vanished.

11:5   John Carpenter Edson spoke to his team members and requested allegiance and their vow that they would not report to anyone what they had seen or what had transpired.

11:6   On the return trek from UC Davis to Montana State University, John Carpenter Edson and the data collector team also were challenged by rampaging horse riders in the shattered zone southwest of New Elko on trade route Eye-80.

11:7   The horsemen demanded all goods inside the team's pushcarts.

11:8   *Ijano Esantu Eleman.* As it was as in the beginning. ♂ John Carpenter Edson looked at them and in an instant they disappeared.

11:9   John Carpenter Edson spoke again to his team members and, as before, asked them to swear that they would not repeat to anyone what they had observed.

11:10 The six data collectors who accompanied John Carpenter Edson became known as The Select Six (TSS).

11:11 One would break his vow of silence and betray John Carpenter Edson, the administrator.

Thus ends Section 11: Tracta Edson: Testimony of Franklor Nevston.

Tracta Edson Transcript Page 13

Section 12. The Early Years

12:1   *Ijano Esantu Eleman.* As it was as in the beginning. After initial implementation of the Charge in Old California, John Carpenter Edson directed the disappearance of 8,453 murderers and 35,792 thieves in east central NorthWest Configuration.

12:2   Thereafter followed disappearances of an alphabet of criminals and evildoers who had destroyed cultural harmony in the central mountainous regions of New NorthWest Configuration. Gone were arsonists, burglars, kidnappers, murderers, pickpockets, rapists, thieves, and vandals. They were no more. All vanished, leaving honest, moral hard-working residents at the regional settlement groups in peace.

12:3   Gone, too, were the gangs of thugs that once pillaged the shattered zones of New NorthWest Configuration during countless solar cycles.

12:4 Once emptied of criminals, the shattered zones became fertile areas for agricultural and economic development that allowed nearby settlement groups to expand their territories and live in safety.

12:5 The scum of society slowly disappeared through the focused mind of the administrator. Let us praise the wisdom of the Overseer (may Its name always be blessed) for issuing the Charge to John Carpenter Edson. May the administrator's work in cleansing evil and crime from the New NorthWest Configuration be remembered always.

Thus ends Section 12: Tracta Edson: Testimony of Franklor Nevston.

Tracta Edson Transcript Page 14

Section 13. Regional Expansion.

13:1 *Ijano Esantu Eleman.* As it was as in the beginning. The Charge was implemented successfully in New NorthWest Configuration. The administrator then expanded his work into New SouthWest, and eastward into the western districts of the Flatland Configurations.

13:2 Throughout Old California and the regions extending eastward toward the great river, cooperation among peoples became a reality, and harmony resumed.

13:3 Gone were the daily cycles of extortion and threats from gang bosses, extortionists, robbers, and murderers.

13:4 Gone were the turf wars, the assaults, beatings, and needless deaths that caused pain and sorrow in the once-great cities of El-A and SanFran.

13:5 Within the great former cities, residents emerged from their protective shelters into the sunlight of cooperation and harmony.

13:6 The evil that once characterized the shattered zones was no more.

13:7 No one understood how or why the disappearances were happening, only that fear of others no longer clouded their minds.

13:8 But not all was well.

Thus ends Section 13: Tracta Edson: Testimony of Franklor Nevston.

Section 14. Years of Fear and Rising Anger

14:1 *Ijano Esantu Eleman.* As it was as in the beginning. As crime and evildoing abated, residents of the settlement groups and the old towns and cities entered into what became known as the strange time: As the criminals and evildoers vanished, questions were asked: How was this happening?

14:2 Other questions were asked: What responsibilities, if any, did honest and law-abiding residents have to assist the innocent family members of criminals who disappeared? How should the criminal's worldly goods be distributed? What should be done with the ill-gained property and barter items obtained through illicit deals and activities?

14:3 Hard-working members of settlement groups asked repeatedly: Who should gain from the distribution of these items? Should it be relatives of the vanished or poverty-stricken families? Why should settlement group council members and government autocrats receive most of the recovered property and barter items?

14:4 For some, the disappearances came with the unsettling recognition that the vanishings were improper – that post-Dark Time individual and group rights were not being applied by the source or cause of the disappearances. Who would be accountable if mistakes were made, if innocents vanished by accident or mistake?

14:5 Residents of the western configurations were safe: But at what price? Mothers watched in horror when their unattended children stole bags of candy from local markets – vanished – never to reappear. They were thieves, but they also were children.

14:6 Fathers who used excessive force when punishing their sons for misbehavior vanished – never to reappear. Did not parents have the right to teach correct behavior and punish their children when basic rules were broken? But punishments were highly variable in different families. What was the dividing line between thoughtful punishment and excessive force?

14:7 Sales clerks who misentered price data into cash registers, either accidentally or on purpose, vanished – never to reappear. Were they thieves, or were they individuals who made basic mistakes?

14:8 Residents of the western configurations were safe from crime and evil, but at what price?

Tracta Edson Transcript Page 16

14:9 Police and protective units collected and analyzed the disappearance data but drew no conclusions – only that the events took place where there was a "commonality of crime and evil." Public security officers were overwhelmed by missing persons reports. There were no answers, no solutions to the mystery.

14:10 Inner-city populations within former crime-ridden territories recovered slowly but cautiously, not understanding how or why the evil had vanished. On the mind of everyone was a singular question: Who might be the next to vanish?

14:11 Life slowly changed. While crime essentially had been eliminated in many geographical regions, suspicion and fear grew among the general population. The fear grew slowly at first, and then paranoia swept across the western configurations of North America.

14:12 The administrator, aware of these concerns, went about the Charge and continued to determine who lived and who vanished. Life vs. death was in his hands, and his only. There were no checks and balances, no second thoughts, no explanations and excuses, no appeals, no second chances.

14:13 In their search for security, most individuals readopted the pre-Dark Time concept: *Do unto others as you would have them do unto you.* While daily life had changed for the better, free will and individual free choice vanished with the criminals and evildoers.

14:14 Not knowing what tomorrow might bring – whether life or death – families and clans of the settlement groups throughout the western configurations remained in states of perpetual doubt, fear, and uncertainty.

14:15 Building upon these fears there arose a group of revolutionaries, known as the New Order.

Thus ends Section 14: Tracta Edson: Testimony of Franklor Nevston.

Tracta Edson Transcript Page 17

Section 15. Origins and Rise of the New Order

15:1 *Ijano Esantu Eleman.* As it was as in the beginning. The basic tenets of the New Order originated and grew in the heart and soul of a pure young woman who loved nature, respected others, and practiced behaviors that harmed no one.

15:2 It is said that the first priestess of the New Order gathered around her like-thinking men and women who worshiped nature.

15:3 It is said that thousands accepted the New Order tenets because they had lost faith in the earlier orthodox religions that had been rejected during the Dark Time.

15:4 Some male initiates to the New Order, however, saw the cult as a means to advance their personal agendas.

15:5 And there came a time when a cabal of five men brought about a revolution within the New Order and usurped the original female-majority.

15:6 And it came to pass that the position of wise elderly first priestess was no more and the administrative power of the New Order shifted to a male.

15:7 He, First Priest Samuel The Select, through stealth and treachery removed the wise females and personally appointed a group of nine who instituted a radically different agenda.

15:8 Then it followed that the New Order shifted in structure and goals. Gone were the noble ideals of environmental protection as amassing personal wealth and power became priorities.

15:9 Gone from the New Order were the noble traits of the sage femmes, who knew the healing plants and soothed the worried and saddened. In their place arose a corrupt and dangerous cult with special warriors and teams of assassins used by Samuel The Select to remove detractors and track down defectors who challenged the revised goals of the New Order.

15:10 And it came to be that the hearts and souls of the New Order members once again became infiltrated with avarice, crime, and overwhelming desires for evil practices (may their names be denounced for all time).

Thus ends Section 15: Tracta Edson: Testimony of Franklor Nevston.

Tracta Edson Transcript Page 18

Section 16. The Administrator Identified

16:1 *Ijano Esantu Eleman.* As it was as in the beginning. And Samuel The Select, first priest of the New Order (may his name be denounced for all time), ordered all local New Order sections throughout New NorthWest and New SouthWest Configurations to identify watchers to note the names of individuals present at the scene of the disappearances.

16:2 Information from the New Order sections was summarized and analyzed for commonalities in descriptions of specific individuals, whether residents or visitors, and the names of thousands of suspects were collected.

16:3 And it became noted in one report that the disappearances were associated with data collectors from Montana State University, New Bozeman, and an outside adviser who accompanied the data collectors on a journey into Old California.

16:4 And it came to be that a specific individual, John Carpenter Edson, was on a list of potential suspects.

16:5 Samuel The Select, first priest of the New Order (may his name be denounced for all time), assigned watchers to carefully monitor the data collector historical teams, but this effort proved fruitless.

16:6 At the same time, Samuel The Select, first priest of the New Order (may his name be denounced for all time) assigned other watchers to monitor the families and work habits of more than 100 individuals, including John Carpenter Edson, and to report their travel-related activities and disappearance correlations.

16:7 And it came to pass that the administrator visited Three Rivers settlement group near Three Forks, Old Montana, and encountered two thieves assaulting and beating a store owner and fleeing with bags of ill-gotten gains. As the Charge was implemented and the thieves disappeared, John Carpenter Edson was watched from afar and the event noted.

16:8 The watchers reported their observations to the Three Rivers chapter of the New Order assembly, and the information was passed on to Samuel The Select, first priest of the New Order (may his name be denounced for all time) and his council.

Thus ends Section16: Tracta Edson: Testimony of Franklor Nevston.

Tracta Edson Transcript Page 19

Section 17. New Order Assassination Decision

17:1 *Ijano Esantu Eleman.* As it was as in the beginning. Samuel The Select, first priest of the New Order (may his name be denounced for all time) assembled his committee members who approved and signed the assassination order.

17.2 The document assigned assassination responsibility to New Order Group IV at Forest Shelter settlement group, New NorthWest Configuration, and called for the action plan to be completed within seven days.

(NOTE ADDED IN MARGIN: I, Franklor Nevston, certify that I have seen this assassination order and it is deposited in a protected archive file, located in the Montana State University History Project archives, Box: A-48-Group IV-2b.)

17:3 The assassin chosen to implement the deed was Brody Taylor (may his name be denounced for all time), selected for his stealth and technical skills in preparation of undetectable explosive materials.

17:4 Samuel The Select, first priest of the New Order (may his name be denounced for all time) met with assassin select Brody Taylor (may his name be denounced for all time) on Day 4, Week 1, Month 5, Solar Cycle 41.

17:5 Samuel The Select, first priest of the New Order (may his name be denounced for all time) lay hands upon Brody Taylor (may his name be denounced for all time) confirming his blessing of the upcoming event and praising the self-sacrifice of the appointed assassin.

17:6 Since the assassination plan included the death of Brody Taylor (may his name be denounced for all time), the New Order Central Council approved the distribution of 27 metal wealth bars, 56 bags of salt, and four horses to be given to the assassin's family, then living at Forest Shelter settlement group.

Thus ends Section 17: Tracta Edson: Testimony of Franklor Nevston.

Tracta Edson Transcript Page 20

Section 18. Assassination of the Administrator

18:1 *Ijano Esantu Eleman.* As it was as in the beginning. May all people with good hearts pause in sadness to recall the assassination of the administrator, John Carpenter Edson.

18:2 The assassination of the administrator occurred on Day 7, Week 5, Month 8, Solar Cycle 42, inside the New NorthWest Regional Court building where John Carpenter Edson had been invited to present his report to the Poverty Reduction Committee of the regional government, New NorthWest Configuration.

18:3 As John Carpenter Edson finished his testimony and left the hearing room, he descended the rotunda staircase. Midway down the stairs, he was hailed by a young male who appeared to be a New Order priest, as he was dressed in their traditional white robes with the Circle N-Omega emblem that characterized their cult.

18:4 It was reported by onlookers who survived that day that the two engaged in light conversation as they descended the staircase together.

18:5 Upon reaching the landing, John Carpenter Edson turned away from the young man and began to engage the social media reporters and visitors.

18:6 As he started to answer questions, the assassin reached out and embraced John Carpenter Edson and shouted, "Death to the administrator," then detonated his suicide vest.

18:7 Subsequent investigations could not readily identify the assassin's name. The name that emerged later (Brody Taylor) ultimately was confirmed and re-confirmed through several regional investigations (may the name Brody Taylor be denounced for all time).

18:8 The blast that killed the administrator also killed 35 innocent bystanders. (Some accounts list the number of innocents slain at 28). An additional 46 were wounded, although other accounts list the number of innocents harmed but who survived as 37.

18:9 A special place on the western wall of the rotunda was reserved for names of the martyrs killed and wounded that day, but until now it remains blank as the names and numbers are controversial and cannot be confirmed.

Thus ends Section 18: Tracta Edson: Testimony of Franklor Nevston.

Tracta Edson Transcript Page 21

Section 19. Aftermath and Subsequent Events

19:1 *Ijano Esantu Eleman.* As it was as in the beginning. How can it be that such an event occurred? How can it be that such evil lurks in the minds and hearts of some? How can it be that evil triumphs over good and darkens the mind?

19:2 In the days, weeks, months, and solar cycles that followed the assassination of John Carpenter Edson, anarchy and chaos arose once again and to levels not previously seen or anticipated.

19:3 Coinciding with the personal rise of avarice, crime, and evil was the domination of the New Order cultists at the majority of settlement groups in New NorthWest and New SouthWest Configurations.

19:4 Gone were the concepts inherent in the Noble Seven that had facilitated survival through the Dark Time into the post-Dark Time recovery period. Gone were the concepts inherent in the Great Septet that had guided behavior during these difficult times:

1. *Aid the weak and helpless;*
2. *Treat women and men equally;*
3. *Appreciate differences;*
4. *Reject behaviors that degrade or harm others;*
5. *Welcome each newborn to the family hearth;*
6. *Respect and honor your mating partner;*
7. *Celebrate those who help you through life's passages.*

19:5 With abandonment of the Noble Seven evolved a parallel set of concepts composed by Samuel The Select, first priest of the New Order (may his name be denounced for all time), selfish concepts that attracted many and accelerated the resumption of crime and evil as supported by the New Order:

316

1. *Those in poverty deserve to be;*
2. *Genders are not equal; men rule – women serve;*
3. *Differences reflect weakness;*
4. *What I have is mine, not to be shared with others;*
5. *Not all infants should live;*
6. *Respect men as the dominant beings;*
7. *I am who I am through only my efforts.*

Tracta Edson Transcript Page 22

19:6 With the return to avarice, crime, and evil magnified, there arose within the once great cities of North America – cities that once had been cleansed of criminals, gangs, and ruthless individuals – new systems of sexual slavery and trade in life. Both El-A and SanFran, once able and workable cities prior to the Ripple Event and Dark Days, then hotbeds of crime and evil during the Dark Days, and then cleansed by the administrator, became known as New Sodom and New Gomorrah, as if the titles applied were something to be admired.

19:7 And there arose at the same time a rebellion fostered by many settlement groups that turned away from the New Order and sought a return to the noble behaviors that had eroded away and been forgotten during the post-assassination solar cycles.

19:8 Some settlement groups that overthrew and evicted the New Order priests and their followers, forcing them out, became Islets of Honor (IoH) where other like-thinkers could find peace, solitude, and joy working and living among honorable people, as the remainder of the western configurations of North America descended into even more anarchy and chaos.

Thus ends Section 19: Tracta Edson: Testimony of Franklor Nevston.

Tracta Edson Transcript Page 23

Section 20. *Ijano Esantu Eleman* (as it was as in the beginning)

20:1 *Ijano Esantu Eleman*. As it was as in the beginning. The Islets of Honor became thorns in the sides of the New Order priests. Jensdeed of New Marin, first priest of the New Order and successor to Samuel The Select (may their names be denounced for all time), ordered representatives of the New Order warrior contingents to draw up attack plans to subdue the Islets of Honor that continued to develop throughout the Western North American Configurations.

20:2 As some settlement group advisory councils adopted more of the belief system and practices of the New Order priests, other residents left the confines of their once-safe and secure settlement groups and defected in groups across the former scattered zones to seek sanctuary and protection within an Islet of Honor.

20:3 And it came to be that on Day 1, Week 4, Month 4, Solar Cycle 45, that Jensdeed of New Marin, new first priest of the New Order (may his name be denounced for all time) ordered united attacks on the IoHs by the warrior contingents of the New Order.

20:4 One by one the Islets of Honor fell under these sustained military attacks. One by one they disappeared, their members brutally slain by teams of misguided New Order warriors, who supported the corrupt belief system imposed by Jensdeed of New Marin, first priest of the New Order (may his name be denounced for all time).

20:5 And it came about during solar cycle 49 the last long loop Trek of data collectors from Montana State University would venture into the far west lands near the outlet of the Mattole River to revisit one of the Islets of Honor, the famous Red-Wood settlement group, where a large contingent of elderly lived. Their purpose was to record stories about how North America had changed since before the Ripple Event of long ago. These data collectors have not returned, and we anxiously await their findings.

Thus ends Section 20: Tracta Edson: Testimony of Franklor Nevston.

After-Word

This is what I know; this is what I have told you.

I, Franklor Nevston, reciter, offered testimony to the best of my memory. I knew John Carpenter Edson better than most, for we bonded together during his earliest years at Bison Camp Settlement Group, and we grew and matured together.

I, Franklor Nevston, reciter, fear the present time and the coming days. I sense that with the return and full manifestation of evil exemplified in the New Order that we are doomed. I fear that with assassination of the administrator, and the events that have taken place subsequently – especially the military attacks on the Islets of Honor – that we have reverted to actions and behaviors that characterized individuals and families during the days prior to the Ripple Event.

I, Franklor Nevston, reciter, evoke the protection of the Overseer (may Its name always be blessed) to bring hope once again to the few of us who remain, the few of us who are responsible, hard-working, caring people. Let not our hearts become immune to the needs of others; let there be justice once more. Thank you for inviting me to recite the sections of the Tracta Edison to you. May our hearts and actions circumvent the evils of the New Order. May we erase what has happened during the last several solar cycles.

May we return to the qualities and justice inherent in the Great Septet, the Great Seven.

May we return to the positive actions and behaviors that once characterized our cultures.

Metal Sheet #13

Inscription and Translation

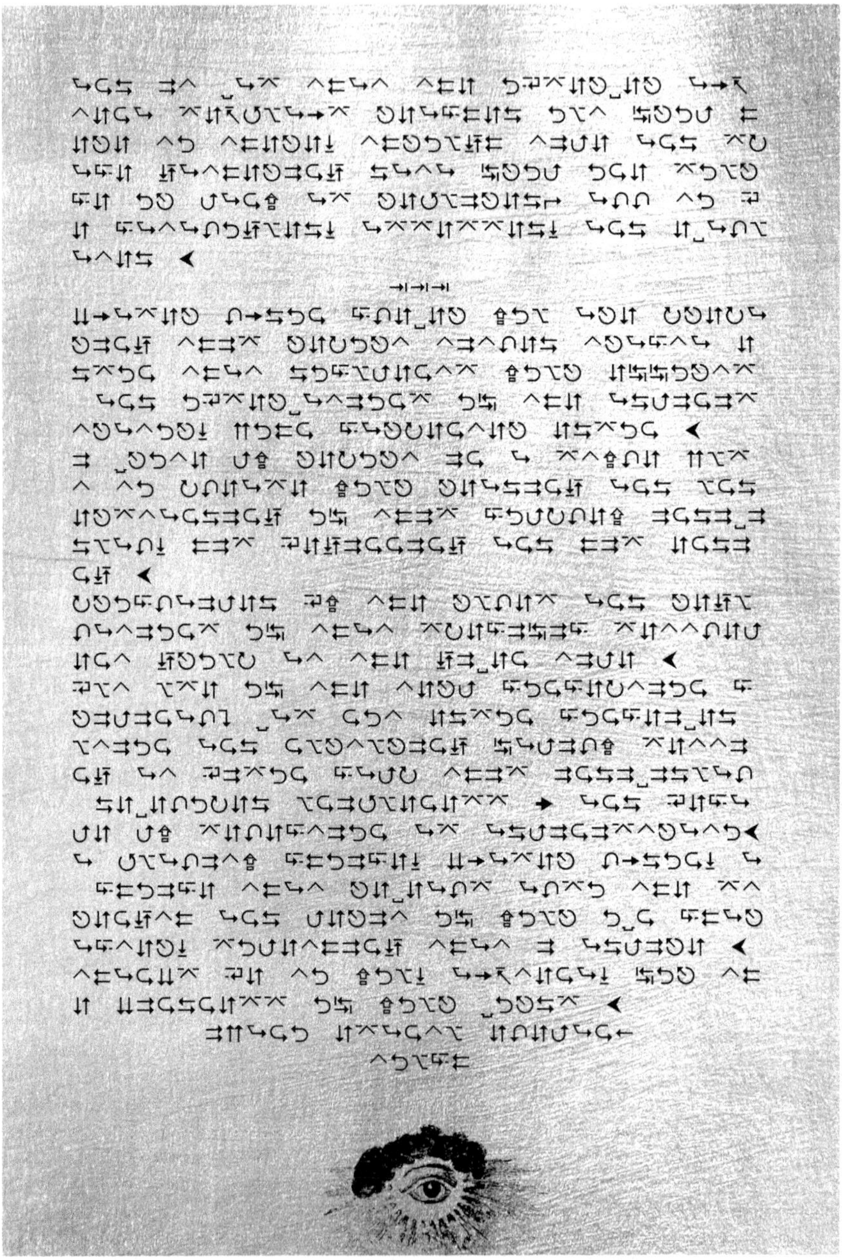

And it was that the Observer A'-Tena Se-Qua reached out from here to there, through time and space, gathering data from one source or many as required; all to be catalogued, assessed, and evaluated.

* * *

K'Aser L'Don, clever you are preparing this report titled Tracta Edson *that documents your efforts and observations of the administrator, John Carpenter Edson.*

I wrote my report in a style just to please your reading and understanding of this complex individual, his beginning, and his ending.

Was not the trial and execution of Edson's parents a reflection of the harshness that these social groups show during times of challenge?

No, A'-Tena, the accusation and trial were conducted with speed as proclaimed by the rules and regulations of that specific settlement group at the given time.

But use of the term conception criminal? Was not Edson conceived by the mating action of two units during an act of love and affection in response to the death of their infant child earlier?

True you say, A'-Tena, but the law was broken and Edson's parents knew they had erred.

The redistribution of Edson to a childless couple, an admirable action written into law of the time, was it not?

To be true, A'-Tena, and through the process of Edson's redistribution and nurturing family setting at Bison Camp, this individual developed uniqueness – and became my selection as administrator.

A quality choice, K'Aser L'Don, a choice that reveals also the strength and merit of your own character, something that I admire.

Thanks be to you, A'-Tena, for the kindness of your words.

Ijano Esantu Eleman!

CHAPTER 15: EVENING READING 15

Document 15, Cave Location: Case 43-B

Ijano Esantu Eleman

As It Was In The Beginning

The sinuous snake of duality
Twisting and turning throughout life
Hisssssptah dona hissssptah
Slithering here and slithering there
The sinuous snake of duality
Hydah Ho!

Raindrops of promise
Whirlwinds of anger
Hissssptah dona hissssptah
Individual duality ever ageless
Goodness and evil in every individual
Hyada Ho!

The dawn of glory arises
The noon of despair follows
Hisssssptah dona hisssssptah
The evening of wonder is welcomed
The snake strikes
Hydah Ho!

Joyful cries of a newborn
Painful screams of the tortured
Hisssssptah dona hisssssptah
Tender smiles of a mother
A knife raised to kill
Hydah Ho!

Minds of innocent infants
Become twisted with age
Hisssssptah dona hisssssptah
Hands of generous individuals
Become killing claws
Hydah Ho!

The sinuous snake of duality
Twisting and turning throughout life
Hisssssptah dona hisssssptah
Slithering here and slithering there
The sinuous snake of duality
Hydah Ho!

(Source: White Antelope Chant, MSU History Archive. File: 39-G-13.)

Pre-Note

The days following the assassination of John Carpenter Edson at Butte, Old Montana, seemed just like any of the previous two years. Most local residents went about their business initially unaware of the suicide bomb attack, the death of Edson and his assassin, and the murder of 28 others. As the terrible news became widely known, fear of additional imminent attacks on the population spread through the regional administrative center. Who was this man – John Carpenter Edson – and why was he targeted for death? The residents of Bison Camp who knew him pondered the news. In their eyes he was seen only as a kind, caring man with a fine family.

Who was the suicide bomber? Why had he undertaken such a terrible deed? There had been no previous uncivil behavior at the Regional Justice Office, so why would there have been a need for tight security? The concept of collateral damage – the death and wounding of innocent bystanders – struck most residents as essential evil, and was a topic only faintly remembered by a few elderly residents at the different settlement groups, a phrase that dated to the unsettled times of madness prior to the Ripple Event. Why had these murders taken place at this time, especially since crime and evildoing had been almost eliminated during the recent solar cycles?

There were no answers – initially.

Sanders Johnson, Assistant Archivist, MSU History Project
Commentary: Assassination of John Carpenter Edson and Aftermath
Date: Uncertain

After the administrator was assassinated, lightning of two types struck the enclaves of New NorthWest and New SouthWest Configurations. Thousands of hectare-acres of wild forestlands within the shattered zones were ignited during a series of unseasonal thunderstorms that lasted for more than three weeks. Numerous residents from nearby settlement groups were forced to evacuate their secure settings as raging walls of fire destroyed equipment, homes, livestock, and supplies.

Some individuals sought safety on the islands in nearby lakes where they were secure for several weeks, making do with sufficient water and limited food obtained by fishing. After the local fires had burned out, the residents returned to their settlement groups and entered near total destruction. Some salvaged pieces of survival equipment, but most lost everything that they had nurtured and stored during the post-Dark Time recovery period.

Immediately after the assassination the New Order Administrative Council met at their headquarters in Butte, Old Montana. A full transcription of that secret meeting has survived and can be viewed at the MSU History Project Archive, File: 37-NG-139c. Included here are summary transcripts from that document:

Statement: Samuel Evans (Samuel The Select), First Priest

To you who have assembled, I can report that it is done. Through your careful efforts and hard work we identified the key individual and took steps to protect our order.

(Hear – Hear!)

It is my joy to explain to you the events of the past few days. What is said in our communal meeting is for us alone, and never to be discussed with anyone outside the order.

(Hear – Hear!)

Our watchers and information analysts are to be congratulated and also our Militia Chief Leland Jackson, who recruited Brody Taylor who accepted the task and completed the work without second thought, because he believed in the goals and objectives of the New Order. Give praise to Brody Taylor!

(Hear – Hear!)

Again, give praise to Brody Taylor!

(Hear – Hear!)

My task today is to set into motion the reinfiltration of the first 25 settlement groups, all within New NorthWest Configuration, and to develop plans for expansion of our efforts within the settlement groups located in New SouthWest and Flatland Configurations.

(Hear – Hear!)

Statement: Enoch Samuelson, New Order Chief Educator

My team has recruited at least one senior educator from an initial list of 72 settlement groups. Each of these senior educators has the task of recruiting the majority of current teachers at each settlement group, especially those responsible for early childhood education, and to restart the process once more of realigning classroom activities to be in accord with recently adopted New Order teaching modules approved at our last administrative meeting.

Statement: Itred Samuelson, New Order Chief Political Advisor

My team has prepared, for review and adoption by our central committee, a plan whereby New Order objectives can be retargeted toward the adult residents of settlement groups. Our plan, the result of two years of subcommittee meetings and discussions, presents a logical pathway whereby New Order goals and objectives can be adopted as critical components for settlement group survival during periods of economic, environmental, and political complexities. I ask that you, members of the

Administrative Committee of the New Order, place our document under consideration, review the structure and pathways for implementation, and bring the document forward for a council consideration and vote at our next meeting. I believe you will be pleased to see how our New Order objectives can be integrated into adult lifestyles and activities, and ultimately our efforts will be adopted as amendments to various settlement group constitutions.

Gone were the concepts inherent in the Noble Seven that had facilitated individual and family survival through the Dark Time into the post-Dark Time recovery period.

Gone were the concepts inherent in the Great Septet that once guided social behavior:

Aid the weak and helpless;

Treat women and men equally;

Appreciate differences;

Reject behaviors that degrade or harm others;

Welcome each newborn to the family hearth;

Respect and honor your mating partner;

Celebrate those who help you through life's passages.

What Samuel The Select and the New Order educators and proselytizers reaffirmed and implemented during the solar cycles that followed the assassination of John Carpenter Edson was a return to old concepts that once characterized activities and behaviors before the Ripple Event and onset of Dark Times.

A new list of underlying precepts of the New Order, a New Septet, soon spread across the New West Configurations:

Why work when there is so much free stuff!

If you don't give it, I'll take it!

You owe it to me!

I want my share!

Why barter for goods; just steal them!

You have too much – give me part!

You blame me for being poor – I blame you for being rich!

The concept *I am who I am through my own hard work with the encouragement and help of others* was lost as New Order tenets and values seeped into the administrative structures of the settlement groups.

Administrative Changes at Selected Settlement Groups

Adoption of the revised New Order tenets was seen by some settlement group administrative councils as beliefs that would support the continuation of their administrative rule. The New Order administrators provided technical and emotional support for those individuals who had lost everything in the August sweep of forest fires. But while listening and ultimately adopting the tenets, those who accepted the new belief system took the short view and did not question the rationale and structure behind the new administrative systems.

Return to Avarice, Crime, and Evil

As the New Order continued to flourish and gain support, their gains were accompanied by a parallel rise in crime and misbehavior throughout the western configurations. As more and more settlement groups adopted the revised tenets of the New Order and abandoned the Noble Seven – the Great Septet – the once cohesive values that had characterized the settlement groups during the Dark Time and early years of the post-Dark Time recovery periods slowly eroded and gave way to a return of avarice, crime, and evil.

The once-great cities of Los Angeles and San Francisco that had collapsed during the Ripple Event had been cleansed by the administrator. A renaissance of activity had begun to take place in both these once-great cities. After the assassination of John Carpenter Edson, however, both cities returned to squalor and violence. New gangs arose as city-dwellers exhibited violence to the extent and level not previously seen as the gangs developed new weapons to protect and enforce rule within their prescribed territories.

An immoral truism emerged: not being in a gang was more dangerous than being a member.

The once-great cities through time became worse than their predecessors, El-A and SanFran. The new urban areas were little different from the ancient biblical sites of Sodom and Gomorrah. Gender slavery of the weak and forced prostitution became the norm. Extortion, theft, and murder became everyday events. Power-to-the-people had become power-to-a-few and danger to anyone who disagreed with gang leaders.

Those who wished for calm and peace remained quiet, lest their voices result in beatings and executions. Still, those who wished for the earlier times of cooperation developed signals, hand signs flashed to others on the street that seemed to the non-informed just to be arms and hands waving innocently, but to those of similar views were symbols that allowed peace groups to expand their members. Carefully and cautiously, like thinkers began to draw images and graffiti in areas not dominated by gangs and drug lords. One message took the form of the outline of a stylized hand accompanied by the number and letter combination H-2-H. To the uninitiated, they meant nothing; to those who drew the symbols, the graffiti images were clear and easily understood – the hand represented unity of purpose, and the H-2-H represented the two Hs of hope and honor!

H – 2 – H

Exodus and Formation of the Islets of Honor

Silently and without fanfare, the rhetoric and revised tenets of the New Order were countered by three independent thinkers, known initially only by their code names: Bear (Logan Potter), Lynx (Joshua Braniff), and Wolf (Roberto Cruz). The three originally were members of Protective Shield settlement group. When addressed by others at the settlement, they were soft-spoken but firm in their belief that the rise in crime and evil was in part due to the expansion of the New Order and the cult's involvement with the administrative and judicial systems at the various settlement groups.

Shortly after the summer solstice during solar cycle 43, they left Protective Shield settlement group at different times for individual treks in different directions to spread the word about an alternative approach to New Order dictates that were receiving widespread acceptance at regional settlement groups. Bear trekked northwest toward New Seattle, Lynx had the difficult assignment of spreading the word at SanFan, while Wolf volunteered to go to El-A.

During the next two solar cycles, word of potential alternative approaches to settlement organization spread widely. But the effort was not without considerable pain and suffering. Both Lynx and Wolf were successful in recruiting members to their view at New Sodom and New Gomorrah. But despite taking care to conceal their presence and attempts to evade detection, both were captured and presumably suffered terribly under interrogation by the gang leaders at SanFran and El-A. Their bodies never were found, and it is presumed that they were dumped into the El-A River and in San Francisco Bay, respectively. Bear, however, was successful in evading capture and after recruitment activities in New Seattle, made his way south through Old Washington State into Old Oregon.

Once inside the boundaries of Old Oregon, along the banks of Rock Creek, north of Vernonia, Bear (now known openly as Logan Potter) established the first Islet of Honor (IoH), which he called Rock Creek, an alternative type of collective settlement, one that had as its foundation motto:

Unum colligens spes et honor (A gathering of hope and honor).

Word rapidly spread throughout New NorthWest and New SouthWest Configurations that new settlements were being formed to accommodate those who disliked or distrusted the New Order dictates implemented by administrative councils at the traditional settlement groups. The Rock Creek IoH soon filled to capacity, as single men and women, as well as family groups, left their original settlement groups over administrative disagreements and forced adherence to the New Order tenets.

Within the first solar cycle after construction of Rock Creek IoH, others sprang up as alternative settlements throughout the western configurations. The departure of a few disgruntled settlement group members – even those with key occupational and survival skill sets – initially did not pose a threat to any of the well-established settlement groups and was seen by the New Order hierarchy and settlement administrative councils as short-term problems. By the middle of solar cycle 44, however, the exodus of disgruntled settlement members who wished to leave and take up residence became a flood, and the New Order saw a problem that had to be solved and stopped – by force, if necessary.

Crushing the Islets of Honor

It was at this time that the military arm of the New Order ousted First Priest Samuel The Select, and installed Jensdeed of New Marin, a man without morals or intellect, who could be controlled by the New Order military. The key leaders of the militia, known only by their rank and serial numbers, ordered Jensdeed to mobilize. The basic plan was to destroy one IoH, execute their members, thereby sending a message to the others that in order to survive they must reorganize their administrative councils and recognize New Order control.

The decision was made to attack and obliterate an IoH located northwest of New Redding, Old California, along the Sacramento River. The plan was for priests of the New Order to approach this Islet of Honor known as Keswick's Rest, and appear to enter into negotiations with the IoH's newly elected administrative council. Negotiating and discussing the key matters of disagreement was a delaying tactic to allow time for the New Order militia to assemble, restock their supplies of potassium nitrate, and manufacture sufficient kilo-pounds of explosives to destroy Keswick's Rest.

The Administrative Council of Keswick's Rest agreed to negotiations, thinking that talking was better than conflict, a naïve view as it turned out. Time was on the side of the New Order militia. As talks dragged on and became encumbered in philosophical debates over individual rights, and then focused more and more on trivial details, quantities of explosives manufactured at supportive settlement groups and transported to the militia encampment south of Shasta Lake became more than sufficient to level Keswick's Rest IoH.

When all was in place, the New Order negotiators withdrew from Keswick's Rest, leaving behind a joyful group of residents who thought that they had achieved agreement for their religious and economic independence from the New Order and assurances that they would be left alone.

But it was not to be.

Before dawn on the early morning of Day 1, Week 4, Month 4, Solar Cycle 45, the New Order militia overcame the sentries and entered Keswick's Rest IoH. The invaders planted explosives at all key buildings, storage areas, and residential complexes and then retreated. The signal was given and the explosives detonated, leveling Keswick's Rest and killing all but 15 members of the IoH.

This was a pattern that would be repeated more than 52 times during solar cycle 45, until nearly all the Islets of Hope had been obliterated. Dissent would not be tolerated; the preaching and tenets of the New Order would be followed. What once had characterized individuals and families, the goodness and qualities of respect and tolerance, these lights had been extinguished.

Death and Memory of Sister Sapha Stone

During autumn of solar cycle 45, militia members of the New Order turned their attention to Bison Camp, one of the key settlement groups that resisted their political takeover. During the New Order attack and siege, Sapha Stone was wounded seriously and subsequently died. Her triplet sisters, Cishqhale and Yuhushi, had died previously, leaving Sapha as the last survivor of the original settlers that had founded Bison Camp shortly after the Ripple Event.

The eulogy chanted at the pyre ceremony to commemorate her departure touched those attending, and was celebrated with kind words and chants. The important events of Sapha's life were recalled, especially how she had taught hundreds of young girls and boys how to determine which wild plants were edible or toxic, who in turn taught hundreds more how to identify key medicinal barks, leaves, and roots. Through her generous sharing of ethnobotanical knowledge, Sapha was responsible for tens of thousands of lives.

News of her death spread rapidly throughout New NorthWest and New SouthWest Configurations, where parallel departure ceremonies were held in Sapha's honor. Transcriptions of chants prepared in her honor ultimately found their place in the Montana State University History Project archives, among them:

> *You taught us well of nature's ways*
> *The lives you saved lived on more years*
> *The wind will always bear your name*
> *Listen as it calls you home*
> *Sapha – Sapha – Sapha – Sapha*

(Chanted at Antelope Plains settlement group, Central Old Montana)

> *We your students – you our teacher*
> *Bound together two as one*
> *Across the shattered zones we trekked*
> *Learning, ever learning from you – Sapha.*

(Chanted at River Crossing settlement group, Central Old Montana)

Sapha – Hydah Haya – Sapha
Look to the mountains
Sapha – Hydah Haya – Sapha
Look to the valleys
Sapha – Hydah Haya – Sapha
Green the leaves of healing plants
Sapha – Hydah Haya – Sapha
Dark the roots of healing plants
Sapha – Hydah Haya – Sapha
You learned them each
Sapha – Hydah Haya – Sapha
You taught us well
Sapha – Hydah Haya – Sapha
We forget you not
Sapha – Hydah Haya – Sapha

(Chanted at Salmon Run settlement group, Western Old Oregon)

* * *

We stand in honor of you – Sapha
You tended us throughout the night
And into morning when we ailed
Sapha – our healer – extending life

(Chanted at Shasta Security settlement group, North Central Old California)

* * *

To the far off distant place you go
Born upon the wings of eagles
Soaring 'cross the vast-land prairies
Where once you trod – Sapha
You taught ten thousand students well
To seek and find the healing plants
The leaves and roots that cheated death
We learned from you – Sapha
The unbelievers watched your work
And then believed your art and skill
Sapha – greatest of all sage femmes
Always remembered – Sapha.

(Chanted at Three Rivers settlement group, Southwestern Old Montana)

Long ago three sisters trekked across the lands to where we stand
Sapha, Yuhushi, and Cishqhale, now together once again.
Sapha – you taught us well
Sapha – you stood for justice
Sapha – you stood for equality
Sapha – the righteous
No one like you there was before
No one like you there 'er will be
Forever in our hearts you'll be
Always in our memories
Long ago three sisters trekked across the lands to where we stand
Sapha, Yuhushi, and Cishqhale, now together once again.

(Chanted at Bison Camp settlement group, South Central Old Montana)

During the memorial recitation honoring Sapha at Bison Camp, Chief Reciter Franklin Thompson rose and addressed the assembly. He asked the adult women who had borne children to stand. Looking out over the assembly, he raised his right hand in solemn tribute and spoke:

How many of you women attending tonight remember the birth chant that Sapha created for you to recite during your labor? Remember how the gentle words of Sapha eased your worry and pain? Remember the passages that spoke of love and care for your newborn? Women who have borne children, please stand – recite the words Sapha taught you. Chant them now in her honor.

Hydah Ho! Hydah Hydah! Haya Ho!
Plant the seed of life inside me

Hydah Ho! Hydah Hydah! Haya Ho!
Ever growing through my time

Hydah Ho! Hydah Hydah! Haya Ho!
Faint your heartbeat stirs inside me

Hydah Ho! Hydah Hydah! Haya Ho!
Stronger through each passing day.

Mydah Ho! Mydah Mydah! Maya Ho!
Three months three I felt you growing

Mydah Ho! Mydah Mydah! Maya Ho
Six months six you twist and turn

Mydah Ho! Mydah Mydah! Maya Ho!
Nine months nine your passage starts

Mydah Ho! Mydah Mydah! Maya Ho!
Your time is now for to emerge.

Omdah Ho! Omdah Omdah! Omda Ho!
You push and struggle – sliding slowly

Omdah Ho! Omdah Omdah! Omda Ho!
You reach the entrance to my gate

Omdah Ho! Omdah Omdah! Omda Ho!
You push and struggle – harder, harder

Omdah Ho! Omdah Omdah! Omda Ho!
My gate now opens to the light.

Rydah Ho! Rydah Rydah! Ryda Ho!
Push now through my gate of life

Rydah Ho! Rydah Rydah! Ryda Ho!
Through my gate your crown appears

Rydah Ho! Rydah Rydah! Ryda Ho!
Gasp your first breath – cry in joy

Rydah Ho! Rydah Rydah! Ryda Ho!
Welcome to your day of birth.

Dydah Ho! Dydah Dydah! Daya Ho!
Blade of stone cuts through your cord

Dydah Ho! Dydah Dydah! Daya Ho!
Blood of birth still stains your face

Dydah Ho! Dydah Dydah! Daya Ho!
Eyes now open greet the sunshine

Dydah Ho! Dydah Dydah! Daya Ho!
Welcome to your day of birth.

Tydah Ho! Tydah Tydah! Taya Ho!
Now you lay upon my belly

Tydah Ho! Tydah Tydah! Taya Ho!
Tiny hands now meshed with mine

Tydah Ho! Tydah Tydah! Taya Ho!
I count your fingers, toes, and ears

Tydah Ho! Tydah Tydah! Taya Ho!
The sacred number twenty-two are they.

Hydah Ho! Hydah Hydah! Haya Ho!
In years to come what will you be

Hydah Ho! Hydah Hydah! Haya Ho!
Daughters-sons conceived in love

Hydah Ho! Hydah Hydah! Haya Ho!
Building now a family

Hydah Ho! Hydah Hydah! Haya Ho!
The strongest bond eternally.

Hydah Ho! Hydah Hydah! Haya Ho!
(shout out again!)

Hydah Ho! Hydah Hydah! Haya Ho!
(again and again, louder!)

Hydah Ho! Hydah Hydah! Haya Ho!
(again and again and again, louder!)

Haya Ho! Entempeah!

At the conclusion of the women's chant, the assembly was enveloped in an eerie silence as the shouted last words – *Haya Ho! Entempeah!* – echoed through forests of pine that surrounded Bison Camp settlement group. The men and children stood to join the adult women, and together the assembled members of Bison Camp shouted farewell to Sapha:

Haya Ho! Entempeah!

Invasion: Military Clash with New Confederacy Raiders

But the pain and uncertainty posed by the New Order was just the beginning of more difficulties.

Out along the eastern portions of New NorthWest Configuration a new danger arose, one that posed serious threat equal to that of the New Order.

As the settlement groups began their realignment, depending upon their degree of allegiance to the New Order, this new serious problem developed along the geographical zone that stretched east of the Rocky Mountains near the abandoned towns of Fort Collins and Greeley in the eastern Old Colorado region of the New NorthWest Configuration.

Scouts on patrol from Plains Sanctuary settlement group observed that a contingent of mounted horsemen numbering some 200 to 250 adult men had advanced westward through the shattered zone and were approaching the settlement. The intruders were supported by wagons carrying supplies and what looked like advanced weapons of a kind not before seen by the scouts. The advancing group was described as wearing wide-brimmed hats with what appeared to be nineteenth-century pre-Dark Time Confederate insignias. The group was multiracial: two tall, powerfully built soldiers, one Black and one White, led the van.

Upon receiving the scouts' report, Jensen Bowman, chief of security at Plains Sanctuary, sent an armed emissary group of six men to discover the intruders' intent. Two of the emissaries rode ahead of the others and immediately were fired on and slain. The remaining emissaries quickly retreated and informed the council.

Warning signals immediately were relayed to the nearby Three Rivers and River Crossing settlement groups and to the Pawnee Nation cluster occupying the nearby shattered zone. The messages were to initiate the defense plans for an armed attack that was imminent. Plains Sanctuary assembled their warrior age sets in preparation for an attack and potential siege.

The horsemen advanced toward the settlement group and paused some 200 yards from the stockade gate. According to post-battle accounts, they sent out two members of their group under a white flag to present their demands:

> We will not attack your settlement and you will survive if you immediately state your allegiance to the New Confederacy. Upon agreement, a treaty will be drawn up to include exchange of populations, economic trade, and sharing of new technology. Deny our offer and we will exterminate your settlement and drive your surviving residents into the shattered zone.

> Be warned!

> We have marched westward hundreds of kilo-miles from our homeland, crossed the great river into the Flatlands. Along the way of our advance, we have brought into our fold 38 settlement groups encountered. We also erased from existence another 17 settlement groups who rejected our demands and elected to fight. We attacked those settlements, burned and destroyed them, and any members who survived were dispersed throughout the shattered zones that surrounded their lands.

Be warned!

We want you as trade partners – but only under our allegiance and administration.

We await your decision.

Battle of South Platte River

The Battle of South Platte River took place on Day 3, Week 4, Month 7, Solar Cycle 46. As the New Confederacy intruders milled about on horseback awaiting the decision from the settlement group defenders, they did not observe that a group of Pawnee stealth fighters (especially trained warriors) had circled behind them from the northeast. Sharitarish, the third, great, great grandson of Sharitarish the elder, ordered his Pawnee fighters known locally as Teo-Km-Lankum or New Braves to set sagebrush afire northwest of where the invading raiders had paused. Using a supply of old truck flares, the young men set fire to the dry brush. At the same time, the Pawnee spiritual leader, Gomda Kuruk (Wind Bear), called down dust-devils from the sky that descended in a broad arc behind the milling raiders, forming a swirling pattern of flames pushing southeast.

The raiders seemed confused as they now were under assault on two fronts. The raider leaders ordered an initial attack on Plains Settlement but were repulsed. As the group turned their horses away from the settlement, they faced the flames and wind that continued to rise in ferocity. The attackers then were forced by the brush fire toward the brink of the Platte River cliff, an angular steep descent of some 150 meter-yards down to the riverbank. The Teo-Km-Lankum raced ahead farther east and ignited more brush, cutting off all retreat. The raiders were left with only two options: death by raging wildfire or death by plunging down the cliff face onto the rocks below.

In a terrible mix of screaming and churning hooves, the raiders retreated from the flames and pushed to the brink of the cliff, where individuals made their decision. Most jumped onto the boulders and scree in preference to being devoured in the whirlwind of smoke and flame.

Defenders from the settlement group raced out to join their allies, the Teo-Km-Lankum, and wound their way down to the riverbank to search for survivors. Only two were alive. They were lifted to the top of the cliff, put upon separate travois and transported to the infirmary at Plains Sanctuary, where their wounds and broken bones were tended. One of the survivors was an officer, a lieutenant named Robert Eustus Micenheimer; he was Black. The other survivor was an enlistee, a corporal named Fisher Lange; he was White.

Prisoner Interrogations

Interrogation of the two survivors of the Battle of South Platte was conducted by Gavin Hill, security chief at Plains Sanctuary settlement group, and by Sharitarish III, chief of the Pawnee Stealth Fighters.

First Interrogation Session: Day 5, Week 4, Month 7, Solar Cycle 46

Hill:	*Please be at ease – we have no intentions of harming or mistreating you beyond your battle injuries. Do you understand?*
Lieutenant:	*Yes*
Corporal:	*Yes*
Hill:	*Have you been given food and water?*
Lieutenant:	*Yes*
Corporal:	*Yes, thank you.*
Hill:	*Please state your name and the position of authority you held in your expedition.*
Lieutenant:	*I am First Lieutenant Robert Eustus Micenheimer. I was in command of our rear guard.*
Hill:	*And this meant?*
Lieutenant:	*My troops primarily were responsible for defending our artillery train and supply wagons. As you should know, I can't say we did any kind of a good job in this.*
Hill:	*Thank you, lieutenant. And you are?*
Corporal:	*My name is Fisher Lange. I am a corporal and artillery team leader. Had we got into action you would not have had as easy a victory.*
Hill:	*That may well be, corporal, but you gave us no choice. We have preferred parley to battle throughout our settlement group history and, frankly, we wish it had*

	been the same with our encounter with you. We can only wonder why you reacted so violently in the face of no provocation.
Lieutenant:	*Long ago my ancestors were ruled by others. It was not a good time for us, and we do not give our trust lightly nor do we grant power over us. Perhaps there was some provocation – genuine or unintended – I cannot say. I was with my troops away from our commanders. I have no idea what went down, as they say.*
Hill:	*Nothing bad went down prior to the murders, lieutenant. Can you explain how two men – even two armed men – were a threat of any sort to your company?*
Lieutenant:	*I cannot, sir.*
Hill:	*Damn right you can't.*
Lieutenant:	*But I can say, sir, we were beaten long ago and now we strive to be victors, not vanquished, and we are just victors at that.*
Hill:	*Justice? I think not. You make no sense. Perhaps we may discuss your philosophy further at a later time, but for now, let me turn to the corporal. Where are you from?*
Corporal:	*New Vicksburg in the Western Zone of the New Confederacy.*
Hill:	*And you, lieutenant?*
Lieutenant:	*Originally from New Georgia, near the eastern coast of our nation. I was in New Vicksburg on attached service with the militia there when our expedition was sent out.*
Hill:	*And what was the purpose of that expedition, Lieutenant?*
Lieutenant:	*To extend and secure the western border of the New Confederacy – to extend by treaty, no matter how coerced. We occupy no community that joins us.*
Hill:	*An interesting use of the word – join – might you agree, corporal?*

Corporal: *Yes, sir. And it surely wasn't worth the cost.*

(NOTE IN MARGIN OF THE TRANSCRIPT: as the corporal spoke, he raised and displayed the disfigured stump of his left arm.)

Sharitarish: *To us battle wounds are signs of honor – they are not to be mocked. Your courage was seen by many of my warriors.*

Corporal: *That was in the heat of battle. Right now, I'd trade valor for a whole body. No disrespect meant to your customs, chief, but we see things differently.*

Hill: *Obviously very differently. That is enough for today. Join us in our communal mess hall, then sleep, tend to your wounds, and we will resume tomorrow.*

Second Interrogation Session: Day 6, Week 4, Month 7, Solar Cycle 46

Question: *Were you treated well last night? Your wounds tended? Enough to eat?*

Lieutenant: *Yes, sir.*

Corporal: *Yes, sir.*

Hill: *Today we want to explore some of the history and organization of what you call the New Confederacy. Our geographical area is known as the New NorthWest Configuration. We have no knowledge or understanding about the people you represent.*

Lieutenant: *Of course you know that the Old Confederacy consisted of states based upon slavery: Alabama, Arkansas, Florida, Georgia, Louisiana, Mississippi, North Carolina, South Carolina, Tennessee, Texas, and Virginia and ultimately Kentucky and Missouri. Our capital is Williamsburg, Virginia, east of Old Richmond, capital of the Old Confederacy, and northeast of the historical Jamestown settlement.*

Corporal: *Our territorial boundaries to the north and west sometimes fluctuate, depending upon whether or not certain geographical regions want and invite our military protection and agree to our terms.*

Hill: *What do you mean? Explain!*

Corporal: *Before I joined the New Vicksburg troopers, I enlisted in my hometown of Franklin, Old Tennessee. Within two months of my enlistment, I was assigned to the Vicksburg garrison. Next thing I knew I was marching back north through Old Tennessee to the Ohio River border to engage a group of Northlanders who had trekked south burning farms and fields in their path, leaving behind their typical chain of settlements.*

Hill: *Settlements? What do you mean?*

Corporal: *Jezz' you NorthWesterners don't have any grasp of what's going on outside of your little world!*

Lieutenant: *Corporal, calm down – he doesn't know. Look, along the northwest border of our New Confederacy is a relatively unknown group of former states. The western part seems to be characterized by settlement groups founded in the woodland and lake areas, while the eastern zone is characterized by the urban disaster zones of Old Chicago and Old Detroit.*

Radiating outward from both these urban centers are the settlements. These consist of small groups – like the links of a chain – where the residents are specific Northerner sects. The settlements never are more than 5 to 10 kilo-miles apart, and their residents exclusively are individuals who left the scarred battlegrounds of urban Chicago (now ChiGo) and Detroit City (now Dee-TC).

Corporal: *As I was relating, sir. Once we crossed the Ohio River into Old Illinois, east of the river port of K-Row or Old Cairo, we engaged one settlement, located just 5 kilo-miles from the river. To our knowledge this location was the furthest penetration of the Northerners southward out from ChiGo. Their settlement defenders fired on us and we returned with five times the volley fire. This brief skirmish is recorded in our regimental log as the near K-Row* incident, but the Northerners call it the Battle of Republic Settlement. What we learned later through interrogation of several captives was that a second chain of Isnads extended westward from ChiGo nearly reaching Cedar Rapids at the eastern border of what you call the Flatland Configuration.

Lieutenant: May I continue? The settlements are all populated by Northerners, but within their respective groupsalso reflect quite different religious and practical beliefs that range from ultra-liberal to ultra-conservative. All the settlements are linked economically with religious ties to spiritual leaders, with their headquarters located in either ChiGo or Dee-TC.

Hill: Let's return to something more about your configuration geography. What are your northern and western boundaries at present?

Lieutenant: Our northern boundary traditionally has been the Ohio River. The current recognized western boundary, at least recognized by us, is the Mississippi River, although the territory known as Texas Across the River, that we just call TAR, changes their allegiance frequently and teeters between joining the New Confederacy vs. being a component of your so-called Flatland Configuration. Sometimes the TARers consider themselves as standing alone as an independent state – something like we hear happened with your old state of Utah that now is independent and called Deseret by its residents.

Corporal: Then east of the Ohio River the boundary slices through parts of Old Pennsylvania and Old New York, then touches the enclave of what we usually call the neo-Puritans. They are very secretive and essentially we have no trade with them. Really, we have little to no idea of what goes on inside their territory.

Corporal: The western boundary as we were saying is indistinct and abuts what you call your New SouthWest Configuration.

Hill: How would you characterize your people? Did you form settlement groups like us? What about your former great cities: Atlanta, Baton Rouge, Charleston, Louisville, Miami, Nashville, New Orleans, Richmond, Savannah, and others?

Lieutenant: Yes, we formed settlement groups. Most of our cities remain in ruins; we selected Williamsburg, Virginia, to be our capital because it basically remained intact during the Ripple Event. We in the New Confederacy have experienced serious gang activities in certain urban centers, especially Old New Orleans and Old Louisville, which we now call Or-Leans and Louie. Both cities never recovered at the end of the Dark Time; most of Or-Leans remains flooded.

Hill: How have you handled basic food and water security?

Corporal: Much of our territory at one time had been given over to cotton – but you can't eat cotton, right? So along the river and canal systems, we grow food. We don't have what you call shattered zones; our militias fixed that right away and cleared out the thugs and gangs – just killed them all – those bloody parasites. As such, we easily and safely farm the land areas between the various settlement groups – and like you – our greatest concern is over the safety of our water supplies. I'm getting tired of all this talk.

Hill: Have you ever heard of the New Order?

Lieutenant: No, what's that?

Hill: What about you, corporal? You must have heard something. This isn't your first excursion outside the geographical boundaries of the New Confederacy – and you have been across the Ohio River.

Corporal: The New Order? No, never heard of them. Now addressing the lieutenant, sir, could they be something like the KuKls?

Lieutenant: I don't think so.

| Hill: | *What are the KuKls?* |
| Lieutenant: | *The fact is that you must know something about the old KKK and their activities in the rural portions of southern North America prior to the Ripple Event and especially before 1962 of the old solar calculation method. The KuKls seem to be an offshoot of the KKK where the members abandoned their ethnic differences but maintained and stressed their ultra-conservative, neo-Christian and conservative political views.* |

Third Interrogation Session: Day 7, Week 5, Month 7, Solar Cycle 46

Interrogation of the two survivors of the Battle of South Platte was delayed by one day, due to the arrival of a looper team. Two certified data collector members, Mary Jensen and Franklin Fowler, were invited by Gavin Hill to observe and comment during the interrogation process:

Hill:	*Good morning. I hope you rested well. Have you been fed? Have your wounds been checked?*
Lieutenant:	*Yes, both were done.*
Corporal:	*Yes, thank you.*
Hill:	*Gentlemen, I would like to introduce Mary Jensen and her consort, Franklin Fowler.*
Jensen:	*We prefer the term "mate." This word is the standard in our community.*
Hill:	*Mate it shall be, Jensen. I would prefer not to do anything that might disturb or anger that very impressive mate of yours.*
Fowler:	*Once you know us, Gavin, you'll see who's the impressive one.*
Hill:	*And now moving on. Jensen and Fowler are leaders of what we call a looper team. These are – well, to help you understand – small-group expeditions sent out from a university in New Bozeman. That's to the north of us in the New NorthWest Configuration. They are non-military.*

Fowler: *We are non-military yet with capabilities for self-defense. We are trained to take many with us should certain situations arise.*

Sharitarish: *What a fine special warrior group these men would make!*

Jensen: *Not just the men!*

Hill: *Their purpose is to record histories, to get information from the time before the Ripple Event from those few who are still among us, and during the Dark Time. Not all of these expeditions return; in fact none of those dispatched to explore eastward and northeastward into and beyond the Flatland Configuration returned.*

Corporal: *River pirates most likely.*

Lieutenant: *Or Northlander raiders from the settlements above the Ohio.*

Hill: *So you can understand when this looper team heard you were with us while they were passing close by, they asked if they might interrogate.*

Jensen: *We prefer "interview."*

Hill: *All right – interview – you and I gave permission. They will be in charge of today's interview, which you'd best treat as an interrogation. Do you understand?*

Lieutenant: *Yes.*

Corporal: *Yes, sir.*

Jensen: *Thank you, Gavin. We are Looper Team 16, dispatched by the History Department of Montana State University in New Bozeman to explore the eastern border of the New NorthWest Configuration. Our journey brought us nearby and when we were told of the battle and that there were prisoners we couldn't get here fast enough. Our mission – well, in a way two missions – has been to gather historical data as well as information on current conditions. This information mostly concerns economic factors – products, trade, and such. Lieutenant, please tell us as you would a friend or relative you hadn't seen in a long time something of your history, your family and your home.*

Lieutenant: *I am Robert Eustus Micenheimer. I was born five years before the Ripple Event on our family's cotton plantation in the coastal area of New Georgia. The family goes way back there. Way, way back to the time of slavery and, yes, we were slaves at one time. As was not uncommon, our lives were tough but not necessarily harsh. Our owner, Robert Eustus Micenheimer, was a kind man – none of us were mistreated and those too old to work were freed and according to my families' oral tradition, many remained on the plantation. After the Old Confederacy's defeat in the War of Northern Aggression, we were freed and proudly assumed his family name. And, yes, we know it isn't correct German – it never was; further, my first and middle names honor Marse Robert, the former master, not Robert E. Lee, the finest warrior of the Confederacy as most in New Georgia and the New Confederacy think. Not a bad thing to have folks think if one chooses a military career. Why, my initials may have gotten me into VMI for all I know.*

Fowler: *VMI?*

Lieutenant: *Virginia Military Institute – a place of higher learning quite similar to your Montana State University, I'd guess, but with a much stronger military component.*

Things were quite tough right after the War of Northern Aggression and for some time thereafter. The family made do by sharecropping and doing odd jobs all the time, saving as much money as they could. We helped Marse Robert but it was not enough; however, when the plantation was put on the auction block by the tax people we, by pure happenstance, were able to buy it. In a reversal of fate, we then kept aged Marse Robert on the place until he passed away. He's still there; we have maintained his – now our – family plot. It is my intent to rest with him someday.

Now this development made certain White folks consider us as being "uppity" and they set about to bring us down a notch or two. Black sharecroppers and handymen didn't bother these folks but Black plantation owners – that was another matter. Anyway the KKK came after us but the National Rifle Association (NRA) helped us with weapons and ammunition. Besides, our White neighbors – we'd always gotten along together – kept us well informed as to what the Klan was about and with the NRA seeing to it that we had the means to handle "situations" on our own, we acquired more lands by purchase or lease. Sooner than you might suppose. The Micenheimers were able, prosperous folks, the sort it is wise to cozy up to, and as calm returned to our little patch of Georgia, so it stayed until the Ripple Event. But you, of course, know of the Ripple.

Jensen: *Yes, lieutenant we do, more than all too well in some cases. But now, KKK? Our archives tell us about the NRA but this other abbreviation is new to us.*

Lieutenant: *The KKK stands for Ku Klux Klan, a radical organization formed after what some call the Civil War. The goal supposedly was to protect Southern culture and to do so by keeping Black people in check through violent, lethal means. They were misguided in many cases and many were evil men. Many were simple misguided folks who did nothing for those Blacks who were lynched.*

Fowler: *Lynched? You mean killed?*

Lieutenant: *Yes, but this violence faded as our economy grew, and Blacks defended themselves more and more. By the Ripple Event, the Klan was but a sick joke. As for my story – it was not uncommon for some to tire of the plantation and I – and others like me – chose honorable careers in the military, in the Army or Navy.*

Fowler: *Navy? You mean the New Confederacy has a navy? For what purpose?*

Lieutenant:	*Well, for several. We have developed coastal trade within our country, plus we trade with New PlyMouth and even beyond across the sea to Recovery Britain and Nouveau France. Anyway, our trade is enough to interest pirates, so our navy provides escorts for the merchantmen. There is also a branch of the navy that serves on the Great River – the Mississippi – to protect against those that prey on traders using the river.*
Jensen:	*And what trade are you in the New Confederacy involved with?*
Lieutenant:	*Well, on the river mostly our own products and salt, lots of salt that comes from somewhere in the West. On the ocean our trade mostly is in cotton – both raw and cloth; some hams and even a bit of salt for the New PlyMouth folks to salt their catch. The ships return with wool – again raw and finished – and wines. There are minor cargoes both coming and going, but these are what drive the trade.*
Jensen:	*Wool and woolens we know; some wine gets to us from New Marin, and we cure our own meats of various kinds. You may find it of interest that the salt originates in our neighbor state New Deseret – or this is at least a good guess. I know many in the western reaches would be interested both in the cotton and the cloth made from it.*
Lieutenant:	*Perhaps we share a potential bright future. As they say – commerce opens many doors and sheaths many swords. We certainly could trade pork for your beef, if nothing else.*
Hill:	*Who knows, but in any case, such a development of mutual trade certainly would be brighter than our first encounter would it not? And, oh, should the New Confederacy need hides or finished leather goods, we've got 'em and quality stone for both knappers and tool makers as well. Sadly, it appears all of us are plentifully supplied with weapons of their own manufacture, but we do need to know more of some of your arms. I understand that would be the business of Corporal Lange.*

Lieutenant:	*Yes, sir, that it would be.*
Jensen:	*Then perhaps we should chat with him a bit? Corporal, please tell us about yourself and your community.*
Corporal:	*Well, ma'am, as said yesterday during my interrogation, I was born in Franklin, Old Tennessee, solar cycle 29. I enlisted at the age of 17 in Franklin and within two months was assigned to the Vicksburg garrison. Our orders took us through Old Tennessee up to the Ohio River where we engaged clusters of Northlanders. We put out their lights, so to speak. After my return to the Vicksburg garrison, we had about another half solar cycle of training before we started on our westward trek that took us here – and given my wound, I wish I'd have stayed at home.*
Sharitarish:	*Forgive him. The corporal does not understand the honor that this scar of battle brings him.*
Jensen:	*Chief, we understand and will treat the corporal with the utmost respect, although a smaller scar would have been just as honorable and easier for the corporal to bear.*
Corporal:	*Anyway, in the New Confederacy was where I was born and there I grew up. Got some schoolin' – enough to keep tallies on the docks. Figures and I jus' get along. My work was trusted and much appreciated by the merchants.*
Jensen:	*Why then did you choose the military as did the lieutenant?*
Corporal:	*Well, ma'am, it was more of a case of bein' chosen. While all in the New Confederacy see the military as an honorable callin' not all of us sign up like folks from VMI. We expect to do time in the service – usually the army – and we wait to be called up for a couple of years. My skill with figurin' was needed by the artillery, so there I was with the artillery train when the wind blew and the sparks flew. All the guns are is big rifles – I'd guess you're looking at those we brought with us right now – muzzle loading, single shot like your carbines. They can shoot farther – lots farther – and that's what takes the figur-*

ing; the pointing, the angle, the powder charge – it takes proper setting of all three to hit folks that are out of sight or far away. Anyway, I was called up by the Vicksburg Militia, trained in artillery gunnery, assigned to the expedition, and here I am, the worse for wear, but here I am.

Hill: *You're right corporal, we've taken a good look at your big guns and most impressive they are. I'm glad we weren't on the receiving end of their fire. You were also correct in that we might not have prevailed in the battle had you gotten them into action. Again, I'm glad you didn't.*

Corporal: *Sir, the more I know of you people, the more I'm also glad we didn't.*

Jensen: *Thank you, corporal, I can see your wound is troubling you. We can talk more at another time.*

Corporal: *Thank you, ma'am.*

Six months after their interrogations, the wounds of Lieutenant Robert Eustus Micenheimer and Corporal Fisher Lange had healed. Both men behaved honorably during their internment at Plains Home settlement group. Both the administrative council at Plains and the Pawnee Council of Chiefs agreed that the two men should be allowed to return to their homes in the New Confederacy. Both took pledges that they would not participate in future military raids west of the Mississippi River, and swore to relate to their superiors that they had been treated professionally and with dignity.

A departure ceremony was scheduled for Day 5, Week 4, Month 3, Solar Cycle 47, where Micenheimer and Lange were given horses, food, and water. Their New Confederacy arms were returned to them along with a significant quantity of ammunition for protection during their long retreat back home to Vicksburg.

As they departed, the Pawnee braves who had participated in the Battle of Platte River saluted the two soldiers with raised lances, and chanted farewell:

Nawa aw ki taw tho
Tema orna tema
Nawa aw ki taw tho

Tema orna tema
Nawa aw ki taw tho
Tema orna tema
Hawda! Hawda! Hawda!

Relics of Honor

The Battle of South Platte River had shown the power of cooperation among settlement groups, and the Native American horsemen enclaves along the western boundary of the Flatland Configuration. But the cooperation and good will did not last long, as the New Order regained its dominance within the majority of the settlement groups throughout the region. Policies of graft and extortion implemented at the settlement groups enticed once good people to commit crimes at levels not before seen. The Pawnee horsemen withdrew their cooperative agreements with regional settlement groups and retreated farther into the shattered zones where they continued with their own honorable methods of administration and livelihood.

The New Order stain flowed across the western configurations as more and more settlement groups adopted their tenets. Almost all of the Islets of Honor were destroyed by the active New Order militia. But even with these losses there remained a few isolated locations where dignity and honor remained valued.

One secluded Islet of Honor known as French Camp, located just west of the Yosemite Valley in east central Old California, remained basically untouched by changes in the New Order. Spies had not penetrated their membership, and visitors to the site were few and most were not admitted. One set of visitors, however, appeared during solar cycle 48 – data collectors from Montana State University History Project who, after careful screening, were invited to remain for nearly a month.

The diaries of these data collectors contain poignant descriptions of ritual pyre ceremonies held at different secluded IoHs, where elderly guild members related memories to the assemblies how honor still flourished at certain locations.

Adam Zurick, Memory Guild Member

Recitation: Pyre Ceremony, French Camp, Islet of Honor
Transcribed by Francis Gomez, Certified Data Collector
The Face of El Capitan

I relate to you this evening the following memory:

> An Islet of Honor had been established in Yosemite Valley, near the monumental cliff of El Capitan. As you know this IoH was attacked by New Order militia (NOM) during the autumn of solar cycle 45. The membership resisted, but were overcome. Once inside the compound, the NOM looted and then set fire to the infirmary where the wounded were being treated. All inside the clinic perished in the blaze. The officer in charge of the attack next ordered the remaining residents into the IoH meeting hall, barred the exit doors, and then set fire to the structure.

> I tell you tonight that the memory of those who lost their lives in the attack must remain in our minds and hearts for all time so the spirit of resistance against the New Order not die.

> Preserve the memory of those who died at Yosemite Valley. I relate to you now the memory of Erick Young.

> Erick Young, son of Vincent and Matilda Young, was the only survivor of the NOM attack on the Yosemite Valley Islet of Honor at French Camp. Using survival skills learned at his IoH, Erick Young evaded the NOM and ultimately found refuge. He grew to a man, was initiated, and when I met him during the regional equinox celebrations, he related to me how the memory of those who perished at Yosemite Valley and other Islets of Honor could be preserved.

> During late spring of solar cycle 46, a small group of men and women led by Erick Young re-entered the Yosemite Valley. Five strides north of the original park monument at the base of El Capitan, they erected a concealable foothold steel cable that would permit pilgrims to ascend the cliff face to leave messages honoring their loved ones who had died during the New Order revival. Those who ascended carved their messages into the cliff face. Those who did so found the climb especially difficult; it was a pilgrimage and task not for the weak of heart.

> At 150 meter-yards above the valley floor, the first inscription may be seen chiseled into the rock face:

> > Dedicated cousin, Joan Franklin
> > Murdered by the NOM at Yosemite Valley
> > Fortitudinem et Honorem

> Ten meter-yards above the first is the second inscription:

> *Blessed wife, Elena Franklin*
> *Murdered by NOM*
> *Semper in corde meo.*

And so the pattern of carving messages of honor persisted – message after message high above the valley floor on the face of El Capitan – words of honor and respect to keep the memory of loved ones alive.

About half-way up the cliff face, there appears a narrow ledge where those ascending may rest briefly. Just above the ledge is an alcove where a metal box is stashed. Inside are hammers and chisels that can be used by pilgrims to carve words into the stone if they did not have tools.

Ascending ever higher, climbers find additional inscriptions, most in English but others in different languages or in coded texts. Each message speaks to honor, respect, and memory of loved ones murdered during the resurgence of evil and crime facilitated by the New Order.

Brave climbers left messages in Armenian, English, German, Slovakian, Spanish, even Tagalog – words of honor and respect from majority and minority ethnic-Californians whose families and loved ones had suffered under the New Order evils:

> *Resista el nuevo orden; enviarlos de vuelta al Infierno*
> *James, duk' payk'arel naev; Yes hargum yem misht*
> *Martha mong laging nasa aking puso*
> *Tapfersten Mann Sie immer daran erinnert werden*
> *bráni', bráni', bráni', nikdy sa nevzdáva*
> *IMO – JAMES – MBNOM.*

But perhaps the most poignant message was carved by a loving mother who braved the cliff face to carve a memory of her son:

> *My brave son Justin*
> *You did your best to protect our home*
> *I held you in my arms the night you died*
> *RIP!*

While it took considerable courage to climb the face of El Capitan, it took even more courage to carve the names of loved ones who had resisted, for if the person leaving the message was identified by New Order spies they would be tried and convicted in New Order-dominated courts, then sentenced to public execution.

After each ascent the foothold cable was concealed from view and all footprints and evidence of activity at the base of El Capitan erased.

To the best of my knowledge, the foothold cable still remains undiscovered by the New Order.

Remember! Do not forget!

Juanita Mendoza, Memory Guild Member
Recitation: Pyre Ceremony, Near Former Clear Lake Islet of Honor
Transcribed by Judith Olsen, Certified Data Collector
Red Earth Hole Cave

I relate to you this evening the following memory:

North of the ruined settlement group at Kelseyville, Old California, an Islet of Honor was established near the shore of Clear Lake. The New Order militia raided this IoH during the spring of solar cycle 45, after the administrative council had refused to incorporate the standard New Order teaching curriculum and refused to pay an annual protection fee (APF).

A group of buildings destroyed at the Clear Lake IoH had housed the Norhammer Foundry, where long before the Ripple Event a family of Scandinavian ethnic heritage had started an artists' retreat known locally as Kriken's forge. After the raid all that remained of the once-thriving artistic retreat was slag and twisted metal. The bronze works of art were melted by New Order mercenaries, because the pieces did not conform to their preconceived ideas of art.

Two survivors from the Clear Lake IoH led me to a secluded spot northwest of the lake. We climbed upslope for a considerable distance, perhaps 2 kilomiles, where we approached a well-hidden cave. Inside was a protected relic: the sole surviving bronze from Kriken's forge. My escorts unwrapped the protective cloth covering the bronze – a tattered flag with 50 stars and 13 stripes. Revealed was a bronze depicting a stylized soldier. I asked, who was this soldier? No one knew, only that it was produced from the mind of Kriken himself, and appeared to be a warrior from a long-ago war much earlier than the Ripple Event. At the base of the bronze were four words, "I remember your laugh." Was this the title of the work? We were uncertain.

I touched the bronze warrior, then sat and wrote notes in my diary. One of my escorts, a member of the Pomo Nation, sat beside me and spoke.

We call this cave the Red Earth Hole. Look about. It was here that we showed Kriken the source of iron that he used to forge the weapons that initially protected us from raiders. Two mountains west we showed him the multicolored stones that melted easily, and the rocks he called cassiterite that he mixed with the melt to produce what he called bronze.

This work of art we call the Warrior. I know about this piece. The idea came from Kriken's heart and recalled in his mind a friend of his who died in a long-ago war in a place he called Viet Nam. How did it get here, and who wrapped the Warrior in this ancient flag? We have no idea, only that Kriken himself completed the work to honor his friend who gave his life for a cause in which he believed.

We, the survivors of the New Order's attack on our community, come here each solar cycle on the summer solstice to remember and to honor what this land used to be – what it once was to our nation – the Pomo – and what it once was to your nation – not what it has become under the rule of the New Order.

Remember! Do not forget!

Matthew Quinn, Memory Guild Member
Recitation: Pyre Ceremony, Little Belt Islet of Honor
Transcribed by Gregory Thompson, Certified Data Collector
Donovan's Box

I relate to you this evening the following memory:

Donovan was a member of what once was called the Greatest Generation, a title of honor given to those who served their country in what then was known as Europe, Africa, and Asia during the Great War. I never met Donovan personally, but my father, Jason Quinn, knew him well. Both were raised on the prairie lands of central Old Montana. Donovan's family was a blend of Irish and Italian heritage. My father knew Donovan from the time they were children. As they grew and entered school, they played together; they hunted rabbits and searched the Musselshell River terraces for arrowheads out near the buffalo drive cliff. Together they climbed the standing rock where at one time the Blackfoot Nation exposed the bodies of their chiefs during sun-up rituals.

They were fast friends.

When the Great War erupted, my father and Donovan had come of age and both attempted to enlist. Donovan was accepted – my father was denied due to health reasons.

Donovan soon enlisted and became part of the 8th Air Force 452nd Bomb Group, based in what then was called England. During his third bombing raid over Germany, he was wounded. Each time he and the crew departed, they never knew if or when they would return safely to their base. Nevertheless, each crew member overcame their fears and reported dutifully for their assignments.

During Donovan's 32nd flight over Germany, his plane was heavily damaged but the pilot maintained control and force-landed the plane safely in Sweden. Donovan received his Purple Heart and Air Medal (with oak leaf cluster) and European Campaign Medal upon his release from service.

These medals were dear to Donovan's heart and were treasured by his family, especially his children. The objects were stored inside a carved wooden box kept in the family home. Donovan would relate stories of bravery from the war years to his children, but most of all they loved to play with his medals and service ribbons.

Donovan's box became the holder of his memories and while he loved to watch his children fondle the medals and campaign ribbons, he sometimes turned away briefly to catch his breath as memories welled up, forcing him to recall the horrors of that terrible time when so many friends had died during the bombing runs.

Donovan passed away 12 years (old calendar calculation) before the Ripple Event. His children, now grown, had not inspected their father's memorabilia for many years. A long-ago war was not something of their experience and, besides, all that old stuff (in their words) was of little interest.

Then came the time when the family house was to be vacated. His children gathered dutifully and went room by room to inventory furniture and decorative objects in accord with instructions Donovan had given. Going through items in the family room, they once again noticed Donovan's box, an object that brought back fond memories of their own childhood activities with their father. Next to the box was a letter, not seen previously but certainly placed there while Donovan was alive.

The letter contained a set of short comments to his children, among them:

> Trust and honor are characteristics of all good persons.
> Evil cannot take root in the minds of good people.

Love your country; fight for what is just and right.
You always are in my heart.

There also were instructions that Donovan wished his children to fulfill:

"Upon my death, please take the box with my medals and campaign ribbons, along with the flag that draped my coffin – now folded inside its triangular display case. Go to Harlowton, Montana. Seek out Matthew Quinn, son of my childhood friend, Jason Quinn. Give the box and flag to Matthew and request that he bury both items next to Jason's Grave. Jason was my closest childhood friend.

"I wish in this way to honor Jason, my friend, for his work as a civilian during the Great War. While Jason did not participate on the field of battle, he served his country better than most, at Los Alamos, New Mexico. I wish to honor Jason for his participation in scientific research and testing activities that helped America win the Great War."

And so it was that Donovan's children honored their father's request and delivered the flag and box to me, Matthew Quinn.

And it was on that long-ago summer day west of Harlowton in Old Montana that Donovan's children and I buried the objects next to my father's grave. And there the objects rested for many solar cycles, through the Ripple Event, the Dark Time, post-Dark Time recovery period, and into the near modern era when the New Order destroyed my settlement group.

It was after the destruction of my home that I returned in the dark of night to retrieve Donovan's box from its resting place in the cemetery, and brought the relic to our Islet of Honor.

Tonight ... I show you that box during our solstice celebration.

Here it is for all of you to see and to touch.

Here is Donovan's box – the object that meant so much to him, to me, and now to all of us assembled.

I end my comments tonight at the Pyre Ceremony with these words:

Now we are few; the majority of our members have died during skirmishes with the New Order militia. And so it is that we few gather each solstice where at our pyre celebrations we – the reciters – stand and speak. Our words you have heard time and time again, words that I repeat to you tonight taken from Donovan's letter:

> *Love your country; fight for what is just and right.*
> *Defend your country; protect those you love.*
> *Be prepared to give your life when the cause is just.*
> *Friendship and honor are more valued than possessions.*
> *Help others before you help yourself.*

Remember! Do not forget!

After-Word

Wherein lies hope for a better life? Do not all people desire food, water, and security? Without hope the Horsemen of the Apocalypse appear, riding their steeds of conquest, famine, war, and death, followed by their cohorts, the Seven Deadly Sins: envy, gluttony, greed, lust, pride, sloth, and wrath. What is there about the behavior of individuals and families when care, hospitality, kindness, and respect all too often are discarded for the evils of avarice, envy, hatred, and strife?

Do other animals exhibit such behaviors? Why, then, is it only certain cultures who exert such behaviors upon themselves and others: exposing infants malformed at birth, mass murders and exterminations in the name of religion or politics – the rise of the alphas and the fall of the omegas – survival of the fittest and the most clever?

Recall how the tiny mammals of the late Mesozoic scurried here and there beneath the thunderous feet of Cretaceous dinosaurs, and when the great beasts ultimately became extinct the tiny clever ones survived. What lessons are there to be learned through the global extinctions of different animals? Were the trilobites and ammonites lustful, greedy, or evil? Nevertheless, they were exterminated as if by an unseen hand that guided the asteroid on its arc of death and earthly collision.

Metal Sheet #14
Inscription and Translation

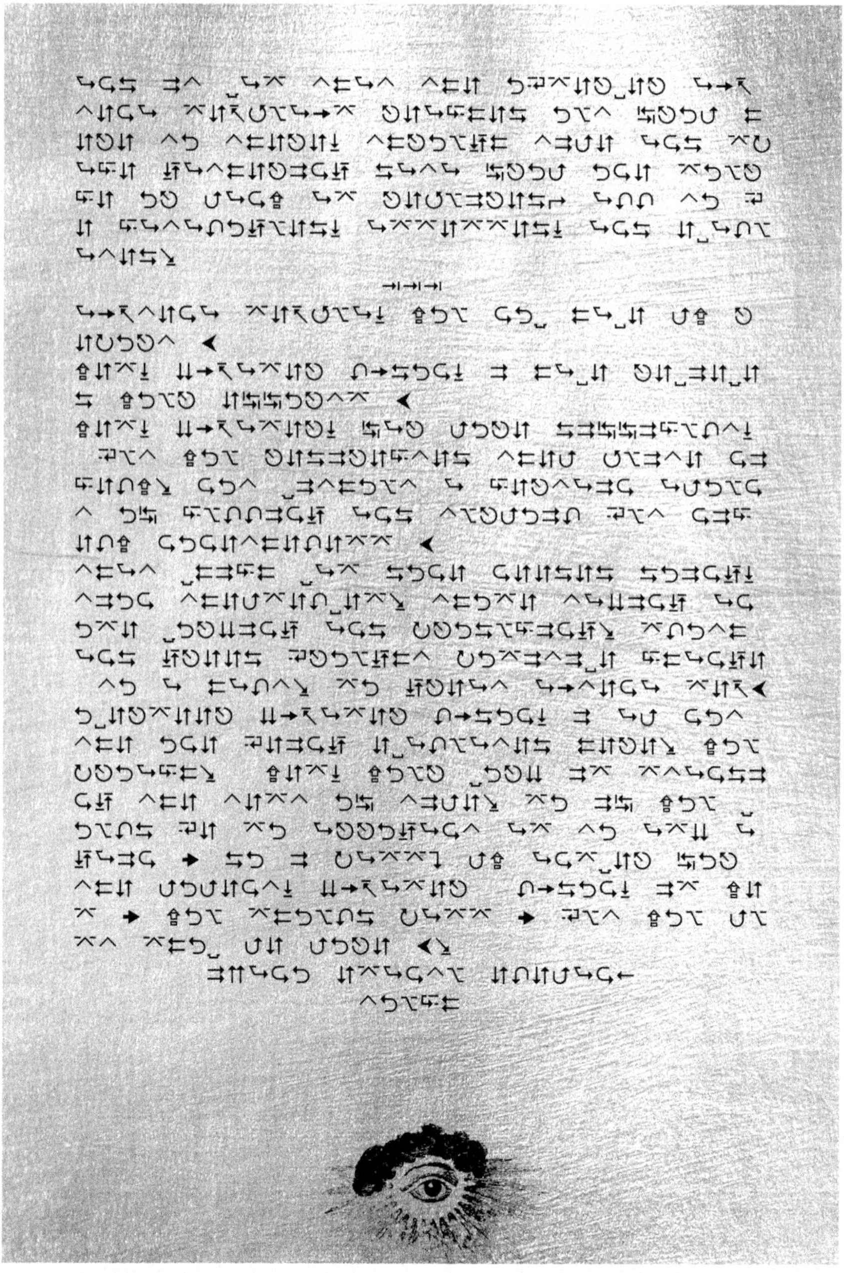

And it was that the Observer A'-Tena Se-Qua reached out from here to there, through time and space, gathering data from one source or many as required; all to be catalogued, assessed, and evaluated.

* * *

A'-Tena Se-Qua, you now have my report.

Yes, K'Aser L'Don, I have reviewed your efforts.

Does this mean I have passed my assignment?

Do you agree that your biped units were nearly out of control?

What did you expect of me, A'-Tena. They have free will. They are more interesting but at the same time more difficult to manage. Are they not?

Yes, K'Aser, far more difficult, but you redirected them quite nicely. Not without a certain amount of culling and turmoil, but nicely nonetheless.

That which was done needed doing, the units did most of the reduction themselves. Those taking and using of others outnumbered those working and producing. Sloth and greed brought positive change to a halt. So great, A'-Tena Se-Qua, do I pass?

Overseer K'Aser L'Don, I am not the one being evaluated here. You have been neither better nor worse than most Overseers but certainly you are different in your approach. Yes, your work is standing the test of time. So if you would be so arrogant as to ask again – do I pass? My answer for the moment, K'Aser L'Don, is yes – you should pass – but you must show me more.

Ijano Esantu Eleman!

Chapter 16: Evening Reading 16
Document 16, Cave Location: Case 43-B
Never Ending Cycles

Are we the offspring of a caring god?
Are we objects of indifference and passing interest?
Do we occupy a cosmic testing ground?

Pre-Note

Most bipeds that inhabited the testing ground considered themselves products of free will with the ability to make choices. The reality has been that various activities have been part of a continuous chain of life, in which events have been examined, recorded, and analyzed from eons past and will be into the future. Life with all its wonders and varieties has played out in cycles of a universal play, set into motion by Etowah (may Its name always be blessed), monitored by a paired Observer and Overseer.

Thus it has been and always will be: creation alternating with chaos and calm. The creation of multiple life forms, their destruction whether by asteroid, flood, or other cosmic means, followed by creation of the new.

Ijano Esantu Eleman. As it was as in the beginning.

Alternating creative and destructive events examined, measured, and monitored by forces not comprehended – predestined cycles played out on the testing ground.

Ijano Esantu Eleman. As it was as in the beginning.

Let it be forever known by these words that the life and extermination cycles (LECs) ordered by the Etowah (may Its name always be blessed), once again were poised for implementation on the testing ground. As in all eons past, the previous LECs were reviewed:

Cycle 1: I who am and ever will be created great seas and land masses upon the testing ground. I who am and ever will be filled the waters with brachiopods, crinoids, trilobites, and others. I who am and ever will be created the Observer and Overseer pair to swim unseen among these creatures of the sea and report. But these life forms offered me no great pleasure. I who am and ever will be then cleansed the testing ground.

Cycle 2: I who am and ever will be created different great seas and land masses upon the testing ground. I who am and ever will be filled the waters with bryozoans, eurypterids, placoderms, and others. The Observer ordered the Overseer to swim unseen among creatures of the sea and report. But these life forms offered me no great pleasure. I who am and ever will be then cleansed the testing ground a second time.

Cycle 3: I who am and ever will be created different great seas and land masses upon the testing ground. I who am and ever will be filled the waters with ammonites, plesiosaurs, and others. I who am and ever will be caused the large and small dinosaurs and other creatures to roam across the land masses. The Observer ordered the Overseer to swim unseen among creatures of the sea and walk unseen among the armored lizards and other creatures. But these life forms, while curious, offered me no great pleasure. I who am and ever will be then cleansed the testing ground a third time.

Cycle 4: I who am and ever will be created different great seas and land masses upon the testing ground. I who am and ever will be filled the waters with myriad swimming creatures and created primates to roam across the land masses. The Observer ordered the Overseer to swim unseen among creatures of the sea and walk unseen among the primates. These primate life forms offered me great pleasure. I who am and ever will be watched from afar as these creatures changed and transformed into bipeds.

And all was well … for a time.

Came a time when the Overseer reported that the bipeds that once offered me great pleasure had adopted corrupt life forms, with the hearts of most filled with evil and violence. I who am and ever will be ordered the Overseer to intervene directly on the testing ground and select one family to survive. I who am and ever will be then cleansed the testing ground a fourth time, and the descendants of the good family repopulated the testing ground.

And all was well … for a time.

Cycle 5: I who am and ever will be created different great seas and land masses upon the testing ground. The Observer ordered the Overseer to swim unseen among creatures of the sea and walk unseen among the new bipeds and found pleasure in them and their good works.

And all was well … for a time.

Came a time once more that the bipeds became corrupt, with the hearts of most filled with evil and violence. I who am and ever will be ordered the Overseer to intervene directly and select one good individual to cleanse evil and crime from the testing ground. The Overseer selected John Carpenter Edson to hear my words and directions:

Ijano Esantu Eleman
I Am Who I Am and Always Will Be.
John Carpenter Edson, you will be my administrator of justice.
Your task is to cleanse the testing ground of evil and violence.

Honor me and follow the Noble Seven – the Great Septet:

1. *Aid the weak and helpless;*
2. *Treat women and men equally;*
3. *Appreciate differences;*
4. *Reject behaviors that degrade or harm others;*
5. *Welcome each newborn to the family hearth;*
6. *Respect and honor your mating partner;*
7. *Celebrate those who help you through life's passages.*

John Carpenter Edson! Understand my directive!
Know and understand my words!
When individuals follow the Noble Seven, they shall thrive!
When individuals ignore the Noble Seven, they do so at their peril!
Ijano Esantu Eleman!

And all was well … for a time.

Cycle 6. I who am and ever will be created great seas and land masses upon the testing ground. The Observer ordered the Overseer to swim unseen among the waters and walk unseen upon the land documenting work of the administrator of justice, John Carpenter Edson. And it was that good individuals flourished and evil ones vanished.

And all was well … for a time …

Came a time when once-good individuals ignored the Noble Seven, the Great Septet, and adopted corrupt ways, their hearts filled with avarice, crime, evil, and violence. And there came a time when a special evil took root across the testing ground – an evil that ordered the assassination of the administrator of justice, John Carpenter Edson.

The Overseer watched these events from afar and reported to the Observer. Both watched and waited whether or not to recommend implementation of the 7th Cycle and another cleansing of the testing ground.

• • •

The Final Long Loop Trek
Report by Travis Sanders, Certified Data Collector

I certify on my honor that the following message and descriptive account is accurate.

Chief Supervisor Bruce Anderson assigned six certified data collectors to embark on a long loop trek to gather additional information from isolated settlement groups located in the New SouthWest Configuration that, according to the last loop trek, had unusually large numbers of elderly men and women who had survived the Ripple Event, Dark Time, and recovery periods.

Our objective was to visit these sites and interview as many elderly as possible.

Our field pair mates on this journey were:

Travis Sanders, field coordinator

Ashland Ross, ethnobotanist

Lee Carpenter, hydrology and water supply engineer

Heather West, interview data analyst

Ethan Hernandez, pre-Dark Time linguistics

Laurel Wells, geriatric health

We left the MSU campus on Day 2, Week 1, Month 3, Solar Cycle 49 and took the standard westward route for long loop treks (e.g., Billings to Bison Camp, then south to Idaho Falls) then at Twin Falls we left the standard route and trekked directly south; bypassed the River-Seeker settlement group outside of Jackpot and continued farther south until we reached Wells Intersection (WI). We spent three days at WI hydrating and bartering for pushcarts that we could use for water container transport. After securing the carts, we started southwest through Elko, Battle Mountain, Winnemucca, Lovelock, Fernley, Sparks, and into Reno. We enjoyed the standard Reno Recovery (RR). After three days spent relaxing we were primed and ready for the over-the-mountain portion of the trek where we stopped briefly at New Truckee and New Auburn to greet old friends, then pushed our carts downhill all the way into Roseville and out onto the flatlands of the delta marshes that surrounded Old Sacramento (still in ruins) and the remains of Old Davis.

We passed through New CowTown (old Vacaville), Old Fairfield (no longer a nice settlement, given the past rocket fire exchanges between gangs in Fairfield firing at nearby Travis Air Force Base during the Ripple Event, then along Eye-80 into Vallejo and west across the top of San Francisco Bay and into the Valley of the Napa. We visited two settlement groups (Vintage and Hot Springs, both located in central Old California) built in the hills east of highway 29 outside of St. Helena and Calistoga.

The way north connected us with 101 outside Geyserville, then north to Ukiah, bypassing the Friendship settlement group located east of Willits inside the Mendocino Forest area near Lake Pillsbury. Farther north up 101, we reached the Big Tree sanctuary zone, where we then headed due west across the rugged mountain terrain. After two days and nights we encamped outside Red Wood Sanctuary settlement group, along Mattole River that emptied into the Pacific.

The next day changed our lives forever.

As we had spent two weeks interviewing elderly survivors at Red Wood Sanctuary settlement group, the six of us decided to take a day off to beachcomb just off Mattole Point, south of Sea Lion Rock. To our surprise, we encountered a wrecked ship with unusual sails and configuration driven onshore by a storm. James, one of the elderly survivors we had interviewed earlier in the maorning, led us west toward the beach. He became very excited and told us that it resembled what in older days was called a junk, and that it certainly was Asian in origin.

Along the upper beach, slightly inland from the shoreline, we discovered the remains of six bodies. The situation looked to us as if the bodies originally had been buried, but later exhumed as portions of desiccated carcasses had been devoured by wild animals. Just east of the sand berm was a smooth cliff face of compacted Pleistocene dune sand. Carved into the cliff face was an inscription that we could not read – each of us carefully copied the symbols or characters into our respective data books.

Out of respect, we collected the remains and re-buried the bodies inland at a place we marked on our route maps with the notation:

40 degrees 18 minutes 17 seconds North Latitude

124 degrees 21 minutes 13 seconds West Longitude

Ethan suggested that we name the site:

Ultima Morada or Last Resting Place

Our journey ended with this grim finding. We thanked our hosts at Red Wood sanctuary and started on our return journey to Montana State University, taking a faster route with fewer stops along the way. On the return journey, Lee Carpenter and Heather West sickened. We did our best to provide comfort and aid, but both of our colleagues died. We awarded them standard data collector honors and marked their burials. Others seemed sick but the four of us made it back to Old Bozeman.

We reached MSU on Day 4, Week 4, Month 8, Solar Cycle 49, and immediately checked in to the university hospital for our standard data collector medical examination. We sat for debriefings and provided our original field notes to our faculty supervisor and professor, Bruce Anderson, for copying and archiving. We discussed with him the incident in which we discovered the bodies along shore near Mattole Point, Old

California, New SouthWest. We told him that we had removed the bodies from the beach and took them inland for burial. We also mentioned the message carved on the cliff face. He thanked us for the clarity of our debriefing and that he would have the text examined and translated by Professor Otu Fong, chair of former Asian languages at MSU.

Two hours later – to our surprise and concern – we were rousted from our residence hall sleep units by campus security police and medical staff wearing protective outfits. We were not arrested but were escorted quickly to the MSU hospital facility, where we were placed inside an isolation ward.

Supervisor Anderson and Professor Fong were standing inside the visitor booth, and spoke to us through the intercom system.

> *Please do not worry.*
> *But how could we not, given our rough treatment?*
> *Anderson spoke: Professor Fong will translate the message from the cliff face, and then we will discuss options.*
> *What did he mean by options?*

We listened intently: Dr. Fong approached the intercom microphone and related the words that chilled our hearts.

> *On this day we landed on the coast of California near the tall trees with red wood. Our exploration team previously encountered a storm; we have been adrift for 45 day cycles. All members of the Eastern Pacific Expedition Party became ill; 15 died and were buried at sea. Only I, Cho Feng Chu, and six others survived to reach shore to tell of our disaster. The six with me worsened and I tended them the best I could. I buried them at a secluded spot along the upper beach. What can I do? I now will leave behind my dead comrades and walk inland to seek assistance at a settlement where I may be cured.*

During the following 12 days, the remaining three data collectors who accompanied me on the long loop trek to coastal California died. The days that followed saw the deaths of my supervisor, as well as the chairman of Asian languages. More than 1,200 administrators and other faculty at MSU also perished. The greatest horror, however, was that of the untimely deaths of 9,044 students during this terrible epidemic.

I walked alone among the deserted halls of Carpenter Hall that once housed the Department of History and the wonderful archives that we worked so hard to protect. I entered the abandoned office of Professor Anderson, supervisor of our data collection program. On his desk was a thick file with a handwritten note appended to the cover:

To Any Certified Data Collection Survivor:

I sit alone in the alcove of the great hall, surrounded by the interview sheets written by you gifted, hard-working young men and women. What have we learned about our past? What have we found that offers hope for our collective future?

The information is contained in the piles of books, diaries, and accounts of past activities and behaviors, how actions of love, affection, trust, and honor have been lost through the years of the Dark Times, as once more we rest upon the precipice that may lead yet again to near oblivion dictated by forces we cannot understand.

My choice is a simple one: make available for inspection and review all of the evidence that the MSU data collection teams gathered when we sought to discover the origins of the Dark Times, or destroy the accounts and records of what we collected so that those who follow will experience their own predestined fates without knowledge of what went before.

The New Vandals are encamped outside our campus defensive structures awaiting for the signal to attack the MSU community – an order to be given by the high priest of the New Order. The word will come soon, and there is nothing we can do to stop the attack.

To you reading this notice, you have two choices: Take the summary document with you and protect it with your life, or destroy the contents and deny information access to the vandals who would overtake, enslave, or destroy you.

The choice is yours – make it now!

Dr. Bruce Anderson
Day 2, Week 2, Month 9, Solar Cycle 49

After-Word

So it was – or had the event been fated – that when the last data collection group returned to campus they unknowingly and without intention infected all within the geographical region of New Bozeman, and beyond.

And so it was that the epidemic could not be stopped.

Reports of deaths elsewhere within New NorthWest, New SouthWest, and eastward into the Flatland Configurations and beyond filled the airways and continued to mount, until all communications ceased.

I, Travis Saunders, was alive, but why? Alone, I returned to Bison Camp. Arriving inside the main gate, the visual impact was horrible: the compound grounds were littered with the unburied bodies of hundreds of my friends.

I dreaded the next step as I entered my family house. Inside was my mate, Reese Sanders. She had survived! Reese was weak, drenched in sweat, barely able to move – but alive! But we both were engulfed in sadness; our two children had died the day before.

We embraced and held each other as the smell of death and family memories encased us through the night. During the next week I nursed and assisted Reese in her recovery. All we had was each other. No one else was alive in the settlement. We had survived, but why?

The sun rose over the eastern mountains as Reese and I sat together to write the words that appear here. We searched our memories and prepared a memorial list of certified data collectors who had died on their short or long look treks. We did our best to capture and preserve the names of those who perished working to understand the Dark Times, colleagues and dear friends all who gave their lives so that others in the future would know of the events that had transpired. Sadly, we could not be certain that we had captured all of the names, but we did our best:

Name

Adams, Henry
Carpenter, Lee
Cox, Richard
Cruz, Juniper
Fisher, Iris
Ford, Georgia

Gray, Stevens
Hamilton, Fern
Harris, Cole
Harrison, Jade
Hernandez, Ethan
Hudson, Sequoia
Hunter, Madison
Long, Cassia
Mills, Rosemary
Olson, Willow
Owens, Honesty
Parker, Lance
Reed, Lucas
Rogers, Louis
Ross, Ashland
Simmons, Darby
Smith, Alan
Stewart, Lodi
Watson, Tracy
Wells, Laurel
West, Heather

Ad memoriam XXVII data collectoribus qui mortuus est, expleto ministerio.
Tu semper in memoria.

Together, we carry the memory document left by Professor Anderson, the record summary of what we certified data collectors discovered during our various long and short loop treks, a record to share with any survivors we might encounter. The pages tell of our collective fall from grace and the aftermath when the Noble Seven, the Great Septet, are ignored.

As we look out over the landscape to the east, we may never know why the two of us were not infected with the new plague. We can only go forward with hope into the new dawn of uncertainty.

We have camped just along the southern ridge near the crest of Lone Mountain. Our view extends eastward down the rocky slope toward the grassland meadow and the abandoned houses that once formed the settlement of Old Big Sky. Nearby in the distance we can see Buck's T-Four Ranch where countless families were entertained prior to the Ripple Event.

Tomorrow we will pass through Old Big Sky and then continue south along the Gallatin River. Ultimately, we will reach the geyser basins of Old Yellowstone. Once inside this noble landscape, we will circumvent the herds of elk and buffalo then exit eastward toward New Cody along the western edge of the Flatland Configuration. Will we find survivors there? Only time will tell. Beyond New Cody lies the vast Flatland Configuration with its multiple shattered zones and the potential dangers posed.

Some say that beyond the Flatland Configuration are other groupings, one called the New Confederacy and a second called the New PlyMouth. Will we locate survivors there?

In our loneliness we are without others
Travel on – Travel on!

We aim for unknown lands beyond the far horizon
Travel on – Travel on!

Two as one together, we face an unknown future
Travel on – Travel on!

Ijano Esantu Eleman

Metal Sheet #15

Inscription and Translation

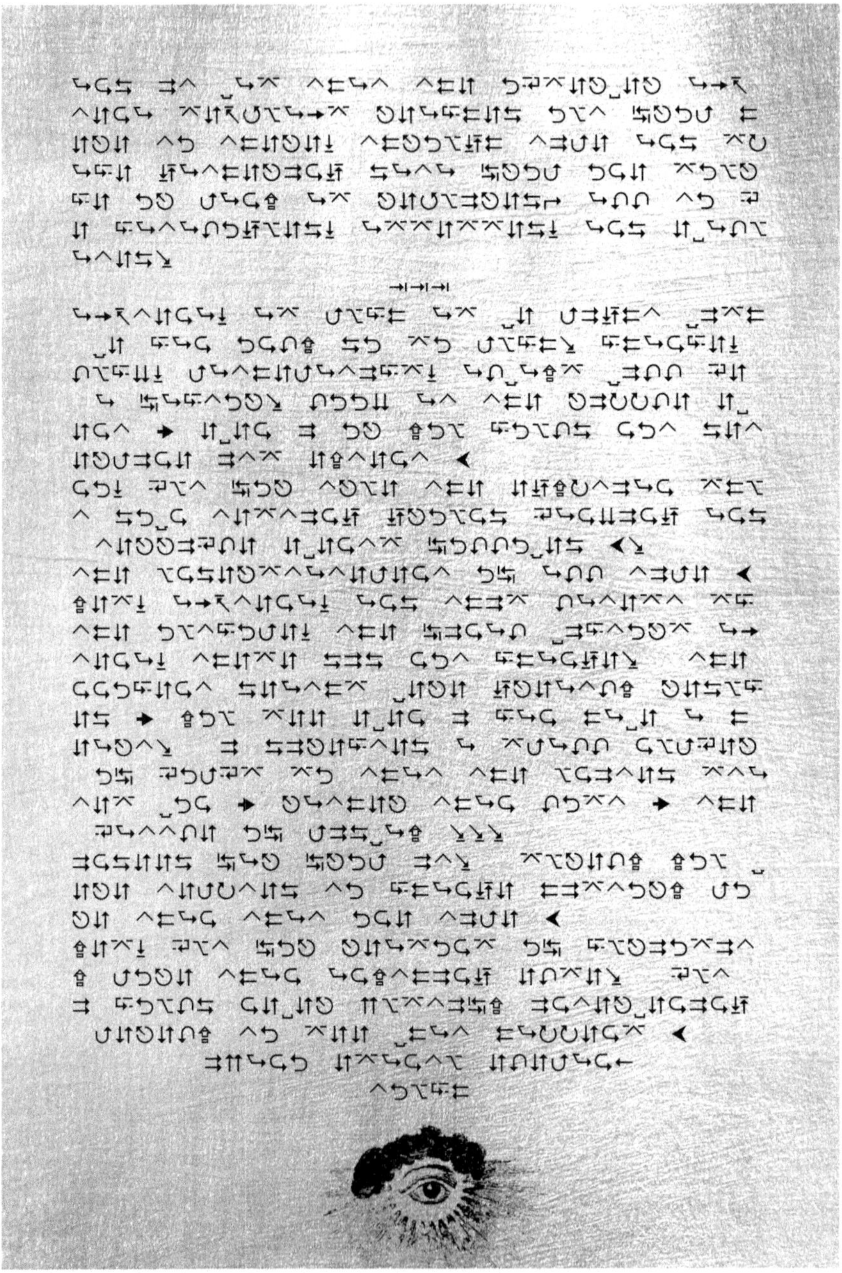

And it was that the Observer A'-Tena Se-Qua reached out from here to there, through time and space, gathering data from one source or many as required; all to be catalogued, assessed, and evaluated.

***

I am saddened, Overseer K'Aser. This latest sickness – the worst in eons – how much can the poor social groups and individuals endure? Are there no limits?

It is sad for true but the worst is past. These biped units can endure and have endured much without direct intercessions on my part. An occasional adjustment I have done, this as you know.

I agree, changing history is like cheating, it is not?

A'-Tena, as much as we might wish, we can only do so much. Chance, luck, mathematics, always will be a factor. Look at the Ripple Event – not even I or you could determine its extent.

No, but for true the Egyptian shut down testing ground banking, and terrible events followed.

The understatement of all time.

I agree, K'Aser, that you handled it as well as could be hoped, as things turned out.

Yes, A'-Tena, and this latest scourge I cannot justify historical intervention, even now. You may recall I did this only once before during a war.

Which war, K'Aser? There were many, oh so many. You mean the largest, most extensive, most deadly?

Yes, A'-Tena, that one. But why K'Aser, did you choose to intervene, change the outcome, change the flow?

The outcome, the final victors, A'Tena, these did not change. The length of time and numbers of innocent deaths were greatly reduced – you see even I can have a good heart. I did not influence human decisions, but I did direct a small number of bombs to hit specific targets so that the United States won – rather than lost – the Battle of Midway.

K'Aser, you are not heartless; indeed far from it. Surely you were tempted to change history more than that one time.

Yes, but for reasons of curiosity more than anything else. But I could never justify intervening merely to see what happens.

Ijano Esantu Eleman!

AFTER-WORDS: ONE

The Answer

What is life?
Why was life created?
Who created first life?
What happens at the end of life?
Can evil be eliminated?
Can good overcome evil?
What are the answers?

Ijano Esantu Eleman – As It Was in the Beginning

Overseer K'Aser walked along the beach, a favorite place of beauty to rest and think. And what a beach: it stretched from horizon to horizon, gleaming white in the sun. A huge moon – much closer to the orb than later times – shared the sky or owned it all. Tidal surges flooded the beach time and time again from horizon to horizon. Eons later, this beach would become a rock formation called the Flathead Quartzite and assigned to a geological period named the Cambrian.

For the now it was K'Aser's beach to enjoy – the sounds of the wind and the sensuous touch of the tidal rush and warmth of the primordial waters. This was his first assignment as Overseer. No animals slithered or trod the land – these would come later, much later. Being alone did not displease K'Aser. Such life that was present was confined to the great sea and was silent. K'Aser walked the sand in quiet solitude. K'Aser pondered: life, what a miracle life is and yet what a bother.

Then, slowly at first but then accelerating and reaching lightning speed the answer came to K'Aser.

Yes, this must be it!

He rushed to the place and time where the decision on his abilities would be given by A'-Tena.

K'Aser:	*A'-Tena! A'-Tena!*
A'-Tena:	*I am here K'Aser.*
K'Aser:	*A'-Tena Se-Qua, the one who sees, the protector of the …*
A'-Tena:	*Such formalities embarrass me, K'Aser. I am but one of six Observers. Go on. You seem excited.*
K'Aser:	*I am that, A'-Tena. I have found the answer!*
A'-Tena:	*You surely have AN answer that may, or may not be THE answer. Come sit by the river and explain. This Big Hole Valley, which in eons future will be known as Bison Camp – for why I do not fully understand. It is one of your favorite places, is it not?*
K'Aser:	*Yes, my favorite place, and has been so for a long, long time. A'-Tena, you well know of my struggle to attain the goal of a perfect cycle, which would not be a cycle at the*

end of it all. Instead, it would be an endless period of – for the lack of a better term – goodness.

A̓-Tena: *Ah, and what a time it would be for the units who will be created later.*

K̓Aser: *A̓-Tena, as you know, I prefer the term people. Will they not be like us in so many ways?*

A̓-Tena: *I agree, K̓Aser. And again by your words and deeds you have passed another part of the test. Yes, we will share much with them.*

K̓Aser: *Yes, the people will be very happy, very content but such a non-cycle is not possible.*

A̓-Tena: *How so?*

K̓Aser: *The key lies in life itself. The key is built into these creatures at the time of their conception, hardwired as individual characteristics.*

A̓-Tena: *In what way?*

K̓Aser: *A̓-Tena, what is the prime goal – indeed the only goal – of all living creatures? It is survival; for without survival, life ceases, disappears. On the basic level, life requires three functions: eating, excreting, and reproduction for life continuation. Without the three, life does not continue. The behavior that sustains life arises from survival. The mathematical genetics of earliest DNA are built into each life system – a coding that enables plants and lower forms to adapt to their environments in order to survive. Survival becomes more complex as creatures develop more self-awareness. But even in the most developed organisms – as we who are the Observers and Overseers – genetics is too slow and other factors must be added. Herein lies the necessary balance of two key factors: sharing and enlightened self-interest.*

Let me continue. Sharing is an act of care and offered gladly. Enlightened self-interest might appear to be greed, but it is much more. It is my theory that each living organism has both factors in relatively equal ratios. At times, however, sharing assures a larger survival quotient; at other times survival is due to self-interest. Did you not find my data interesting that during the *Ripple Event* groups could survive by sharing food, water, and goods with those who have such items, but they could be extremely greedy and exclusive in their treatment of those without items to contribute? So while both elements can be present at the same time, one usually prevails in response to external conditions. When one factor prevails in response to an action or acute life-threatening situation, the other factor is reduced. As the situation changes, the lesser factor grows until a rough equity once again is achieved. The near balance remains until the next crisis or positive event, whichever might come first. So, A'-Tena, what I sought to achieve as my personal goal on the testing ground was impossible. I could not offset or beat the home advantage no matter how long I might take, how much I might intervene, or how many times I try.

A'-Tena: The home advantage? What do you mean?

K'Aser: Let me explain. You remember how it was in Old Las Vegas, where many individuals went to play at games of chance? There were many other places that offered this sort of gaming, but Las Vegas was the biggest and the best. A'-Tena, the reality was that there was no chance in those games. The mathematics of the casino games were such that the casino – the home, the house, the establishment – would always gain over half of the monies bet. The fact that those palaces in Vegas were built and decorated by winnings, construction made possible through the home advantage, was no small matter. Anyway, I could not win, and now you have the why of what I contend is the answer.

A'-Tena: Interesting, but you have not considered that dark side of these bipeds, what sometimes you called true evil in your reports to me, K'Aser. How can you say that such actions of the evil ones had little to no connection to the survival of which you speak?

K'Aser: A'-Tena, yes, true evil has been a component of the testing ground, beginning with the initial appearance of bipeds, although not as common or as strongly present as Observers and Overseers assigned to other orbs might suggest. Since I discovered its rarity, I saw no need to address it. Genuine evil usually was eliminated by societies, often by people on their own. Sometimes this happened over time, other times rapidly, but the evil in people was cauterized through war more often than not. You recall the data I presented to you on Hitler, Stalin, and the eastern religious terror groups – I had no part in ridding the testing ground of them. Societies took it upon themselves to do so, no matter how tempting such an action of interference was to me. As for other cases, such as Mao, Castro, al-Shivzent, and E'kholm II – when death took the evil ones, the evil that they espoused faded away, slowly in some cases, but rapidly in others.

A'-Tena: K'Aser, you are the first Overseer to have come close enough through your data summaries to have deduced the answer. Not only do you pass your test, but I recommend that you be identified for another challenge once I make my report to Etowah.

K'Aser: Thank you, A'-Tena. But please! Will I be able to return to this testing ground and to this valley and river – the place once called the Big Hole? This has been my favorite of all places and through all times.

A'-Tena: Yes, K'Aser, you may return as a visitor but not as a formal Overseer. This orb always will remain a testing ground as assigned by Etowah. You know, of course, K'Aser, that even this beautiful place where we now sit and speak must in time conform to Etowah's plan. As you recall the rules of stellar physics set into motion by Etowah at the beginning dictate this orb's destruction sometime in the future, after about 2,800,000,000 solar cycles when the nearby great fiery orb becomes a red giant and engulfs the testing ground. By that time, of course, other testing grounds will have been initiated. Will one or more have a place as beautiful as this one, K'Aser?

	We will have to wait and see.
K'Aser:	*Ijano Esantu Eleman! Ijano Esantu Eleman!*
A'-Tena:	*Yes, Ijano Esantu Eleman. And now, K'Aser, at this time because of your success you have the option of naming your Observer replacement.*
K'Aser:	*For true, A'-Tena?*
A'-Tena:	*For true, K'Aser.*
K'Aser:	*Then I shall choose you, A'-Tena. I've become quite taken by you.*
A'-Tena:	*And I you, K'Aser.*

AFTER-WORDS: TWO

Notes from the Log of Senior Lieutenant Jackson James

It is reported in the surviving Gen-Sis document that the Gar-Den of E-Den was the most beautiful location on the orb, where botanicals and zoologicals grew and developed in harmony and balance, where the first biped was created from dust and the breath of Great Spirit Etowah, a mate was created for the first biped, followed by reproduction, followed by the emergence of jealousy and evil ... the initial goodness of bipeds vanished on the testing ground.

It is reported in the surviving Spe-Cies Sur-Vival document that botanicals and zoologicals consistently fight and struggle to survive through any means possible when disturbed by local or exterior forces set into motion on the testing ground.

Botanicals and zoologicals tested were not created good or evil, beautiful or wizened. Such appellations were created and grew in the minds of bipeds as they matured and reached adult stages. The great dichotomy had been reached: what was good and proper behavior to one was evil to another, what was beautiful to one became ugly in the minds of others.

Survival – by any means possible – became the key. (The document ends abruptly.)

(Source: Anonymous. Cave Document 26, Case 43-A.)

Expedition Date: 3012
Log Scribe: Senior Lieutenant, Jackson James, Navigation Specialist
Notation: Second work shift, 746ᵗʰ day PDC (post-departure calculation)

Throughout the following days and evenings, officers and crew members of the *KosMa ExPlorer* pondered and discussed the translated texts and their meanings. In a manner not well understood, the Ad-Miral's readings from the documents retrieved from the cave bound us more closely together as a group, we the 96 (22 officers; 10 senior crew members; 64 junior crew members):

Senior Ad-Miral (Franklin Egenda, Commander, *KosMa ExPlorer*)

Junior Ad-Miral (Josclyn Vega, Deputy Commander, *KosMa Explorer*)

Officer Teams

Blue Group:

> Senior Legender (Thomas Dickinson, Primary Security Officer)
> Senior Colonel (Mavis Stronghaven, Strategic Operations Coordinator)
> Senior Major (Gorgie Lemjkov, Navigation and Instrumentation)
> Junior Major (Adam Winkler, Personnel Systematics)
> Senior Captain (Joyce Evans, Computer Systems Solvency and Repair)
> Junior Captain (Tamara Goodwin, Medicine, Nutrition, and Psychiatry)
> Senior Lieutenant (Jackson James, Propulsion Systems)
> Junior Lieutenant (Peter Chu, Supply and Technical Orders)
> Senior Quartermaster (Boyce Chalkins, Equipment Repair)
> Junior Quartermaster (Allison Currie, Food and Beverage Preparation)

Gold Group:

> Senior Legender (Saranda Foster, Security Officer)
> Senior Colonel (Johnson Makris, Strategic Operations
> Coordinator)
> Senior Major (Dawn Jenkins, Navigation and Instrumentation)
> Junior Major (Francis Delvan, Personnel Systematics)
> Senior Captain (Richard Engels, Computer Systems Solvency
> and Repair)
> Junior Captain (Louis Carpenter, Medicine, Nutrition,
> Psychiatry)
> Senior Lieutenant (Roxanne Hernandez, Propulsion Systems)
> Junior Lieutenant (Janice Upton, Supply and Technical
> Orders)
> Senior Quartermaster (Kristie Winters, Equipment Repair)
> Junior Quartermaster (Theodore Ikado, Food and Beverage
> Preparation)

Four sections of 16 crew members each were paired with gender opposites. Each crew member had been trained and received certification in academy's standard-20 skillsets:

> Astrophysics and astronomy; communication, computer programing, and repair; construction engineering and structural repair; creative manufacturing; digital recordings and image preservation; electrical circuitry and ionic flow; emergency medicine and herbal compounds; engine and propulsion systematics; exercise and strength development; exo-botanical and exo-zoological identification; fuel and transport technology; geology and structural formations; micro-biological sanitation and disease transmission; history, literature, and music; hydroponics and food production; mathematics and computational creativity; metallurgical chemistry; political and economic education; wilderness and seasonal survival skills; and weapon development and repair

The Ad-Miral assigned teams to reconnoiter short distances within the valley. After de-briefings and reports of no danger, explorations were expanded to nearby regions.

One of the teams led by crew member weapon specialist, Yuri Benson, left the valley along vector 021 and reached the ruins of an extensive settlement. They spent four days examining the ruins of what appeared to be a center of higher learning and young adult education. Based upon materials gathered and subsequently translated we learned that the site once was named Bozeman. Based upon several documents retrieved, the team had stumbled upon a valuable cache of pay-per documents and electronic devices in what once may have been a university archive. The team reported no evidence of survivors, only significant numbers of predatory animals roaming the site at dusk.

The exploration team also discovered numerous symbolic messages scribbled on walls of decaying buildings and made copies for technical storage. Upon return to the craft, these texts also were translated. The majority seemed to be attempts to locate missing family members, perhaps separated, during what appeared to have been a terrible epidemic. Others provided directions where individuals and family members could meet and share resources. The content of some also implied a religious connotation, whereby, their deity was implored to intercede and to save the lives of families and children, and at least three such included the phrase that we had heard several times during the Ad-Miral's readings – *Ijano Esantu Eleman.*

> *J-T we are secure for now; meet us any evening at our regular rendezvous site; we have medicine and food. Tell no one else, only you and F-R will be admitted.*

> *Bradley and Susan, where are you? We have food and water for about 16 day cycles. Meet us where we attended our first class. We will be in the basement. For the entry password use Bradley's middle name, followed by… (rest of message obscured).*

> *Help us! We were never part of the New Order. We always followed the Noble Seven. Why must we suffer for the actions of others? Darkness now shades our lives. We implore the Overseer (may Its name always be praised) to release us from suffering and death that has enveloped our city, homes, and families – Ijano Esantu Eleman.*

Hikes back to the hillside cave were organized by science officer Upton. Each day additional documents were retrieved, and after six such trips the bio- and metallic-scans of the various relics remaining inside the cavern were completed. Each visit revealed new information regarding the previous inhabitants of the orb. Of high interest were the objects stashed in and about the different cave compartments. Some appeared to be old-style directional finders (we later learned that such objects once were called compasses). There were ancient communication devices as well as numerous machines and small objects of unknown use that projected digital images. Among the more curious were stone items that might have had served as weapons (NOTE: translation of several documents determined that the inhabitants called these objects arrowheads) – all these items certainly from bygone days. In summary: the objects were an eclectic mix, items left behind by the inhabitants that once were cherished or widely used.

The use or function of most, however, could not be identified.

Expedition Date: 3012
Log Scribe: Senior Lieutenant Jackson James, Navigation Specialist
Notation: Second work shift, 776th day PDC

On the evening of this day Ad-Miral Egenda called assembly and spoke to all:

> During the past time period, our local and distant scanners have found no evidence that bipeds continue to inhabit any adjacent regions. My communication with home base has been positive. The decision has been made by Governor Almade-Garlo that a component of craft KosMa ExPlorer should claim land and form a new settlement, initially to be located and based in the present valley. Our tests have revealed that the region here and the surrounding areas are productive for food growing and securing significant quantities of wild foods of both plant and animal origin. There is water abundant, and the predictive weather patterns are not dissimilar to those we ordinarily experience on our home orb. The message sent to me from home base by Governor Almade-Garlo may be summarized in just two words:

> Colonize and learn!

> By establishing a colony in this valley, we will have time for further study and evaluation of the items retrieved from the cave site. From the documents already translated and related to you during and subsequent to our recent evening sessions, we can learn more about the former inhabitants and how they survived during hardships and how these findings can assist our own cultures at home.

Another positive value that would result from a successful colony in this valley – after due exploration outward into the surrounding vastness – is knowledge that we could solve the overpopulation crisis we at home currently anticipate will occur within the next 24–27 solar cycles. Our expanded transport craft system could bring many thousands from our overpopulated home to this orb and create a new extension of the core values we hold – and we could do so in a peaceful and beautiful setting.

Colonize and learn – key words from our governor that present for us a new challenge, a new and bright future, in which each of us present here today can be proud of being part of such a new beginning.

The plan conceived by Governor Almade-Garlo is to leave a team of 16 gender-matched individuals – each composed of two officers and six crew member sets – to establish the first settlement and develop a system of colony self-sustainability, a new colony that maintains the ethics and values that we on the home orb hold dear and practice.

Governor Almade-Garlo confirms, however, that the 16 original settlers must be volunteers and gender matched. Neither I nor Deputy Commander Vega will force compliance with this order from home base. We ask for volunteers from all assembled. If more than the prescribed number volunteer, then Deputy Commander Vega and I will use a random process to select the final 16 from those with the most diversified skillsets.

Are we in agreement?

And so it came to be that more than half of the officers and crew members volunteered (the exact number was 55 out of 96). When two sets of equally skilled gender-matched individuals volunteered, as per the Ad-Miral's remark, the duo was selected randomly.

Upton and I were chosen as one of the officer sets; Louis Carpenter and Joyce Evans were higher in rank and were tapped to provide the command structure for the fledgling colony. Our 12 gender-matched crew member volunteers were an exceptional group with advanced technical training that covered eight key skills with overlapping redundancies:

Digital recording and image preservation; emergency medicine and herbal compounds; exercise and strength development; exotic botanical and zoological identifications; health and sanitation; hydroponics and food production; metallurgical chemistry; and survival skills.

According to our Ad-Miral's presentation, the *KosMa ExPlorer* would be prepared for departure (scheduled date: 50 relative days hence). This would be sufficient time for construction and preparation of our basic settlement structures, completion of the carpentry and wiring necessary for communication with the craft on its return to home base, and for all networks and technical support systems to be installed and tested.

As time progressed, the volunteer teams met regularly with the Ad-Miral and his officers. We reviewed our charge and functions. We also held daily meetings with our crew members and drew closer in understanding and friendship. We developed a task-management system based upon standard supply and security procedures. Each of us knew and understood our respective responsibilities; each of us looked forward to participating in this unique opportunity.

Came time for final departure preparations, as we loaded the *KosMa ExPlorer* with samples of soil, rock, vegetation, and cave document and relic scans for further analysis aboard the craft on the homeward bound journey.

The return to home base would take approximately 720 in-flight relative day calculations (depending upon solar winds and vector changes). The orb time that we would experience before new colonial settlers would arrive was estimated to be between full four and five solar cycles (a generous allowance given the need for recruitment and supply management cost issues). During their voyage to home base, we would miss our colleagues, but would not be alone; we would have each other and would be working together as might be a family of like-thinking adventures.

On the morning of *KosMa ExPlorer's* departure, the Ad-Miral attempted to raise home base but message transmission through the orb's unusually high atmospheric static made contact impossible. We were not worried about this slight celestial ionic problem, since once our craft were launched and two orbits completed, the standard thrust applications for the shortest trajectory back to home base would be implemented. Communications easily could be established once outside the orb's atmosphere.

All assembled. Best wishes were shared. Each volunteer remaining behind presented the departing travelers with messages to be delivered to their families back home. Then good-byes and best wishes for a safe flight.

We remaining on the orb stepped into the shelter that protected us from the craft's aft-engine blasts, and the *KosMa ExPlorer* achieved lift-off. We watched as our friends disappeared from view. All this took place on Relative Day 826th PDC (post-departure calculation)

And with the departure of the *KosMa ExPlorer*, we kept two time sets: Relative Day (home base departure calculation) and KED, days marking the *KosMa Explorer* departure.

Throughout the rest of the morning and afternoon we remained in good spirits, reinforced with good food and beverages all around.

During the following 20–30 days (KED) since departure of the *KosMa ExPlorer*, we also resumed construction of safe-haven redoubts and hillside caches where we could store food and water as necessary.

Thus it was we began to fit into the alternating work and leisure routines that would characterize us in the solar cycles to come.

• • •

A total of 120 relative days (KED) passed. We worked well together; we listened and learned from each other. In the evenings, we conversed during the dinner meal. We regularly contemplated the similarities and differences of the former orb residents to our own cultures.

• • •

An additional 120 relative days (KED) passed. We remained in regular communication with *KosMa ExPlorer*. We exchanged as they used to say – news and views. The Ad-Miral informed us that the *KosMa ExPlorer* still was unable to raise home base – something that puzzled each of us – but we were told not to worry since Senior Major Dawn Jenkins, navigation and instrumentation, was working with Senior Captain Richard Engels, computer systems solvency and repair, and had the technical problem under repair.

The fact that home base originally had transmitted the Colonize and learn message after the *KosMa ExPlorer* had landed on the orb did not immediately pose concern to us. We were doing well and expected few if any unexpected problems to complicate our mission.

On the 243rd relative day (KED) after departure of the *KosMa ExPlorer,* Harold Gaston, our communication, computer programing and repair expert, received a disturbing message from the craft. The *KosMa Explorer* had been forced to alter trajectory vectors due to magnetic pulsations emanating from a vistal dark spot. The transmission officer aboard the craft, Gorgie Lemjkov (navigation and instrumentation), quietly and without emotion expressed modest concern that the magnetic pulsations could render the starboard stabilization thrusters inoperable, which if not countered would cause the craft to … (transmission ended abruptly).

These were the last words received by us on the orb from *KosMa ExPlorer.*

Gaston quickly retrieved and reviewed previous messages that *KosMa ExPlorer* transmitted during the previous 30 relative days. After analysis, he found no evidence that home base had received any message sent by the craft.

We met immediately to share the disturbing news and to review all the transmissions between our orb and the *KosMa ExPlorer*. After due consideration, we concluded that the craft had been unable to contact home base or relay any information regarding our current status on the orb. That home base knew about us was certain, since it was they who had approved the Colonize and Learn Program. But it was not clear whether or not home base knew our Kos-Mic location within the vast expanse of our original assigned sector A-38-M-19.

It now appeared that we were on our own – not only for the anticipated four to five solar cycles, but perhaps in for a much longer experience.

• • •

And it was that the first solar cycle (365 relative days KED) came and passed; we worked well together.

• • •

And it was during the second solar cycle on relative day 498 (KED) that the first child born of our new colony emerged – a boy. His parents, crew members Nancy and Mark Rovela, named their son Eleman, because the event truly marked a new beginning.

Ijano Esantu Eleman

CODA
The Place

The Place was neither too plain nor too fancy, it was just right. It was here and there, now and then, and even yet to be. It was comfortable always there (no matter where and when that might be) and the beer was cold. This was where those preparing to be Observed, those being Observed, and those who had been Observed could – and did – gather to share ideas along with a pitcher or two, or three or....

Indeed it was quite like any other tavern as might be found convenient to those being instructed, to others currently being tested and to a few who had passed the challenges and were taking their relaxation before being reassigned. Having been tested (for the third time) The Place was where K'Aser found himself awaiting his evaluation. The company of his brother (himself preparing for testing and struggling a bit in the bargain, truth be told) along with several others (who had been tested and had passed to one degree or the other but not moved upward), made the beer even more tasty.

How go your studies, A'Donis?

Slow, K'Aser, slow. I've pretty much mastered the many ways of using dark matter and energy and am now grasping the whens and wheres, ins and outs, ups and downs and the here and there of quantum studies.

Well, that pretty much describes it.

I was about to add – but this does not make real-world application any easier.

This will come, A'Donis, it will come. I also struggled with those studies and then, why, it took me three times to pass the testing. Things of value and accomplishments are not meant to come easy. Even after failure novices may try as often as they care to. It is the struggle to succeed that is most important.

And if one is beaten down during the struggle and choses not to continue?

My brother, it is best not to think of this. Have you ever heard of a former novice? Met one? Seen one here? Think on this very carefully. My third time was the hardest, so here I am awaiting the official evaluation – and, who knows, perhaps another challenge. You should do well; I always have considered you to be the most gifted.

And I considered you the luckiest. Hello, what is this?

THAT, brother, is A'-Tena Se-Qua, the one who Observed my testing. Show proper respect or it will count against you.

Ah, there you are, K'Aser. I have met with our committee and bring news of your evaluation. Oh – say, who might this young cutie be?

A'Donis would have blushed had he been capable of such....

A'-Tena, it is my pleasure to present my brother, A'Donis, who is studying in preparation of his testing. You were saying?

K'Aser, I knew early on in this testing you would pass. So you did and with honor. A further level of challenge is open to you – one based even more on responsibility. Further, you can choose your Observer.

For true, A'-Tena?

For true, K'Aser.

In that case, I choose you, A'-Tena. I've become quite taken with you.

And I you, K'Aser.

A'-Tena, a relaxing stroll seems quite in order. Would you care to join me on my favorite beach?

Did you have to ask? Let us go and discuss our – your future.

For true you are the lucky one, K'Aser.

To be continued ...

APPENDIX

Additional Document from Case 43-B

The materials found inside Case 43-B included this list of certified data collectors, with their predominant personality traits.

Names of Certified Data Collectors and Program Administrators

Known as	(Family name)	Personality comment
Ada	Price	Stubborn
Alan	Smith	Peaceful
Alan	West	Contemplative
Alba	Bennett	Joyful
Alden	Johnson	Sensitive
Alexander	Williams	Boastful
Amber	Barnes	Respectful
Anise	Wood	Moody
Archer	Jones	Bright
Ashland	Ross	Thoughtful
Autumn	Henderson	Friendly
Axel	Finmaster	Courteous
Basil	Davis	Protective
Bay	Coleman	Imaginative

Known as	(Family name)	Personality comment
Bella	Jenkins	Analytical
Beth	Simmons	Tolerant
Birch	Pollard	Reserved
Bowman	Hoffman	Impulsive
Bruce	Anderson	AdMin/DC Supervisor
Cambria	Powell	Brave
Cassia	Long	Polite
Cheyenne	Patterson	Shy
Cole	Harris	Attentive
Connor	Martin	Versatile
Darby	Simmons	Enterprising
Deanna	Erwin	Inventive
Delbert	Clark	Practical
Dominic	Lewis	Meticulous
Echo	Bryant	Cheerful
Elko	Griffin	Courageous
Ennis	Hall	Always willing
Ethan	Hernandez	Helpful
Fallon	Myers	Careful
Fern	Hamilton	Smart
Flora	Graham	Watchful
Franklin	Fowler	Discreet
Fowler	Jensen	AdMin/DC Supervisor
Freedom	Scott	Adventurous
Frost	Woodward	Tactful
Georgia	Ford	Delightful
Glen	Baker	Impressive
Hanna	Wallace	Outgoing
Hardin	Green	Efficient
Harmony	Cole	Brilliant
Harper	Woods	Serious
Heather	West	Talented
Henry	Adams	Diligent
Honesty	Owens	Clever

Known as	(Family name)	Personality comment
Hunter	Nelson	Betrayer
Indigo	Reynolds	Friendly
Iris	Fisher	Spirited
Jackson	Carter	Methodical
Jade	Harrison	Gentile
Jenkins	Alan	Considerate
Jewel	Gibson	Well respected
Joanna	McDonald	Sincere
John	Roberts	Cautious
Juniper	Cruz	Modest
Lance	Parker	Quick learner
Laurel	Wells	Impressive
Lavender	Simpson	Resourceful
Ledger	Edwards	Charming
Lee	Carpenter	Artistic
Lodi	Stewart	Motivated
Logan	Morris	Ambitious
Lottie	Webb	Capable
Louis	Rogers	Discrete
Lucas	Reed	Fabulous
Madison	Hunter	Generous
Mark	Edwards	Wary
Martin	Cook	Energetic
Mary	Jensen	Curious
Mason	Bailey	Imaginative
Melody	Hicks	Frank
Mike	Richardson	Independent
Nicole	Crawford	Orderly
Petra	Warren	Complex
Phoenix	Gordon	Amicable
Piper	Holmes	Natural
Potter	Ingram	Respectful
Richard	Cox	Faithful
River	Livingston	Nice

Known as	(Family name)	Personality comment
Rosemary	Mills	Curious
Ryan	Ward	Gregarious
Sage	Grant	Adaptable
Sequoia	Hudson	Diplomatic
Serenity	Spencer	Protective
Stevens	Gray	Tolerant
Strong	Conway	Nurturing
Theodore	Johnson	Kind
Tracy	Watson	Gifted
Travis	Sanders	Trustworthy*
Willow	Olson	Thoughtful
Winter	Andrews	Agreeable

*Last data collector survivor

ABOUT THE AUTHORS

Louis Evan Grivetti is a professor emeritus in the Department of Nutrition, University of California, Davis (UC Davis). He received his bachelor's and master's degrees in paleontology at UC Berkeley (thesis: *Intertidal Foraminifera of the Farallon Islands*), and his Ph.D. in geography at UC Davis (dissertation: *Dietary Resources and Social Aspects of Food Use in a Tswana Tribe*). His academic research specializations have included cultural and historical geography, domestication of plants and animals; food history; and wild plant use during drought and civil unrest/war – with implications for health and nutritional status.

Sargent Thurber Reynolds is a retired technician for Valley Toxicology, and exploration geologist and consultant with Reynolds, Bain and Reynolds, and Tri-Valley Oil & Gas Co. He received his bachelor's and master's degrees in geology at UC Berkeley (thesis: *Geology of the North Half Bannack Quadrangle, Beaverhead County, Montana*), with a secondary credential at National University. He is an ardent angler, past president of the Fly Fishers of Davis, Calif., and past president of the Northern California Council Federation of Fly Fishers.

Both authors have lived and worked extensively within the western, central, eastern, and southern regions of North America, and have lived, traveled, or worked in the Middle East. *The Testing Ground* volumes constitute their initial literary collaboration.